ULTIMATE PREY

A TALE OF BOATS, GIRLS, SLAVERY AND A TOUCH OF PURE EVIL

BOOK 7 IN THE FIREBIRD SERIES

IAN DOLBY

DISCLAIMER:

This is a work of fiction. While names, characters, businesses, events and incidents are the products of the author's warped imagination, places and locales are as correct as possible, but are used in an entirely fictitious manner. Some characters are a composite of several personalities the author has encountered in his travels across Australia as such richness of true-life character could not be ignored. However, any resemblance to actual persons, living or dead, or actual events is unintended, accidental and purely coincidental.

The opinions expressed by the various characters in this story are deemed appropriate for their role and should not be assumed to be those of the author. I ride bikes and embrace the right to freedom of the open road on two wheels for everybody.

Published in Australia by Silverbird Publishing

First published in Australia 2024
This edition published 2024
Copyright © Ian Dolby 2024
Cover design, typesetting: WorkingType (www.workingtype.com.au)

The right of Ian Dolby to be identified as the Author of the Work has been asserted in accordance with the Copyright, Designs and Patents Act 1988.

Dolby, Ian
Ultimate Prey — Book 7 of the Firebird Series
ISBN: 978-0-6487179-5-9
pp394

ABOUT THE AUTHOR

I was born and raised on the Gold Coast, Queensland where my extended family always had boats. My love of sailing came from this background and developed through a series of racing catamarans that in turn led to the purchase of an old 47-foot wooden, engine-less, monohull yacht that had been built in Ireland in 1905 and had taken part in the Dunkirk evacuation. I lived on this boat at a marina in Rushcutters Bay, Sydney Harbour for several years and my engine-free adventures on this wonderful old boat may one day appear in writing.

The love of flying dragged me away from the boating scene, and after 38 years of glider, aeroplane and helicopter flying, I have retired to live in country New South Wales with my partner, who is my Chief Editor, and our two cats. While my writing has evolved from a part-time hobby to become a full-time occupation, it is no less enjoyable while the story lines keep coming to mind.

With heart-felt thanks to Luke, for your inspired cover layouts and publishing assistance. I couldn't have reached # 9 and still be writing, without your help and guidance.

Also with thanks to Brian, for your beta-reader skills and enthusiasm for my scribblings. Sometimes I need a push forward.

CONTENTS

PROLOGUE

The violent storm which sank the decrepit Indonesian fishing boat crammed with Vietnamese refugees, blew itself out almost as quickly as it had formed. Although short-lived, the storm produced howling winds which quickly whipped up a mess of steep, white-crested waves, which seemed to come at the boat from all directions, one of which contemptuously rolled the boat on its beam-ends, whereupon it partly broke apart, rapidly filled with water and sank. With it went ninety-three of the ninety-six persons aboard, along with their hopes and dreams of a new life in an untroubled land. After weeks of too little food, and seriously weakened by sickness from the contaminated water supply, most of the hapless passengers and crew were unable to keep themselves afloat in the rough conditions and quickly succumbed to the seething maelstrom. Life-jackets were something it seemed that the captain had only read about in a newspaper.

As a clear, crisp dawn broke over a now quiescent, but wreckage-strewn sea, there were just three survivors clinging desperately to a water-logged hatch cover, nervously looking for a sign of the sharks which had been nosing around since the boat sank. Coincidentally, they were all who remained from one large family. The initial terror which had gripped them when the gale of wind and crashing waves had torn the frail craft apart around them, had given way to a hopeless, fatalistic acceptance of their delayed fate. As they contemplated just letting go of their flimsy, improvised lift-raft and surrendering to the promise of eternal peace in the cool, green depths, they saw, like an apparition, possible salvation in the form of green trees, apparently growing out of the endless heaving ocean.

If they could have peered through the sharp eyes of the solitary seagull circling overhead looking for food, they would have seen a small island about five hundred metres away, with the barren, rocky shore of the mainland visible as a faint brown stain in the far distance. Because their eyes, blurred and burning from constant salt-water splashing, were only centimetres above a constantly heaving water level, their range of vision was short. However, as they drifted closer, the trees lost their ethereal appearance and proved to be firmly attached to land as more details slowly emerged into view. Behind the scrawny trees growing near the beach, the gentle slopes of the tiny island were covered in low bushes, twisted and moulded into weird shapes by the cyclones and storms which routinely blasted the hardy vegetation with torrents of salt-laden air. The contrast to their lush green tropical homeland couldn't have been more extreme, but at this stage, any dry land which didn't heave up and down, and was full of bitey things trying to kill them, was a vast improvement on their current circumstances.

Being the hardest worker, the woman was the least debilitated of the three, so it was she who kicked feebly with her bare feet, slowly driving their water-logged, make-shift raft across the general current flow sweeping them past the island, and into a small, shallow bay where a white sandy beach promised salvation. Her man tried to add what he could to her efforts, as did their sole-remaining child, a scrawny, sixteen-year-old girl. By her parents dispassionate reckoning, Hanh had always been considered the least promising of their five children, but she was all that was left of the next generation of the Tran family.

Although well-used to adversity, the Tran seniors were nevertheless mentally numbed by the scope of the tragedy which had stripped them of their life's savings and their best four children. Despite all their plans for a bright and safe future in the Great Southern Land being in tatters, Hanh's parents resolved to do whatever was necessary to make some sort of a new home for themselves and their sole child. The harshness of their former life had conditioned them to expect tragedy as a daily occurrence, and unlike many who had found their way to the southern continent without the benefit of legal entry papers, they weren't afraid of hard work. The boat owner's agent, to whom they had paid the equivalent of two years wages for the journey, had delivered a friendly warning.

'Many Australians are very different to us in their outlook and approach to life. They know they have the best country in the world, but they expect to work as little as possible, while enjoying the highest standard of lifestyle. Many have the expectation that what they don't do today, somebody else will do tomorrow. Most are told by their worker unions that they are only allowed to work 35 hours each week, in addition to which they have so many holidays, it would seem they have little time to work at all. For many, if they don't like the idea of working at all, they don't, and the Government somehow pays them a wage anyway.'

He paused, encouraged to see that he had his audience's rapt attention. 'But please remember these words. No matter how you see Australians behaving in regard to working, you must work for a living. You are not expected to use the Government's paid, no-work scheme. If you try to, be prepared to be severely abused. Australians have come to expect any foreigner to work at least twice as hard as they do and not complain.'

For the Trans, being paid for not working was a concept they found utterly impossible to comprehend, although conversely, working and not getting paid was a situation they were all too familiar with. Consequently, they were mentally prepared to work hard, or to do whatever was necessary to get ahead in this vast and frightening land which promised so much.

Finally, the feeble kicks of the Trans were able to drive the make-shift raft toward the northern end of the shallow bay. The water there was shallow a long way from shore, built up by sand washed out of a small creek which meandered down from the low hill in the interior. Therefore, it was with immense relief that the Tran parents felt their feet touch the soft, white sand more than fifty metres from shore. Between them, they dragged the soggy hatch cover, bearing the slender, shivering form of their youngest child, ashore beside the little creek mouth.

They were delighted to find it was pure, fresh water and drank their fill, marvelling at the wonderful taste after weeks of the foul-smelling and tasting liquid aboard the old fishing boat. They helped their girl-child to the fresh water and laid her in it, using the clean, white sand to cleanse her body of salt while she drank.

Thanks to the decent knife Mr Tran always wore on a thong around his neck and was the only weapon and tool they possessed, a rudimentary hut was soon built using the hatch cover as a roof. It was bound firmly to a small tree on one side, and propped up by dead branches on the other, with walls quickly made from interwoven, green, leafy branches. The bush food they found was unfamiliar, but applying the basic rule that bitter taste probably wasn't good and sweet was, they gathered enough to ease hunger pangs. More familiar and trustworthy was the copious supply of shellfish, like oysters and mussels, which were easily gathered each day. Large empty shells became water and cooking containers. Some old survival skills learned in the military, like fire-lighting the hard way, came in handy and it was Hanh's daily task to collect firewood and keep the fire well alight to build up a deep bed of coals which would last the night.

Although her parents had started out in better shape than Hanh, the abundant, healthy diet and food-gathering activity soon had all three feeling and looking better than they had been in many months.

By the end of the first week, they were exploring further and discovered the creek was fed by a tiny lake nestling near the top of the low hill, and that the island was narrow, about five kilometres long. Unsure of what wildlife might be on the island, they made some rough spears with knife-sharpened and fire-hardened tips, and carried them whenever they left the camp.

On the eighth day, when they rose as usual with the dawn, they were surprised and nervous to find a motor boat moored in the little bay. As their camp was not well concealed, they decided it would be better not to try to hide, and went to sit peacefully on the beach opposite the boat. To Dai Tran's experienced nautical eye, the boat was about seventeen metres in length, had good, sea-worthy lines with a low cabin-top forward, a raised wheelhouse amidships, and a long, low cabin behind it stretching to the stern where a small dinghy was hoisted on davits.

The morning sun was well above the horizon behind them before there was any sign of movement, when a man appeared on deck, checking around the boat. He wore just a pair of shorts and had a good tan. It wasn't until he was checking the anchor chain that he spotted the small family sitting on the beach watching him. After inspecting them for a few moments, he must have decided that they were harmless and raised his hand in casual friendly greeting. The three castaways repeated his gesture, so the big man called aft and shortly, a woman came up on deck.

They both watched the family for a few more minutes, before going aft to launch the dinghy, which they beached near where the Trans were seated.

Up close the man was tall and well-built, with broad shoulders and a smooth, bald head, while the woman was attractive, of medium height, red-haired and a well-fed, rounded body. She wore bikini pants, a T-shirt, and had a friendly face with a spray of freckles across her nose.

In return, they saw three small, skinny Asian people who looked, to their eyes, in need of a good feed or three.

The two adults looked old, but were probably not, while the young girl was very pretty, with a slim, developing body.

Dai Tran spoke in broken English as they stood to greet the

Australians. 'We shipwreck. Only t'ree escape. Need help, please.'

With a calculating look, Frank eyed the scrawny man, his wife, then the skinny daughter.

'Yes, you sure look like you need help,' he replied in a deep rumbling voice. 'What'd you reckon, Nora?'

His red-headed wife nodded, 'Yep! Sure do, but are you thinkin' what I'm thinkin'?

He nodded slowly, almost thoughtfully, his usual deliberate thought processes working on the situation. 'Yeah, maybe. If I was a mind reader!'

Nora sighed deeply and theatrically. 'Oh Frank! I was thinking that if they can't pay anything for us to rescue them, we might be able to score a servant girl.'

'Jeeze, Nora,' Frank exclaimed, 'you really do cut right to the guts of it, don't you?'

Nora shrugged. 'Might as well. Matey here doesn't speak much English and their not in any position to bargain or even argue.'

It was obvious who was the tough one of the two, as she looked straight at Dai, and at odds with her friendly appearance, asked baldly, 'This rescue business can be very expensive. How much money do you have?'

Dai looked helplessly at his wife, Long, who lifted her hands in the universal gesture.

He looked back at the woman, 'I just tell you. We have nothing. All gone when boat sink. No money – no extra clothes – no children – just Hanh.'

She nodded slowly and with a calculating grin, said, 'Alright, this is good. Seems like it's negotiating time.'

Dai Tran was no fool and quickly caught the drift of the conversation. He also recognised the looks the big man was casting at Hanh, so with his mind firmly in survival mode and suppressing the few fatherly instincts remaining, he haltingly said, 'We lose erey'ting in storm. You go Darwin... take us Darwin. You keep Hanh for servant... hard work girl! This my trade. Only trade.

Nothing left.'

While Frank processed the pros and cons of the deal, Nora giggled gleefully. 'Good deal, my smelly little friend! You tell your daughter now, that she's going to stay with us after we drop you two off in Darwin. I want to see her reaction.'

Dai nodded and told Hanh in Vietnamese that she now belonged to the Australian couple who would keep her safe and fed, in return for her doing the house-work. But if Nora was expecting a violent reaction from the girl, she was disappointed.

Hanh just shrugged, since to her, it was an amazing stroke of luck to be offered a home and food, in return for doing what she would have had to do anyway. And so far, these Australians didn't seem bad people. Since they hadn't hit them yet, that was a really good start.

She gave another philosophical shrug and walked over to stand facing the Wrights, her back physically, as well as mentally, to her parents.

'There we go,' Nora crowed, delighted with the result of what she thought was her shrewd bargaining, 'that's excellent. C'mon, Frank, let's get going. The sooner we're at sea again, the better it'll be for us in case these people change their mind and cause trouble.'

Causing trouble was the very last thing the Trans were going to do, and Frank was about to point that out to his wife, but as usual, he avoided an argument by settling for a shrug before walking back to the dinghy behind their scrawny new crew member, her parents trailing listlessly behind.

It was always better to let Nora have the last word.

On an overcast morning, just twenty-four hours later, the *Sea Witch* slipped quietly into Darwin harbour, and with their new passengers out of sight below, Frank told the harbourmaster that their last port of call was Point Sampson near Karratha. He made no mention of the rescue, although he did make a genuine effort to find a suitably quiet place to land their two adult refugees where they could slip away and blend in with the population of what is the most vibrant and cosmopolitan city in Australia. He and Nora noted there was a notable shortage of affectionate goodbyes from Hanh's parents as they simply waved, then walked away up the old wharf without a single glance back. After re-fuelling and re-provisioning, the Wrights and their new crewmember left the next day to continue their slow, clockwise circumnavigation of the island continent.

CHAPTER 1

BURNETT HEADS

Twelve-year-old Jake woke to the sound of a rowdy magpie doing his semi-melodious best to convince someone to give him a feed. As the tenacious tendrils of sleep swiftly cleared from his brain, he swung out of bed and stepped over to where his ten-year-old brother, Will, was still fast asleep. Although the sun was barely above the horizon, Jake could feel the warmth radiating through the thin canvas walls of their bedroom, which was part of the annex attached to the side of the family caravan.

The two boys and their parents had been staying at the caravan park in Burnett Heads for the last few months, where their dad worked as a shipwright at the local marina, although there was little call for his excellent boat-building skills. That was of little concern to the boys who were delighted that their dad took them fishing on weekends, weather permitting, and also that the park was close to where the waters of the Burnett River met the open South Pacific Ocean. With the river shoreline comprised of sandy beaches and patches of mangroves, it proved to be the perfect adventure playground for two young boys who loved fishing or just being on and around the water.

Jake had to shake his brother's shoulder hard to wake him, but finally got a mumbled reaction. 'C'mon Will. Get your arse into gear. The rain's stopped. If we want Dad to take us fishing, we've gotta catch some bait.'

'Yeah, yeah. Gimme a minute.'

Three minutes later, the boys were excitedly pedalling their bikes along the narrow dirt track which skirted the school oval just next door to the caravan park. As always, Jake carried their prized circular bait net in a plastic bucket, while Will carried another battered old bucket they hoped to fill with baitfish. They knew that returning with a good supply of bait and an undamaged net guaranteed their father would take them out fishing in their four-metre tinny.

Their favourite place to net some fish was a small beach on the southern side of the wide mouth of the river. A low mangrove-covered spit of beach at the seaward end caused the interaction of wave action and tide flow to leave all sorts of flotsam on the beach. This day there was plenty to inspect after the last three days of heavy rain which had kept the boys unhappily confined to the van, wasting their precious school holiday fishing time.

With a tidal range often more than three metres, the Burnett River usually flowed strongly, and much more so after rain, so the boys were careful not to wade out too far, and like the careful big brother he was, Jake made sure Will kept in the shallow water.

Their dad had taught Jake how to cast the circular net and he'd become quite the expert. Although the water was still muddy from the rain, several throws later, Will's bucket was slowly filling with fingerling mullet and other good baitfish. On the next throw, as Jake hauled in on the net's drawcord, he felt a heavy load and said a rude word.

'What's up, Jakey?' Will asked, watching his brother struggling to haul in the net which the tide flow was trying to drag from his grip. 'Is it snagged?'

'No, it's still moving a bit, so it can't be a snag. It's bloody heavy, though, so it could be a mud-crab. I don't want the bugger to tear it or Dad will go nutso.'

Slowly, Jake managed to drag the net in, cursing when he saw what looked like a lump of funny-coloured seaweed the size of a basket-ball caught in the fine mesh. As he carefully dragged it into shallow water, he was surprised how heavy it felt for a bunch of weed. Finally, managing to pull it in far enough to be out of the drag of the current, he then carefully opened the net out and reached down to lift the weed-ball free.

Just before his hands reached the object, a small wave caused the weed strands to float apart, hideously transforming the seaweed ball into long, tangled lengths of hair firmly attached to a human head! To further add to the horror, the head was displayed with empty eye sockets, and a gaping mouth made worse by having had the lips nibbled away by crabs, showing the teeth permanently bared in the hideous parody of a broad grin.

For a few moments, the boys were struck dumb and immobile, then Will screamed and both boys jumped back, adrenaline pumping, their hearts racing with shock.

Despite an empty, churning stomach threatening to produce a rising tide of bile, and with commendable presence of mind, Jake said, 'Quick, Will. Go get Dad! He'll know what to do. I'll stay here and make sure it doesn't drift away.'

Will was only too happy to escape the presence of the silent, grinning horror at his brother's feet and ran for his bike. With help organised, Jake stumbled on decidedly unsteady legs along the beach to the nearest scatter of driftwood, selected a long branch and used it to anchor the drawcord of the net to the sand. He then retreated far up the beach and sat, trembling with shock while hugging his knees, unable to tear his eyes away from the grisly bundle gently washing back and forth in the low waves. To Jake's fevered imagination, the head seemed to be nodding as though happy it had been found. This would form the basis of a series of nightmares for many years to come.

While their dad was at the beach within ten minutes, it was a further twenty minutes until a blue-uniformed police officer made his way across the beach to where the boys were huddled with their father.

Thirty seconds later, the young officer, his face pale with shock, was on his radio talking urgently to base, his words causing two detectives up-river in Bundaberg, to curse as they hurriedly abandoned their breakfast and headed east in unaccustomed haste.

CHAPTER 2

'Adam's Accountancy, this is Eva. May I help you?'

'I certainly hope so!' was the cryptic reply from a marvellously rich, baritone male voice, with a slight chuckle. *'My name is Russell Beal and I have a young lady here who insists on talking to Mike Adams if he's available. She claims that he's the only one who can help her.'*

'That sounds rather mysterious, Mr Beal. What's her name and where are you?'

'I'm sorry, I'm not explaining myself very well. It's very confusing for me too, as it's not every day I get to save someone from drowning. I'm on my boat anchored beside Crusoe Island near Jumpinpin, and just twenty minutes ago, I saw this girl in the water, being swept past me by the outgoing tide heading for the bar. She was having a hard time just keeping her head above water, let alone making headway to shore, so I jumped in my dinghy and managed to pick her up. She was quite exhausted and I had a terrible job getting her aboard. Her name is Hanh.'

Although intrigued by the story, Eva was getting a bit frustrated. 'This is an interesting story Mr Beal, and I'm very glad you were able to save her life, but why are you calling us instead of calling the police? We're just accountants. The police will be happy to come and pick her up and sort out the how's and why's.'

'Oh dear. I'm really not explaining things well, am I? It's all a bit of a muddle. The problem is, you see, she's just standing in my cockpit, dripping wet, shivering with cold and won't let my wife or me touch her.'

'Yes. I can see how that might be very distressing for all three of you, Mr Beal, but once again, why are you calling an accountant?'

'I'm sorry. Bit upset by all this mystery myself. Anyway, the important bit I forgot to say is that the only thing Hanh would say was that I had

to call Mike Adams and to say the name, 'Samantha Bartlett'. Does that mean anything to you?'

'Ah, finally. Yes, it does, Mr Beal. Will you let me speak to Hanh, please?'

'Sure. Good luck with that.'

Moments later, a trembling, soft female voice said, 'Is that Mike?'

'No Hanh, I'm Eva, Mike's secretary and partner. But I can put Mike on if you'll wait a moment.'

'Yes, please Eva.'

Eva pressed buttons and Mike's voice sounded, 'Yo! Sweet-cheeks!'

'I'll give you sweet-cheeks, boyo! But anyway, this is a weird one, Mike. I have a young lady called Hanh on the phone. She's on a boat up near Jumpinpin and the boat's owner has just rescued her from the water. She won't say anything to him except she asked for you by name and used the words, 'Samantha Bartlett'. Does this mean what I think it means?'

'It probably does. But damn it! We're not supposed to be running a collection agency for abused females. Still, I suppose we can pass her on to Sam. Where did you say she is?'

'Somewhere up near Jumpinpin on a boat. But she wants to speak to you, so get the where details from the bloke who picked her up. His name's Russell Beal.'

Mike sighed theatrically, 'All right, put her through.'

There was a click, then Mike said, 'Hi Hanh. I'm Mike Adams. How can I help you?'

'Hi Mr Adams. I can't say too much at the moment, but are you able to get me to Samantha Bartlett? Or at least in touch with her?'

'Yes, I can do that Hanh, but I need to talk to Mr Beal first, please.'

.... 'Hi Mike, this is Russell Beal.'

'Gidday Russell. This is all very weird as you well know. However, I do know Samantha Bartlett, who has a habit of looking after stray waifs, so I guess we'll have to collect Hanh if she's on your boat. Where's the closest place we can meet up?'

'*For a start, Hanh's not exactly a waif, but that'll do for now. The closest pick-up point will be Jacob's Well, a small village about half-way between the Gold Coast and Brisbane, and east of the freeway. I can be there in less than an hour. When you get to the village, you'll find there are three jetties on the waterfront, but I'll be at the end of the middle one, which has a bait shop and store at the head of it. I'll be in a fifteen-metre cruiser with a white hull and blue upper works.*'

'Okay, thanks Russell. I'll get going shortly.'

'*I really appreciate this, Mike. We feel a bit helpless at the moment not knowing what's going on, and Hanh is apparently unable or unwilling to tell us anymore. See you there.*'

Mike looked at Eva, now sitting quietly on the other side of his rough wood desk formed from slabs of bleached driftwood, with an excited grin on her pretty face. He sighed and said, 'Any clients due for the next couple of hours?'

She shook her flowing mane of red hair and smiled.

'Nope – and of course I'll come with you. This sounds way mysterious… very exciting, so I can't wait to hear the story.'

Accepting that he was out-manoeuvred, Mike nodded resignedly, so they closed up the office, set the phone to forward to Eva's mobile, and were soon in the car heading north on the M1 motorway.

The sleepy little cluster of weekender fishing shacks which originated around the well of the long-departed Jacob Gross, had succumbed gracefully, if unwillingly to the inevitable march of progress by turning into a thriving village flanked by two marina complexes. The waterfront was front and centre and as promised, there was a power boat with blue upper-works parked at the end of the centre jetty with a bait shop at the head. A pleasant-looking, middle-aged bloke with a tanned face and an easy smile had walked down the jetty to meet them and poked out his hand as Mike and Eva approached.

He gave Eva an appreciative look which just avoided being lecherous. 'You look like Mike and Eva… I hope?'

Mike couldn't help chuckling, 'Good call, Russell. I'm pleased to meet you.'

'Likewise, Mike. Eva, you look as lovely as you sounded on the phone.'

Eva made a little curtsey at his courteous comment. 'Thank you, kind sir.'

Mike gestured at Russell's boat, 'Before we meet your catch-of-the-day, would you mind running through what happened earlier in a bit more detail?'

Russell did, but couldn't add much more to what he'd told Eva over the phone. 'She still won't say anything to Joy or me, apart from your name and this Samantha woman. Your name was the only one listed in the phone book, so you copped the call. She's at least inside the saloon now, but won't sit down, and won't change into dry clothes, although Joy managed to get her to take a big towel to wrap around herself. That seems to have helped her stop shivering.'

'Have you ever seen her or heard her name before?' Mike asked casually.

Russell's smile didn't falter, 'Nope to both. Joy and I live aboard full-time. We do have a town-house in Tedder Avenue at Main Beach, but we enjoy the boat life too much to stay ashore for any length of time.'

Mike nodded, satisfied with his statement. 'That's understandable. She looks a lovely boat.'

Russell beamed, 'Thanks Mike. Nice to hear others appreciate what we think is something special.'

'I know Hanh hasn't said anything, but do you have any idea where she might have come from?'

Russell shook his head. 'No. That was the second thing Joy and I discussed. We were anchored on the northern side of Crusoe Island, in the main channel leading to Jumpinpin Bar. The tides run really strong there and the Bar itself is bad news most times. Plus, there are always lots of sharks in the area.

We were anchored near the east end of the island, closest to the bar, with a couple of other boats anchored well upstream of us, but they were too far off to see any names or details. They were just there, if you know what I mean.

When I first came on deck early this morning to do my usual security check, I simply noted them. It wasn't long after that when I saw a person splashing weakly in the water as she was carried past us by the current. Luckily, my dinghy was already in the water, so I was able to chase after her pretty quickly. After I got Hanh aboard, we spent some time trying to warm her and trying to get her to speak, so I forgot to see if both the boats upstream of us were still there.'

Mike nodded, 'Are there any houses on any of those islands upstream?'

'No. Absolutely nothing around there. Further north there's a lot of development, like on Warren Island, but around the Crusoe area the islands are mostly tidal swamp – mosquitos, sandflies and mangroves. Not even nice to go for a walk on!'

Mike looked thoughtful, but had no more questions. 'Thanks Russell. I guess that gives us a bit of background.'

Russell smiled. 'Good. In that case, come aboard and meet the girl. I'll bet she's been checking you out from behind the tinted saloon windows. She's been very intense about you and this Samantha girl.'

They followed him aboard, being greeted by Russell's wife Joy. She was short, attractive, with a happy, bubbly personality.

'Please come in and meet Hanh,' she said quietly. 'I do hope she'll be more open with you than she has been with us.'

Standing on a thick throw rug by the dining table was an unusually tall Asian girl with very long, black hair cascading down her back in damp, salt-sticky strands. She was remarkably pretty with flawless skin, although it was hard to judge the rest of her as she was swaddled in a huge towel that could almost do duty as a storm sail.

Mike smiled at her and stepped slowly forward, his hand outstretched as he softly said, 'Hi Hanh. I'm Mike Adams. How can I help you?'

At his words, something seemed to crack in the girl as her facial expression softened and some tension visibly left her body as she firmly grasped his hand.

A tentative smile flittered across her face. 'Hello Mike. Lovely to meet you and thank you for coming so quickly. I'm sure things will be alright now if you can get me to Samantha.'

She greeted Eva with a quick smile and handshake.

Mike looked at Russell, who shrugged. 'Can I have your contact details, please Russell? Just in case there's any other info we might need.'

While Russell wrote out the details and handed them to Eva, receiving Mike's card in exchange, Hanh stepped into the cockpit and took off the towel, handing it to Joy.

'You can keep it if you want,' Joy said.

'No. That's okay. I'm only damp now. Thank you both very much for rescuing and looking after me.'

Mike tried hard not to stare too much, since she was only wearing a very small bikini and there were a lot of lovely-shaped girly bits it was having a lot of trouble trying to contain. Eva came down with a minor fit of the giggles at his expression, as Hanh calmly stepped off the boat onto the jetty, waiting patiently while Mike and Eva hastily said their goodbyes to Russell and Joy.

As Russell shook Mike's hand, he commented, 'I, ahh… hope things work out alright with her. I'm sure there's a very strange story behind all this, so if or when you find out, we'd really appreciate hearing from you.'

'We'll do that, Russell, you've more than earned it. It's been good to meet you both and thank you. Cheers for now.'

In the car, Eva found an old towel for Hanh to sit on.

'You can wait until we get home to tell your story, if you like,' Mike said, letting Eva drive.

Hanh gave him a big smile that really lit up her pretty face, 'Thanks Mike. And thanks to you too, Eva for being so nice. Russell and Joy were lovely, but I feel much happier now we're away from that area. I would prefer to wait until we get to your place, then I'll tell you what's been going on. It's a long story. But I will be able to see Samantha at some stage, won't I?'

'Yes, not a problem, although we need to hear what's behind all this first. That's how things work with Sam and us. She trusts us to check her occasional clients out first.'

Hanh seemed comfortable with that and sat back, gazing at the passing scenery in a relaxed manner as the kilometres slipped by.

CHAPTER 3

GOLD COAST

Hanh loved the look of the old Queenslander that Mike and Eva called both home and office, and appreciated being shown to a spare bedroom where Eva brought her an assortment of clothing which was a close enough fit. After a welcome shower, a comb-out of her long hair and clad in a pair of Eva's shorts with a loose top, she joined Mike and Eva in the kitchen for a mug of hot, sweet tea.

The story she told of the shipwreck which had killed her siblings and changed her life forever was heartbreaking, and nearly had Eva in tears. Then hearing how she'd been traded by her parents, and became boat-maid for Frank and Nora Wright was equally distressing, even though she stressed that the Wrights always treated her well, with no abuse, sexual or otherwise involved.

Then she told of an incident which darkened the tone of her story still further. The Wrights had parked in a marina in Yeppoon for a while, as they made their way slowly south to avoid the summer cyclone season. A stranger, who had berthed his boat close by, had stopped to chat one day, and was invited aboard by Nora.

'I was asked to serve them drinks, and this dude creeped me out straight away by the way he stared at me. I might as well have taken my clothes off to save him the trouble! I got out of sight as quickly as I could by retreating to the galley, waiting to be called for the next round of drinks.

Anyway, I heard them chatting about the usual boat stuff for a while, like where they'd been and who they'd bumped into. But then I overheard him bragging to Frank and Nora about what a great setup he had on his boat, where he had four girls who did all the work and were sex-slaves as well. Although Frank and Nora had treated me really well up to that point, I was a bit shocked when they started asking him lots of questions, making it sound like they were really interested in the idea.'

Mike looked troubled. 'Did this guy suggest they should get you to do the same? The sex-slave bit, I mean.'

'Yes. He did exactly that. He just came right out and said they should get me to do the same. Then Nora asked how he kept his girls from running away. So, then this creep, Gary Turner is his name, told Frank and Nora that all it needed was the right sort of attitude adjustment, and the girls stayed put.'

Eva looked puzzled, and Mike said, 'That's all a bit wild, but nothing really illegal so far, just so long as the girls stayed there voluntarily. But what sort of attitude adjustment was he talking about to make them want to stay there doing all the work and providing sex on demand?'

Hanh shrugged. 'I don't really know much about that side of things, although the black plastic collars all his girls wore must have had something to do with it. He'd simply told them that if they tried to leave the boat, it would set an alarm off. That would mean that the girls weren't staying on a voluntary basis, wouldn't it?'

Mike and Eva looked puzzled as they tried to work out what the collars meant, so Hanh hurried on with her story.

'But to cut a long story short, it didn't take much for Turner to convince the Wrights to do a swap with him for a week or so as a trial. The deal was that I had to go to his boat, and one of his girls came to the Wrights. He encouraged them by saying it would let them 'expand their sexual horizons', since all his girls were conditioned to do whatever they were told and couldn't or wouldn't run away. He gave them a small box which he said was a portable controller-transmitter to hook-up to their power supply and would keep the collar functioning. He also bragged that he already had a bunch of like-minded, live-aboard boaties who he'd supplied with girls, and the scheme was going really well. He had a partner with a small shore-based crew who scouted for suitable homeless new girls off the streets, and let him know when they'd picked up some good prospects.'

She paused to take a drink of water before continuing.

'The way he explained the deal, was that after they'd been trained, girls were initially sold outright, but the owners were free to then swap or trade them with other members of the scheme if they wanted some variety. He boasted that his fee for the service was very modest in comparison to the fun and enjoyment the participating boat owners would get from the arrangement.

Other than that, I didn't really understand all the other stuff he said to the Wrights.'

Mike thought a moment, shaking his head in disgust. 'What a foul scheme and definitely illegal! But why didn't you bug out straight away, Hanh?'

She paused, marshalling her thoughts. 'Probably because at first, apart from the collar thingy, the environment wasn't much worse than being with the Wrights, and I had other girls to talk to, so that was really great! There was also one much younger girl I made good friends with, and I suppose I sort of started looking after her. Then even when the sex stuff started, I guess I didn't want to run out on my little friend, Vivian.'

While Mike thought that over, Eva asked, 'But where did the girls come from?'

'From what I heard the girls talking about, they'd been living on the streets or shelters in various towns and cities in south-east Queensland, or crashing with friends for a few days at a time and were offered a new start on life. I did hear that some were backpackers who'd overstayed their visas and were broke, or were illegal immigrants like me. Anyway, they were all homeless, in a bad situation, and not in a position to make a fuss with the police. With the Wrights, I was in a very comfortable environment by comparison. However, once Gary got these other girls aboard and away from civilisation, he put the collar on them and they always stayed.'

Mike nodded, 'That's close enough to kidnapping as doesn't matter by using the threat of the alarmed collars, but perhaps not as bad as it could be, seeing as how the girls were doing it tough living on the streets.'

Hanh nodded, 'Yes. That's how it seemed to me at first. Then later, I guess I was in too deep to make any clever plans to get away. I mean that apart from sex when he wanted, we were never physically abused or beaten.'

Getting over her shock at the simple but diabolical nature of the scheme, Eva asked the question. 'But why just boaties? What's the significance of that?'

'Yes – I heard the Wrights ask that question. Turner's answer was that since boat life was a much more self-contained existence than on land, it was heaps easier to have sex-slaves than in suburbia where everybody wants to know your business. Boaties really respect each other's privacy, so it's easy to do whatever you want. The real advantage was that anybody seeing a flash boat with naked or half-naked girls running around wasn't going to think it even slightly unusual.'

Mike sat back in his chair, his head spinning, and when he glanced at Eva, she looked equally as stunned. 'So, to summarise, this Gary Turner has set up a business, essentially kidnapping homeless girls off the street, forcing them to be sex-slaves, strapping electronic collars around their necks, then selling them to other live-aboard boaties?'

Hanh nodded seriously. 'Yep! That's about it.'

'Fuck!' was Eva's succinct comment.

'Tell us more about the collar,' Mike said.

Hanh shrugged. 'It was just a black plastic collar. It was almost like a fashion accessory. We were told it contained some electronics which would trigger an alarm if the collar was taken too far from the transmitter on the boat.'

Mike nodded. 'That makes sense. It would trigger a proximity alarm and that's what would be keeping you all aboard, but surely it became uncomfortable?.'

Hanh shook her head, sending her now-clean, long, silky hair rippling in waves. 'No, not at all. It wasn't tight and being very light, it didn't hurt or leave marks or anything, but it was locked. Every two weeks, we had to sit for an hour with a device held against it to charge the battery.'

'How about showering?' Mike asked. 'Was it removed for that?'

Hanh shook her head. 'No. We were told it was waterproof, but if we tried to cut it off, or got too far away from the transmitter, it would set the alarm off and bad things would happen. We always supposed that meant we'd cop a beating.'

While looking worried, Mike was still a bit sceptical. 'Didn't you think that maybe he was just bluffing? I mean, you've described a very sophisticated device, even though the tracking ones the police use, go around an ankle.'

Hanh nodded. 'I know what you're thinking, and of course I did. But the day after I went aboard and was fitted with my collar, Turner gave me a demonstration. He had a spare collar, a white one for some reason, although all the others I saw were black. He had his head girl, Mary, who kept the records and was like a trustee, put it in a metal box with a tight-fitting lid, and after a few seconds, there was an ear-splitting howl from a siren-type thing in the transmitter. I guess the box blocked the signal and set the alarm off. That sort of convinced us not to try to get away.'

Eva became upset again and Mike muttered, 'Bloody hell, what a rotten, stinking mess. But you obviously managed to escape. How did you manage that?'

Hanh gave a grim smile. 'Early this morning, as I was starting to make Turner's breakfast, there was a beeping sound from my collar. He swore and muttered something about yet another faulty one, then fetched his little toolkit and another collar. For some reason, he unlocked my faulty one first and removed it, but before he could replace it with the new one, I bashed him in the face with a can of peaches I was about to open. The rim cut his forehead really badly and he fell down with blood pouring down his face. He seemed very dazed, so I didn't stop to think, just ran out to the stern and jumped overboard. There was another boat in the far distance, downstream which must have been the Beal's, so although I can't really swim, the strong current was at least carrying me in that direction. I just sort of did a dog-paddle sort of thing to stay afloat. I didn't really have time to look back to see if I was being chased, but apparently he didn't or couldn't until I was too far away.

By the time I was swept down past Mr Beal's boat, I was getting really tired and was just about ready to give up and let myself sink, but luckily he saw me, chased me in his dinghy and hauled me in.'

She shrugged, 'That's about it. Turner made a mistake… I got lucky and escaped.'

Eva and Mike looked at each other, communicating silently in a manner which to Hanh was both lovely and quite uncanny.

'One last very important question,' Mike said. 'How did you get Sam's and my name?'

Hanh gave a short laugh. 'That was a real coincidence. A couple of months back, Mary, I think I said that she's sort of the head girl on board Turner's boat as well as the book-keeper, had a teen magazine and she let me read it. There was a short article about a girl and a friend on the Gold Coast who had helped a couple of abused girls get out of their family situation. Your names just seemed to stick in my mind.'

Mike considered her words, then nodded and said, 'Please excuse us for a short time. We need to make some phone calls. But if you need something, we'll just be in the front office. You can hang out here, or go in the lounge room and look at TV. We'll be back shortly.'

Hanh nodded, apparently happy to trust them. 'I will see Sam sometime soon, won't I? You did promise.'

Mike grinned, 'Oh, yes. You will certainly be seeing Sam. Either today or tomorrow, but there are some elements to this situation which need closer attention than we can supply.'

Hanh sat back, looking satisfied that things were under control, as Mike and Eva headed for the office up front and the phone.

Once at his driftwood slab desk, bleached pale grey by years of exposure to sun and salt-water, Mike said, 'We'll let Sam know what's going on, but this is a very nasty situation, so I reckon we need to drop this in Harry's lap first. It's way too big for Sam to try to handle, given that it's nowhere near your average abused, runaway-girl situation.'

Eva agreed. 'Good thinking. And Sandy might have to get involved officially. If Hanh first saw this Turner character up at Yeppoon, he might have been up and down most of the east coast, making his sales pitch to those with a taste for this… whatever this sort of rotten perversion is called. It's almost like paedophilia, except it would seem that most of the girls are over eighteen. And have gone willingly. At least at first, it would seem.'

Mike looked thoughtful, 'Yes, you're right, although they're still being abused and kept under a sort of duress. I suppose sexual slavery is the right term. It certainly isn't paedophilia. But the collars and this brain-washing – coercion or whatever it is, adds a new and very unsavoury dimension to the whole thing.'

He called Sam, catching her supervising the collection by couriers of the latest example of the amazingly detailed, scale military aircraft and ship models which she made for various museums and collectors world-wide. The fact they paid handsomely for the privilege of owning a Bartlett original, as her repeat customers had begun to call the models, meant she had a six-figure annual income and Mike was her accountant.

He explained briefly that he and Eva had just collected another girl from an abused situation.

'However, there are some very nasty and much wider criminal implications involved this time,' he explained, 'probably involving many other girls, so it's not just a case of sorting out one girl's abused mental issues. This is going to have to involve Harry and Sandy.'

'*Oh… that serious?*'

'Very much so, I'm afraid. I'll explain more when we see you, but this girl, Hanh is her name, read that story about you and had our names, so she wants to meet you to make sure she's going to be looked after. She is Vietnamese but has very good English.'

Sam gave her usual throaty chuckle, 'That bloody magazine article! Gross embarrassment! I thought it was a good idea at the time, since it might have made a few waverers take the first step in getting out of their bad situation, but it seems to have had a sting in its tail! Okay, I'll contain my curiosity for the moment. Do you want me to come over now?'

'I haven't called Harry yet, but come over sometime soon please, if you're not too busy, just to say hello and reassure Hanh that you are real and we're doing all we can to help her and all the other girls. We need to get Harry and Sandy moving on this immediately before the trail gets cold.'

'*Okay. I'll just finish up making sure the couriers don't break something, then come on over.*'

He hung up, then immediately dialled another number which he knew as well as Sam's.

CHAPTER 4

GOLD COAST, HARRY

Having just finished an oil change on both generators, I was relaxing in the cockpit with what I considered to be a well-earned frosty bottle of beer, when the phone rang.

'Harry's Knock Shop. Press 2 to hear today's tasty-tart specials.'

'*Very funny, mate, but I need to see you, Sandy and Jasper as soon as you can make it. My place, if you don't mind.*'

'Wow! This must be the full-on, serious Mike. Not even a 'Gidday' for my trouble?'

Mike chuckled, '*Yeah, sorry. Gidday mate. How's it going?*'

'That's better. Going well, thanks. We fixed all the minor problems from the shake-down cruise and are ready to go again.'

'*Considering that the shakedown trip was close on 7,000 nautical miles, and took you nearly to Antarctica, I'm not surprised you had a few minor problems.*'

'Yeah, well that's where you've got to go when you buy outside Australia. But I wasn't going to let some random delivery crew have all the fun. Anyway, is this something official or low-key private?'

'*Low-key for now, but almost certainly official before long.*'

'That's more like it!' I enthused. 'We've been back for six weeks and already we're getting bored. If it might turn official, I'll get Sandy to knock off early and pick me up. We should be there in thirty minutes or so.'

'*That'll be great, thanks Harry. But no uniform for Sandy if you don't mind.*'

'Hmmm. It's like that, is it?'

'*Just get over here Sport and stop stuffing around.*'

'You've got it, big dog! Woof!'

Mike gave the phone's handpiece a puzzled look, then grinned at Eva as he hung up. 'I think that means Harry's bored already. Anyway, I guess we'd better let our guest know what's happening.'

She smiled indulgently, 'Good thinking, 86. Two more strangers and a giant moggy might be a lot to handle on the back end of a rather fraught day, so we'd better explain the whole setup before they arrive.'

They found Hanh in the lounge room listening to rock music on the radio, and led her back to the kitchen, which as usual, turned out to be the nerve-centre of the house.

Mike sat across from Hanh, and quietly said, 'Based on what you've told us so far, I've called Sam and two of our friends, Harry and Sandy, who have helped people at various times with the more serious stuff we've come across. We reckon this situation falls very much into that category. Together with Harry's cat Jasper, they're are coming over to talk with you and get the story first hand. Harry is a retired SAS Major and lives on a big catamaran with Sandy, another couple and two cats. He's become very good at fixing-up nasty situations like this, but I have to ask you one important thing – how keen are you to see Turner and his mates sorted out properly, or doesn't it matter too much to you?'

Hanh's eyes flashed with emotion and a sudden tearing of her eyes, although she otherwise kept control. 'The Wright's kept me as a maid for two years, which I didn't mind as they were quite nice, looked after me and the work was easy. I had my own cabin and plenty of time to myself, although as an illegal immigrant, and for my own good, I was never allowed off the boat. I was never abused, and they respected my privacy. Then we ran into that piece of scum called Gary Turner, with his big, flash boat and his sex-slave network. The day I got swapped for one of his girls was when my life really did go down the tubes. He's insatiable where sex is concerned, often wanting it twice a day, every day! He made all the girls aboard run around naked most of the time unless we were at a marina. When I suggested to you earlier today that it was easy to become complacent and not fight back, the main reason was that his penalties for disobedience were very painful and humiliating. The alarm collars were additional deterrence, and both things tended to focus our attention on doing exactly what he wanted. I only escaped because I took advantage of a moment when he got careless – something he rarely did. I had additional motivation to escape, as I knew he'd already done a deal to sell me to a boating couple, and was just waiting for them to arrive and take delivery. I'd sat in on the initial meeting with them when the deal was done and it really freaked me out. They talked like I wasn't there, and sounded like a pair of raving lunatic sex maniacs. The woman was as bad as the man when they talked about what they'd planned to do with me. However, all this is a very long way of answering your question. The short version is that I'll do anything it takes to see that bastard shut down and preferably suffering what he's put me and all those other girls through! No punishment is too much for an evil, sadistic bastard like him!'

For the first time, her steely reserve cracked and she bent forward, her face in her hands, heaving sobs wracking her body.

Eva looked uncomfortable and put an arm around her, but in contrast, Mike remained unemotional and unmoved by her tears, and just waited until she recovered.

'Thanks for that explanation, Hanh,' he said quietly as her sobs subsided, 'I needed to be sure you would totally support any plan Harry comes up with. He is very good at handling this sort of problem as he believes in strong, direct action, doesn't tolerate fools and in general, isn't the sort of character you mess around. His lady, Sandy, is a serving Police Inspector, although she's coming here in an unofficial capacity for now.'

Hanh sat up in alarm, wiping tears away. 'Hang on! I can't afford to be involved with the police. I'm still an illegal immigrant!'

Mike made patting motions with his hands, 'Don't worry. I can promise you Sandy won't be concerned with that in the slightest.

She'll just want to hear everything about Turner, what he does, his contacts and plans. Every and any detail you can remember will be very helpful. All of us, including Samantha, will be working together to stop this foul scheme of Turner and his cohorts, and rescue the other girls. Anyway, as I said earlier, this is the way we do things, but I can promise that nothing will jeopardise your freedom.'

Eva added her thoughts, 'Sam will be here shortly, don't forget, so she might make you feel more comfortable.'

'That's good! It was her story which inspired me to take the first opportunity to bust out.'

CHAPTER 5

GOLD COAST, MIKE'S PLACE

Sam was the first to arrive and for a few moments, Hanh wondered who the tall, attractive blonde teenager was. That was until Mike led her over and introduced them. Hanh was suitably apologetic for getting her involved, but Sam weaved her usual charming magic to put her quickly at ease and they were soon talking as though they had known each other for years.

While they were chatting, the back door buzzer went off again.

'In here, Harry, the door's unlocked.' Eva called.

Hanh had a minor freak-out when a huge black cat, very lean, but with the general proportions of a medium-to-large dog, and with vivid green eyes, bounded into the room with a loud 'merowl' of pleasure at seeing Sam, nuzzling her face as he stood with his front paws on her knees, purring loudly with delight.

She was further disconcerted when Sam bent down and appeared to whisper a brief something in his ear, causing Jasper to turn his head to inspect Hanh carefully.

Jasper's appearance was followed by a tall and tanned, sandy-haired man with a lean, wiry body. His hair was in careless disarray, but that seemed to suit the enigmatic smile that hovered on his face. He was very casually dressed in an old, well-worn pair of shorts and a T-shirt which had several holes in it and a stylish pattern of ancient paint blotches across the front.

He was followed by a tall, strikingly-beautiful woman with the most glorious mane of thick, auburn hair cascading down her back. She was also dressed casually, in very tight jeans and a pre-shrunk T-shirt, bearing the logo for Bintang beer.

We greeted Sam, Eva and Mike like the good friends they were, then I introduced myself and Sandy to Hanh. 'And this is my cat, Jasper. He's an Indonesian jungle cat who was supposed to have been bred with a normal house cat to make him domesticated, but it didn't work very well, which is why he's so big and eats like a horse. Despite the cross-breeding not working, he's reasonably civilised, until he decides he doesn't like someone or just basically forgets his manners.'

Jasper turned away from Sam and gave a good-natured 'huff' in my direction.

'But,' I went on with a disarming grin, 'once you're properly introduced, then he's on your side... big time.' I went through Jasper's introduction routine and to her credit, Hanh stood up to the crotch-nuzzling part of the introduction with only a slight lurch backwards, impelled by Jasper's damp nose. He then captivated her by sitting back and holding up his right paw to shake hands.

'There you go, furball' I said, 'another member of the family to protect. I hope you're up to the job.'

That earned me another 'huff' as he closely inspected his new charge who was still a bit cautious, but despite that, she was obviously feeling the usual sort of strange connection with him.

I looked around at the others. 'Okay guys. What's the go with the urgent call?'

Eva waved us all to the kitchen dining table, another large slab of bleached driftwood on sturdy legs which had room for ten with space to spare, and set about making tea and coffee.

Mike and Eva seemed happy for me to take charge of the meeting and I saw Hanh give me a careful, calculating look as I opened the questioning. Having told her full story once, and answered Mike and Eva's questions, she was able to tell her tale fairly coherently and concisely. I clarified a few points along the way, and noticed Sandy jotting down her thoughts in a small notebook.

When she finished, I asked, 'How many boaties do you think have been involved in this scheme so far?'

Hanh had that answer ready, 'Not certain on the number of people, but because Mary looked after the books for Turner, she knew of forty-two boats which have been supplied with girls, and while most have just two people aboard, that could have changed since the transaction. Virtually all boats have just one girl… except for Turner's boat, *Poseidon*, of course.'

That raised my eyebrows. 'Did you learn where these boats were when Turner sold the girls?'

She thought a moment, 'I think that Yeppoon is the furthest north he's been, so from there to the Gold Coast is probably the range of sales sites, but naturally, the customers could have gone anywhere after they received their girl.'

'And do you know if any other girls have escaped?'

She shook her head, 'None that I've heard of, I'm afraid. The collars, plus the brain-washing or whatever it was that he did to the other girls to make them so compliant, seems to have been an effective deterrent.'

'Yes, I can understand that. But it seems like he didn't do any brainwashing on you? Or not that you were aware of?'

She shook her head, swishing her long hair about her shoulders. 'No, he didn't Harry. I just had the collar and his warnings not to stray. Or else!'

'That's interesting. But it's the collars which bother me the most. Were there any markings on them that you could see?'

Hanh shook her head. 'No, sorry. The spare one Gary was going to put on me was just sitting on the galley bench when he unlocked the faulty one around my neck. It was plain black plastic and he had to go to the main control panel to unlock it. I did notice that there was a tiny red light on the front of the collar buried in the plastic, which flickered briefly every ten seconds or so. It fitted together so well you could barely see the join.'

I thought some more, then said. 'Okay. That's enough for now thanks Hanh, but I need to know that you are totally willing to trust Sandy, Jasper and me as much as you trust Sam, Eva and Mike.'

Hanh seemed to think for a few moments before she nodded, 'Yes, I do.'

I smiled, 'Excellent! Mike has told me that you really want to see this character nailed, so I'd like you to stay here with Mike and Eva for now, until we work out a few details. When we've done that, I'll let you know what's happening. I'd prefer if you didn't go wandering the streets of sunny Southport too much, but I'm sure Eva will want to take you shopping for clothes and other stuff in some quieter places.'

Eva smiled and Hanh nodded, 'Okay Harry. I'll be good. But don't leave me waiting too long, please. And if we go shopping, what do I use for money? I've got nothing except the bikini I swam away in.'

'Don't worry about that. I'll cover the money side, but for now, Eva will pay for whatever you need. For the other, I expect we'll have a plan to discuss with you later today or tomorrow. Will that be alright?'

She smiled, 'Oh, yes. That'll be great, thanks.'

With that settled, we left, leaving Sam behind to get to know Hanh better, and ease her mind that she really was now on the side of the white hats.

Before we drove away, Sandy commented, 'I know what you're thinking, dearest, but this really is a crime in progress, and as such, should be handled officially.'

I laughed, 'I'm going to agree with you, but with one proviso.'

'Which would be?' she asked suspiciously, knowing how much I favoured direct and brutal action against all low-life's who preyed on children, teenagers, females of any age, or other vulnerable persons.

Paedophiles of any description incurred my especial wrath.

'As I see it, there are two crimes being committed at the same time. The girls are being detained against their will, by using an alarm collar and possibly some form of brain-washing or coercion – and the girls are being sold or traded to other sicko's! Kidnapping and sexual slavery are illegal in most civilised countries and certainly are here. Therefore, until we find out more about this and who's involved, we need to keep the investigations very quiet. Remember that Victorian paedophile business? That involved officials at all levels. Here we've got one escaped girl, three more presently on Turner's boat, and at least forty-two more out there on other boats. If we were to make too much of an official fuss, and it reached the wrong ears, they all could be made to disappear overnight. Because most are on boats, they could even be bopped on the head and tipped overboard which would instantly cover tracks. Therefore, I reckon you should mention the situation only to your Superintendent, Bob Casey, just to let him know what you're working on, and I'll do the same with my controller in Canberra.'

Sandy looked happier. 'Lovely, thanks dear. I can handle that. My life is always easier when Bob knows I'm doing actual police work and what it entails. But have you got a plan for dealing with this?'

I tried to look suitably thoughtful. 'It's forming, but needs some refinement. Let's go bring our crew, neighbours and bosses up to speed while I get our ducks in a row.'

Sandy and I lived with two of our good friends, Alex and Bree, who were former mercenaries, onboard our 83-foot sailing catamaran *Firebird*, which was moored a couple of hundred metres out from the Southport Yacht Club.

Dave and Corrine, our other very close friends, lived on their 100-foot Italian sports cruiser *Seeker*, parked much more conveniently in a berth at the Yacht Club marina which made it much easier to go visiting.

The gleaming royal-blue colour of the hull enhanced the

low, sleek lines of the massive boat which had super-luxurious accommodation, and a ridiculous amount of horsepower hiding in its spotless engine room.

Climbing up the steps to the cockpit, we found Corrine, barely wearing a micro bikini, propped up in the corner of the comfortable cockpit lounge reading a magazine. From an open hatch in the floor nearby, came a series of curses, followed by the upper half of the well-developed body of the blonde, ex-pro surfer who was Dave, the co-owner of *Seeker*.

In contrast, Corrine looked about 16, was small in frame, but supremely fit. Like me, she's also ex-SAS and had been in the Middle East desert as a sniper and close-combat expert. The end of both our military careers came when bad intelligence caused her and her squad to be ambushed by a Taliban patrol, and she was badly wounded in the subsequent firefight. That was when I turned up and managed to pull her out of a very dodgy situation which was rapidly going south. It was during that furball that I'd stupidly let myself get shot several times, an action which somehow prompted my superiors to suggest I should be awarded the VC, along with a medical discharge for both of us from the Service.

We both had a set of nasty-looking scars as a permanent reminder of the occasion.

'Hi Harry… Sandy. Beer, wine, tea?' asked Corrine.

'Much too hot for tea, Mouse,' I replied obliquely.

'I'll get them,' Sandy offered, heading for the cockpit fridge, very familiar with where everything was.

'Social or business?' Dave shrewdly asked, noting Sandy's standard of dress.

'Business,' I replied, popping the top off an ice-cold long-neck.

'Oh… outstanding! In that case, I'd better climb out of this hole and have a beer as well.'

I made a phone call to Alex and Bree on *Firebird*, suggesting they should come over ASAP so we didn't have to repeat things, and to bring a couple of bottles of Sandy's newest favourite wine, Lillypilly Sauvignon Blanc.

Once everyone was comfortable and suitably hydrated, it didn't take long for us to outline the situation Hanh had escaped from, and even less time for Corrine to remark, 'I'm guessing that both of you will inform your bosses, while we plan our own response. Hopefully, the bad guy is still in the area.'

I grinned and pointed my empty bottle at her. 'Well put, Mouse. That's exactly the case.'

She grinned, 'I'll even go one step further by guessing that your new cunning plan will be a sting operation, and you want me to play the part of a teenage sex toy so we can infiltrate the operation.'

I shook my head admiringly. 'Can't fool you for one second, now can I, Mouse? That about sums it up in very broad terms. What's everyone think?'

'Not much else we can do,' Dave chipped in, 'although if we do meet this Turner character, I'm not happy for Corrine to have one of those collars wrapped around her lovely little neck. He sounds like the original sleaze-bag.'

Corrine put an adoring expression on her face. 'Gee, Dave. That's so romantic. Maybe you do like me a little bit after all.'

'Yeah, well. You know how it is – some days you aren't too bad to have around.'

As Corrine had sometimes played the part of a young, innocent girl in previous operations, Dave's response was predictable and quite justified, but as usual, Corrine trotted out a series of arguments which counted his protests.

'I can look the part and can look after myself. We certainly can't put Hanh at risk again, not now that she's just escaped from all that crap.'

Sandy, as she often did, played devil's advocate. 'Good basic idea guys, but what level of opposition are we looking at? If this Turner character has been organising this for several years, won't he have some sort of security and protection set up? The partner and his recruitment crew who Hanh mentioned, would do for a start!'

That made everyone think for a few minutes, until I said, 'Good point, but I still think this is a small operation. Maybe just this Turner bloke, his small shore team and perhaps whoever is supplying the proximity collars. However, one of the big questions for me is… where do these bloody collars come from? There might be a lot more to this than meets the eye. Like… are they made locally or overseas? According to what Hanh has said, they're very sophisticated devices, and although our authorities use the ankle bracelet version, they're a lot bigger than these slim neck bands. I don't know of anyone using a collar as a tracker or proximity alarm before this, and really, why would you want to? There's something very odd about them.'

'Exactly my point!' Corrine exclaimed triumphantly. 'To find out, we need to get a good look at one, and the only way that's going to happen is if I get one around my neck. I mean, what's the big deal? I jump overboard when a boat is going past and they pick me up. I say I've been mistreated and don't want to go back.'

That reasoning caused a further spate of grumbles from Dave, which Corrine smugly ignored.

Sandy chipped in again. 'The sting might work, but how do we track Turner down so we can tempt him with Corrine? We don't know his boat or what he looks like, and we can't have Hanh aboard to identify him. We only know its name.'

That succinct observation quietened discussion for a few moments, until I spoke slowly, while my mind raced, 'Not necessarily…'

'Oh, bugger it, Harry! No, no and no way!' Sandy interjected. 'I really hate it when you say things like that. It usually means someone else gets to stick their head in the noose yet again!'

I grinned, patted her denim-clad leg and uttered the other words she hated, 'Don't worry, my darling lady. I have a cunning plan.'

'Gee, that makes me feel better already! Things are going to be fucked-up before we even start!' Sandy replied sarcastically.

As always, I ignored her sarcasm and added, 'We know Turner was in the area this morning, although he's sure to have moved away from the Jumpinpin area by now. If we were to just revert to our usual undercover role of being degenerate wealthy boat bums, boozing and wenching our way around Australia, we'll attract Turner to us like flies to a dunny door. However, first we need to get Hanh's co-operation, and quickly.'

'What for?' Sandy asked in her most reasonable tone, which I knew from long experience meant she was about to be anything but.

I gave her my best 'gee-whiz' grin. 'Because we need to have her along to identify Turner and his boat. We're going to pose as her rescuers, and when we catch up with Turner, no matter what he says, we're going to refuse to give her back. We might, however, after a lot of arm-twisting, offer to let him take a substitute!'

All eyes focused on Corrine for a few moments. 'That still means using Hanh as initial bait,' Sandy said with a sour expression.

I smiled gently at my dear lady, 'It's the only way were going to find the bad guy, dearest – by letting him find us. With Corrine, Bree and Hanh acting the part of young, fun girls, we head north and try to mingle with as many groups of boaties as we can. We can tell the story about how we recently added to our collection of young girls by finding this girl floating past and saved her, but she refused to tell us where she came from.'

I looked across at Bree, sitting quietly beside her devoted partner, the giant South African ex-mercenary, Alex Chetty. 'Please excuse me for volunteering you for this role Bree, but it's just for appearances. You can easily pass for a young adult.'

Bree laughed, which eased the tension. 'Good on you Harry, and thanks for the sort of backward compliment. I'll play the part as long as I don't have to go with Turner. I don't really like collars.'

'Thanks Bree and no, you definitely won't be leaving the boat. We'll refine the plan a bit more as we go, but it won't be a difficult part to act. I just hope Hanh will be willing to come along. She'll be a vital part of the operation.'

Alex spoke up in his deep, slow rumble. 'If she does agree,

protecting her from Turner at all costs will be essential.'

'That's a given, Alex.' I replied. 'I've already promised that we'd protect her and that's what will happen.'

It was Dave's turn to ask, 'Tell me more about this plan to get Turner to take Corrine aboard instead of Hanh?'

I expanded on the plan which was still forming in my mind as he spoke. This was, by now, a familiar process to all of them, as I find it highly beneficial, even essential, to run my ideas past those who were going to be involved in making them work.

'When we trip across Turner, he's going to arc-up about us having his runaway slave, but we're going to stand firm. We saved her – we keep her. Finders keepers, losers can get stuffed and all that crap. He can rant and rave all he likes, but when he settles down, we could confirm our level of degeneracy by reluctantly offering to let him have Corrine as a trade. We can make up a legend to explain her origins and say that while we've had her for a while, she seems to be getting tired of us. We're certainly fed up with her bitching about everything all the time. Hanh has proved to be much more compliant and agreeable. But as long as Turner has Corrine, we have to stick very close until we can find out more about his sex-slave scheme and these collars.'

As an action plan, it was very thin on detail, but at least it was a start.

'What's going to be the timetable?' Alex asked. 'As you said, Turner can't be too far away. It seems we should move as soon as possible.'

'Yep. You're right,' I replied. 'At the latest, we should leave by early tomorrow morning, if we can get everything organised.'

There was no disagreement to that, so after a bit more discussion, Sandy had the last word. 'We'd better go back to Mike's right now to explain this plan face-to-face, to make sure that Hanh will go along with it.'

'Also,' she added, 'we need to talk to our respective superiors as soon as we can to get their approval.'

We did that job first. While Bree and Alex went back to *Firebird* to check the food and booze supply, I called my base in Canberra, giving my controller, an unseen lady who had come to like to be called 'M' and always seemed to be on duty, a rundown of the situation. She must have been quite senior in the pecking order, because she immediately approved my plan to move forward, and to do what we thought was necessary to infiltrate this slavery ring, as she called it. Naturally, I had first call on all or any Federal resources as necessary.

Sandy called Bob Casey, the station Superintendent, and as the afternoon was slipping away, asked him to stay in the office until she returned with me in tow.

He and I were old friends, based on several successful previous operations, some of which had involved us borrowing some of his officers to supplement our forces or bolster our legend.

Although injuries to his staff on those operations had been minimal, he was always wary of any of my plans which involved some of his staff, Sandy included.

After we explained the situation, he looked at Sandy, gave a theatrical sigh, and said, 'Very well, Inspector. This seems a worthy investigation and due to the number of other girls out there, I can appreciate the need to keep it very low profile, despite the implications posed by these collars.'

He swivelled his gaze to me, glaring from beneath his famously large, bushy eyebrows. 'I trust, Harry, that apart from Inspector Thomson, you don't need to borrow any of my staff for this operation? You would seem to have sufficient personnel in hand.'

I coughed gently, causing his brow to immediately crease into a deep frown, 'Well, actually Bob, since I'm still developing the plan, I was thinking that even taking our full crew, we could use at least one more female who looks very young. If you happened to have such a person, that is?'

His eyebrows bristled to complement the frown, so I hastily added, 'She'd only be there as window dressing, so to speak. She wouldn't be expected to have close encounters with the enemy, for instance, if I may use a military term.'

He de-bristled slightly, and looked at Sandy. 'Hmmm. Well, Inspector. Do you agree that the additional person is necessary?'

My request was news to Sandy but she stoically supported me and lied glibly. 'Oh, yes sir. Very necessary. For the plan to work properly, we need to have a good supply of our own young ladies, so we can appear to be in a position where we could release one without interfering with our usual degenerate lifestyle. Our cover lifestyle, I mean, sir,' she added hastily.

He glowered at me, obviously thinking of the many young policemen and women I'd borrowed in the past and returned quite morally corrupted. Once they got a taste of the sort of life and action I seemed to attract, they became addicted, wanting more, while returning to traffic or general duties was pretty tame afterwards.

In my defence, I'd always returned them in more or less the same condition as they'd been received. Well, mostly the same anyway. I can't help what they think!

With another long-suffering look at me, he sighed, 'Very well then. Do we have someone who would suit this unusual requirement, Inspector?'

Sandy tried to look apologetic, something which doesn't usually sit well with her. 'Well, sir… coincidentally there is a Constable, Regina Morgan, who does fit that description rather well. She hasn't been at this station very long, but has an excellent record so far.'

Bob rubbed his eyes in frustration. 'Bugger it Harry. You're doing it again. All right Inspector, I'll approve the transfer of Constable Morgan to your direct command, and leave it to you to brief her.'

I rose and sketched a salute, 'Thanks Bob. I appreciate your assistance once again. We'll look after her.'

'Now why doesn't that reassure me,' he growled to the room in general as he shooed me out the door with a wave of his hand, Sandy following me back to her office.

CHAPTER 6

'I think we just gave Bob a new set of grey hairs,' Sandy said with a quiet chuckle, sitting at her desk, while I sprawled in one of the two visitor's chairs. 'Shall we check out this Constable now if she's here?'

'Yes, please,' I said, 'the sooner we get this bunfight rolling, the better. To save time, I'll call Mike and explain the plan to Hanh. If she agrees, we can pick her up in the morning.'

I did that, giving Mike and Hanh a heads-up on the plan at the same time. To my relief, Hanh agreed immediately. While I was sorting out our precious bait, Sandy phoned the front desk and was told Constable Regina Morgan was presently in-station, buried deep in the file archives shuffling dusty papers, but would be sent up immediately.

I pushed my chair back against one wall, out of direct view and we waited.

Within five minutes, there was a polite knock on the open door and a uniformed police-woman stepped inside, coming to attention one pace inside. She was slightly breathless, her brownish hair dishevelled, and a broad smear of dust bisected by a dribble of perspiration adorned her left cheek.

'You wanted to see me, Inspector?'

Her voice was light and clear, and at first glance certainly looked like she should have still been at school. She was probably right on the minimum height for a female officer, with a slim build and was pretty. I noted approvingly that her breasts were reasonably compact and her hips slim, reinforcing her overall appearance as a young adult. Because of that, she'd probably copped a hard time at the Academy.

Sandy smiled, in an attempt to put her at ease.

'Yes Constable, I did. Thanks for coming up promptly. But first, I'd like to introduce Commander Stevens of the Commonwealth Police.'

Constable Morgan turned smartly, slightly taken aback to see a tall, tousled-haired man, clad in casual shorts and an old T-shirt, sprawled inelegantly in the other chair.

She recovered quickly, bobbed her head and said, 'A pleasure to meet you, Commander,' before turning to face Sandy again.

Sandy tried not to grin too much as she added, 'Purely as a by-the-way, Constable, the Commander out-ranks both myself and the Superintendent.'

'Yes, ma'am, thank you. How may I be of assistance to you and the Commander?'

'You can start by closing the door and taking a seat, if you would. We have a lot to cover and very little time to do it.'

We waited until she had done so, then Sandy said, 'If you are agreeable to what the Commander and I are about to tell you, you will be transferred from General Duties to my direct command, effectively immediately, on an undercover assignment. However, that is wholly dependent upon you volunteering for this assignment. I'll let the Commander explain further.'

Regina kept an impassive look and politely swivelled her chair to face me.

I chose my words carefully. 'As the Inspector has said, we are inviting you to be part of an undercover operation, which is still very much in the early planning stages, but which, due to circumstances, is forcing us to move quickly. You have, shall we say, certain attributes which make you a desirable part of the plan.'

She looked about to ask a question, so I held my hand up.

'Hold the questions for a few minutes if you will. All will be revealed, but we need to get past this first bit. This operation may have an element of risk, at this stage we don't know how high, but in your case, probably somewhat comparable to that if you were sent to sort-out a domestic disturbance. Being an undercover operation, there will be a large element of role-playing required, as we all need to get deep into our cover roles very quickly and stay there, regardless of what happens around us. That's how undercover works. You may find yourself going along with, or even taking part in illegal activities, but you must never break your cover unless instructed to do so by a superior officer. The other thing about undercover, is that role-playing starts immediately you sign up. Once we are away from this station, there must be no hint of Service protocols at any time. That means no saluting – no Sir's or Ma'am's. I'll be Harry and the Inspector will be Sandy. Forget that just once at the wrong time, and we're all in trouble with a blown operation, or worse. You also won't be able to communicate with your partner, friends or family for the duration. It's like you and your normal life will be put on hold for the weeks, or however long the operation takes. We also can't take a time-out or a work-break until it's over. Some people can't handle that and it won't be held against you if you don't think you can. There are obviously bad guys involved, although at the moment we don't know just how bad they are or how many we might be up against. Apart from the Inspector and myself, there are another five persons on our team, none of whom are police officers, although three, plus myself, are ex-military. I must add that this operation is approved by Superintendent Casey, however, should you think it's not for you, you may return to General Duties immediately, and no record of this conversation or your decision will appear on your record – although you may not speak of this particular conversation to anyone. Unfortunately, that's all the information I can offer until you volunteer for the operation.'

Constable Morgan sat for a few moments, apparently digesting the information and my warnings, then said, 'No problem sir. I'm in. I volunteer.'

I smiled at her and Sandy. 'Excellent, thank you Constable. Please note, Inspector that Constable has volunteered for the operation, which is nameless at the moment.'

Sandy smiled briefly. 'So noted, Commander. Welcome aboard, Constable.'

I picked up the lead again. 'In that case, we'll give you a briefing so you know what we know. But first, I must ask – is there anyone at home who will be concerned or bothered if you are away and out of contact for a while?'

She returned my smile, her face lighting up with excitement. 'No sir. No partner and no cat. I share a flat in Broadbeach with another constable, and we expect to be moved around on the job. She won't be concerned if I say I'm going away for a few weeks or longer. Jealous, perhaps, but no problem. My parents live in Sydney and are used to not hearing from me for weeks at a time.'

I nodded, 'That's good. Now, what do your friends call you? Gina?'

She blushed slightly, 'Actually, I'm usually called Reggie.'

I grinned, 'If you're happy with that, Reggie it is.'

We spent the next fifteen minutes telling her what we knew, which wasn't a great deal, before giving her the rough plan.

'I hope you don't mind boats or cats, because you'll be living on our boat for the duration, and we've got two cats. I also hope that modesty won't prevent you spending your day in a bikini, weather permitting. I have to add that your role may sometimes require you to wear even less, depending on the circumstances.'

She held a commendably straight face, and said, 'Yessir. I understand that, in the line of duty, I have to look and act like a sex-crazed, drug-loving, air-headed bimbo. I also wish to state that I won't have a problem being in a bikini or less. I don't know much about boats and I like cats, but if I may ask, how far do I have to take the role-playing?'

Sandy looked puzzled for a moment, then gave a small grin.

'Oh. I see. Ah… only what would be expected if we have the bad guys aboard or possibly watching. You can play up all you like or not – it's up to you. Mostly, it's best if you act as though you're on a free pleasure cruise and are determined to enjoy yourself. That will be the best cover as it's virtually the truth. If it's any consolation, we don't exactly live rough – on or off the job.'

Reggie nodded. 'I think I understand. I presume I'll have some time to get used to things?'

I picked up that query. 'No, I'm afraid not, although moving aboard tonight will help if you can do that. If Hanh will get with the plan, she'll come aboard in the morning, then we need to get going in case this Turner character moves too far out of the area to take our bait.'

She nodded. 'I understand and I'll do my best to fit in. It's all a bit overwhelming at the moment, but I'll be fine.'

'Do you have your personal vehicle here?'

'Not today, sir… sorry, Harry. My flatmate is on the same shift this roster, so we came in hers.'

I looked at Sandy. 'No problem. We're done here, so we'll take you home and wait while you pack. I forgot to say that from the moment you leave this office, you cannot say anything to anybody about what you're doing or where you're going.'

She nodded understanding, and as we let Reggie walk out ahead of us, I looked at Sandy.

'Will she be okay?'

She smiled and nodded. 'Yeah. She'll be fine. I checked her record and she can look after herself very well, despite her looks and size. She's rated well with weapons and fair to good with hand-to-hand combat.'

I nodded. 'Maybe you can sharpen her manual skills a bit once we get going.'

We found Reggie waiting in the carpark, and were soon on our way through the traffic to Broadbeach in our slightly rusty old Falcon. Her shared flat was in a plain, two-story block of four built with pale brick, and was typically slightly messy and pleasantly lived-in.

'What should I pack,' Reggie asked.

'Just casual clothes, bikinis and some warm stuff like trakkie-daks and tops, but leave the cocktail dress behind. Bring enough for at least several weeks. If you need anything else, we'll buy it on the run. Bring your official ID, weapon and handcuffs, but no uniform. We have plenty of .40 calibre rounds and spare magazines aboard. Pack it all in soft bags, please.'

Sandy and I hung around in the lounge-room while Reggie bustled about collecting stuff, and to her credit, was ready in about ten minutes.

'I left a note for Mandy, my flatmate, to say that I was going to be away on assignment for a few weeks and that I'd fix up the rent when I got back.'

Sandy whipped her little note pad out and made a notation.

'I'll take care of that for you.'

Fifteen minutes later, we had parked at the Yacht Club, and were walking down one of the long marina jetties. Reggie looked a lot like our daughter, trailing along behind with a bulging backpack and a smaller carry bag, her head swivelling around looking at all the insanely-expensive, white fibreglass on display. I thought I heard her mutter, 'fuckin' hell' a couple of times, and murmured to Sandy, 'I think she's gonna fit in okay'.

I turned to Reggie. 'We're going to check in with two more of our crew first, then we'll go out to *Firebird*. The kitties will be getting hungry.'

'Oh, okay.'

She was gobsmacked when we stepped across onto the stern board of the 100-foot-long Italian power cruiser, *Seeker*.

'You can dump your bags down here for the moment,' I said, 'we'll get picked up in our dinghy shortly.'

Dave and Corrine were waiting in the cockpit, having spotted us coming down the jetty.

They made Reggie welcome and Corrine took her on a quick tour of the boat, while Sandy and I filled Dave in on the latest.

When the girls returned, Reggie looked even more stunned by the sheer opulence of the interior of the big boat. I said to Dave and Corrine, 'How about you guys come over for a BBQ in about an hour. We'll get Reggie settled in and see if anybody has more bright ideas for this slightly sketchy plan.'

Dave and Corrine were happy with that, so we collected Reggie's bags again and waited for Alex to collect us.

The sun was settling low on the horizon as we pulled up at the stern steps of our 83-foot catamaran, and I let the ladies climb the steps to the cockpit where Bree had drinks ready.

While not as long as *Seeker*, *Firebird* was more than twice the width, which made for an imposing first impression. I carted Reggie's bags up to the cockpit, suffering Jasper's and Krazy's enthusiastic greetings, even though I'd only been away a few hours.

Reggie promptly retreated down the steps when my huge black cat jumped up onto the stern daybed beside the stern steps to inspect her with his serious look, but was soon won over by the introduction process and his solemn paw shake. With Krazy perched happily on her shoulder and purring loudly, she was introduced to Bree, who took the additional guest in stride.

'Which cabin for Reggie, Harry?' Bree asked.

'Ah… Dave and Corrine will have the port midships queen, so Reggie can have the starboard forward twin, thanks Bree. I'll do the tour and induction in a moment. Oh, nearly forgot. Dave and Corrine are coming over for dinner as well. We can just have a BBQ seeing as you weren't prepared for three extra guests.'

Used to my usually erratic habits, she smiled indulgently. 'All good, Harry. I've got dinner in hand. You go settle our new crew member in.'

I grinned cheekily at her, 'Yes, Boss-lady.'

Reggie wasn't sure what was going on, but seemed to pick up

that life on board was rather laid-back. Accompanied by the two cats, I led Reggie across the mini-ballroom space which was the combined lounging, dining and galley space, pointing out stuff on the way. 'Stairway aft on the right goes to the cabin Sandy and I share, while Alex and Bree have the one over there on the left. The forward set of stairs on the left leads to another queen cabin where Dave and Corrine will bunk, and forward of that is the laundry and workshop, with another twin cabin forward of that.

This forward stairway on the right leads to a twin-bunk midships cabin, with another twin-bunk cabin forward of the shared bathroom. I might put you in the forward cabin for now, but you can have the middle one if you want. Hanh will have whichever cabin you don't want, but you'll be sharing a bathroom.'

Reggie loved the layout and was impressed by the comfort and spaciousness, and promptly stated, 'The forward cabin is fine for me.'

'Good-oh. If you have any problems, you can access our stern cabin via a door in the midships cabin, or go back up to the saloon and down the aft stairway. There are bathrooms everywhere. For safety and ventilation, we ask that you leave cabin doors open, and only close bathroom doors when you're using them.'

I gave her the briefing about power and water conservation and explained that we were almost exclusively an electric boat.

'We do have a pair of small diesel generators for emergencies, but our power mainly comes from solar, wind and hydro-regeneration from the electric motors when we sail, which is most of the time. We make our own water, so it's very pure. There are a lot of things on deck to trip over, so I'll give you a brief topside tour now, and a better one tomorrow when we get underway.'

She dumped her bags in the forward cabin, used the bathroom briefly, then joined me in the saloon. I showed her the laundry, workshop and the twin cabin forward of that, then checked out the galley where Bree was busy stirring something cooking in a large pot which smelled terrific.

'I don't know much about boats,' Reggie said, hesitantly, 'but I'm more than happy to help with any of the house-keeping chores.'

Bree gave her a big smile. 'I usually do the cooking, but a hand with all the other stuff will be great, thanks. I let the guys look after all the string-pulling boat stuff.'

With that settled, I took her on deck and delivered the usual caution about moving carefully topside and always hanging on with one hand. She loved the peaceful panorama of the calm water reflecting the myriad lights which turn the Gold Coast into a fairy-land at night, accompanied by the soft, sonic background mix of surf and traffic roar.

'This is so peaceful, Harry. It's like we're in another world, yet the Gold Coast is right there. I can see why you live on a boat. It's fabulous.'

I smiled, 'Yeah. It is, although when it blows and rains, getting ashore isn't so comfortable or glamorous. Under those conditions, we tend to stay aboard, although Sandy does have to go to work sometimes.'

The evening meal was some sort of Hungarian Goulash served with rice and tasted great. Bree was born to be a gourmet chef. We could have made another fortune by offering meals at 'Harry's Café Mittout de Wheels.'

Afterwards, with a round of NQ teas on the table, I suggested an itinerary for the morrow.

'I've told Mike and Hanh about our plan and she's happy to help, so if she joins us in the morning, Dave and Corrine, you move in as soon as you can. Mouse, you had better bring as many of your toys as you can too, since we don't know what we'll be facing. Sandy or I will go collect Hanh. Then we can get straight into degenerate boaties mode and get going as soon as we're stocked up.'

Bree smiled at me, 'Already made up the lists, Harry. We can hit the supermarket first thing, and should be back by the time you get Hanh.'

'Oh, great. I don't think we'll have to stray too far from civilisation this trip, but if we can get Corrine on Turner's boat, we need to be prepared to stick very close like he's our newest bestie. At least until we find out what's going on.'

I looked at Sandy. 'Is *Dragonfly* still aboard?'

'Yep. I'll charge the batteries, and there's plenty of fuel and oil.'

I said to Alex. 'I think the generator tanks are full and everything else seems ship-shape.'

'Yes, Harry,' he rumbled, finally remembering not to call me Commander, which had been his normal habit, despite all we'd been through together. 'Everything is in top condition.'

There was a palpable air of excitement coming from our group as each mentally prepared to face the unknown foe. 'Okay. Bring on tomorrow.'

CHAPTER 7

UNDER-WAY

The next morning, while Sandy, Bree and Alex looked after the re-supply run, I was knocking on Mike's side entrance at 07:30 and found Hanh in the kitchen cleaning up after breakfast.

'Hi Harry, I'm packed and ready to go. Eva took me shopping yesterday afternoon so I have more clothes than I've ever had before.'

I smiled at her upbeat manner. 'Thanks for doing this, Hanh. I didn't like to involve you so closely, but it seemed the only way to attract Turner's attention, and your presence will make the swap with Corrine much more feasible.'

Eva bustled into the kitchen to make coffees. 'We've got a 08:30 customer,' she explained, 'so we have to be quick.'

'No problem. If Hanh's ready, we have to go anyway. We need to get to Moreton Bay ASAP, before Turner decides to head further away from the area where he lost Hanh.'

I looked at Hanh, but what I said was as much for her ears as it was for Mike and Eva.

'In return for your help with this plan, I need to make it clear that we have no intention of letting Turner anywhere near you, let alone getting his grubby paws on you. We have enough crew, including Jasper, who are firmly committed to making sure you stay very safe at all times.'

Hanh responded with the familiar intensity we'd heard the last time the name of her captor and tormentor was mentioned. 'If it's going to help nail that rotten bastard, I'll do absolutely anything.'

I smiled, 'That's what we like to hear, but you do understand that we can't just grab him the first time we find him? We need to find out who's supplying these collars, and if there's more to this foul scheme than just sex and money. I have a nasty feeling there's something deeper behind all this. Therefore, we need solid evidence, which in turn means we will have to stick close to him and demonstrate our degenerate lifestyle as expected.'

Hanh nodded seriously. 'Sure. I understand all that and nothing will be a problem. Just knowing that I won't be abused or hurt again, will make whatever I need to do a real pleasure.'

As Hanh had said, Eva had taken her shopping and made sure she had all the clothes, make-up and supplies she would need, packed in a pair of soft bags. While Eva processed my credit card to pay for everything, and Hanh fetched her bags, I said to Mike, 'I'll call Russell Beal and ask him to keep an eye out for any boat with one guy and a bunch of young girls aboard.'

'Good idea. But make sure he keeps quiet about it, although I don't reckon Turner will hang around after losing a girl like that.'

I considered his words, 'I'm not so sure. In his place, I'd want to know whether Hanh survived or not, so he might at least still be in the area. It's a pity Hanh didn't get a better look at his boat.'

'Yeah. Something more than just its name, *Poseidon*, would be better. That was a very broad description she gave – thirty-five of her paces from bow to stern adds up to about sixty-odd feet, with a centre wheelhouse.'

I shrugged. 'It's better than nothing and will have to do for starters.'

With Hanh in tow, we headed back to the boat and installed her safely aboard. While Sandy and Bree introduced her to the crew and showed her around the boat, I called the number Mike had given me.

'*Russell speaking.*'

'Hi Russell. My name is Harry Stevens and I've been given your number by Mike Adams.'

'*Yes, Harry? What can I do for you?*'

'My crew and I have your rescuee, Hanh, aboard my boat. We're in a position to both care for and protect her. Without going into too many details, I can also tell you that we're trying to locate the person who was holding her, but we could use your eyes to help with that search.'

'Hmmm. I'm glad to hear that someone is looking for him, but I wouldn't like to do anything which would put Joy and me at risk, Harry. As a retired lawyer, I'm not a very gung-ho type, I'm afraid.'

I laughed. 'No problem, Russell. We're willing and more than capable of doing the gung-ho stuff when and if it comes to that, but as you're part of the live-aboard boating community, I'd appreciate any sighting you might make or hear of a boat which is around sixty-five feet long, named *Poseidon*, with a centre wheelhouse and a single guy with several young girls aboard.'

'Oh. Sure. That's doable. How can I contact you?'

I gave him several mobile numbers, including *Firebird's* SatPhone.

'You can call anytime you see or hear of something which might be our target, but where are you now?'

He chuckled, 'We haven't gone far. Just up the bay to the Myora anchorage. Joy didn't like the mozzie hordes that hang around the swampy islands near Jumpinpin. After a few days at Myora, we thought we might head further north to the Great Sandy Straits.'

'Good choice. Do you think there's there any chance that this bloke, his name is Gary Turner, by the way, could be still anywhere around the Jacob's Well area?'

'No, Harry. Since we passed Hanh on to Mike and Eva, we stocked up and motored up here to Myora, but we've not seen a boat like that. I must confess that I've been quite intrigued by the story Mike passed on, so we've been keeping an eye out.'

'Sounds good and thanks for that. We're about to depart Southport now, so we might head straight for Myora as well and catch up. It's a good starting point for us. I'll give you some more info when we meet.'

'Lovely, thanks Harry. Looking forward to seeing you there.'

YACHT CLUB CARPARK

A well-built man, dressed in shorts and a T-shirt was sitting on the grass verge beside the Yacht Club car park, a long fishing rod angled out toward the water. At a casual glance, he was just another hopeful wetting a line, although a more detailed look would show that he didn't reel in very often to check his bait. Dark shades and a cap pulled low over his eyes shielded where he was looking. Which in this case, was at a man and two women getting in a dinghy tied to the marina jetty.

'Yeah, Rob.'

'Hey, Korey. I just spotted the girl with an older couple getting in a dinghy at the Yacht Club. I can't see which boat they're going to, there's too many others in the way, but I'm pretty sure she's going to one of them.'

'Good work. Stay put and see if any boats leave within the next hour, then come back. I'll let Gary know.'

'Roger that.'

By the time I finished chatting with Russell, the girls had organised everything below for travel, including stowing all the new supplies. Dave and Alex had hoisted the dinghy at the stern, checked all the sailing lines and were ready to drop the mooring chain. Unlike a normal boat with diesel engines, I had set *Firebird* up to be fully electric, including dual electric drive motors in each hull, and electro-hydraulic sail controls. A large, but lightweight lithium battery bank stored the power supplied by a combination of solar, wind and hydro-regeneration when we sailed.

Consequently, once Alex dropped the mooring chain, getting underway was as simple as turning on two master power switches, and advancing the twin throttles. There was no vibration – just a faint hum coming from below the cockpit floor while a gentle boil of water showed behind each stern. If necessary, acceleration could be quite brisk when the power was applied quickly, but in the confines of the anchorage, less was usually less stressful.

Once in the main north channel passing the bustling and noisy helicopter operation at Marina Mirage, then the trawler basin, and with SeaWorld coming up on the right, I pressed the appropriate buttons and hoisted the tall mainsail and the self-tacking inner staysail. Turning the drive motors off, I selected the regeneration mode and the system automatically set the propellor pitch to the most efficient angle to make the motors act as generators.

The last of the light westerly land-breeze moved the two slender hulls along at a steady eight knots for now, which was nearly silent and very comfortable. It also let Bree prepare and serve a welcome morning tea of one of my favourites – fresh scones with real whipped cream and jam.

Both Hanh and Reggie were fascinated by the whole un-fussed process and our silent, effortless movement under power or sail. Sandy took both girls up forward onto the expanse of trampoline netting between the slim bows, which was a favourite place to sit or lie when in motion, watching the water slip past just below.

With the air temperature steadily climbing, Sandy had already stripped down to a bikini, a sight I always admired, as did many of the guests on several cruise boats we slowly overhauled. Once past the Seaway and the opening to the ocean, Sandy must have suggested to the other two that this would be a good time to get into undercover mode. They went below briefly, Reggie re-appearing in a suitably brief and neatly-filled bikini, while Hanh, with greater experience of the required role, came back in just a pair of brief panties. She was tall for an Asian girl, and was very nicely built. I gave both a smile of appreciation, causing Reggie to nervously ask, 'Should I take my top off too?'

'Only if you're comfortable being topless,' I replied. 'If you are, then it won't hurt to get a bit of sun on your rather nice pale bits.'

She grinned in return and took her top off, before re-joining

Sandy and Hanh up for'rard. It wasn't long before Corrine joined them, also topless, followed by Bree, but she kept her bikini top on as always.

Still, it was a much smaller bikini than she normally wore, and really didn't cover or hide much.

Alex was happy to take the wheel, so Dave and I wandered up to join the ladies.

'What's the plan now, big dog,' Corrine asked, eyeing me cheekily.

I sat, attempting to conceal the bulge in my shorts. 'Russell Beal, the chap who rescued Hanh, has already checked the Jacob's Well area for any sign of Turner, so I said we'd meet him at Myora, which will be a good overnight anchorage. We can visit Peel Island, Dunwich and all the usual anchorages over the next few days, generally just showing ourselves, and hopefully we'll get a sight of him.'

'How long will we stay around Moreton Bay?' Sandy asked.

'Probably only four or five days. It'll take some time to visit all the popular anchorages, although there's no need to go to all the major marinas over toward Brisbane. There's too many of them and they're mostly just parking places for little-used, expensive boats.'

Dave and I stayed and chatted with the girls for a while, as Alex steered us north up the narrow passages inside South Stradbroke Island. I was keen to see how Reggie and Hanh settled in with the other girls, and was encouraged that Reggie relaxed quickly in such a different environment. It was hard to picture the young-looking girl who was lounging back, nearly naked in a group of strangers, as being the uniformed Constable from just yesterday.

Hanh also appeared relaxed, without any trace of the nervousness Mike had told us about. She must have meant what she said about being happy to do whatever was required, now she knew she was protected from bad guys.

Once we reached the Jumpinpin area, the channels became too narrow and winding to sail safely, so we stowed all sail, and switched the motors back on until we cleared the bulk of Warren Island and entered the bottom end of Moreton Bay proper.

With more sea-room and with the south-east sea breeze kicking in nicely, the motors were shut down and sail hoisted again, including the huge Code Zero, which tended to look like a football field sized chunk of light-weight fabric. Our speed increased nicely to around twenty knots, and less than twenty minutes later we cheekily sailed into the shallow, sheltered bay of Myora, just two miles northeast of the township of Dunwich on North Stradbroke Island. Only one boat was anchored there, a powerboat with a white hull and blue upperworks. It was the work of just a few minutes to furl all sails and engage the drive motors again, before making a more sedate approach to the Beal's boat.

We anchored close-by and Russell and Joy came over in their din-ghy. I noted that the girls stayed true to their cover and remained mostly undressed, and even Reggie appeared unfazed, appearing to be almost relishing her role.

Russell and Joy were introduced all around, and greeted Hanh like an old friend. In turn, she thanked them again and hugged them, Joy grinning at Russell's discomfort at being hugged by the near-naked young lady.

I'd talked to Sandy about how much to tell the Beal's about our mission, and we decided that given his legal background and their boating situation, they could be trusted allies, and would be vital additional eyes and ears in our search. Therefore, we sat them down and gave a full briefing while Bree and Hanh organised lunch. I left out my ACP background and let it be assumed that I was loosely attached to the Queensland Police. The Beal's admired our cover and said that we looked totally convincing as a group of degenerate boaties. High praise indeed!

Russell chuckled after he'd chewed a chunk of sandwich and washed it down with a swig of beer, 'I must admit, Harry, that I didn't really know what to expect when this large, low and very red catamaran suddenly swerved into the bay at full speed under sail. I guess you need the big crew to stow all your sails so quickly. And I love the mufflers on your engines. We couldn't hear a thing when you motored up to us.'

I had a chuckle. 'Actually Russell, Alex did the whole thing without leaving the wheel. Nobody else had to lift a finger. The whole sail-handling process is fully automated and the drive motors are all electric.'

He was suitably stunned, so I had to lift one of the engine room hatches at the rear of the cockpit. The opening revealed a steep set of steps leading down into an open, uncluttered space with full standing headroom. There were two sets of blue-painted motor stacks standing up from the floor like a pair of sixty-litre oil drums, and two of the three reverse-osmosis water-makers were mounted against the forward bulkhead.

Reggie and Hanh, keen to see more of the boat, came down as well, but even with four of us down there, it wasn't too crowded.

Russell was amazed by the lack of obvious machinery. 'Is this it?' he asked. 'There's no oil or grease in sight, no fuel smell at all and I could eat off the floor.'

I smiled, 'It's easy to keep the area clean without diesel fuel, fumes and oil everywhere. The light-weight lithium batteries are in two big banks, one in each hull and forward of here. There's a small back-up diesel generator in a small, sealed compartment in each hull aft of here, which are vented overboard, so no smell. They rarely get used, although I test them every couple of weeks. Most times, we can live at a mooring or sail for extended periods without using any fuel at all. We have a limited range of electric only motoring at night or in very bad weather, but overall, that's not been much of a problem. We can fire up the generators to extend our range considerably if really necessary.'

Russell was noticeably distracted by the close presence of the two girls who still hadn't put any more clothes on, and soon beat a hasty retreat back up to the cockpit.

'Bloody marvellous, Harry. I've heard of boats with all-electric systems, but this is the first I've seen. And obviously, you've tested it thoroughly.'

I grinned, 'The delivery trip was roughly seven thousand five hundred miles in some pretty terrible weather with virtually no problems.'

That raised his eyebrows. 'That sounds like a good story.'

'It's a very long story, I'm afraid, but I can give you the short version. The long version will have to wait until I can talk Sandy into writing the book. But no rush. We'll stay here tonight, then go poke our noses into some of the more popular anchorages tomorrow.

CHAPTER 8

That morning, some 350 kilometres north of the Gold Coast, Detectives Tom Webb and his partner, Harriet Butler, were seated at their usual table in a café in the main street, finishing up breakfast. Tom was in his 50s, divorced and putting on more weight than he liked. Harriet, being in her early 30s and keen to make headway in the Service, was fit although short and stocky in build. Harriet was also new to detective ranks and had a lot of respect for Tom who acted more like her big brother than a colleague.

As usual, they were talking shop, with the main topic being the gruesome discovery of the female head on the beach at Burnett Heads just two days ago. They'd been on duty at the time and had attended the scene. With no urgent matters pending that morning, they were happy to linger over coffee, especially as the outside windows were freshly-speckled with rain, and the hissing of passing vehicle tyres on the wet pavement grew louder.

All was peaceful until Tom's mobile phone rang and he cursed when he saw the caller was the dispatcher.

'Yeah, Ellen. Wot's the go?'

'*You two are the go,*' was the short answer. '*The rest of the bits that presumably used to be attached to your female head have washed ashore around the corner on the Burnett Heads' main beach. A couple of tourists walking in the rain came across it not long ago, and they're freaking out. The local constable will meet you at the end of Scott Street and take you to the remains. The ambos are nearly there, and the boss says hustle, please. There's a crowd building and TV are on the way.*'

'Terrific. Okay, Ellen. We're rolling. Cheers.'

Twenty minutes later, they had joined two uniformed officers and a growing crowd of thrill-seeking gawkers clustered around the headless torso of a naked female. Apart from some nibbling of flesh by small fish and crabs, the torso was surprisingly intact, although it looked like it had been in the water several days. That allowed Tom and Harriet to note that along with the head, most of the neck was missing as well, and although the separation wasn't a clean cut, it didn't seem to have been chewed off by fish or sharks either.

'Remember the head we saw,' Harriet commented, 'if I recall correctly, it didn't have much neck either.'

Tom considered her remark. 'Yeah, you're right. At the time, I thought that whoever cut the head off must have left the neck attached to the torso. But it looks as though the whole thing is missing.'

Harriet squatted down and peered closely at the raw, bloodless wound almost flush with the shoulders.

'Look here, Tom. What's that line of discolouration around the edge of the neck opening? Could it be traces of a tattoo? That might help with an ID if a good lab could get a sample.'

Tom squatted beside her. 'Good pick-up. I didn't notice the same marks on the head, but there wasn't much to see anyway. We need to get the Coroner's opinion on this. She might be able to make something of those marks. Apart from the obvious, there's something very nasty about this, so we'll let the ambos take her back to Bundy. There's nothing else left here to see. It's no accident and not the original crime scene.'

Tom gave a nod to the ambos, approving the removal of the sad remains of what had been a fit and shapely young girl, then they followed the ambulance back to Bundaberg.

Four hours later, the Superintendent of the Bundaberg station called his two detectives into his office. Waving a sheaf of papers at them, he exclaimed in disgust, 'What a clusterfuck this is turning out to be! The Coroner doesn't know what those marks around the base of the neck are, so she's sent tissue samples to a specialist lab in Melbourne. We might get an answer in a few days, if we're lucky. Now that she's got the two bits together, she confirmed that 90% of the neck itself is missing so that was a good pickup by you two. Why the hell would anyone cut a head off in the first place, then go to the extra trouble of removing most of the neck?'

Tom shrugged, 'Dunno, boss. It's a weird one alright. We'll talk to everyone along the water-front, but the way the tide runs in the river, she could have been dumped in almost anywhere.'

'Well, the report says the torso had been in the water about four or five days, so you'd better do some asking around. Oh, and there was evidence of heavy amphetamine use shortly before death, plus she'd had recent sexual activity with several partners. I don't know if that'll help.'

Harriet cleared her throat gently. 'Ah… if the body had been in the water that long, why was there so little flesh loss due to marine life. I would have thought it would have been perfect shark bait. The river's full of those rotten bull sharks.'

Both Tom and the Super puzzled over that but got nowhere.

'Good point,' the Super finally conceded, 'maybe it was tangled in mangroves where the bigger fish couldn't get at it.'

Tom agreed. 'If all the blood was drained before the torso was dumped in the river, that might cut down on its appeal to the bigger fish.'

The Super gave a macabre chuckle. 'I would think that cutting a head off would cause a fairly rapid and complete blood loss!'

'Yeah, righto boss. Fair call.'

While brainstorming was an excellent problem-solving technique, they soon found they were going around in circles, so with little more to discuss, the two detectives headed back to their shared office, autopsy report in hand. Once there, Harriet commented. 'Given that the head was found just inside the river mouth and the torso on the beach, it's logical that the two bits were dumped further up the river at the same time and washed down with the tide and the recent heavy rain runoff, although the lack of nibbling by fish and crabs on the torso is a puzzle.'

Tom nodded glumly. 'Yeah. You're right. It's a bloody puzzle all right. We'd better get some uniforms to help with questioning. This is going to take days.'

CHAPTER 9

The tall, thin man was reclining comfortably in the cockpit of his boat, anchored in picturesque Horseshoe Bay at Peel Island in Moreton Bay. The peace of the beautiful setting on that late afternoon was disturbed by the ringing of his phone, although it was promptly answered by an attractive girl clad only in brief panties. After a short exchange, she came aft and handed him the phone, saying, 'It's Mr Yanos, Gary.'

He nodded and said, 'Thank you, Mary… hello Korey. How are you this lovely day?'

'*Yeah, terrific Gary. But I'd be a bloody sight better if that blasted girl hadn't escaped! Have you seen or heard anything about her?*'

'No Korey, I haven't and before you ask, I've tightened security for the times when I've got to change a faulty collar. You need to get your supplier to improve the build quality, mate. This is the third one that's been faulty.'

'*Yeah, already done that. Any chance she's been picked up by somebody?*'

'I've put the word out, discretely, but there's no sign of her so far. There's a very good chance she drowned. She couldn't swim, the current was strong and the area is well-known as a breeding-ground for sharks. But just in case, I'm moving every few days.'

'*I really hope for your sake that she's shark bait, Gary. It would be most unfortunate if she was to turn up somewhere telling tales. I don't want my 'Grand Plan' buggered up.*'

Gary poked a face at the phone. 'I know, I know. Just put your goon squad on the case. Ask around on shore, and I'll keep doing the same amongst the boaties.'

'*Yeah, I'm already doing that. Are there any other problems I need to hear about?*'

'Ahhh… yeah. There is as a matter of fact. It seems that one of our customers up at Bundaberg had a girl fall overboard a few days ago.'

'*Oh shit! Did he get her back?*'

'Nope. The idiot couldn't get to the control panel in time and in this case, the device actually worked as advertised when she drifted too far away. It was their fault entirely and they've acknowledged it. He, two other mates and his wife had an extended heavy session with the girl and they overdid it a bit with the drugs. The girl was so far out of her tree, she just walked over the side. Apparently, they were far enough downstream from other boats and the town that nobody saw or heard anything. Unfortunately, they were also close to the shore and the body hung up in mangroves on a falling tide. They managed to get to it a couple of tides later and let it wash downstream, hoping a shark would grab it.'

'*Stupid pricks! You're going to have to improve your briefings. The clients have got to be told they can't let these girls just wander around the boat if they're pissed or drugged. I suppose they want a replacement?*'

'Yep, sure do. They'd been having a lovely time with their young playmate. But they'll be paying top dollar for another one.'

'*I hope they take full responsibility.*'

'Yeah. They know that and have, as I said. Very sorry! Won't happen again! All that crap.'

'*Well, hopefully there won't be much evidence for the cops to see.*'

'No. Not if the result is what we were told by your supplier. But the coppers will go nuts over a beheading.'

'*Yeah. You'd better keep low profile for a while, just in case. Which reminds me. I've just received another box of collars. You said you were getting low on stock.*'

'Yeah, great. I was down to the last collar and transmitter.'

'*Where do you want them sent?*'

'The Redland Bay post office box number by Express Post, please. I'll pick 'em up tomorrow when I move on again. I've got to work out where to meet the Gibson's somewhere and give them their replacement girl.'

'Okay. Just remember – low profile for a while and don't take chances.'

'Yeah, mate. I'm in control of things.'

'I've heard that before. This time, you'd bloody well better be.'

The man passed the phone to Mary, his head girl, to replace in its charging base. But as she took it, and despite the anger he felt at the discussion with Yanos, he let his eyes drift over her well-toned body and lingered on the wispy pair of panties she wore. A familiar tingle spread down his body, so he drawled, 'Why don't you head up to my cabin Mary. I think you could help me improve my mood in the nicest possible way.'

Despite smiling at him, Mary felt a knot form in her stomach. Although he treated the girls well in all other respects, when it came to sex, he was almost insatiable and tended to be somewhat rough. Luckily, he wasn't into S & M, but a prolonged session with him left her sore for days. That was one benefit of having other girls around to share the load.

However, sometimes fortune smiled on her. As they passed through the wheelhouse, his hand already painfully tweaking the nipple on her bare right breast, the phone rang again.

He was tempted to ignore it, but then gave a curse, pushed Mary away and grabbed for the offending device and rudely barked.

'Yeah, wadda you want!'

'My, my. That's not a very nice way to greet the bearer of good news. Can't have bad manners like that, now can we?'

'Stick it Korey, right up your bum – sideways for good measure! What good news is there that you couldn't tell me five minutes ago?'

'Because I didn't have it then, did I? Anyway, I just had a call from one of my guys. We've found the girl you so carelessly misplaced. Alive, and getting on another boat with what looked very much like her new owners.'

'Ah, shit! What boat and where?'

'Southport Yacht Club is the where. Don't know what boat yet. They *got in a dinghy and my man couldn't see which one of the moored boats they went to. I may have more info in an hour or two.'*

Without further words, he was gone.

His work-out session with Mary forgotten for the moment, the tall man returned to the cockpit, phone in hand, a foul stream of curses spilling from his mouth. Mary faded away, rubbing her sore breast, knowing from painful experience that in this mood, he could become seriously violent and probably would, so it was best not to be in a bedroom with him for the next few hours. If she could avoid it.

MORETON BAY, QUEENSLAND, ABOARD FIREBIRD

With *Firebird* anchored close to *Barrine*, the Beal's boat, Bree, Hanh and Reggie had returned to the bow area, where Hanh had started talking about her time with Turner.

'It's so different here to the *Poseidon*, and not just in size. Everyone is so happy and cheerful, it's like a new world.'

'Well, you're part of this world now, so relax and enjoy it,' Bree replied.

Sensing an opportunity to probe a little more deeply into the psyche of this lovely, but enigmatic girl, Bree sat Hanh down on one of the padded seats right up in the bow, a favourite position when they were sailing, which offered a spectacular view back over the boat and a thrilling, swooping ride at sea.

Leaning back against the railing beside it, with Reggie beside her and Jasper in a Sphinx position on the deck, his bright green eyes fixed on Hanh's, Bree casually asked, 'So, how did it all start for you?'

Hanh took a deep breath, making Bree afraid she was going to clam-up, but apparently she really wanted to tell her story and slowly it came out.

She and Reggie heard in fine detail of her time with the Wright's, after her rescue from being shipwrecked, a time which was really quite pleasant in hindsight. At that stage, she wasn't expected to take part in Nora and Frank's rather bizarre sexual practices, although she couldn't help but see them quite often.

Then the first chilling encounter at the Yeppoon marina, with Gary Turner watching her with those dead eyes from his boat or from the wharf. This was followed by the meeting when he parked

Poseidon alongside the *Sea Witch* and came aboard, which was when he talked the Wright's into letting him train the blossoming 18 year old to be a lot more than just an unpaid crew member.

She told in explicit detail the procedures Turner used to break the will of the girls he collected, and although he didn't indulge in any of the weird sexual practices she'd seen that Nora Wright loved so much, the tale of Turner's version of sexual behaviour training horrified and disgusted Bree and Reggie. Their disgust was increased by the tale that they had to wear plastic tracking collars all the time.

Keen to lighten the discussion a little, Bree asked, 'What about the other girls you mentioned – where did they come from?'

Hanh poked a face. 'Wherever his mongrel partner, Korey Yanos, could find homeless, desperate girls who weren't drug-dependant. Some like me, were illegal immigrants, a few were backpackers who'd overstayed their visa, but most came from broken, abusive families. He offered what seemed like a great deal at first by giving them a free home with other girls for company, where they were fed well, had a comfortable bed at night and didn't have to do a lot of work. The glamour and interest of living on a big, luxurious boat that was usually parked in beautiful, secluded anchorages always appealed to the girls he roped in. And after the life they'd been living, once they'd settled in, having sex with him wasn't such a bad thing. He played it smart by rarely choosing young girls. Nearly always those in the 18 to 20-year-old age bracket. Although he has this one slightly older girl, Mary, who seems to be a long-termer. She does his bookwork, acts like his secretary and helps the new girls to settle in and avoid getting into trouble.'

'You mentioned this circle of boaties he's created. How did that come about?' Hanh shrugged. 'I don't really know how it first started, although Mary said that in the early days after she was there, Gary usually tried to anchor in lovely places where a lot of other boaties were gathered. Like on weekends and at school-holiday time. She said he would invite couples on-board for five o'clock drinks and she'd hear him brag about how good it was to have lovely girls on board to help out with the chores and cooking. Being decent, family-oriented boaties, most of those he invited didn't come back again, since he has the social skills of a rabid cane-toad, but despite that, some must have seen the potential of having a trained girl around, because Mary remembers some of them coming back several times and having private talks with Gary. They were the ones who usually ended up taking a girl and money changed hands.'

'Doesn't Mary want to get away?'

Hanh shook her head. 'Doesn't seem to. She actually seems fairly happy where she is. I mean, she's never offered for sale, or anything like that. In fact, she's treated better than the others, although she spends just as much time in his bed, or anywhere else that takes his fancy, the fuckin' deviate! She told me that her life before this was a living hell with a very abusive father and brother who had been having sex with her continually since she was just 11 years-old. Therefore, by those standards, as bad as he is, life with Gary is most likely an improvement, and as I said, many other girls were from a similar environment, and viewed the new situation as an improvement.'

They were silent for a short time while Bree, who'd had a similarly-abusive upbringing, mentally digested all that info, until Hanh asked, 'Do you mind me asking – what's the go with Harry? I mean, he seems such a nice, funny guy, but he gets very intense sometimes. What's his background?'

Bree nodded, 'Yes, he is deep and doesn't talk much about himself, but I do know he's ex-military. He and Corrine were in the Aussie SAS in Afghanistan and other Middle East areas together. Corrine was a sniper and was with a squad which was ambushed by the Taliban. Harry, although a Major, took another squad out to rescue them and was shot while retrieving Corrine who had been badly wounded. In the process he deliberately diverted fire from the rest of the squad so they could get to better cover, then brought Corrine out slung over his shoulder.

Apparently while he was dancing back and forth drawing fire away from the rest of the squad and despite being shot twice himself, he also managed to shoot two Taliban heavies who were near the top of the SAS hit list. For all that, he was awarded the VC, but both he and Corrine were medically discharged.'

Hanh's eyes widened, 'I've heard of that award. That's like the highest award for bravery under fire, isn't it?'

'Yep! That's exactly what it is. If you see Corrine and Harry in swimming gear, you can't miss their scars. They aren't pretty!'

'But that doesn't really explain why he has such a strong interest in my situation, as well as the other girls I've told you about. Is there something else lurking in there?'

Bree shrugged, 'Yes, I'm sure there is, but I don't know what it is. It must be something further back in his earlier years. All I know is that he gets very worked up about any abuse affecting kids or young women. Alex and I have been involved with him and Sandy on a few operations now, and the best I can say is that he has an extremely low tolerance of people who do the wrong thing by others. Particularly if those being victimised aren't in a position to stand up for themselves. You definitely do not want to be on the wrong side of Harry.

Alex and I have seen military service, but we've never seen a pairing like Harry and Corrine. When provoked, they're two of the most ruthless people I've ever known when it comes to dealing with bad guys.'

Hanh looked thoughtful, 'Oh. Well in that case I do hope I stay on his good side. And on Jasper's too for that matter.'

The big, black cat at their feet lifted his head and pulled his lips back in what passed for a grin, but as that only served to display his long, white teeth, it usually terrified those who didn't know him. Bree bent down and gently scratched his whisker pads, something he loved, starting an immediate loud purr which seemed to vibrate through the deck.

'I don't think you'll have any problem here,' she said. 'As Harry said earlier, you're under Jasper's protection now, which means that if anybody threatens you, they'll have to fight off Jasper first. And I know for a fact that he's never lost a fight. Lovely pussy that he is!'

Hanh smiled, 'That's good to know. But is he really an Indonesian jungle cat? I've never heard of such an animal.'

'Oh, yes. He really is. He was supposed to have been crossed with a domestic cat, but the cross-breeding process got a bit muddled or maybe the breeder just skipped that bit and he's the result. He's a very impressive pussy, although most times he just a normal cat like little Krazy.'

Jasper yawned as if the discussion was boring him, then laid his head down onto the front paws and closed his eyes.

Hanh shook her head in wonder. 'It's almost as though he understands us. That's weird.'

Bree laughed, 'Actually, although no one seems to know how, he does understand. Particularly stuff that Harry says. It's just one of his unusual traits. You'll see more in time, I'm sure, but don't underestimate Jasper's level of understanding.'

As if to underscore Bree's last remark, the subject of their words gave a loud 'huff' which blew against Hanh's foot, making her jump.

'What was that for?'

Bree laughed, 'It's just his way of replying. Sometimes he seems to be saying, 'don't be stupid'. He does that to Harry a lot. Or he might just be agreeing with something you said. Like now.'

Reggie asked, 'How long has Sandy been with him?'

'Oh, they go way back. They originally met on some small operation Harry was doing with the police, but about a year later, she was involved in the take-down of a huge paedophile ring which Harry uncovered in Victoria.'

Reggie looked wide-eyed. 'Really! I've heard a bit about that. It involved senior police, celebrities, high-level clergy and politicians. I didn't know Harry and Sandy were involved.'

Bree gave a knowing look. 'Actually, Dave and Corrine were somehow involved as well, although I still haven't heard the full story. But since we became tangled with him, Harry has been very kind and generous to Alex and me.'

Reggie wriggled around, visibly getting quite excited. 'I've heard stories that other officers from Southport have been on special operations involving boats, but no one will say anything about them. Were you and Alex on any of those?'

Bree smiled coyly, 'Maybe. But I can't say anything either. You'll have to ask Harry or Sandy. They might tell you.'

Reggie nodded, 'I'll do that. But you seem to have a great life, living on board this fantastic boat. It must be hard to get a job like this.'

Bree laughed, 'This isn't a job, silly. We choose to be here. This is our home. Thanks to Harry and Sandy's generosity by sharing equally whatever we earn from operations, we can afford to go anywhere we like, or even have our own boat if we wanted. But we choose to stay with Harry and Sandy. We've become like a family and life is much more exciting and rewarding.'

Reggie wanted to hear more, but Bree felt she'd said enough and headed aft to start preparing the evening meal since Harry had invited the Beal's to join them.

POSEIDON

As the light over the western end of Peel Island faded in a spectacular display of deep orange shading to purple, Gary Turner's phone rang.

Having been on edge all day, he grabbed it before Mary had a chance.

'Turner.'

'Oh, dear. We are Mr Grumpy Bum today. Lighten up, dude. It's bad for your digestion.'

'How fucking long does it take one of your moronic fools to work out what boats are leaving that blasted yacht club?' Turner demanded.

The voice hardened considerably. *'Careful Gary. Neither my staff or*

I take kindly to abuse. You will conduct our exchanges in a civil manner. Nothing in our agreements is set in stone, my prickly-arsed friend.'

'All right, all right. Don't get your panties in a twist. What information do you have?'

There was silence for a few moments. *'Very well. My man reported three boats left the marina within an hour of the first sighting of your misplaced girl.'*

'She wasn't misplaced…'

'Don't interrupt me, Gary. Now, as I was saying, there was a fifty-foot sports cruiser, a forty-something-foot typical old wooden Queensland Moreton Bay boat, and a large, red catamaran. They all left from the far side of the anchorage, so my man didn't see how many people were on board. There were no other indications which one might have had the target aboard. That concludes my report, except to say that your parcel is at the Redland Bay Post Office awaiting collection.'

The abrupt hanging up of the phone didn't improve Gary's mood in the slightest, causing the four girls aboard to cringe at the thought of what they would all be forced to endure that coming night.

NEXT MORNING, FIREBIRD

After a very pleasant evening with the Beal's, we left around mid-morning the next day, to start showing our face at the popular anchorages in the southern section of Moreton Bay. One Mile, a small, but very popular anchorage close to the township of Dunwich on North Stradbroke Island, was crowded as usual, but a careful swing through the tight pack of moored and anchored boats didn't reveal any boat matching Hanh's rough description. Then it was a short sail across to Horseshoe Bay on Peel Island, where the white beach is made of such coarse sand, it's almost like a fine gravel. Nevertheless, it was always a favourite of mine, being a beautiful spot and a great anchorage, although not a comfortable place to be in strong southerly winds.

There were many boats of all sizes anchored there, including a bunch of small, open ones pulled up on the beach – the occupants camping ashore. The island used to be a quarantine station around the middle of the nineteenth century, and was then a leper colony for the first half of the twentieth century, with many of the original buildings preserved by the National Trust. We didn't see a boat like our target, although as we approached Horseshoe Bay from the east, I had noticed a large boat departing at speed toward the south-west.

He was much faster than we were with the light breeze blowing, so I didn't bother trying to chase him.

I recognised and briefly spoke to some friends from a previous visit and promised to return that evening so they could check out our new boat. They were part of a wholesome, fun-loving group of nudist families who kept to themselves by parking up in a sheltered pocket at the east end of the bay. Since they were regular visitors to the area, I thought it would be useful to ask them some casual questions about boats with lots of girls aboard.

That in turn, started me thinking about what other boats we could be looking for which might be part of the Turner Girls-for-Sale enterprise.

After reluctantly leaving our happy nudist friends, we motored around the east end of the island staying well out from the shallow bank of sand and rock, which was an excellent place to catch mud crabs, heading for the Lazarette Gutter on the north side. It was a confined, shallow anchorage with a narrow entry channel, and gave direct access to the old buildings of the quarantine station and the leper colony. Although offering excellent protection from strong south winds, there weren't many boats braving the shallow water, but now my mind was working on the problem of identifying girl-slave boats, one stood out.

It was around forty-five-foot, a comfortable-looking power boat with a high bow to handle the short, steep waves which were generated by strong winds and storms crossing the bay. It probably had a single diesel engine and two or three cabins. As we slowly eased past, looking as though we were trying to find a place to anchor, but couldn't find enough room for my mini aircraft carrier-sized cat, a man and woman appeared in the cockpit.

They might have been in their fifties, both tanned and lean. The woman was in a brief bikini which she wore very well, while her husband just wore shorts. Behind them in the shadows of the cockpit canopy was a young girl, late teens or early twenties, wearing just panties. Maybe she was a late, unplanned pregnancy, maybe a granddaughter, or maybe something else entirely, but significantly, nobody was smiling.

That by itself was unusual, as the boating fraternity is normally very close, filled with happy, relaxed people always ready to chat or socialise.

'Good morning,' I called, as with furled sails, we eased past in silence, just metres away.

'Gidday,' was the unwelcoming reply.

'You might be able to help me,' I continued, pulling the throttles to stop. 'I'm looking for a mate of mine. He's got a sixty-five-footer with several young ladies aboard. You haven't seen him, have you?'

I was rewarded with a flat stare and an equally flat, 'Nope.'

I waited a moment in case he needed time to think of a few more words, but apparently that was a forlorn hope.

'Oh. Okay then. We'll just be on our way in that case. Bit tight in here for us. Maybe we'll see you again soon. We could have a drink or two.'

'Maybe.'

POSEIDON

The phone rang on Gary Turner's boat *Poseidon*, which was still ploughing its way steadily south-west toward Redland Bay. As usual, Mary picked it up and brought it to Gary who stood at the wheel.

'It's Mr Colling, Gary.'

'Yeah, Warren, what's the go?'

'Just had a bloke on a big red cat, asking about a mate of his with a sixty-five-footer and a bunch of girls aboard. Know him?'

'No. But he might be bad news, or maybe just wants another girl. He also might be the bloke who picked up my lost girl.'

'But he's already got a heap of girls running around on the thing. Proper fuckin' harem it looks like. Do you want Millie and me to shut him down?'

'Settle down, Warren. Kerb that blood lust! Let's see what he's up to first. But maybe you can keep an eye on him for me? I don't want him to get too close just yet. I've got a delivery to make up at Tin Can Bay.'

'Yeah. Can do. He won't be hard to follow. He stands out like a stiff cock in a nunnery.'

'Thanks Warren. Lovely thought, old mate. That'll be fine. Call me.'

MORETON BAY

After that sparkling conversational encounter in the Lazarette, the rest of the morning was spent visiting a couple of other anchorages and sailing slowly and quietly through the collection of boats, showing ourselves and the girls, and having a good look around. I didn't bother with the very large marinas on the mainland, since they were mostly just parking stations for deserted, seagull-crap encrusted, seldom used boats. The ones we wanted to see were in use, out on the various islands and harbours.

As we headed north of Peel Island, along the west edge of the Amity sandbanks, heading for Tangalooma on Moreton Island, Dave, who was sitting inside at the chart table, called me in.

'Have a look at the radar,' he said quietly. 'There's a boat that's been following us since we left Peel Island. At first I thought it was coincidental, but those other two anchorages we came to, he'd stop some distance away until we left, then pick up our tail again.'

He pointed out the sharply-defined blip, just on a mile away, faithfully following our wake.

'Good pickup, mate. Let's have a closer look at him.'

I flicked two switches on the panel, and on the masthead, some 34 metres above us, a pair of small, water-tight clamshell doors opened, exposing a stabilised, 4K camera with both daylight and infra-red modes, massive zoom, full tilt and pan, and auto-track. As the razor-sharp image came up on one of the screens set into the panel facia, I moved the mini joystick to look back down the line of our wake. Keeping the wide-angle view, we quickly located a white boat in the distance. Then I twisted the stick and the lens zoomed in at a vision-disorienting pace, but it had the desired effect of filling the screen with the bows-on view of the boat glued to our wake.

At that angle, it was hard to make out details, but after watching a while, we did see a girl come onto the foredeck and spread a towel out. I zoomed in again and she filled the screen. She was definitely the girl we'd seen on the boat in the Lazarette Gutter, standing behind the taciturn man and his shapely partner. She was attractive and had just removed her panties, getting ready to lie on the towel.

'Are you guys looking at porn again?' Corrine asked, stepping between us and peering at the screen. 'Oh, goody. You are. She's rather nice. Lovely tits and a really nice shave job. Is that the boat that's been following us?'

I gazed fondly down at her, only wearing revealing, lacy panties. We had some good history together, but she was Dave's girl now. 'Yeah, Mouse. That's the bloke we spoke to in the Lazarette. It might be a coincidence, but no way is that girl their daughter. I'd bet the only fun being had aboard that boat is provided by the girl and I reckon she's not enjoying providing it. Anyway, let's keep an eye on them and see what happens.'

I didn't bother pointing out that she wore a distinctive black collar around her neck.

Since the wind was light, we sailed steadily on, our tail maintaining the same separation.

When we reached Tangalooma Resort, the site of the old whaling station in the 1950s, I decided to drop anchor among a bunch of other boats.

I couldn't help but notice that our own girl collection had taken to acting the part of party animals with a vengeance, and looked to be really enjoying parading around topless and playing up to all males they saw, thereby attracting a lot of attention.

I let Alex cope with the sail stowing and anchoring stuff, something he was supremely qualified to do, while I stayed watching the camera with Corrine and Dave. Our gabby friend followed us most of the way into the anchorage, only turning when he saw we were anchoring. He headed one mile north to the other popular anchorage called The Wrecks, a line of old coastal cargo ships and dredgers, deliberately sunk just off the beach to provide a wave break for bad weather and an excellent dive attraction at any time.

At such close range, we were able to get a detailed look at the boat broad-side on and took some photos of the couple for the record. Both the man and the woman were lean, fit-looking types with hard expressions and I didn't trust them at all.

I called the crew together in the cockpit.

'We'll stay here tonight, so you can go ashore or do what you like, but don't forget our cover if you talk to anyone ashore. We older types are the wealthy, degenerate yachties who've attracted the company of several lovely young ladies who also like the good life.'

There was a good laugh at that.

'We also seemed to have attracted our first nibble of interest from a couple on a boat with a girl who almost certainly isn't their daughter. They're likely to be one of Turner's customers and hopefully, to judge by the way they followed us all afternoon, have already been in touch with him. That could also mean that he's still in the area, in which case, we might stay here a day or two to see if we get more of a response from the bad guys.'

That wrapped things up for now, as Bree set out a late lunch of sandwiches, and to stay in character, the bar was opened, although everyone took it very easy.

Afterwards, Dave, Corrine and Reggie swam ashore, which wasn't far since Alex had nosed us in close to the beach and anchored with both bow and stern anchors holding us steady. They lazed around on the beach for a while, chatting with resort guests and day visitors. Hanh didn't want to mingle in public, and with a possible associate of Turner just up the beach, I didn't blame her. Since Dave hadn't shown his face that morning in the Lazarette Gutter, I had asked him to leave the girls and go for a run up to the Wrecks.

We knew from camera surveillance that our tailing boat was still there, anchored amongst seven or eight others.

An hour later, they swam the few metres back out, with Dave reporting there was little movement aboard the *Gideon* as the forty-footer was called.

POSEIDON

Early that evening, the phone rang on *Poseidon*, was answered by Mary and passed to Turner.

'Yeah, Warren. What's happening?'

'*The red cat is anchored off Tangalooma Resort. We're just up the beach at The Wrecks. Do you want anything to happen?*'

'Do they know you've been following them?'

'*Nah. No way. We've hung well back all afternoon. They've been too busy tossing down cocktails and fooling around with the girls to spot us. We were never closer than a mile behind except when they anchored and we kept moving past.*'

'How many on the boat?'

'*I saw two or maybe three guys, an older woman and about four girls. The older chick looks a top piece of work too. They all seemed to be having a great time. Typical cashed-up party boys, with lots of pissed girls.*'

'Did you confirm that sighting of a tall Asian girl aboard?'

'*Oh, yeah. Sorry. There is one there like that. Big tits for an Asian, too. I thought they were all skinny little things.*'

'Not all of them, Warren. And to answer your question, I want to play nice for now. They seem to be innocents who happened to pick up a girl from the water. Therefore, I need to talk to them about getting my property back, but I have to make another handover first. How about in the morning, you go visit and ask them nicely to stay in the area for 48 hours. I'll have the clients meet me at The Wrecks.'

'*Okay.*'

'Let me know if there's a problem.'
'Okay.'

FIREBIRD

For safety, we backed off the beach fifty metres, before re-anchoring for the night. I took the normal precautions against intruders by letting Jasper roam loose, but didn't turn on the perimeter-defence system, which had the potential to deliver a lethal current to any uninvited visitors.

Later on, after an excellent BBQ dinner, and when activity ashore had retreated to the disco and various bars, I took Jasper and Krazy for a run on the beach. I went some distance toward the Wrecks to be away from curious eyes, and let them run and play in the sand for twenty minutes, burning off their excess energy.

Next morning dawned cool, bright and still, the surface of the water like mirrored glass, with the anchor chain hanging vertical and clearly visible lying on the sandy bottom. I was first on deck doing my usual check-around, quickly joined by Jasper and little Krazy. There was little problem in having Jasper causing alarm in the anchorage, as from any distance over twenty metres, he can pass for a medium-sized lean black dog. Or as that was what people expected to see, that meant they invariably did. I washed off the pussies toilet mat and gave the decks and fittings a brief freshwater hose-down. Reggie was next up, climbing up through the deck hatch above her cabin.

She had on a tracksuit top against the chill, but still looked very fetching with her legs bare and apparently little or nothing on under it.

'Good morning,' I greeted.

'Morning Harry. It's really lovely here. You really are so lucky to be able to go where you want on this fantastic boat.'

'Yes, I am,' I admitted.

She started to ask something, but over her shoulder, I spotted a familiar boat quietly nosing into the anchorage from the north side.

I stopped Reggie's question with a, 'hold that thought a moment, please Reggie. We seem to have a visitor.'

She started to look around, so I said, 'No. Don't turn. It's that bloke we spoke to yesterday. You know – the really chatty one. Looks like he's going to come close for a real chat.'

I casually perched on the port bow seat, sipping my brew, with Reggie leaning on the rail close-by. I freaked her out slightly by addressing Jasper directly. 'A bad man is coming over here, boy. Go hide, but make sure you get a good look at him when you can.'

He gave a soft 'huff', before looking at the boat burbling slowly in our direction. As it approached on our left side, Jasper slid into a low crouch, rounded the far side of the cabin and disappeared inside.

Reggie looked shocked. 'I can't believe Jasper understood what you said, yet he did exactly as you asked. How can he do that?'

Keeping my eyes on the man's upper body protruding above the approaching wheelhouse, I replied, 'I can't explain it. He just does. He'll understand you too, if you tell him something directly, or ask him to do something important. Anyway, keep your eyes and ears open. I might need a second opinion on this little chat.'

The man selected neutral and coasted to a stop just a couple of metres away, his boat reflected as a perfect mirror image of the original in the dead still water.

'Good morning,' he offered, 'we meet again so I thought I'd say hello.'

I'd already seen that he was medium height and build, with a shock of dark, unruly hair like a small mane, which he kept tossing out of his eyes. It seemed to be an affectation which branded him a tosser, literally and otherwise by my standards, but there was a gleam of wild intelligence in his eyes. He spent a lot of time visually undressing Reggie, an process which took little imagination given what she wasn't wearing, and seemed to approve.

For her part, she eased closer to me and I felt her shudder in revulsion.

However, I could bung on an act just as well, so I pasted a fatuous smile on my face and said, 'Well hello to you again as well. What a jolly fine coincidence. We must have that beer I promised. How about you come over later with the rest of your crew? It's a bit early just yet, even for us. Ha, ha.'

He cracked a wintery smile for my jovial efforts.

'Maybe. But I have a message for you from the bloke you were asking about – the one you said was a mate of yours.'

'Oh? Oh, yes. Well, he's not really a mate, as such. I just heard about him from somebody else. He's the one with all the girls I presume. Although I must say we have rather a good collection this time ourselves, eh. Haven't we Reggie darling?'

I made a show of patting her tight little rump fondly, then kept my hand firmly in place.

She rose to the occasion by saying in a little girly voice, 'Oh, yes, Harry. You've been wonderful. We're having such a lovely time.'

She even managed to slur her words slightly and finished with a silly little giggle to confirm the impression of a gullible young girl, still slightly out of it on booze and drugs.

He looked closely at her again. 'Hmmm… yes. I'm sure you are. Anyway, I'm Warren and a friend of the bloke you asked about. He'd like to meet you, but has some other business to organise first. He asked if you wouldn't mind being up at The Wrecks the day after tomorrow at about 10:00. We'll be up there as well.'

I beamed vacantly for a moment, then said, 'Oh, yes. Lovely. That sounds like fun, so why not? This is a nice place to hang around, so we'll be there. Thanks Warren.'

He gave me a strange look, then nodded and using his feet, selected forward gear and with minimal fuss, drifted back toward The Wrecks anchorage again.

I reluctantly removed my hand from Reggie's bum.

'Pardon me being overly-familiar with your lovely little bum, but it seemed called for under the circumstances. That was a really good act. Now he's convinced you're a brainless bimbo, still half out of your tree from booze and drugs. And by the way he was undressing you, it's a good thing you had panties on under that jersey.'

She grinned and said, 'Panties. What panties? But I didn't really mind, Harry, so long as he doesn't get his hands on me. I'm just glad it went well.'

I nodded soberly, sipping at my cooling tea. 'Yeah. It did. That's some useful info and a solid bite on the hook by Mr Turner. Let's go tell the others when they get around to dragging their sorry arses out of bed.'

She laughed, 'You're funny.'

We'd just returned to the cockpit when the boat's mobile phone rang.

'Harry's Café de Hulls. Pie floaters on special, today only. Puns are free.'

'*Very droll, Harry. It sounds like you're out of bed.*'

'Good morning, M. Lovely to hear from you on this beautiful morning in paradise. Don't you wish you were here?'

'*I do, as a matter of fact, dear boy. But this is in the nature of a heads-up, not a social call.*'

'Roger. Go ahead.'

'*On your behalf, I've been browsing police reports of accidents involving young ladies in Queensland. Nearly all are what I would class as relatively normal, like drowning, vehicle accidents and shootings, but there is one in Bundaberg which you might like to look into. The severed head of a young lady was found at the mouth of the Burnett River a few days ago, and the rest of her was washed up on the ocean beach not far away a day later. Apart from the separation of the head from the torso, there were no other injuries. The only odd thing was that there was no neck attached to either body part.*'

'Yes. I can see how that could be a bit unusual on two accounts. And although I'm not sure how it could be related to this case, it's worth looking into. Do you have the names of the investigating officers?'

'*Of course, dear boy. Don't I always?*'

'You are a wonder, M. What would I do without you?'

Typically, she ignored that bit of gratuitous flattery and just read out the names.

'I guess Sandy and I could whiz up there, take a look and have a semi-official chat. We have a couple of days to kill, waiting for a meeting with Mr Turner. At his request, I might add, so he seems to have taken our bait.'

I passed on a summary of what had happened over the last few days, accepted her congratulations on achieving a quick reaction from the bad guys, and promised to update her when I knew more.

While Bree and Reggie cooked breakfast, the rest of the crew slowly surfaced. I checked the ferry and flight timetables, made some notes, measured some distances, then thought some more.

As breakfast was being served, I updated the crew on the chat we'd had with Warren, the invitation to meet with Gary Turner, and the disturbing information from my controller, the mysterious lady who really liked me calling her 'M'.

'And your latest cunning plan would be?' my dear lady asked sweetly.

'As soon as we've finished eating, Alex and I are going to haul anchors and head for Brisbane. You're going to pack an overnight bag for us so we can go to Bundaberg, view these remains and have a chat with the detectives.

When you're ready, I'd like you to call the Bundy detectives in your official capacity, and request a viewing and the chat. Say that it might be associated with a couple of missing girl cases you're working on. That should keep them happy in the short term.'

She nodded, so I added, 'While you're on the blower, we'll also need a taxi at the Kirra Street wharf, Pinkenba, for about 10:00, to run us to the airport where we'll collect a rental car which also needs to be booked.'

'How about I take care of the bookings,' Reggie volunteered, 'while Sandy talks to the Ds.'

'Even better, thanks ladies. Now, let's get moving.'

Within five minutes, we were motoring silently out of the anchorage, and ten minutes later, had all sails hoisted and filling nicely in a strengthening south-easterly breeze.

CHAPTER 12

BUNDABERG

Our course was a straight line for the mouth of the Brisbane River, so I left Alex and Dave to get us there while I made sure all bookings were okay, and used the internet to verify a few other thoughts. Sandy reported that the Bundaberg detectives would be delighted to see us later that afternoon, while Reggie said she had the taxi and the rental car booked.

Less than two hours after leaving Tangalooma, Alex was gently nosing *Firebird's* slim, red bows up to a small patch of sand beside the public boat ramp across the river from the Lytton oil terminal.

'We should be back here around midday tomorrow,' I said to Dave and Alex, 'but I'll give you plenty of notice. It might be better to stay away from Tangalooma for now, so maybe try Horseshoe for the rest of the day and tonight. Give the pussies another run if you would.'

'No problem,' Dave said, 'it looks like being a nice day, so we might even get everyone wet and give the bottom a bit of a rub to get the weed off.'

'Ta mate, that'd be great. See you tomorrow.'

The taxi was waiting and whipped us around to the Arrivals terminal where the rental car outlets were. Fifteen minutes later, we were heading north up the expressway for the four-hour drive to the rum capital of Australia.

'What exactly got you so interested in our case, Inspector?' Tom Webb, the lead Bundaberg detective asked, when we met at the police station and were shown to a utilitarian conference room. Sandy and I had discussed the best approach and decided on a close version of the truth.

'We have a witness to what appears to be a well-organised sex-slave ring, where several individuals are acquiring homeless or illegal immigrant girls, then selling them to live-aboard boating couples.'

He nodded, his partner, Harriet Butler, busy taking notes. 'And how did the ACP become involved Commander?'

'Inspector Thomson called us in because these girls are being sold exclusively to boating couples. Therefore, they are highly mobile and could go anywhere. Additionally, I've been involved with the Queensland Police on several previous operations because I'm in the fairly unique position of being able to move freely within boating circles.'

He smiled knowingly, 'Yes. Bundaberg may rate as the back-blocks, Commander, but behind closed doors, your name has been mentioned in connection with that outlaw motorcycle gang war some time ago. That was, I might add, a particularly nice piece of work, but a lot seemed to remain untold.'

I tried very hard to look suitably modest, as I replied, 'Unfortunately, a lot will have to remain untold, Tom. There was some nasty stuff going on which we wouldn't like the public to hear about.'

'Understood, but since it happened almost in our backyard, I'd really appreciate hearing more, if you could indulge me at some stage. Anyway, to get back to the matter in hand, we're still intrigued where you think a connection might be.'

I tried to get more comfortable in the rather basic visitor chair. 'After being alerted by my people early this morning, I did some research into beheading crimes. It would seem there are two main reasons to go to the extreme of cutting off someone's head, and it's not just to kill them. There are much easier ways to do that as we all know. The most obvious one is a terrorist group wishing to make a high impact political statement on international social media. The other is to conceal the victim's identity. That is, the head and fingers are removed and disposed of somewhere they won't be found. Unless there are very distinctive tattoos, the body is unidentifiable.

However, your situation doesn't fall into either category because the fingers are still attached and there was no effort to dispose of the head somewhere well away from the body. So, the question remains – why cut it off in the first place?'

Harriet spoke for the first time, drawing the obvious conclusion. 'Because the head and torso were found not far apart, it raises the possibility that the beheading wasn't a deliberate part of the killing, although how the hell do you accidentally cut off someone's fucking head?'

I rewarded her with a big smile. 'Exactly. That's the question. That is what has had us puzzled. Why cut the head off at all? Despite Hollywood's more graphic portrayal of extreme violence, it's not an easy business to cut through the neck and spine. Even those blokes with the big two-handed swords and the black hoods often can't do it with one stroke. And whatever method is used, I can assure you, it makes a fearsome mess.'

That statement earned me a speculative look from Tom, and a rather sick one from Harriet.

I shrugged, 'In my experience, it's a highly un-necessary complication if the killer isn't after publicity or wants to prevent identification.'

Tom nodded slowly, 'Good point, Harry. So, how do you explain the missing neck?'

'At this stage, absolutely no idea. Perhaps we could visit the coroner. Now, if possible?'

Tom drove, and a few minutes later we went down an unmarked laneway behind the General Hospital. World-wide and out of necessity, morgues are situated close to the main hospital, but invariably hidden from casual sight. It's considered bad form to remind the paying, ever-hopeful customers out front, that sometimes despite the best efforts of dedicated medical professionals, shit happens.

It was a long, low, single-story building, with a pair of flower gardens filled with a riot of colour either side of the glass entry doors. That was the first and only touch of gaiety. The small foyer had a scatter of uncomfortable-looking chairs, a reception counter with a white-coated technician seated behind it scribbling in a ledger, and a passage-way leading deeper into the bowels of the building. A glass window was set into the corridor wall, covered by a thick curtain on the other side.

'Evening, detectives,' the technician called cheerfully to Tom and Harriet, 'what's your pleasure today?'

I've never worked out where hospitals find people to do this work. When faced with a soul-destroying job, they are usually cheerful when dealing with other professionals, or suitably serious when a grieving relative or loved one has to perform the dreadful task of identifying remains. Perhaps the attitude is a shield to keep them sane. Whatever the reason, they don't get paid enough.

'Gidday Shane. These officers are with us and we need to look at our beach girl again, please.'

'Okie doke. Follow me.'

The first door down the corridor past the curtained window opened straight into the chemical-laden and chilly air of the autopsy room. Although I was all too familiar with blood and gore, I preferred to keep it at arm's length. Therefore, I was grateful that no work was underway at the time and the place was spotless, as is normal between jobs. The pathologist's office in the corner was empty as Shane led us to a wide side corridor where a bank of small, square stainless-steel doors was set into the wall. Barely hesitating, he went to one and opened it, releasing a flood of even colder air.

'Do you need a detailed look, or shall I leave the tray here?'

Tom looked at Sandy and me with raised eyebrows.

'Just here will be fine thanks,' I said hastily.

He pulled the drawer all the way out, flipped the covering sheet down past the feet and stepped back. I found it less unsettling to see that the head had been placed in roughly the right place in relation to the rest of her body, but with the neck missing completely, the remains were still a bizarre sight and Sandy kept back a pace. I was keen to see the strange discolouration the detectives had noticed and thought might be the remains of a tattoo.

As well as the strange, dark markings, the edges of the wound weren't a clean cut, but rough and jagged, almost like a bite, so I mentioned that to Tom and Shane.

'Yeah. Dr Cook noted that during the autopsy. She's still puzzled how the head was removed. A boat propeller could have done this, but would have left other marks on the body, not just neatly removed the neck. Even hacking it off with a machete, axe or large knife would leave a series of smooth, stepped cuts. This does looks more like a bite, except there aren't any tooth or claw marks. It's just a ragged wound. Or two wounds to be precise, allowing for the neck removal.'

'The report mentioned traces of amphetamines in the system, but how about semen?'

Tom looked a bit shamefaced, 'Oh, yeah. It was in the autopsy report, but I forgot to include it in ours. My bad. There was quite a lot, as though there may have been two or more partners, and not long before death. Vaginal only – nil by mouth.'

'Sounds like she had quite a party just before she died,' I noted dryly. 'Sex, drugs and rock 'n roll.'

My attempt at humour fell like a lead balloon.

'Okay,' I said to Tom, 'that's all for us, thanks.'

We'd almost made it to the external door, when it banged open and a cheerful young lady strode in. 'Hello again, Tom. Just visiting?'

'Hi Mickey. Just showing my colleagues our beach girl.'

He introduced us to Dr. Michaela Cook, who insisted we call her Mickey. 'Everyone does. No ceremony around here,' she said with a charming grin, 'but you're just the people I wanted to see.'

She brandished some sheets of paper at us, looked around to make sure no other live customers were present, then waved us to chairs.

'More comfortable and warmer than my office. I've just got the results back on the tests of the flesh around the torso neck area and you need to hear what they found.'

Like all good doctors, she had a talent for theatrical flair, and paused briefly.

'The markings aren't a tattoo, but an explosive residue mixed in with a quantity of polyethylene. The explosive compound is pentaerythritol tetranitrate or PETN. The lab has no further information on the plastic, unless it was the container for the explosive. Does that mean anything to anyone?'

I sat down heavily, attracting Sandy's attention who didn't like the grim expression on my face.

'What's up, Harry?'

'Unfortunately, I know exactly what it is. Many military personnel do.'

Mickey gave me an impatient poke with her foot.

'C'mon expert. What the hell is it?'

I looked up at her. 'It's a very fast explosive used in many forms, but the one I'm most familiar with is called detcord or detonator cord. It looks like a coloured length of thick clothes line, often blue or yellow, depending on the manufacturer. It can be wrapped around a small object like a door knob or a pipe and does a great job of cutting that object. If someone has wrapped a length around this girl's neck and set it off, it will do exactly what we just saw inside.'

'Oh, fuck!' was Dr Cook's unprofessional, but accurate response.

The others seemed to have similar feelings, but refrained from expressing them.

I stood and shook Mickey's hand. 'That's enough to create and connect a few dots. We'll go now, thanks Mickey, but I must ask you and Shane to say nothing about this to anyone else. No discussions with colleagues please, until further notice. You can take that as being official from the highest levels. Keep your reports totally confidential for now, copied to Tom and Sandy only. This has just escalated into an active murder investigation with possible terrorist implications, so any loose talk could have serious consequences for my people and me.'

She nodded soberly, 'I partly understand, Harry. Good luck and perhaps you could let me know the outcome of all this when it's over.'

I smiled. 'I definitely owe you that, Mickey. Bye now.'

I led the way outside into the welcome fresh air and settling twilight.

'Sorry to keep you two from home and partners,' I said, 'but perhaps you could spare a little more time for a quick summary of what we've learned. A quiet pub lounge might be best, if you can make a suggestion?'

Tom and Harriet both smiled, obviously happy to be outside. 'Yeah. Good idea, mate. After all that little lot, I feel like a beer or two before heading home.'

'I'm in,' Harriet added, 'that little revelation just raised a heap of questions.'

We collected our rental car from the station carpark, and followed them to a pub just off the main street. It looked like it had recently been done up, but there was still plenty of old varnished wood walls and antique light fittings to make it feel homely. The chairs in the lounge were new and comfortable, while heavy carpeting kept the noise down.

Once settled with beers and wines in hand, Tom said, 'Okay Harry. We have some new information which won't really change how we'll proceed with our investigation, but I don't want to trip over whatever you're doing. So, what can you tell us?'

I looked at Sandy and was happy to get her nod of approval. I've never liked keeping stuff from the local guys and girls as it causes unproductive tensions, and prevents a free exchange of information which can really mess up an investigation.

'Alrighty. What we have going is an undercover sting operation trying to bust a sex-slavery operation. I have my own boat, a sailing catamaran which we've crewed with four young-looking girls. That's in addition to Sandy. One is a constable from Southport, two are ex-military, and the other is an escapee from the main organiser, a bloke called Gary Turner. There are two other guys to add muscle, although we are all posing as a bunch of drunken degenerates with too much money, time and booze on our hands. We have a meeting with Turner scheduled for the day after tomorrow. We figure he'll want his girl back, but we're going to say we rescued her and want to keep her. We then plan to offer to let him have one of ours, a lady who can easily pass for eighteen or less, but is ex-military and is extremely lethal in close combat. She's also a sniper and an explosives expert.

The plan is to get her aboard Turner's boat as a slave, then we all stick close to him while our girl finds out what's going on, and how best to shut him down for good. Unfortunately, this stuff with the detcord has just upped the stakes by a big margin.'

They nodded, but then Harriet asked, 'But how does the detcord fit in with the sex-slave thing?'

I looked at her and Tom. 'What I haven't mentioned so far, is that our rescuee has told us that all the girls sold by this Turner dude have had plastic collars fitted to them once his shore-based pick-up crew deliver them to his boat. The girls were told that if they strayed too far from the centrally-mounted transmitter, an alarm would sound. Therefore, they couldn't run away, but after what Mickey just told us, I think there must also be a length of detcord inside the plastic, with a mini-detonator triggered by the proximity sensor. Therefore, while there most certainly is a proximity alarm set off by the girl straying too far from the transmitter, there's also an explosive cutting charge which will neatly remove the girl's head and neck. This explains why the neck is absent. It was totally destroyed in the blast! That also explains the presence of the polyethylene in the dark residue that Mickey had tested.'

That thought stunned them into silence, so I went on, 'I was puzzled all along why the girls didn't just take a chance of an alarm sounding and jump overboard when a boat was passing close-by, but not if their head was going to be removed. If a girl gets too far from the central transmitter on the boat… bang! Lights out!'

Tom and Harriet were still shocked by the concept. 'I've seen some low things in my time in the service, but this has got to be the pits,' Tom said in disgust. 'I hope your girl knows what she's getting into.'

'Oh, she does. Although, with this new information, I'm inclined to cancel the plan. The risk is too high. We'll just have to come up with another plan.'

The discussion wound down after that, so after Tom and Harriet were sworn to secrecy again, they went to their homes, while Sandy and I had an excellent feed of pub-grub where we were, then went to find a motel. We found one just a few blocks away which was very comfortable, although we hadn't allowed for the main railway line which ran through the middle of the city just a block away. Still, we were tired and slept well regardless.

An early start next morning, with breakfast at a roadhouse on the way, had us back at the boat ramp by 11:30, watching Alex nose the bows of our lovely red cat, gently up on to the beach – Dave was waiting with the boarding ladder.

'Where to, Boss?' Alex asked, as we eased away from shore.

'Back to Horseshoe Bay, please Alex. We have a lot of re-planning to do.'

On the way, we brought the crew up to date on our findings, with everyone shocked to find out the sinister truth about the collars. Even just re-telling the story about the report from the forensics lab in Melbourne, when Sandy and I realised what the simple words really meant, sent chills down my spine.

Dave asked a few good questions. 'As we said the other day, these things must be very sophisticated, especially with explosive inside them. So, where are they made, and who supplies them?

Does Turner have yet another partner who might be a mysterious background person?'

'Good questions which we'll have to find the answers to sooner rather than later. However, the big problem is this infiltration plan. Mouse, we can't risk letting you have one of those things strapped around your neck.'

That produced the expected heated protest from Corrine, although everyone else was totally in favour of making sure she kept her head firmly attached to her shoulders.

When she settled down, she asked, 'Okay. So, how do we go about finding out what's going on if we don't have someone on board able to relay info to us?'

I looked at her fondly. 'At the moment, Mouse, I don't know, although a few thoughts are drifting around. The only thing I will say is that unless we discover a way you can disable one of those things by yourself, you're not going.'

The highly animated round table discussion carried on as I sat back thinking, letting all their words float past me as my mind churned furiously with the deadly problem.

I had one thought and unthinkingly interrupted someone to ask Hanh, 'There must be some control on the transmitter to turn the collar off completely. That's what happened when yours malfunctioned, right? Turner had to make sure it was off and safe before he removed it from your neck. Did you happen to see what he did?'

She thought a bit. 'He went to the panel and did something, because there was a soft buzz, then the thing clicked open, but I don't know what he did. I'm sure it wouldn't be anything as simple as just pressing a button.'

Sandy chipped in. 'No, of course not. So how do we find out how to do it? We can't just ask Turner, and we're not going to be able to ask to sign up to have one of those things aboard, because in our case, there's obviously no need to. Warren has already seen that every female aboard is here by choice. No coercion required, so no collar needed.'

I nodded, a cunning, devious plan slowly taking shape. Sandy noticed my preoccupation and for once, held back the sarcastic comments and left me to firm up my thoughts.

After a while I asked Corrine, 'Do you have your special first-aid kit with you?'

'Of course, Harry dear. As that catchy commercial says, '*I never leave home without it!*'

'Excellent. Therefore, this is what we're going to try to do.'

Although we were almost at Peel Island, I asked Alex to change course to head direct for The Wrecks on Moreton Island. Then I explained my plan to the crew. Our two newbies thought it was crazy, while the others, more used to me and my wild plans, just thought it super-flaky at best.

Which was about normal for their opinion of all my plans.

I also outlined plan 'B', in case they thought plan 'A' was too far out, although they did agree that 'B' could bite us on our collective bums later on.

I briefed Alex and Dave separately. 'Regardless of what happens, we don't let Hanh leave the boat, and we don't let anyone try to take her.'

Jasper got a scaled-down version of that briefing, including a bit about staying out of the sight of any visitors, unless one tried to grab Hanh.

With a brisk south-easterly breeze kicking up small white-caps all over the bay, the slender hulls of *Firebird* offered little resistance and we cruised comfortably at well over 20 knots. The distance to The Wrecks was covered in less than one hour of exhilarating sailing. Reggie and Hanh loved the sensation of speed, especially when laying on the trampoline netting, while looking down at the flashing water just below, giving little shrieks when chilling spray was flicked up across their mostly bare bodies by the breeze.

Approaching the shoreline of Moreton Island, the breeze diminished and with the big code zero foresail furled early, our speed dropped rapidly. Dave scanned the anchorage with binoculars and soon picked out the forty-foot boat we'd first seen in the Lazarette Gutter. It was anchored at the southern end of the chain of old ships forming the artificial reef.

While providing a superb fish haven and therefore a great dive site, some wrecks still had their rusty upperworks exposed, making the otherwise pristine area a bit of an eyesore.

'Sail in, Harry?' Alex asked with a grin.

'Go for it. Let's get fairly close to him – say about forty metres or less.'

'You got it!'

He furled the small inner staysail, then started the big main boom-furl system rolling the mass of expensive fabric into the boom. As the main diminished in area, the boat slowed even more, until with about half the sail still up, Alex rounded up directly into the breeze, the flapping sail acting like a brake as we passed beside the *Gideon*. We halted close to, and diagonally upwind of Warren's boat, at which point Alex released the anchor. The drag of the sail slowly moved us backwards, laying out the chain and digging the anchor well into the sand bottom. He furled the rest of the main and the parking manoeuvre was complete.

'Nicely done, sport.' I grinned, 'that should have attracted some attention.'

'It was quite good, wasn't it,' he grinned back, pleased with himself.

CHAPTER 13

THE WRECKS

We'd attracted attention, all right. Heads were popping up all over the anchorage and not just because of Alex's slick parking style. Eighty-three feet of low-slung, Ferrari rosso-red catamaran doesn't exactly lend itself to stealth mode, except in the silence department. Maybe we should plan to only sneak into anchorages at night. Nevertheless, I was sure we'd be able to use our silent mode to good effect sometime soon.

The crew on *Gideon* weren't proof against curiosity, and three heads were poking above the cockpit rim as we settled into place about ten metres back from them.

Adopting my best vacant look, I waved cheerily, 'Hello Warren. What an absolutely marvellous sail we just had. Terrific breeze. You'd have loved it.'

He had the decency to wave back, so I decided to go ahead with phase one of my diabolically-cunning plan 'A'.

To Reggie, I grinned as I said, 'here's where you get to put your acting skills to good use. As Warren saw you up close the other morning, you're coming with me to say hello. I'd be obliged if you'd wear just a light gauzy shirt – borrow one if necessary from one of the other ladies, with nothing on underneath. It'll be similar to what you had on the other morning, but a lot more see-through.'

She grinned cheekily. 'Sure Harry. I'll just be a minute,' as she and Bree disappeared below.

Sandy raised one eyebrow, a trick I'd yet to master and envied enormously.

'While you were snoring your head off the other morning, Reggie was on deck with me when Warren came calling. She wore something similar, a track-suit top if I remember correctly, and he couldn't keep his eyes off her. Therefore, I want to keep him as off-balance and keen to get to know us as possible.'

She nodded understandingly, but then couldn't help herself. 'I believe you dearest Harry, but everyone else would say you're just a dirty old man who likes semi-naked young ladies hanging off his arm when you go visiting.'

Disarmingly I nodded. 'Too true, my darling girl, as do you. It could almost be said that I'm looking after your interests as well.'

She laughed, smacked my arm and gave me a quick kiss on the cheek as Reggie re-appeared, a wispy, thin white shirt decorously covering her to mid-thigh. That was until she moved or the breeze pasted it against her body when it became nearly-transparent, making me realise why Warren had trouble looking at me the other morning.

She noted my looks and grinned. 'Okay, Harry?'

With an effort, I lifted my gaze. 'It's so okay that if you went ashore like that, even here, you'd be arrested for indecent exposure.'

'Oh, goody. Just right, then.'

Which sort of explains why Superintendent Bob was so concerned about his female staff being corrupted by being on *Firebird*.

As we motored slowly across to Warren's boat, I said quietly, 'Just smile a lot. I'm only going to invite him and wifey back for the promised beer. How it goes after that depends on his reaction, but you may have to play up to him a bit.'

She flashed a quick smile. 'No problem. I can be a good little bimbo.'

I nosed up to his stern board and Reggie grabbed a support chain to hold us there.

Beaming smile in place, I called, 'Hello again. We just popped over to invite you all to come and have that beer I promised you the other day. Cookie-lady has got some lovely pre-dinner snacks ready, so you're all welcome anytime you'd like.'

With slightly sour expressions on their faces, Warren and his wife stood just inside the cockpit, and as expected, Warren's eyes were fixed firmly on Reggie who managed to hold her shirt in such a way so that it stuck against her body most of the time. Interestingly, his wife was also checking her out in an equally appraising manner. They exchanged a meaningful glance which I only caught because I was looking for it, then Warren nodded.

'Yeah, righto. We could come over for a couple of beers. Give us five minutes or so.'

'Oh, lovely,' I said, clapping my hands briefly and flashing a beaming smile, 'and bring your young lady too, if you wish. We'd love to meet her.'

He frowned and lapsed back into talkative mode. 'Yeah. Maybe.'

'Okay then. See you soon.'

Reggie pushed off and pretended to slip, bending over way more than was really necessary to recover, but it was noticed by both Warren and his wife.

Once clear, I said softly over the soft purr of the electric outboard motor, 'Nicely done, Reggie. It looks like you'll have to play up to both of them now, and forget that vow to keep his hands off you. But we'll make sure you're not alone with him at any time!'

She nodded, 'Yeah… thanks for that. I reckon she's almost as creepy as he is. But do you really think he'll bring the girl? He'd have to de-activate her collar to take her that far from the boat.'

'That's why I asked. I'm pretty certain he won't take the chance she might claim refuge with us.'

Back aboard, I found Bree and Hanh had made trays of tasty snacks and glasses were on the table for beer and wine. The crew were already sipping on their own drinks, and the girls were dressed down as much as seemed reasonable. Which meant that all were topless and with as little as possible covering the bottom bits.

I looked around and said in mock shock, 'Bloody hell. We'll never get rid of them once they see you lot.'

Sandy poked her tongue out, 'Ha, ha, Harry… very funny.' She wore just a beautiful, colourful wrap from Port Vila in Vanuatu tied almost obscenely low around her hips, and open all the way up one side. She looked terrific and I said so, earning a quick kiss. 'Keep that up and I might just whiz you off to my boudoir afterwards.'

'Promises, promises!'

Ten minutes later, the dinghy left *Gideon* with just two people aboard. It quickly covered the short distance and I let Reggie take the bow-line. Warren introduced his wife, Millie, and they met the crew. Millie was tall and lean, with what looked like an all-over tan. She wore short shorts and a bikini top, and at least made a decent effort to be sociable by smiling and chatting to everyone.

She happily accepted a glass of wine and sucked it down like grapes were going out of fashion. Warren was a straight beer bloke, accepted a tall cold one, and answered Dave's questions about his boat with short replies.

Still, both of them got stuck into the snacks like they were starving.

'Your girl didn't want to come?' I asked Warren, sucking hard on his second beer.

'Nah. She's not much for socialising. Reads too many books and listens to music all the time.'

So many words, all at once suggested that the beers had well and truly loosened his tongue. 'Pretty girl – although I didn't see much of her.'

He gave me a strange look, something feral stirring deep in his eyes, then nodded slowly. 'Yep. She's pretty, all right. But you blokes seem to be doing alright for yourselves. Got some good sorts here.' It was even longer than the last statement.

'Oh, yeah. They're not bad. We never seem to have much trouble getting a high-spirited crew to come sailing.'

'Get a fresh lot each time, do you?'

'We try to, but we only found two new ones this time. Reggie, the little girl who came over with me earlier, and Hanh, the tall Asian girl. They're turning out to be really good, and fit right on in with the way we like to play.'

Again, there was that flash of… something hungry and feral, in his eyes. 'So, both those are new? Where did you get the Asian girl from? She's tall alright.'

'Now that's a really strange story. We were down near Jumpinpin, when we saw a girl struggling in the water. She was being swept past us, downstream toward the bar and didn't seem to be able to swim very well, so we fished her out. She said she didn't have a home, and scrubbed up rather well, so we kept her. She's a good cook as well.'

The feral gleam came again. 'Did she say why she was in the water and where she came from?'

I screwed my face up into a look of puzzlement, as if I was having trouble sorting through my brain-fog. 'That's the other really odd thing. She won't say anything about how, why or where she came from, but otherwise, she fits right in and she's lots of fun to have around. When girls fit in with our crew as easily as she does, we don't ask too many questions. She'll do anything we ask, but to be fair, I'd have to say the same about little Reggie. She's been terrific. Just incredibly grateful to have a comfortable place to stay.'

His mouth twisted into an openly feral grin. 'That good, eh?'

'Oh, yeah! The pair of them more than make up for Corrine over there. I think she's been here too long and is getting a bit grumpy. Can't have grumpy-bum, fun-chicks around. Spoils the mood, if you know what I mean.'

He looked appraisingly at Corrine. 'She looks pretty bloody good to me. Maybe she just needs a new home.'

'Maybe. I'll have her get us another beer.'

I signalled Corrine with a bottle hoisting motion, and made a nod toward Mille as well. Millie happily surrendered her near-empty glass and Corrine took it to the small bar at the forward corner of the cockpit, where she filled Millie's glass and took her time struggling to pop the caps on fresh beers for Warren and me.

She handed Millie her wine first, then stepped close to Warren and handed the beers over. Warren ran his eyes over her mostly exposed body and made with that nasty grin and eye flash again.

'Thanks, girlie. You're looking after me very nicely.'

I held my breath a moment, waiting for the explosion. If there's one thing Corrine absolutely, positively cannot tolerate, it's to be called 'girlie'. In his previous mercenary life, Alex saw her kill a man even bigger than he is, with her bare hands, for just that reason.

But Corrine had always had steely control when she needed to, and apart from a flicker of a grimace, she smiled. 'No problem, Mr Colling. Just call if you need anything else.'

An instant bulge appeared in Warren's shorts, as he tilted his bottle and chugged nearly half in one go. 'That is one very sexy little lady,' he remarked, not taking his eyes off her.

I laughed, 'Oh yes. Even when she's being a grumpy-bum, she certainly is that.'

I clinked my bottle against his. 'Here's to lovely, sexy fun-ladies.'

He automatically took another big drink in response to the toast. I looked over to where Millie was chatting with Sandy and Reggie, noting that the level of her wine had dropped dramatically. Corrine glanced at me and let her eyelids droop slightly.

'Why don't you take a seat, Warren. I find that it's a much better height to inspect the lovelies, eh?'

He sat and gave a slurring chuckle. 'Yeah, why not. Even though you're a stuck-up prick, I like the way you think.'

Sandy took my cue and sat Mille down before she fell down. Two minutes later, both were deeply asleep and Corrine was opening her 'first-aid kit'.

Hanh's eyes were wide open and Reggie asked, 'What's going on?'

'Stage one of the master plan. This bit is Corrine's insurance policy,' I replied, as Corrine swabbed between Warren's toes, and slipped a fine needle attached to a small syringe under his skin. The liquid she injected was a pale-yellow colour. On the other side of the cockpit, Millie was allowed to rest peacefully.

'Okay everybody,' I said, 'please back off into the saloon, stay totally quiet and out of sight. Just Corrine and me for now, thanks.'

Corrine took a standard, plain black plastic hair-band from a locker under the bar, and slipped it around her neck, the open section out of casual sight to the rear. She also removed her lacy panties.

Several minutes later, Warren stirred and struggled to sit up, but we'd sat him comfortably in a supportive chair, so when I quietly said, 'Stay comfortable, Warren. Everything's under control,' he did so without argument.

His eyes stayed open, and roved slowly around the cockpit without any reaction, before looking at Corrine and me, standing in front of him. Speaking slowly and deliberately, he said, 'Hello. I like naked ladies. This one's very nice. I like looking at her.'

'That's good Warren, because she is very pretty and very sexy. But there are a few questions I'd like to ask you. Will that be alright?'

He gave a vacant smile. 'Oh, sure. No problem. Just as long as the lovely lady stays there. I like looking at naked ladies. I like doing things to naked ladies. What I'd like to do to her is to......'

I hastily interrupted, 'That sounds like it would be really great, Warren, and I really want to hear more about it, but for now I need your help. I've forgotten how to de-activate the collars, so I'd like you to remind me how to de-activate this one on Corrine. It's been making funny noises.'

He gazed at the black plastic band around Corrine's neck for a few moments. 'It'd be a shame to remove that pretty neck before I've had a chance to play with the rest of what it's attached to. We can't have that. What you do is press and hold the green button on the control panel, until it gives three beeps. A green LED will turn on the panel to show the collar is de-activated. The collar will pop open and the LED on the front will flash green every ten seconds as well. To turn it back on, hold the ends of the collar together, then press and hold the button again for three seconds until you hear four beeps and a red LED comes on. Then it's live again.'

'Of course. How stupid of me to forget. Thanks Warren. How

about Corrine sits on your lap for a while. Would you like that?'

His eyes flashed like crazy. 'Oh, yes please. I like her. Do you think she'll like me?'

I leant down and whispered in his ear. 'She's got no clothes on and is about to sit on your lap, Warren. I think she must like you, but you've got to behave yourself. Millie wouldn't like it if you were too naughty with a new girl so soon.'

He gave a weird, evil-sounding chuckle that raised the hairs on my arms and sent shivers down my spine. 'Millie will want to check her out very carefully too. I just wanted to get to her first before she gets ruined.'

'Okay, but you must try very hard to behave for a few minutes. I've just got to go do something, but I'll be right back. Corrine will get you another beer.'

'A beer would be good. I've got a terrible thirst. But is she still going to sit on my lap?'

'Yes. She's still going to do that, just as soon as she gets your beer. But don't try to fool around too much, will you. You haven't bought her yet, so she's not really yours.'

'Oh… yeah well… right. I'll be good. But don't be long. I want to do stuff to her. I like to do lots of stuff to naked ladies.'

I patted him on the head and waved for Reggie to join me in Warren's dinghy. A few minutes later, we were tying up at the stern of *Gideon*.

'What the hell are we doing, Harry?'

'I made Warren tell me the procedure for turning off the collar, and we need to verify that it is correct. Before we allow Corrine to have one put around her neck. Therefore, I need to try to turn off the one on his girl as proof.'

She looked a little bit concerned. 'But what if it isn't correct? Won't the collar explode and kill the girl?'

I nodded. 'Yeah. I'm afraid so, but there's just no other way to keep Corrine safe. She has to be able to turn hers off if we get her aboard Turner's boat.'

'Fuckin' hell. That's pretty cold, Harry.'

I shrugged. 'No other way. I'm not going to risk Corrine with one of those things around her neck unless she knows how to turn it off. Anyway, that's what we're doing and I need you to help keep this girl reassured and quiet if necessary. But we don't have long until the effect of the drugs wears off and Warren falls asleep. If I need to ask any more questions, that'll be too late. We won't have another chance to do this little trick.'

She gave me a dubious look and shrugged, so I led the way inside.

The interior of the *Gideon* was neat and tidy, and the aft saloon was occupied by a girl who looked about eighteen, standing by the table. She was dressed in the standard manner of just a pair of brief panties and a black plastic collar about her slim neck. She was pretty and very nicely built.

'Who are you?' she asked in a scared voice. 'Where are Warren and Millie?'

'Hello. I'm Harry and this is Reggie and we're from the boat next door. Warren and Mille are taking a brief snooze, so we've come here to help you.'

She didn't reply for a few moments and I thought we were about to have a problem, but then as my words sank in, they unleashed a torrent of information I'd thought would take hours to extract.

'How can they be taking a snooze on your boat? And how can you help me?' she asked bitterly, fingering the collar. 'This rotten thing keeps me tied to this boat and at the warped whims of Warren and that sadistic, perverted bitch Millie.'

'What if I showed you how to turn it off? Would that be useful to know?'

She gave a bitter smile, 'That's been my dream since I was grabbed by Turner's man, Yanos and his fucking mongrel bastards.'

'What's your name?' I asked.

She stopped the tirade, and gave another lovely smile, 'I'm Taylor. Taylor Scott.'

'Hi Taylor. My crew and I are trying to stop what Turner and his guys are doing, and your assistance will really help.'

She looked and sounded keen to help. 'Sure thing, Harry. But what can I do?'

'Warren accidently just told me how to de-activate your collar. I need to make absolutely sure the process works.'

I saw from the changing expression on her face, that the implications of what I'd just said were sinking in. I thought she might refuse, but then she gave a shudder and said, 'Okay. Sure. Go ahead. My life is totally fucked if I stay here like this, so if there's even a slim chance to get away, I'll take it.'

I sounded a note of caution. 'I can't permanently release you now. I need Warren to wake up as though nothing has happened, and to come back here and find things exactly as they were when he left. You'll have to go along with your situation as it is for a while longer. We'll be close by, and try to help as soon as possible. Hopefully just a few more days.'

She nodded, 'I understand and I'll go along with your plan, but please come and get me as soon as you can.'

'I promise. We won't forget about you.' Reggie and I gave her a hug, then I went to the control panel in the wheelhouse.

'Hang on, Harry,' Taylor called, 'wait until I'm in the toilet. Just in case the procedure doesn't work. No sense in you being blown up as well.'

With Taylor safely in the toilet, I went through the actions as described and after a few seconds delay, was rewarded by a green LED on the panel. There was a shriek of happiness from the toilet, before Taylor burst out, holding the collar in her hands.

'Oh Harry! Wow! It worked. There was a buzz which made me think it was about to go bang, then the band popped open and I could take it off. Oh, this is just so fuckin', incredibly amazing!'

I took the collar and with Reggie watching, carefully looked it over. It was very well-designed and beautifully made of a smooth, tough plastic. There was a concealed hinge opposite the opening, and a locking clip at the front released by the small electronic package and battery at the front. A tiny green LED gave a brief flash every ten seconds.

As suspected, there was a length of blue detcord moulded into the plastic which would also add to its strength. What looked like a tiny blasting cap was mounted on the micro-circuit board plugged directly into one end of the detcord.

'Take a good look, Reggie. We need to make a sketch as soon as we get back because we forgot to bring our mobiles.'

We stared at it a few moments longer, trying to fix all the details in memory. I hoped Reggie's younger brain was sharper than mine.

'Okay girls. Times up and we have to get back. Taylor, you're going to have to put this back on and I've got to re-activate it. Warren and Millie mustn't suspect anything.'

She looked worried. 'Yeah, got that. But won't they remember being drugged?'

'No. One of our girls has some amazing stuff which wipes their memory of the last hour or so. It's a bit like a roofie, except that the memory is pretty-well complete. People who've been treated wake up thinking they must have drunk too much and had a momentary blackout. Nobody likes to admit to a blackout, so we've found that they usually say nothing and soon forget all about it. That's why everything here must be the same as when they left. They'll still be sleepy when they return, so you can expect them to go to bed early and sleep well all night. Tomorrow, it will be like this hasn't happened. They've been fed, so don't worry about that either. Just try to act normal and we'll come for you as soon as we can, although it may be a few days like I said earlier.'

Reluctantly, she nodded. 'Okay Harry. I wouldn't dare say anything, anyway. I'd just cop a thrashing if I did, so your secret is safe.'

I hugged her again, which wasn't at all unpleasant, Reggie giving me a cheeky grin. 'Good girl. We'll be back.'

I had her hold the collar in place, the open ends together, then punched in the lock sequence. There was a buzz from the collar, and both LEDs turned red. Mission successful.

Reggie and I headed back in the Colling's dinghy to find that Corrine had abandoned Warren's lap as he'd fallen asleep. She'd also put her panties back on.

'Everything alright?' I enquired, sending Reggie down to her cabin to start sketching the collar.

Corrine shuddered. 'If you call being roughly fingered by that piece of crap as being okay, then yes. I'm fine. What an arsehole. I glad he fell asleep so quickly. Anyway, I hope you got what you wanted, since I can't reverse the process.'

'Yep, we did. Sorry we were so long, but all's good. It worked a treat. You can wake them up as soon as you like. We're done.'

'Great.'

She prepared a different syringe, with only a small amount of a different drug in it, but announced to the crew first. 'We all need to be standing around exactly like we were before. It's possible they might notice it's a bit later than they thought, but if we carry on as though nothing has happened, their minds will adjust quite quickly. The new drug will work in just a minute or two, so if I bring Warren a fresh beer, could someone please have a fresh glass of wine for Millie. Take the contaminated bottle and glass away and wash them well.'

Everyone bustled about for a few moments, getting into the approximate positions they were in previously, as she expertly injected the wake-up drug between their toes. Barely a minute later, they woke almost together, although Warren was slower to come out of it than Millie who seemed to snap straight back to full consciousness. While Warren woke up properly, Sandy, Dave, Bree and Alex distracted Millie by standing between her and Warren, telling her some complicated story.

Corrine held a fresh bottle of beer out to Warren. 'Here you are, Mr Colling. One fresh beer as requested.'

He took it, a puzzled expression on his face, but took a long drag at it anyway.

'That's better. I felt a bit funny there for a moment, but this beer seems to be fixing that. How are you doing, Mille?'

Mille's group parted to let her see Warren, sprawled back, the front of his shorts seriously tented, and a fresh beer in hand.

'I'm fine, but you look wasted, you degenerate. I think we need to leave these lovely people alone and get you back to our boat. You need to lie down for a while.'

'But I'm just starting to have fun,' he protested, 'these girls are really nice and are looking after me.'

'I can see that,' she said, pointedly looking at the front of his shorts, as she hauled herself upright with Sandy's help. 'Oh. I'm a bit wobbly too. Definitely time to go.'

Corrine helped Warren up after he chugged the rest of his beer, and with their wobbly boots firmly in place, they managed to flop into their dinghy.

'Thanks for a lovely afternoon,' Millie called, 'you're all very nice people. I'm sorry if Warren disgraced himself with anyone. We'll see you tomorrow.'

Warren steered an erratic course back to *Gideon*, where Taylor appeared, collar in place, to help them aboard.

CHAPTER 14

THE WRECKS, THE MEETING

We clustered in the saloon where Reggie and I were pestered for details of the raid.

I summarised the details for them, to general approval.

'Does that mean you'll let me go with Turner if he'll take me?' Corrine asked.

'Yeah. I'm afraid so, Mouse. I can't object now you'll know how to at least get rid of the damn thing. But it won't help if something blows your cover and Turner pushes you overboard. You've got to be able to get to the control panel to de-activate it.'

'There's always a risk, Harry. And there's still a lot of information we need to get, which won't happen unless I'm close to the source.'

'Yeah… you're right Mouse. So, when Turner fronts up tomorrow, we'll proceed with the plan and see if he wants you.'

I guess we were all a bit on edge that night, since it's not often we have one of our own planning to walk so knowingly into the lion's den. But I had one final bit of kit to organise. Amongst the range of toys and gizmos which we tended to collect aboard after several operations, were a selection of micro transmitters my superiors had supplied some time ago – just in case.

The one I selected was about two centimetres long and less than one wide. It had a quality, voice-activated microphone and a tiny battery which was good for a week or more since it only activated when it picked up speech. A small piece of plastic-coated wire poked out one end to form the antenna, and it transmitted up to three hundred metres or more on a frequency in the FM radio band.

I asked the crew if anyone was handy with needle and thread and Bree volunteered.

I set the gear up on the chart table and asked Corrine for a pair of her bikini panties.

I showed her how to turn it on or off in an emergency by using a tiny magnet which could be worn around her wrist as part of one of those coloured-cord bracelets. Bree then inserted the transmitter into the waistband in the centre front, and sewed a tiny bow over the spot to camouflage the slight bulge.

I checked the frequency by tuning one of the boat's FM radios, until it picked up our conversation with remarkable clarity.

'There you are, Mouse. Good to go and wired for sound.'

She grinned, then stripped off the panties she had on and pulled the wired ones on.

'I can't feel it,' she said, while I studied her, close-up from various angles, and couldn't notice it either.

'You only need turn it off if you think they're running a bug check,' I said, 'which would be very unlikely. Otherwise, just leave it on. It's supposed to be waterproof, so no worries swimming. I'll leave it to you to find the best way to use it, but we'll have a recorder running this end all the time, and we'll be monitoring the radio as well. Just remember to bail out if it looks like a major problem developing.'

'Yes, Dad,' she replied cheekily.

I had trouble sleeping that night as my over-active imagination kept coming up with situations where things might go wrong, then trying to think of ways to counter them.

Next morning, the whole crew was up early, the boat was cleaned up and the girls rehearsed their roles. At around 09:45, a large power cruiser, about 65-feet long, burbled into the anchorage from the north, and dropped anchor close to Warren's *Gideon*. As the tide turned its stern partly toward us, we saw that its name was *Poseidon*.

She was a handsome boat with a graceful sheer line, and a high, seaworthy bow. She also lacked the currently popular, towering fly-bridge structure, which was usually fully-enclosed and made such boats ugly and very top heavy.

We conducted business as usual, with topless girls moving around the decks and jumping overboard into the clear water. We older folk avoided such frivolous activity and stuck to the serious business of watching the girl's antics, while keeping an eye on *Poseidon*.

We saw Warren head across to *Poseidon* in his dinghy, and caught sight of him talking to a tall, thin man clad in what looked like loose white pyjamas. We also saw three or four girls moving about the boat doing various house-keeping jobs. After fifteen minutes of animated conversation, Warren and the other man, who we presumed to be the much-discussed Gary Turner, headed for us in Warren's dinghy.

As they stopped at the port stern platform, Warren called, 'Mr Stevens. This is Gary Turner, the person I said wanted to talk with you.'

Turner had a long, lean face, all angles and could almost be called cadaverous, with bristling eyebrows shading his dark, soulless eyes. There was a freshly-healed, curved scar across his forehead.

With Hanh standing well back in the saloon, I went into fatuous mode.

'Ah, yes. Warren, my dear fellow. I hope you feel better after yesterday. Maybe a touch too much of the old sun, eh? Anyway, good to see you up and about. So, this is the chap you were telling me about? Well, c'mon up then and let's hear what you've got to say.'

I'd asked Corrine to do the tying-up duties, and noticed the scowl on Turner's face was quickly replaced by a speculative look as he examined her very carefully.

'C'mon dear fellow. You can ogle the girls up here just as well as down there. If you've got something to say, you need to get on with it. We've got stuff to do... I think? Don't we? Someone?'

I don't know what he was expecting, but by the look on his face, this wasn't it. "Confound the enemy at every opportunity", the clever general Sun Tzu once stated, a sentiment I was happy to follow.

Up close, Turner wasn't very impressive, and certainly didn't radiate power like so many clever, ruthless men do. He did, however, radiate a feeling of… nothing much at all, which was a very odd thing. By comparison, Warren, with that weird, feral look in his eyes, was far more intimidating than Gary. He seemed to be quite disconcerted at the size of my crew, although I'd asked Alex to stay out of sight for now, along with Jasper, as usual.

Little Krazy girl cat bounded happily about in her normal manner, getting underfoot.

'Tea or coffee?' I asked after shaking his limp, damp hand and seating him at the cockpit table. That excuse for a handshake was another giveaway to his non-personality.

'Oh, coffee, please. White and one.'

He looked carefully around at what he could see of the boat, finally spotting Hanh seated in the saloon.

'Ah,' he exclaimed with a trace of enthusiasm, adding in a commanding voice, 'there's my girl. Come here Hanh.'

She didn't move.

He turned to me, and said arrogantly, 'This is what I wanted to talk to you about, Stevens. You've got my girl and I need her back.'

I waited until Corrine had served mugs of tea and coffee, then said quietly, 'I'm afraid I don't understand how Hanh is 'your girl'. We rescued her from the water near Jumpinpin about a week ago. She said she slipped on the wet deck and fell in. I can understand that. I've nearly done it myself. Ha, ha.'

He shook his head. 'No way. She's mine.'

I turned to the saloon and called, 'Hanh. Would you mind coming here please?'

She only came as far as the saloon doorway.

'Do you know this man?'

'Yes, Harry.'

'And is he your relative or appointed guardian?'

'No, he isn't.'

'Do you wish to go with this man?'

'No, I don't. I want to stay here.'

'Good girl. And you're perfectly welcome to do just that.'

I turned back to Turner, a beaming smile on my face, spreading my arms as though all was well, with nothing more important to worry about except what to have for lunch. 'There. I'm sure that's cleared up the misunderstanding, dear fellow. Hanh wants to stay here, and I must say we all thoroughly enjoy having her... so to speak. She fits in very well with everyone.'

Turner seemed to lose some of his arrogant look ,and fumbled for words. 'But there is no misunderstanding to clear up. Hanh is mine. She was on my boat as part of the crew.'

'Ah, I see. So, you *employed* Hanh to be part of your crew?'

'Yes, yes. That's right. I employed her. The same as the other four girls.'

I turned to Hanh again. 'How much were you paid to be crew on Mr Turner's boat, Hanh?'

She shook her head, not leaving the security of the doorway, 'Nothing, Harry. I was never paid to be crew.'

'Oh, I see. Well, that changes things, Mr Turner. You claim she was employed as crew, so she must have received a proper wage. Therefore, you must have records showing her employment history, taxation deductions, superannuation and all that rubbish that goes along with having employees. Do you have such records?'

Turner looked both annoyed and frustrated. 'No. Of course not. She's just a silly little homeless girl. I looked after her, gave her shelter and food. In return, she had to do work around the boat just like the others. That's how it works.'

I pretended to carefully consider his words. 'Ah yes, I understand what you're saying now. I must apologise for sounding stupid. Please forgive me. However, we couldn't possibly part with Hanh now. She has proved to be a real asset on board and the whole crew appreciate her many talents. Nobody wants her to leave.'

There was a collective murmur of negativity from the crew at that pronouncement.

I waved my arms expansively again. 'There you have it. Total agreement. But I do feel for your plight Mr Turner, as you seem to be in the difficult position of being a girl short of a six-pack, so to speak. But it occurs to me that perhaps there's a way for both of us to reach agreement.'

The sour, stubborn look was back on his face. 'And what might that be? You're claiming someone who belongs to me. There's only one way to reach agreement. She comes with me.'

I gently shook my head, careful to sound contrite and not aggressive, as much as I wanted to rearrange his gaunt face. 'I'm sorry Mr Turner, that just isn't going to happen. But hear my suggestion first.'

'Alright. What is it?' he grumped. 'You might as well have your say before I take her.'

I gave him my best wintery smile. 'Whilst we continue to differ on that point, we appear to share the same taste in cruising with lovely girls aboard. Therefore, I propose a trade. In exchange for Hanh staying here with us, I'm prepared to let Corrine go. While she has been very good at everything she does, she hasn't been happy here for some time now, and that attitude is affecting all the crew. I'm thinking that maybe a change of surroundings will brighten her up.'

I looked across to where Corrine was standing, naked except for panties, a blank expression on her face. 'How does that sound to you, Corrine. You can go with Mr Turner on his lovely boat with other, new girls.'

She pouted and kicked moodily at the rear seat moulding. 'Yeah… whatever. I suppose anything would be better than this place.' She looked at Turner, 'So what's the go with you, then?'

He looked uncertain with the way the conversation was proceeding yet again. 'Well. If I were to agree to this most unusual proposal, you'd come aboard as Hanh's replacement. You'd be crew, just like she was.'

She sneered at him. 'I suppose there'd be the usual strings attached. Like fuck the boss and his friends when required?'

Turner coughed, and almost looked embarrassed. 'Perhaps we can discuss your duties at a later stage, after you've settled in and met the other girls. They're a happy bunch. I'm sure you'll like them.'

The cunning little minx had pushed him straight into agreement.

She nodded slowly, 'Yeah. Okay then. But no kinky stuff. I don't do kinky stuff. Straight sex only!'

His look of bemusement gave way to one of lust. 'No, no! Of course not. Anyway, Mr Stevens, it would appear that we've somehow managed to reach an agreement after all.'

He stood and held his hand out, so I shook it.

'Wonderful! Call me Harry, please. I'm glad we can both be happy. Got to have plenty of happy girls around, I always say. Where do you head next?'

'Oh, right then Harry. Ah… Warren and I were talking about heading for Tin Can Bay and the Great Sandy Straits. Interesting area and there are more like-minded friends up there I want to catch up with.'

I nodded – a happy grin plastered across my face. 'Gee. That sounds like a good spot. We haven't been up there for a long time. We might tag along, if you don't mind. I'd like to meet some of your friends if they think like we do. I like the idea of this exchanging thing now that we've done it. Might be fun to do it again.'

Turner appeared to think that one through, but a look around at my very attractive female crew made up his mind.

'Very well, that could just be a good idea, but be warned – we leave immediately. Follow as best you can.'

'Jolly good. Roger wilco, and all that.'

Warren looked like he had just sucked on an unripe lemon, while Turner frowned, looking like he was trying to work out if he'd just been insulted or congratulated.

By now, Corrine had packed a small carry bag and had joined Turner in Warren's dinghy for the short ride back to Turner's boat, *Poseidon*.

I felt really bad about seeing her go, knowing that he'd have one of those rotten collars around her neck within minutes. To maintain cover, she didn't turn to wave at us, making me feel even worse. I always hated sending my troops into a known fire-fight without being with them, but this was infinitely worse.

Dave was surprisingly upbeat about the whole thing and tried to cheer me up.

'Look at it this way, dude. Sending Corrine with Turner is like sending an Inland Taipan in disguise aboard *Poseidon*. Turner is the one we need to almost feel sorry for.'

I slowly nodded, 'Yeah. I hear you, mate, but I still feel bad. She's going to have to put up with a lot of crap to maintain her cover.'

As Turner had said, the other two boats didn't mess around and were soon underway. Fortunately, they were both displacement-type hulls, only being capable of twelve knots in Warren's case, and about fourteen for Turner's much longer boat. We could hit about fifteen knots under power alone, but that knocked the stuffing out of the batteries pretty quickly. Fortunately, we could easily keep up with them under sail, so long as the breeze was eight knots or more. As it turned out, the slowest boat, Warren's *Gideon*, held a steady ten knots, so we were easily able to pace them under sail alone.

I sat down with the chart and worked out that unless Turner was very brave or incredibly stupid, he wouldn't want to risk crossing the Wide Bay bar at night, so would probably want to stop at Noosa for the night, which was about five and a half hours away.

I left the FM radio on, volume cranked up and tuned to Corrine's radio bug, and was pleasantly surprised when it crackled into life after a couple of hours.

'Hi, guys. I hope you can hear me okay. All is well so far. I've got my collar fitted. Turner is super creepy, but no messing around yet. He told me that if I tried to leave the boat, a very loud alarm would go off. About thirty metres range, was the limit he said. I can only report like this when the engine's running and I'm in the toilet. The other girls are nice enough, but three of them definitely don't want to be here. They were collected by a roundup crew who work for Turner, finding homeless or runaway girls as demand requires. He has one older girl, Mary, who has been aboard a long time, and is almost like a trustee, even though she wears a collar like we do. She looks after the boat's books and the food-supply ordering.

She's the only one who seems reasonably happy with her life aboard, so her life ashore must have been supremely crappy.

The other three say that Turner is an insatiable sexual deviate and an absolute pig. They confirmed he sells girls to other boaties, very occasionally to a single man or woman, but mostly to perverted couples. They're always live-aboards.

I'll wear the wired panties, or leave them laying around again when I think there'll be something interesting for you to hear, so stay tuned.

Bye now.

That gave us some more things to discuss, as we sailed steadily north.

I asked Sandy and Bree to dig out our trusted UAV, *Dragonfly*, and check all systems, in case it was needed.

As expected, and without any radio contact to warn of his intentions, Turner led the way into the shallow, twisting entrance to the Noosa River in the late afternoon, finally anchoring near the main town. It was the same anchorage I'd come to in my old *Firebird* on a previous operation when we were being chased by a bunch of bikie gangs who wanted the large quantity of drugs and cash I'd managed to pinch from them.

We parked ourselves as close as was safe for the sake of Corrine's bikini bug, and as I didn't expect any courtesies from Turner, I wasn't disappointed when he ignored us completely. However, Corrine's bikini bug did manage to pick up one side of a phone call from a guy called Korey.

'What now, Korey?'

… 'Yeah, mate. Maybe two more, if you can. I just replaced the one who got away, but if your boys could find two more, that'd be really good. It was a real stroke of luck getting this replacement.'

… 'No, nothing like that. Just some moron with too much money, too many girls and not enough sense. I'm making sure he stays close for now in case he wants to spend some big dollars when your grand scheme is up and running, excuse the pun.'

… 'There are three young ones and one older chick. She's a real stunner.'

… 'No. No need for collars with that lot. They all seem happy to hang around pissing it up and maybe doing a line or three. I figure there must be some drugs involved, as well as the booze to keep them as happy as they seem.'

… 'Yeah, yeah. When is the master plan kicking off?'

… 'Yeah, okay, okay. Don't get your knickers in a twist. We're supposed to be partners, aren't we? Anyway, we're at Noosa tonight and Tin Can Bay tomorrow.'

… 'It's business. I've got to hand over a girl to replace the Bundaberg fuck-up. They're meeting me there.'

… 'Yeah, I was. But the silly pricks ran over a sandbank and buggered the prop. They're supposed to be mobile now.'

… 'Oh, righto then. See you there.'

There came a loud rustling sound, a soft thump, then Turner said, 'I'm glad you took those pants off, but don't leave them laying around. I don't like the boat to be untidy. No, don't bother to put them on. Like that is just fine.'

It was interesting to know that despite ignoring us, Turner wanted us to stay close. I was relieved that he wasn't going to try to dump us, as long as we played the part of wealthy fools who might want to be talked into spending dollars on whatever this, 'Grand Scheme' of Korey's was.

CHAPTER 15

NOOSA

While we were having a few pre-dinner drinks, I saw activity on *Gideon*, and shortly after, spotted Warren and Millie motoring ashore in their dinghy. Obviously, their girl, Taylor was confined to quarters. Turner and the crew on *Poseidon* stayed aboard.

The last time we visited Noosa in the old *Firebird*, I had taken the crew ashore for a night of wining and dining, which ended up with us all getting hilariously pissed. But this time, we had an at-home piss-up, mostly for show, although a few NQ teas gave everyone a bit of a glow, Reggie in particular getting very giggly. Even Hanh tried one and liked it. Now that her biggest concern, Turner, had been faced down and she felt safe, she was a lot more relaxed and comfortable in her new role.

With the operation properly under way, I decided to keep a discrete night watch, and with seven aboard, it was easy to have two stand a watch of three hours each. My prime concern was to monitor Corrine's radio constantly, since I didn't trust Turner or his associates in the slightest.

I took the first watch and Reggie was happy to keep me company, letting Sandy get some sleep.

We turned all lights out to make it look like everyone was in bed, although there was plenty of light from the town just a few hundred metres away to allow for tea and coffee-making. Jasper and Krazy joined us, delighted to have humans sharing their normally lonely night vigil.

'I hope Sandy doesn't mind me keeping watch with you,' she said, as we settled into the comfortable cockpit chairs.

'Nah. Sandy doesn't mind anything like that. Not a problem.'
'Really? Okay, that's good.'

We passed some time quietly chatting, and Reggie told of her early history and aspirations to join the Police Service. Then we heard the sound of a small outboard motor close-by, and I poked my head up carefully to have a look.

It was the Colling's coming back from their night out, but they had two others with them. Female, by the sound of their drunken giggling.

'Is that yours with the big mast? It looks great,' we heard.

Warren's reply was muted by the outboard's purr, but then the girl piped up again.

'Oh, I like that other big one. Is that one yours?'

She was doomed to be disappointed if size was all that mattered, although from what I'd seen of the interior of Warren's boat, it was very comfortable and well-fitted out. The next few minutes were amusing as Warren and Millie struggled to get their very wobbly guests aboard.

Lights were switched on everywhere, and the same girl apparently had no idea of how well sound carries over water on a quiet night. Therefore, we had a running commentary of what was going on.

It quickly became obvious that both Warren and Millie wanted a lot more from their guests than some light-hearted chat over a hot coffee. At first, the girls seemed to be all in favour of getting rid of unnecessary clothing, and loudly voiced their approval of Warren's erection and Millie's toy collection. Things went quiet for a while, with just the occasional giggle and laugh from the girls.

Then there was the sound of several loud smacks of a hard fist against soft flesh, which triggered a series of loud, terrified screams. As all lights were still blazing aboard *Gideon*, we saw a naked girl, with blood streaming down her front, run into the cockpit, slam sideways into the guard rail, then fall overboard with a great splash.

'Quick,' I said to a startled Reggie, 'grab those towels and jump in the dinghy. I don't know what that stupid prick has done, but she may be too injured to swim.'

Moments later, we were speeding toward the feebly splashing girl, quickly being carried away from *Gideon's* stern by the outgoing tide. Belatedly, Warren appeared in the cockpit, stark naked, still with a formidable erection, but with a long-bladed knife in his hand.

Approaching the girl, I cut the motor and coasted up beside her.

'Fuck off, Harry!' he called, standing up on the cockpit surround, waving the knife and his erection in interesting synchronisation, 'this isn't your business.'

'Slashing pick-up girls shouldn't be yours either, you fucking idiot. Really bad move, dipstick!'

We were beside the girl, but she was in a bad way and kept sliding under, so I slid across and held her head above water until Reggie was able to get hold of her arms and drag her over the smooth, rounded side of the inflatable dinghy.

There was blood all over her front, most coming from a short knife slash across her upper chest. It was too low for her throat, fortunately, but still serious. Reggie had a twice-folded towel pressed against the cut as the girl coughed up salt-water and gasped for breath.

With that under control for the moment, I motored forward a little to where I could talk to Warren more quietly without alerting the whole anchorage, but still kept well out of reach.

'What the hell's wrong with you, Warren? You can't go playing Jack the Ripper with any stray girl you con into coming back to your boat. This is madness and can get the police involved!'

'Get fucked, Harry. You know nothing!'

'I know you're a homicidal maniac, just setting yourself up to get arrested.'

He gave me the finger, then as the other naked girl stumbled into the cockpit, looking for her friend, he arced up again.

'Here you go. If you like strays so much, smart-arse, you can have this fuckin' bitch too! She's a dud root and that makes her bloody useless!'

With that, he grabbed the girl by one arm, gave it a sharp wrench which made her scream in pain, then threw her over the side.

At least she could swim with one arm and awkwardly stroked away from the naked madman who was still waving his cock and knife and spitting curses at us.

I steered to where I could drag her aboard, then headed back to *Firebird*, where most of my crew had assembled. Many hands helped both girls aboard, where they were quickly wrapped in beach towels. Sandy and Bree quickly had the slashed girl laid out on the saloon dining table, where her injury proved to be not too serious. The cut was only shallow, although by the angle, it looked as though it had been aimed at her throat.

The pressure Reggie had applied with the towel had almost stopped the bleeding, so after the cut was painfully disinfected, a series of butterfly adhesive dressings applied to hold it together, then covered with a padded dressing taped in place. With all the blood wiped off her body, she looked a lot better.

Sandy helped her off the table and over to a seat beside her mate, where they clung to each other and cried. The blinds were already drawn over the saloon windows, although I changed the lighting to dim, red night mode so we had total privacy, but I went back out to the cockpit to look over to see what was happening on *Gideon*.

I wasn't surprised to see that Turner was already on board, and appeared to be having a heated argument with Warren. They were keeping the volume low, but the body language was intense.

There were a few lights coming on around the anchorage, so I suggested to Sandy that we needed to keep the girls quiet for the time being until I saw what Turner and Warren were going to do.

As expected, Turner soon broke off the argument and headed our way in his dinghy, so I met him at the stern-board, holding off the bow with my foot.

I sounded-off first. 'I didn't know I was going to be associated with a homicidal maniac who can't keep control of his cock or his knife!' I spluttered with righteous indignation. 'Just what is wrong with that freakin' idiot?'

My approach seemed to fluster Turner, for he waved his hands placatingly, 'It's all right. Warren just gets excited sometimes around females. He has a bit of a coke habit which doesn't help, but he's in control the rest of the time.'

'Bullshit he's in control!' I responded. 'That girl could have been killed. In fact, it looked like he was trying to do just that.'

Turner patted the air again. 'Now, now, Harry. I'm sure it's not that bad. Just a bit of harmless fun that went too far. That's all this is. No need to make a fuss. Everything will be all right in the morning. I'll slip the girls some money and they'll go home and forget all about it.'

I decided I'd made enough fuss for now, so I backed down and replied, 'Do you think so? I certainly hope so. But if Warren arcs up again like that, for any reason, I'm out of here.'

'It'll be okay, Harry. Don't worry. I'll speak to him again and I'm sure he'll behave from now on. So, if you'll just ask the girls to come out, I'll run them ashore.'

I shook my head. 'No way, Gary. Both girls are injured and in shock. My crew have treated them and they'll be staying here for the rest of the night to recover. I'll see how they feel in the morning, but the last thing they want now is to go anywhere near that maniac, or you either, for that matter. You can go get their clothes, however. They were both thrown violently overboard without anything.'

'Oh. Well, I do have their belongings with me since I was going to take them ashore now. I still think they should come with me.'

'Nope. Not happening. They've been through enough for one evening.'

He sat there for a minute, contemplating what to say next, having already found out what it meant when I said, 'no'. 'Okay then, if you insist. But you'd better make sure they aren't going to flap their gums to any coppers.'

I shook my head wearily, 'Don't threaten me, Gary. Your job is to make sure your tame psycho doesn't run amok again or he'll bring your pretty scheme undone very quickly.'

His eyes glittered dangerously in the light spilling from the saloon. 'I'll do my job, Harry. But if you want to be part of what I'm doing – you need to do your part. There's a lot more happening here that you don't know about yet, so don't rock anybody's boat if you want to reap the benefits.'

I nodded reasonably, 'Fair enough, Gary. I'll certainly do my part. But I'm serious about keeping that clown away from me. I don't like psychos. They tend to fuck things up for everybody.'

Without further discussion, he handed up two small bundles of clothing and two purses, then fired up his outboard and headed back to Warren.

I went inside and sat down across from the two girls, still huddled together, but both looking brighter. I'd not taken a detailed look at them before, being rather busy dragging them out of the water. They were both blonde, and it would seem to be natural. They looked to be in their mid-twenties, with short, dishevelled hair plastered to their scalps by sea-water, and very similar in build. In fact, as I looked more closely, I realised that they were most likely sisters.

'Are you sisters?' I lamely asked.

The one with the badly bruised and wrenched arm, which Bree had tied up in a sling, nodded.

'Yes. I'm Sally and this is my sister Kim. We both owe you big time for saving us from that madman. Thank you.'

They had already met the rest of the gang, so I introduced myself.

'Do you mind telling us what happened tonight?'

Sally gave a concise account of two close sisters who went out on the town to have a few drinks and some fun. They weren't sure how they came to meet Warren and Millie, although I reckon it was carefully staged by psycho Warren once he spotted the pair.

Sally was remarkably candid about the group sex play on the boat leading up to where Warren started to get too rough with Kim and Sally screamed.

'He just went crazy,' Sally said, 'he was in Kim and started to choke her. I screamed since she couldn't, and he just reared up and grabbed a knife from somewhere and made a slash toward her throat. I kicked at him when I saw the knife and upset his aim. Kim pushed him off her, kicked him in the gut, ran out the back, then fell overboard. She can't swim very well. I ran out and tried to punch him, but he grabbed me by my arm, swung me around and tossed me overboard as well. That's where you came in. Thank you again.'

I thought about their story and since it aligned closely with what Reggie and I had seen and heard, it made sense. I shuddered to think what was happening to their girl, Taylor, after Warren was stopped short during his near-rape.

'Was there another girl already there?' I asked.

Sally nodded, 'Yeah. Looked like a teenager. Naked, apart from a black plastic collar around her neck. Weird. She didn't say anything at all, but didn't act surprised by what went on. It was like she'd seen it before.'

She gave me a forlorn look, 'I suppose we've been really stupid, haven't we? I mean, falling for the old, 'come and see our boat, have a few drinks and some fun,' line. They just looked like a nice couple who liked to play around a bit.'

I nodded. 'Yep. In hindsight it wasn't the best decision to make. But at the time, I can understand why. Do you live here in Noosa?'

'No. We're from the Gold Coast. We work in a solicitor's office and took holidays together. We've just been driving around, staying at different places for a few days at a time, seeing the country. And so far it's been great. But what's the go now, Harry? We need to report this to the police and get that man stopped before he hurts another girl. Like the one already aboard.'

I looked carefully at her and Kim, seeing two rattled, but intelligent girls, who'd almost taken a step too far over the fine line between fun and fatal consequences.

'How much longer are you on holidays?'

Sally continued as spokesperson, 'Nearly two more weeks. We were going to leave here tomorrow and head for Hervey Bay. A couple of days there, then over to Fraser Island/K'gari to have a look around. There are some nice resorts there.'

I nodded, 'Yeah. Lovely spot. Look, just give me a minute, if you would. I need to run something past the others. Reggie and Hanh will sit with you, but I can promise that you'll be safe with us, and no one will hurt or bother you.'

Since there seemed to be some level of acceptance of my promise, I motioned for Sandy, Alex, Dave and Bree to follow me out to the cockpit, Dave closing the water-tight doors behind us.

Sandy chuckled, 'I know what you're thinking, dear man. But is it the right thing to do?'

The others looked back and forth like they were at a tennis match, until Dave asked, 'What's the go, Harry?'

'I was thinking we need to keep these girls aboard. If they go to the police, the whole operation will be stuffed. This isn't like the two detectives at Bundaberg who know the importance of keeping our operation a secret. The big decision is – how much do we tell them?'

Dave came back with, 'I agree that we need to stop any official reporting, but how can we tell them anything without possibly compromising Corrine?'

Alex, our usual voice of reason, said, 'I think we must ask them to stay, and not to report the incident. To gain their trust, you will have to tell them who we are and what we're doing. They should feel safe staying here, knowing that they are with the authorities and that real justice will be done to the bad guys. It's just a bit unusual having civilians along on an operation. It could create an awkward situation, but we are all so very used to that.'

I bowed my head to him. 'Well said and thank you Alex. Correct and to the point as usual. That's my reasoning as well. Does anyone have problems if we proceed like that?'

After a few moments, there was a chorus of, 'No problems, Harry.'

'Well then,' said Bree brightly, 'I'd better head down, move Hahn for'rard in with Reggie, and make up the two bunks in the cabin ahead of your bathroom, Harry. That leaves just the port for'rard cabin spare in case you're thinking of picking up more stray girls.'

'Great, thanks Bree. Ask Reggie and Hanh to help you, while we have a chat with Sally and Kim.'

Alex's super-efficient lady headed for the midships cabin, collecting Hanh and Reggie on the way. I asked Alex and Dave to stay outside on watch to make sure we didn't have any visitors inbound from either *Gideon or Poseidon*. Sandy went down to our cabin briefly, while I took a seat on the settee diagonally across from the two girls, who were staying semi-decent wrapped in towels.

When Sandy returned, I tried to look friendly and inoffensive, and said to the girls, 'I have an unusual plan to deal with this situation, and a proposition to put to you. Please listen carefully and understand that you're not under any obligation to go along with it, although a lot of hard work and planning will be buggered up if you don't.'

'That sounds like a bit of gentle coercion straight up,' Sally managed to grin.

'Yeah. Sorry about that, but it's the truth. Anyway, the first part of the plan is that we don't want you to go to the local police or make any official reports to anyone outside this boat.'

Sally started to speak but I held up one hand.

'Hold that thought a moment, please Sally, until I explain my request.'

She subsided, frowning.

'Thanks. The reason I ask this is that you've stumbled into an undercover police operation. We *are* the police. Sandy is a Queensland Police Inspector, Reggie is a Constable, and I'm a Commander with the Australian Commonwealth Police. We are all operating undercover in an operation to bring down a sex-slave operation.'

Our audience were dumb-struck for a few moments, so I let them digest the information. At my nod, Sandy held out her Police ID card which Sally inspected carefully as if she'd seen one before.

Sally cleared her throat. 'I guess you're trying to say that we already have given a report to the police.'

I grinned, 'Yep. That's exactly what you've done.'

'Can you explain more, or is that top-secret?'

'Well, it is supposed to be kept secret. That's the whole point of being under-cover. I'm prepared to tell you the story, but I need one commitment from you both first.'

In reply, Sally expressively raised one eyebrow, a trick Sandy could do and I couldn't. Damn it!

'In return for full disclosure, we need you girls to stay aboard for the duration of the operation. This is for your protection as well as that of the operation. If any hint of who we are and what we're up to gets into the wrong ears, it will put one of our crew in serious trouble, and will almost certainly result in her death. These people have killed girls already, although we weren't aware of Warren's nasty little habits before this.'

Sally and Kim looked at each other and exchanged some breathy whispers, before Sally spoke.

'Just to be clear, you want us to stay aboard this boat, under your protection, until you sort out these sex-slavers. Is that right?'

I nodded, 'That's it.'

'For how long? And what about our gear at the motel, our car and stuff like that?'

'I don't know how long, but it could certainly be a couple of weeks or even longer. As for your motel, you said you were leaving tomorrow anyway, so if I run you ashore shortly, you can collect your stuff, check out, then I'll bring you straight back here. You'll have a cabin to yourselves, but you'll be sharing a bathroom with Hanh and Reggie. You'll be regarded as part of the crew, which means we supply all food and booze. You'll have to comply with our rules as we're on the job, but you'll find it's all very laid-back. Very similar to a five-star pleasure cruise, even if I do say so. If you can help out with some housekeeping jobs, that'll be good, because we don't run a maid service. It will also help a lot with our cover if you're also willing to lie around in bikinis like the other girls as much as possible. We're posing as degenerate piss-pots, with too much time and money on our hands, which is why we have so many young-looking girls aboard.'

The girls put their heads together briefly, then Sally nodded and said, 'We're in. What's next?'

'Excellent! In that case, Sandy will show you your cabin and bathroom, and you can get dressed since I managed to retrieve your clothes. You're just ahead of where Sandy and I bunk down, but you take the forward companionway or stairs on the right side. Then we'll go ashore and get your gear from the motel because it's already late. Please tell them you're joining some friends who are leaving town tonight.'

Kim asked quite reasonably, 'Why can't we just get our stuff in the morning?'

'Because the senior bad guy here, the one in the big power boat, is likely to leave at any time after first light, so we need to be ready. He has Dave's girl aboard and we don't intend letting her out of our sight. Literally! I'll give you the briefing on what's going on after we have your stuff aboard.'

'Okay.'

They stood, not bothering to cover themselves with the towels, but it didn't really matter given the events of earlier that evening, and followed Sandy below.

'All fine below?' I asked Sandy when she returned.

'Very much so. So far, they love the boat and facilities, and I gather they're already starting to regard this as an extension of their holiday. They might prove to be a feisty pair, though. I think what they were doing with Warren and Millie was considered normal playtime activity for them.'

'Even better. That'll help them fit in, but we'll have to be careful to keep Turner and the Collings from getting their grubby paws on them.'

'Amen to that, my dear man. And when you get back, you'd better introduce them to Jasper. He wants out of confinement.'

'I can understand that. He's missing out on all the excitement, but you could let him out and tell him what we're doing once we head ashore. He can meet the girls when we come back.'

Ten minutes later, they came back up, dressed in their night-clubbing gear of short skirts and T-shirts. In Kim's case, the high neck just hid the slash across her chest.

'How's the cut?' I asked. 'Are you up to going ashore?'

By way of answer, she pulled her T-shirt up to show that the cut had stopped bleeding, she'd taken the padded dressing off, and just had some butterfly strips covering the deeper section. She also showed a delightful pair of firm, tanned breasts.

I smiled, 'Lovely. And that cut looks a lot better than earlier.'

She grinned cheekily. 'I'm glad you like them. The cut feels much better too, thanks Harry. And I haven't thanked you for pulling me out of the water. I never did learn to swim, so you saved my life. I owe you big time.'

'I'm very glad I could,' I responded, patting her shoulder as she carefully pulled her shirt down, 'but we'd better head ashore before it gets any later.'

I saw no need to try to be covert about the trip, because Turner would half expect a degenerate like me to try to hang onto two fresh lovelies. I also expected he would think that keeping the girls away from the police was a good thing.

The motel didn't think it unusual that the girls wanted to checkout at 01:30, so I had Sally park their car behind the hotel in a public car park where their old Commodore looked right at home. Twenty minutes after coming ashore, we were purring back out to *Firebird*, the rest of the anchorage was dark and quiet.

They had just a couple of soft bags each and a lap-top, so there was plenty of room in their cabin.

'How about I give you the briefing tomorrow?' I suggested. 'We might get a few hours' sleep before we have to move, and we can talk on the way.'

'Where are we heading?' Kim asked.

'Tin Can Bay, initially. The bad guy in the big boat is meeting another boat there. It'll be a five or six hour run, so get some sleep now and we'll talk later.'

Dave and Alex took the watch, so I snuggled down with Sandy and was too tired to fool around. There were a few faint giggles drifting aft from the midships cabin which was a good sign, but I was too tired to notice anything else.

CHAPTER 16

NOOSA – TIN CAN BAY

Dave woke us just before dawn by politely knocking on the door frame, and a naked Sandy let him in. As does any male confronted by Sandy when she's naked, he gave her an appreciative look, then said. 'Looks like Turner is getting ready, so Alex and I might haul anchor and stand by to move.'

I yawned deeply and rolled out of bed. 'Thanks Dave. Yeah, go ahead, I'll have a quick shower and come on up.'

Sandy decided to join me, which messed up the shower arrangements in a delightful way, and was far more pleasant than simply washing myself. Therefore, I was on deck later, rather than sooner, to find that we were already following *Poseidon* and *Gideon* along the shallow, winding channels leading out of the river to the open ocean. I was still getting used to the near-complete silence of *Firebird* under way.

The four girls in the right hull were still in bed, so just Dave, Sandy, Bree and Alex were on deck. Five customers were enough for Bree to fire up the galley, and plates of hot buttered toast dripping with honey were soon on the cockpit table along with mugs of tea and coffee.

The air was totally still, leaving the gently heaving ocean a shimmering mass of small, rolling swell waves and making the orange orb of the reborn sun flash in dazzling patterns – sometimes hurting the naked eye, but always enchanting. With the lack of breeze, we remained under power and were easily able to stay with *Gideon*, the slower boat. I checked battery capacity and was pleased to see we still had 70% in reserve, with the solar panels just starting to generate power. Ten knots of self-generated airflow across the decks were enough to spin the wind generators, so they added a few

139

more amp-hours and extended our range slightly. Nevertheless, I expected some breeze before long.

The first twenty-seven nautical miles were a vista of continuous sandy beach, backed by steep, scrub-covered hill country, very sparsely populated. The scenery became more interesting once past the jutting peninsula of Double Island Point, by which time a south-east breeze had been filling our sails for more than thirty minutes. The four sleeping beauties finally graced us with their presence as we slid quietly past Rainbow Beach, of coloured-sands fame, with Inskip Point and the treacherous, boat-breaking waters of the Wide Bay Bar ahead.

Reggie and Hanh showed Sally and Kim where everything was in the galley and they tucked heartily into a late breakfast.

The swell was still low, and although a wind chop was building, *Firebird* hardly rolled as the slim hulls gently parted the waves with little fuss. The two power boats, in contrast, were already rolling quite heavily and throwing spray over their decks.

'This is absolutely magic, Harry,' enthused Kim, looking much better after a decent sleep. 'I didn't really take notice of the boat last night, but in daylight, it's enormous. And so comfortable. I thought we'd be rolling and pitching all over the place.'

I smiled. 'That's the beauty of a big catamaran. It's only in a very big sea that we get tossed around, and we try very hard to avoid those conditions.'

Both girls wore basic shorts and T-shirts and their well-tanned legs and arms showed that sunburn shouldn't be a problem. They had both scrubbed up very well, compared to how they looked when I was hauling their bleeding, naked bodies out of Noosa harbour.

I thought it a good time to introduce Jasper to his two new family members, and as usual, after the initial fright subsided, he won them over with his affectionate and playful nature. They had met little Krazy cat as soon as they came board last night.

I also gave them a condensed version of why we were doing what we were, which brought them sufficiently up-to-date. It subdued them a lot when they realised how much danger they'd managed to dodge last night at the hands of the Collings pair.

I followed the two power boats as they swung well out to sea to clear the extensive and shallow approaches to the Wide Bay Bar, which was made more interesting because the brisk south-easter was blowing against a strong ebb tide. This made for a very confused sea with short, high breaking waves. Luckily, the swell remained reasonably low, so I was confident we would be able to comfortably sail through with all sail set and hatches and portholes battened down tight.

We slowed down by easing sail enough to hang back, waiting to see if Turner would be sensible enough to wait for the tide to turn as recommended by the local Coast Guard, but he was either very brave or totally ignorant, and elected to run in at his full speed of fourteen knots.

Unfortunately, a displacement hull with generous beam and a square stern, doesn't handle overtaking waves very well, and we were treated to the highly entertaining spectacle of first *Poseidon*, then the slower *Gideon*, doing their best to roll over as they were repeatedly turned sideways by the short, breaking waves. It was only the low height of the swell which saved both boats from being rolled over several times.

Naturally, with the reputation for being a smart-arse to live down to, I waited until they were half-way through their miserable trial by waves, then we just sailed on by, saluting them with raised glasses of beer and wine from the cockpit as we scooted in, *Firebird* sitting flat and tracking arrow-straight in the following sea, as only a catamaran can. The only consequence was that we did cop a lot of water over the foredecks, as the long, slim hulls tended to slice through the waves, rather than over them, producing little pitching movement and almost no rolling.

Once inside the broad area of rough, shallow water which constituted the bar, we reduced sail until the two hapless power-boat skippers motored past, several heads of the crew still hanging over the cockpit sides of *Poseidon*, paying the standard tribute to the boat's cranky, celestial namesake. We smugly followed behind as Turner made his way south along the channels, to finally anchor in the broad, shallow bay on the east side of town. The other side of town was the river, and a lot more sheltered, with better access to shops and services, but as Turner was going to conduct some nasty business, he must have thought the east side would be more private and secure.

I had Alex tuck us in quite close to the other two boats, and when comfortable with our position, I treated the decks and fittings to a brief fresh-water wash to get the salt off. While splashing water around, I was surprised to see Turner launch his dinghy and motor the short distance to our stern, so I wandered aft to meet him.

'That was great fun, wasn't it Gary?' I said brightly, slipping easily back into my silly, rich fool persona.

'Yeah, very,' he replied dryly, 'although you did seem to make the crossing a lot more easily than we did. But I didn't come here to trade boat stories. I wanted to update you and let you know what's going on.'

'Good-oh. Do you want to come aboard?'

'No. This is fine and more private – thanks anyway. I'm waiting for a customer who recently lost their girl and want a replacement. They're happy to pay the money, so I'm happy to supply the girl.'

I looked at him admiringly, 'Wow, Gary. I'm impressed! That's a neat operation you've got going there. Good money too, by the sound of it. Clever work.'

My bit of flattery paid off and the stupid prick seemed to relax slightly. 'Yes. It was a good idea and does work very well. There's a steady supply of girls to be picked up, and most are happy to be off the streets. But I wanted to ask you, did you hang onto those two from last night?'

I nodded enthusiastically, 'Yeah, I did. They're a pair of good sorts once cleaned up, and fit right in. It's a pity Warren can't keep his prick and knife in his pants when he's pissed or high. He could have killed one girl.'

Turner scowled. 'Yeah, that was really stupid, the dopey bastard. He's caused trouble like that too many times in the past. I presume you convinced them not to talk to the coppers?'

'No worries there, old mate. The promise of a boat cruise with lots of sea, sex and booze for free, and they were only too happy to stick around. We haven't had a chance to do too much with them yet, but once the one who got cut up has healed, they'll be looking for fun.'

'That was quick thinking last night, by the way. You handled it well. The delays caused by two dead girls in the harbour would have been a bit too restricting to my plans just now.'

It occurred to me that in reacting so quickly, I might have shown that I wasn't the fuckwit I appeared to be, and made note to self to be more careful. However, Turner didn't appear to find anything odd with that anomaly and carried on.

'But I must warn you that Warren has taken your actions very personally and will be looking for revenge. He has… shall we say, an unstable personality at the best of times. It might be a good idea to stay well away from him for a while, even though you're welcome to continue to travel with us.'

I beamed, 'Well, thank you Gary. That's very kind of you and I appreciate the warning. He certainly was upset last night when he chased the girls out into the cockpit and over the side. Naked he was, and really, quite magnificently equipped if you know what I mean.'

Turner gave a cold grin, 'Yes, quite. I've had the dubious pleasure of witnessing Warren hard at work and while his size is impressive, what he does isn't pretty. Not many of Warren's girls come away unscathed. Those girls last night escaped very lightly. I don't suppose they might be suitable for my operation? I would make it well worth your while to hand them over if they are.'

Sadly, I shook my head. 'Unfortunately, no. I thought of that, but it really wouldn't work. They're on holiday from a law firm and would be missed if they don't get back on time. That isn't what you need, is it?'

'No, it's not. Pity. But never mind. My partner with his shore crew are rounding up more as we speak, so vacancies will be filled soon.'

'Good work. By the way, how's Corrine working out? My crew are happier now she's gone, but I'd feel bad if we'd landed you with a dud.'

He actually smiled, 'Oh, she's really very, very good. Quite spectacular, in fact. You did me a big favour letting me have her instead of that Asian girl, what's-her-name?'

'Oh, good. I was a bit worried she wouldn't work out.'

I was amused by how chatty and relaxed he'd become with me. Perhaps the furball last night had shown him that psycho Warren was a severe liability.

'Just between you and me, she has worked out so well, that my head girl, Mary, has really got her knickers in a twist about it. Not that she gets to wear them very often, ha, ha. In fact, if she doesn't get her act together very soon, I might have to give her the flick.'

'Oh dear. That is a shame. But isn't letting a girl like that go very dangerous? She could talk to all the wrong people… like coppers, couldn't she?'

He laughed, 'Oh no, Harry. You misunderstand. When I let a girl go because she's outlived her usefulness, she stays gone. There's never any chance of them talking again.'

I frowned. 'Oh… I see, I think. I suppose that is the best way. Then there's no comeback, is there?'

'No there isn't. But I also wanted to let you know that we might be here longer than I expected. For at least a couple more days. My repeat customers have been delayed yet again, but when they do arrive, perhaps you and your main lady would like to come over to *Poseidon* to sit in on the transaction. You might find it interesting.'

I nodded keenly, and speaking the whole truth for once with

him, replied. 'Yes, indeed. Thank you Gary. That would be very informative and greatly appreciated.'

'Okay then. I'll be in touch when they arrive, but in the meantime, please remember my warning about Warren. He's got a very mean streak and he doesn't like you very much at all.'

'Thanks for the warnings. I'll do that, Gary, so see you then. Cheers.'

He flapped his hand, then motored away. I went back inside and relayed the gist of the conversation to the crew. Sally and Kim went wide-eyed at Turner's warning, as they were again reminded just how close they'd come to a very nasty end.

To reinforce the point, I delivered a caution to everyone. 'This means we have to be on guard in case Warren decides to act out his coke-fuelled fantasies one evening.'

I looked at Sally and Kim, 'I don't suppose either of you are familiar with firearms?'

'Oh, yes,' replied Sally, 'we grew up on a farm, so Dad taught us to shoot from an early age. Much to Mum's disgust,' she added with a laugh. 'She didn't think young ladies should be running around with guns.'

'Great. How about handguns?'

She shook her head. 'Nope. Just rifles and shotguns. What have you got in mind?'

'We have a few weapons aboard, so I might take you and the pussies to an inlet on the other side of the bay and have a bit of practice. I'd feel better if you can defend yourselves, when and if push comes to shove.'

They actually looked excited, and since it was lunch time, we ate first, before I went to dig out the PMR-30 pistols and a couple of boxes of .22 magnum rounds.

I started Bree on making out a shopping list, allowing for the extra two bodies aboard, then loaded two excited girls, and two equally excited cats into the RIB. Keeping Jasper as much out of sight as possible, we headed south-east across the bay toward a long inlet I'd seen on the chart.

There were a few fishermen about, but none were in the inlet as we pushed right up to the end where a long strip of sandy beach allowed for a clean landing away from the endless muddy mangroves.

With the tide coming in, I set the small anchor well up the beach and turned the pussies loose.

'Won't they run away?' Kim asked, watching the way Jasper's long legs carried him away from us at great speed, leaving poor little Krazy floundering through the loose sand in his wake.

'No way. See how he looks back every few strides to see where she is and where we are? She'll tire quickly, then he'll carry her back. They need to burn off some of the food we feed them.'

I showed the girl the guns, which were compact and lightweight, with a staggered, double-row magazine which could hold up to thirty rounds, although it was more reliable with only about twenty loaded. They been well-taught about gun safety, so that bit was easy. I showed them how to hold the gun with two hands for proper support and aim, then let them fire off a few rounds at a tree. Once they became used to the sharp crack of the magnum round and mild recoil, they proved to be quite competent.

'If you have a bad situation with someone coming at you, don't mess around making threats or saying 'stop'. Just aim for the biggest target, which is their main body mass, and keep pulling the trigger. Re-aim between each shot as the gun will tend to climb up more and more if you don't. The .22 isn't a big round, but with a magnum load behind it, it still has a good punch, especially if you put ten or fifteen bullets into your target. Remember, if a bad guy is coming at you, it isn't so he can say hello. He's going to kill you if he gets the chance, so don't give him or her that chance.'

Both girls looked a bit serious after that advice, and returned to assaulting the tree with renewed determination. I saw perhaps one in three shots hitting the target, which wasn't bad under the circumstances, which is where the sheer number of rounds in the PMR-30 would become a real advantage.

After they'd banged away for a while longer, I called a halt, collected the guns and had the girls collect all the shell casings they could find.

'I don't like leaving traces of firearm practice for someone to find,' I explained as I helped. 'Just in case a bad guy puts two and two together and blows our cover.'

Kim laughed, 'That's right, we nearly forgot. We're supposed to be sex-crazed piss-pots. And you did say we had to act the part, didn't you?'

She grinned when I nodded, 'Yep. That's the idea. The more of each, the better.'

'Terrific. I'm getting to like this gig more and more.'

The pussies were not far away, playing chasies in the soft white sand.

'Bugger. They'll need a good brush to get rid of the sand before Bree will let them leave the stern platform. She's got a thing about sand through the boat. She complains that it always ends up in bed.'

'Ooh, that can be nasty when it gets in the wrong places,' Kim said with a sly grin. 'But we'll brush them down if Jasper will let us.'

'No problem there. He loves being brushed, as does Krazy.'

Back aboard, I cleaned the guns, then when they had finished brushing the last of the sand from Jasper's coat, I showed the girls where they were stowed and where the ammunition was kept.

'Are these the only guns aboard?' Sally asked casually,

'Ahh… no… not really. We do have one or two more, but I won't pull them out at the moment in case someone is watching. There are a couple of 12-gauge shotguns, a .44 magnum pistol, two Glock .40 cal pistols, a 9mm mini-Uzi sub-machine gun, and one Russian RPG with ten or twelve rounds. Oh, and a case of Russian hand grenades. So long as we get the chance, we're well able to defend ourselves.'

'Fuckin' hell, Harry!' Sally exclaimed. 'Where did you get all them from?'

'Oh… we picked them up here and there in our travels. Spoils of war, we call it. They've been very useful at times.'

That comment earned me a pair of very ordinary looks from the fledgling legal eagles.

The afternoon slid gently into drinks o'clock, and our new crew embraced the piss-pot play-acting with a passion, although Alex, Dave and I took it a bit easier, with volcano Warren just fifty metres away.

The drinks session morphed equally painlessly into one of Bree's finger-food snack-fest dinners, where she whips up a series of tasty little snacks and brings out platter-loads of them until everyone is stuffed. We were nearly finished, when there was a crackle from the FM radio tuned to Corrine's bikini bug, so I nipped inside to listen, with Dave on my heels.

'Hey guys. I hope you can hear. A bit of a situation has developed here and I've got to be very brief. Tonight, please be ready to pick up an info package which will be drifting northward on the tide, sometime roughly around 22:00. That time is very flexible as I've got to provide a diversion for Turner. Don't leave base until you hear a loud thud. There'll be some fuss around Poseidon, but please take the RIB with the electric outboard out east clear of the two boats, then hang around a hundred metres north of Poseidon.

You should see a dim white light at water-level drifting north toward you. Don't shag around making the pickup, but be very quiet. The package will explain everything. Bye.'

'What's the hell's that all about?' Dave asked.

I shrugged, 'Dunno, mate. Sounds like she's sending us a heap of written stuff in a container. I don't know why she has to create a diversion though. Maybe Turner's suspicious of her, or something like that.'

'But what's the go with this 'thud' she's on about?'

'I'm not sure. The only thing which comes to mind is that is the sound a grenade makes when it goes off deep underwater, but I'm sure she didn't take one with her from the stock aboard. Anyway, all we can do is to be ready when she said.'

'Do you want a hand?'

'Nah. If it's just a floating container with a light taped on top, I can handle that. I'd rather you and Alex be ready to repel psycho Warren in case he comes calling at the same time.'

'Okay. We can handle that.'

CHAPTER 17

TIN CAN BAY

Ahead of time, I moved the RIB up to the bow on the side away from the other two boats, and was in it and ready by 21:45. There was no movement on either *Gideon or Poseidon*, but ten minutes later, there was the promised, 'thud', which was felt through the water, rather than heard. I immediately turned on the electric outboard and as lights came on in *Poseidon's* cockpit and girls could be seen walking along the side decks with torches, I drove at slow speed out to the east to remain well clear of the spill of light being cast. Once clear of the wandering light beams, I turned north in darkness and increased speed a little, while torches and spotlights continued to be shone over the water around *Poseidon*. Turner himself, clad in a pair of shorts, was directing whatever the operation was with much waving of arms and pointing of fingers.

By the time I was in position, about a hundred meters north of *Poseidon*, the fuss was dying down as lights were turned off one by one and the crew retreated inside. Five minutes after that, only one saloon light was still on, along with a couple of gleaming cabin portholes.

Near the shore, the town lights were relatively bright, but toward *Poseidon* the background was quite dark. Therefore, the faint glow of what could be a small torch showed, as it bobbed its way toward me, borne by the current. As it came closer, there looked to be a slightly lighter-coloured mass beside it, which I took to be the container Corrine had used to carry the message.

I had a mutter to myself. 'Bloody hell, Mouse. What's in that thing, a fucking book?'

I was keeping the motor at low power to just stem the tide, which let me position the RIB so the object floated straight at me. When I lost sight of it under the high bow on the right side, I cut the power and slid forward on my knees to reach over the side and retrieve the container.

That was when the little torch arced up in the air and hit me on the head. I fell back in shock, as containers don't usually throw torches around, but then received an even bigger shock. Two bare arms slapped up over the rounded side, and flailed around, looking for a handhold. Pushing thoughts of giant, killer octopi out of my overly vivid imagination, I lunged forward, grabbed hold of the wrists and pulled hard.

To my surprise, a naked, very well-built young lady, and firmly attached to the arms, almost launched herself out of the water, landing on me as I fell back onto the bottom boards.

Her arms were wildly flailing around and I copped a backhander across my jaw. 'Bloody hell, woman!' I barked as quietly as I could, 'settle down! I was pulling you in anyway.'

As she rolled sideways off me, there was a bump at the bow, which lifted as though we'd run aground, except we were in at least five metres of water. Then along the side where the girl had come over, I saw the tip of a grey fin slide slowly past, making a scraping sound as it went. It must have been a big fin to poke up above the high side of the RIB, and would have been attached to a much bigger shark, so I reached back, grabbed the outboard steering arm, pushed it over and twisted the handgrip.

The electric motor, which produces maximum torque at start-up, leapt into life, dragging the stern down and to the right. There were a series of 'clunks', which savagely jarred the handle, before a great splashing arose in our wake.

I chopped the throttle again and let the boat coast to a noiseless halt, before turning to inspect my latest catch of the day. It was definitely a case of déjà vu, being the third naked young female I'd pulled into this boat within twenty-four hours. This one was still in one piece without any obvious claret leaks, and was very definitely female with some very generous bits in the proper places. She ignored me at first, being busy wiping herself with the dry towel I'd used on the shooting excursion that afternoon.

I looked over to Turner's boat, but the fuss we'd made with the shark had gone un-noticed, so I let the tide carry us further away while I asked a few questions.

'Good evening, young lady. Care to explain what you're doing swimming with the sharks this time of night? Or are you so pissed off with your life, you walked over the side.'

She groaned, 'Give me a break, Harry. This isn't the time to be a smart-arse. I'm freezing fuckin' cold, exhausted from trying to stay afloat long enough to find you, and that bloody shark kept nudging my bum all the way. It feels like he's sandpapered all the skin off it.'

She got to her knees and turned her bum to me. 'What's it look like? Am I bleeding?'

I had to peer closely in the dim light from the little torch, still lying on the floorboards. 'It certainly is a very nice bum, I must say. Definitely one of the better I've been privileged to see. And, yes, you are bleeding, but not badly. There are abrasion marks on both cheeks, but if you sit on the towel to apply pressure, the bleeding should stop soon.'

She stuffed the folded towel under her bum, wincing as she sat back down. 'Fuck me. Corrine warned me you were a smart-arse, but I didn't think you'd be this bad. Anyway, I'm Mary and thanks for saving me. I was about done when you nearly ran over me. That shark was becoming way too friendly.'

Sometimes I'm a bit slow on the uptake, but finally the penny dropped – the light came on, and it suddenly all made sense.

I chuckled, 'Good one, Mouse. This is worthy of one of my plans. I guess I taught you well.'

Mary looked strangely at me. 'Are you alright? If you are, can we head back to your boat – quietly. I'm supposed to be dead, but if I don't warm up soon, I really will be.'

I smiled at her. 'No problem, my curvaceous little water nymph. Home and warmth coming up.

Mary shook her head in wonder. 'Fuckin' fruit loop!'

I curved well east on the way back, and approached *Firebird* slowly and silently from the south. I called softly to warn Dave and Alex.

'No lights at all, please guys. Not even in the saloon.'

'Copied,' came the muted answer.

Dave tied us up and helped Mary out. I retrieved the little torch and followed.

Only the two guys were still up, so I gave a brief report, then said, 'I'll take Mary below to warm up in a hot shower and fix her abrasions. We'll do the full debrief in the morning, but remember, she's officially dead, so she has to stay out of sight.'

'Got it Harry.' Dave said, 'Don't worry about the rest of the night watch. You sort things out with Mary and we'll catch up later.'

'Thanks, mate. See you then.'

Mary was shivering violently as I led her down the aft stairway to the cabin Sandy and I shared. My lady was sitting up in bed with just a bed light on, and got up when we walked in.

She didn't bother dressing, and laughed as she inspected our guest. 'Oh dear, Harry, you've done it again. You have the most remarkable talent for finding naked young ladies in the middle of the night, swimming in the ocean.'

Not waiting for my reply, she held out her hand and said, 'Hi. I'm Sandy and welcome to *Firebird*. May your time here be a lot happier than where you came from.'

'Hi Sandy, I'm Mary, but I'm dreadfully cold and about to bleed all over your beautiful carpet.'

'No problem. Come with me and we'll warm you up in a hot shower. Harry, the first-aid kit, please. The proper one this time.'

I grinned, 'Yes, dear. Real first-aid coming up as requested.'

As Sandy ushered her into the bathroom, I heard Mary say, 'Does he ever stop with the smart-arse stuff?'

'Oh, no. He's always like that. I think it's in his genes. The time to worry is when he stops!'

Ten minutes later, Mary was red all over, but the goose-bumps had gone, along with the shivering fits. She didn't have the slightest qualm about being naked, but as her previous environment probably required that most of the time, I wasn't surprised. Sandy and I inspected her closely all over, and apart from the shark-skin scrapes on both bum cheeks, she was undamaged.

From that inspection, I concluded that she was a very nicely put-together young lady, medium height, short blondish hair, very nice boobies, and like Sandy, a follower of the hairless body fashion – something I thoroughly approved of.

I gently spread a powerful antibiotic cream on the scrapes, which were still oozing slightly, then taped a thin, non-stick dressing over them.

'There. They should heal nicely and won't leave a mark. In the meantime, if we get you a hot coffee, do you feel like a bit of a chat?' I asked.

'Sure,' she replied, pulling on a long-sleeved T-shirt and a pair of trakkie-daks Sandy gave her.

'Let's go up to the saloon,' I suggested, 'but we'll leave the lights off.'

'Tea or coffee?' Sandy asked, as I pointed Mary to the big U-shaped settee and gave her a thin cushion for her tender bum.

'Oh, coffee, please. Black and one.'

'Coming up.'

Dave drifted in from the cockpit to hear her story, which wasn't a lot different from what we'd worked out.

'Gary has really taken to Corrine,' she said. 'I've been his head girl up to now, but just yesterday he gave Corrine that job and said he was going to get rid of me. I thought he meant to sell me to one of his customers, but afterwards, Corrine took me aside and said that he was planning to just push me over the side and let the collar finish the job when I drifted far enough away. He knew I couldn't swim very well.'

'How long have you been with him?' I asked.

'Nearly three years. I was one of his first girls, and was picked up by his partner, a really vicious, slimy bastard called Korey Yanos. I was staying with a few others at a crash-pad, since I hadn't long left home and didn't know my way around the homeless scene very well. I soon discovered that nobody was willing to help me – I guess they'd seen it all before. I was just one more brainless bimbo running from one bad situation into a worse one. Anyway, Yanos turned me over to Gary, but instead of selling me to a customer, he kept me on. Apart from all the usual fucking twice a day, I suppose it was because I was silly enough to say I could look after his paperwork. He hated doing that stuff. Things had been going as well as I could expect in that sort of situation, but when Corrine turned up and I saw how much he liked her, I got really jealous and tried to hurt her, but she was way too fast for me. I had no chance, although oddly enough, she hardly hurt me. Just had some sort of hold on me that sort of calmed me down, but then she gave me the bad news. I was a bit of a mess for a while, until she said she could help me escape, if I did exactly what she said.

The deal was that once away from Turner, I had to tell you guys everything about him and his rotten mates. That's something I'm very happy to do, seeing as the arsehole was going to blow my head off.'

Her head lifted defiantly, a challenging gleam in her eyes, but I saw a hint of tears there as well. 'So here I am. I don't have any clothes or money. Nothing.'

'Do you have a home you could go to?' I asked, keeping a neutral tone and expression.

'No. Mum works as a waitress when she isn't stoned, and my stepfather and brother will just want to fuck me all the time like they always did, so that's out. There's no one else I trust, or anywhere to go.'

I thought a moment. 'In the longer term, we can probably help you get somewhere safe, but for now, are you willing to stay here with us, and not show your face up on deck?'

She nodded. 'Corrine told me a bit about you guys and what you're trying to do, so I'll do whatever I can to help with that. She also said I could trust you with my life, so I guess I'll have to go along with that. I mean – like I'm dead anyway, aren't I?'

She had a bit of a sob session, but got over it quickly.

'Sorry… that's enough of that shit. Just tell me what I've got to do to be able to stay here and I'll do it.'

She glanced around in the gloom of the saloon, lit only by the myriad little LED lights on the various bits of equipment on the nav station and in the galley.

'This place looks better than Turner's, and there's a lot more room, so that's something at least.'

She noticed my pained expression. 'What? What's the matter now? C'mon, spit it out! Been there, had to do that, and copped it all. Have I got to perform for all the boys and girls too? No problem – I can do that… I'm used to it. It'll still be better than being with Turner all the time, and that arsehole Korey when he visits. He's one very sick mongrel when he gets his hands on a female!'

I held up one hand to stem the tirade. 'For Christ's sake! Knock off the tough tart routine for a minute and listen! It's not like that here.'

She still kept glaring at me, as I blew out a big breath in frustration, trying very hard not to start yelling at her. 'Look. I know you've had a tough time and I don't argue with people I rescue from sharks and drowning, so if you prefer, I can run you ashore right now, you can bugger off and take your chances on your own again. Find another crash-pad. In fact, the more I think about it, that's what we'll do. This is a really happy boat, so we don't need a giant pain-in-the-arse bitch whinging all the time. We'll be much better off without you! No wonder Turner wanted to dump you overboard. I'm almost tempted.'

She teared up again immediately, and I copped a stern, 'Harry! Behave!' from Sandy, along with a hard smack across my arm.

I looked at Sandy. 'Well, how else can I treat the silly bitch? Why does she have to immediately bung on the, 'beat me – I'm used to it,' routine when I've already said we'd help her? Why the fucking carry-on? This is bullshit. She's just winding us up.'

That earned me another stern look, so I turned back to Mary.

'Look. To avoid getting into more trouble with Sandy, and strongly against my better judgement, this is the last, final, never-to-be-repeated offer you're going to get from me. The deal is that you're here as crew. Nothing more and nothing less. You're the same as everybody else. You don't have to take your pants off for anybody if you don't want to. Glue the fucking things on if you like, slap on a chastity belt, lock your precious pussy closed and dress up like a nun if that makes you feel safer. You don't have to wear a bang collar. Ever! You'll have your own cabin and get fed three or four times a day, the same as the rest of us. You can drink whatever you can find in the fridges, alcoholic or otherwise. If you want to stay dead as far as Turner and Yanos are concerned, stay off the decks during the day, and down below window-level at night.

The reason for that is we're going to be travelling with them until we find out what their 'Grand Plan' is, then we'll take them down. Permanently. If you want to help with that, then great. If you don't, then you'll still get fed and protected until we can dump you ashore when the operation is completed and all our people are safe.

Apart from the usual boat rules, which you should already know, there won't be restraints of any sort, but if we even think you're going to do something really fucking stupid, like show yourself to Turner or Yanos, one of us will deck you, and you'll be tied up and gagged until we can dispose of you. I won't have you jeopardising Corrine's life or our operation by being thoughtless or stupid. I can promise that we won't stick our necks out to save you again. And one last thing to get through your thick, ignorant skull – there is no payment, or service of any description required for living here and being kept safe by this crew, although keeping your cabin clean and tidy would be good. However, in the very unlikely event that you do decide to stick around, it would be really nice if you made some effort to be pleasant. At least to the others. I don't give a shit as to how you want to behave toward me, but don't disrupt the happy atmosphere we have on the boat. It happens to be the permanent home to four of us, and a temporary one to the others. Try to fuck that up and you'll be dumped ashore super-quick! And if you want to regard that as a payment, that's up to you.'

I was in full-on pissed-off Major mode when I stood, glaring down at her and even Sandy didn't dare speak.

'Just remember that a senior member of this crew, who is also a very close, loved friend of ours, and the love of Dave's life, has literally put her neck on the line to help you disappear out from under the thumb and cock of Turner. She's the one with a bang-collar around her neck tonight instead of you, you ungrateful little bitch! Your belligerent bullshit attitude is a gross insult to her efforts and sacrifice, and from my point of view, that's utterly unforgivable! Now I'm going to bed, so Sandy will show you to your private cabin. Try really hard not to sink us or set fire to the place!'

With that I went below, took a shower to cool down, and climbed into bed, still cursing the mindless stupidity of people who couldn't be bothered to look, listen or think for themselves. I don't often sound off like I just did, but sometimes people who just want to feel sorry for themselves and believe the world owes them a living, need telling. I've never been tolerant of fools, which I'm sure Sandy will point out is a major character flaw, but I really don't care.

On that note, I slipped into a deep sleep, dreaming of gentle seas, warm breezes and cheerful people.

CHAPTER 18

TIN CAN BAY

Next morning, just before dawn, I was first on deck as usual, having an early cuppa with Jasper and Krazy keeping me company. Despite having been on watch last night after all the fuss was over, Reggie wandered up, a steaming coffee in her hand, and a long T-shirt her only covering.

'Good morning, Harry. This is lovely. I've not been here before.'

'Mornin' to you too, Reggie, and yes, Tin Can Bay is a nice spot. Sleep well?'

'Oh, yes. This boat is like a magic sleeping potion. I've never slept so well.'

I grinned. 'Yeah. Boats do that to people. It's one of the many attractions of boating life.'

'Tin Can Bay is a funny name. How did that come about, do you know?'

'The town was originally called Wallu, but was changed to Tin Can Bay in the 1930's. Where the name came from is uncertain, but some say it was derived from an indigenous name, possibly 'tinchin' meaning "mangrove" in one of the local dialects, or more likely 'tinken' meaning 'vine with large ribbed leaves' from another dialect, or even 'tuncanbar', possibly referring to the dugongs that hang about the area, feeding on the sea-grass beds.'

She giggled. 'How do you remember all that stuff?'

'I'd like to say I'm just clever with a brilliant memory, but the truth is, I looked it up on Mr Google and some things just stay with me.'

She laughed, but my attention was over her shoulder where I saw Turner making a rare early appearance, wandering the decks and peering intently over the sides. She noticed my distraction, looked behind and said, 'Dave said there was some fuss last night. What was going on?'

I gave the short answer. 'Turner decided to replace his head girl Mary, with Corrine, then decided to dispose of the old one permanently. Corrine warned her about it in time and cooked up a plan to get the collar off her, presumably re-arm it, then toss it overboard where it went bang as it sank. We got a cryptic message from Corrine, in advance, warning us to be ready to pick up a package drifting north of Turner's boat. I'm guessing that Mary hid under the stern-board until they gave up looking for body parts, then let herself drift away with the tide. I went out there and found a naked girl being chased by a shark. She's down below sleeping. She's a total hard-ball nutcase case, but may be able to help us if or when she decides to talk.'

'Wow. That's really great, Harry. She can tell us everything about him and his plans.'

I felt my face pulling into a grimace. 'Yeah, she certainly should have good intel. Provided she tells us everything. She bunged on a bit of an act last night about how everyone was against her, so I told her a few home truths. I doubt she'll co-operate this morning, but at least Turner thinks she's dead, so that's one more saved from his grubby paws.'

'Oh. Well, breakfast should be interesting, in that case. Oh, look. Is that Turner heading this way?'

She'd spotted Turner's dinghy appear from behind *Gideon* and indeed he was heading our way.

'Yup. That's the man of the moment. This'll be good.'

We didn't need to move, because Turner had seen us and drove straight for the bow where we perched.

He nodded greeting. 'I don't know if you were aware of the incident we had last night, but my ex-head girl tried to get away by jumping overboard. Unfortunately for her, the collar worked as expected, and we haven't seen her since. There are a lot of sharks around here and she wasn't a good swimmer. I don't suppose you've seen any sign of her?'

I shook my head and lied like a pig in poo. 'Aw... that's a shame but no, we haven't Gary. That's terrible for you. Will it mess up your plans very much?'

He gave a mirthless grin. 'Not much. She could have been sold to a new buyer, or used to test out my partner's grand scheme, but I have some new stock arriving soon, so it's not a big problem.'

'Oh, good. I wouldn't like to hear that your plans were messed up.'

'All going well, thank you. Anyway, I've decided to remain here for another couple of days since my customers are still delayed.'

'No problem. We were going food shopping today, and it seems quite nice here.'

'I'm glad you like it.'

Without further words, he motored back to his boat, as Reggie looked at me.

'He's a soulless bastard, isn't he? I don't envy Corrine one little bit. But I wonder what his partner's grand scheme is – the one he was going to use his ex-head girl to try out?'

'Yes. That's the second time he's let slip something about a 'grand plan' or 'new scheme'. Before she buggers off, I need to ask Mary some questions, whether she likes it or not.'

I went back to the saloon, Reggie following, to find the whole crew milling around, with Bree and Hanh starting to cook breakfast.

'We heard most of that through the for'rard windows,' Dave said, 'and it didn't sound as though he has any suspicions.'

'No. I'm pretty certain he's accepted what he saw as being what happened.'

There was a quiet, tremulous voice from the forward port stairway.

'Can I come up now, please? I heard it all too. He was right outside my cabin porthole. I could've touched him.'

Mary's tousled, blonde head showed half-up the stairs, an

anxious expression on her face.

Sandy flashed me another stern look, so I flapped my hand wearily, 'Yeah, yeah. Come on up. You need to eat as meals and drinks are self-serve only, and I need to ask you some questions before you bail out. We can't take you ashore until tonight, so you're stuck here for the day. Suck it up and live with it!'

That earned me another warning glare from Sandy.

Mary slowly stepped up, still wearing the T-shirt and trakkie-daks Sandy gave her, reminding me that she had nothing of her own. In the tinted daylight in the saloon, she looked quite presentable, filling the T-shirt almost as well as Sandy did hers, although she had an strangley timid expression on her face.

Sandy introduced her to the rest of the crew, which made it almost a crowd, since with Mary as temporary guest, we now numbered nine. Hanh gave her a brief hug as the girls inspected her carefully and made her welcome.

I let them chat for a few moments, then as soon as Bree started serving brekkie, I shooed everybody out to the cockpit with their plates of lovely hot food in hand. I pointed Mary to the inside settee where she'd sat last night, and Sandy and Bree joined us, after handing Mary a mug of coffee and a plate of bacon, beans and eggs.

I avoided any pleasantries or references to last night's discussion, focussing just on the facts which might help us. 'We've worked out Corrine's escape plan for last night. Is there anything else odd that happened we should know about?'

'No. Nothing special. Somehow, Corrine knew how to deactivate and open the collars, and told me. Then, when Turner took her into his cabin for a session, I popped the collar off, closed and re-activated it, then tossed it overboard. I was already at the stern, so the moment it went off, I slid into the water and hid under the stern board until all the fuss died down.'

She gave an unexpected giggle. 'I don't know if Turner was more upset by thinking that I'd tried to escape, or by having his session with Corrine interrupted. When he charged out to the stern, it wasn't hard to tell what he'd been doing twenty seconds earlier.'

'Okay. That's covered. What do you know about this partner, Korey Yanos?'

'Just that he's from Melbourne. Says he used to be with an investigation company with a very strange name, and is a total degenerate. He's vicious and behaves like an animal with the girls. He damages every one he's with. Even Turner won't take any girl he's used, they're so fucked mentally, as well as physically scarred.'

'That strange name wasn't Stainless Associates, was it?' I asked casually.

'Yeah. That's it. Weird. But that word suits this whole deal.'

I concealed my misgivings, and pressed on, 'What about this grand plan or new scheme of Yanos that Turner keeps referring to?'

She frowned, 'I'm not sure. I would overhear little things occasionally which didn't make sense. Like, there's an island not far north of here, which is involved with this plan. It's called Slain Island, and is up the Straits somewhere. I know there are firearms involved, both rifles and pistols, and there's a house Yanos has rented in a little fishing village called Maaroom. It's not far from Slain Island. They must plan to bring other people into this place, 'cause one day, Gary had me look up flight schedules from Brisbane to Maryborough. I've not heard what they intend doing on the island, only that it must be worth a lot of money to them.'

'Why do you say that?'

'I used to do the books and one day I pointed out to him that he wasn't doing much better than break-even with the girl-slave racket as the expenses were so high. Korey charges a heap to supply girls. Anyway, he said he was aware of that, but the new plan was going to turn that around very quickly and make the whole operation very worthwhile. I know he's also looking for an extra boat with shallow draft. That bit didn't make any sense to me, 'cause I don't know anything about boats.'

'Hmmm. None of that adds up, yet. Did you hear anything about why he wants to keep us around?'

'Only that you already have a bunch of young girls and seemed to have heaps of money, which it seems about right to me, just looking around.'

I looked at Sandy and Bree. 'Is there anything I've missed? Speak up, since today is our only chance to get insider intel.'

Both shook their heads, so I said to Mary, 'Okay. That'll do. After dark, I'll get Dave to run you ashore. We'll see if the girls can scrounge up some more clothes and a small bag, while Bree will give you a few thousand dollars to get you going. Then you're free to go where you want, but I would strongly advise that you get away from the whole east coast scene as soon as you can. Try Adelaide or any smallish town in South Australia. Korey shouldn't be trawling for girls over there for a while yet.'

She suddenly teared up again. I don't like it when ladies turn on the tears because I don't know how to handle it. Therefore, I'm called insensitive.

'What the hell is wrong now?' I demanded, perhaps more harshly than I should have.

'I... I... I don't want to go!' she sobbed. 'Everyone's being so nice and I'm sorry about upsetting you last night, especially after you just saved me. I was just so upset about nearly being killed and not knowing where I'd go or what I'd do. I've got nothing I can call my own, and I don't know where to go that'd be safe. As I came on this boat naked, I've got nothing to lose, so can't I please stay?'

I looked at Sandy and Bree, who for once were equally un-impressed with her tears, and Bree suggested, 'Perhaps as a trial, we let her stay under the same conditions as Sally and Kim, except she'll have to stay within the saloon by day and down below at night until after lights out.'

'Yeah, perhaps. What are your thoughts, my dear?'

Sandy nodded, 'Yep. Good thinking Bree. Let's try it for a few days and see how it works out. Any problems, we'll just dump her on the nearest bit of dry land, whether it's connected to the mainland or not. Someone else can find her and sort her out.'

I was surprised by Sandy's turn of attitude, either real or bunged-on, but it was easier to have them on my side. I looked back at Mary.

'Okay then, that's the verdict from the Executive committee. You can stay for now while we see if you're going to behave yourself. Remember, if you show yourself at the wrong time, this whole operation is blown and Turner, Collings and Korey will be free to carry on and do it all over again. And they'll be gunning for you in particular. It won't be a quick death, either. I can imagine both the Collings and Korey will have some very inventive ways to make your demise as much fun for them as it'll be agonising for you.'

She turned pale and visibly shuddered.

'You don't need to remind me. I know they're very talented in that way.'

'Very well. You stick with your curfew, do what you can to help around the boat without being seen, try to be pleasant to be around, and perhaps all will be well.'

'What about afterwards? What happens to me then?'

I gave a mirthless bark of laughter, 'You haven't earned the reward of future planning... yet. Just do your best to behave well for the next few days, don't fuck things up for any of us, and we'll see what happens then. In the meantime, Bree will round-up some more clothes for you to wear. The laundry is beside your cabin, so you might like to volunteer to look after that, as the others will be doing a lot of other housework and cooking for you since you can't show yourself.'

She nodded eagerly, thanked us apparently sincerely, then went below, while Bree resumed making out the shopping list.

I went out to the cockpit to bring the rest of the crew up-to-date with this latest information.

'This special project – the island, the rented house, guns and the much greater income all sounds very strange,' Alex said in his slow, deep voice.

'Yes. And it bothers me greatly,' I replied. 'They're planning something a lot worse than sex-slavery, I'm afraid. Let's hope Mouse hears something else soon.'

Ideas bounced around the table for a while, but nothing new came from anyone by the time Bree re-appeared with a large shopping list in one hand, a smaller list in the other.

'Mary has asked for some personal things, so since we're going ashore, I'll get her some clothes as well.'

'Okay. Alex, I presume you're going?'

'Yes, Harry. Unless you need me here.'

'Nah, mate. All good, thanks. Bree will need your muscles to carry all that stuff she's got on the list.'

CHAPTER 19

TIN CAN BAY

The next two days slid past quietly, as Sally, Kim and now Mary, settled into our boat routine. At anchor, there wasn't much to do, boat-wise, apart from basic house-keeping chores. Supplies were re-stocked, Mary stayed out of sight at times of high risk, but joined in with everyone when she could. She must have had a good think about her situation and made a surprisingly successful effort to get along with everyone and do what chores she could. Like doing the laundry, a big task all by itself. She tackled it with enthusiasm and the dark cloud of Turner's oppression finally seemed to be lifting as she appeared to be enjoying life out from under someone else's control.

There was little activity on the Collings boat, although their girl, Taylor, made a few appearances by sunbaking naked on the foredeck. What Warren and Millie got up to, we didn't get to see at the time, although we finally found out the hard way a couple of days later.

Our cover had to be maintained and the younger female members embraced that with a passion. As suspected, Sally and Kim were hard-core party girls and once they saw what standard of un-dress was the norm, they happily stripped off completely and adorned the trampoline netting, and various other areas, along with Hanh, Reggie and Bree who as usual, always wore her bikini. After sunset of the third day of our Tin Can Bay layover, while the evening drinks session around the cockpit table was in full swing, we turned all the lights out so Mary could join in and she made a valiant effort to catch up. We'd got to the NQ tea stage where I told the new ladies the recipe of dark rum liqueur in black tea.

On top of the wine consumed earlier, three NQs sent Kim and Sally a bit silly. Nine around the table made for a decent party and at one point, I noticed Sandy getting friendly with the girls, as sometimes happens when a lovely lady takes her fancy.

Being a bit slow in matters involving females, I must have missed any earlier signals being flashed around, so when Alex and Bree drifted off to bed, followed soon after by Reggie and Hanh, I was surprised to see that Sandy was absent.

Dave noted my searching look and said, 'I think she went to bed some time ago, mate.'

I still didn't catch on, so I went to pee over the stern in the accepted manner, then waved goodnight and headed for bed. Where I found that the bed already held three sleeping bodies. Female ones. Naked even.

Sandy and one of the sisters were occupying not a lot of space, with the other one in the middle of the king-size bed. That left just enough room for me, so I scrubbed teeth, killed the lights and fitted into the remaining space. Which wasn't totally uncomfortable with Sally's warm body at my back, so I did manage to get to sleep for a while, at least. My reward for being such a good boy came sometime in the wee small hours, and the resulting joyous activity woke Sandy and Kim, who happily continued where they'd left off.

There was time for some dozing after that, before starting again with Sally being more than willing to disturb the other two.

I woke for the third time to hear the sound of rain pattering hard on the deck above as the forecast cold front moved through, bringing a chilly wind which set up the usual soft, deep moaning from the carbon mast. It made for an interesting counter-point to that coming from Sandy and Kim fooling around again.

Although I could feel the boat tugging fretfully at its anchor chain, there's something terribly attractive about being warm and comfortable in bed, on a cold, windy and rainy morning. It really makes one want to just stay there and take advantage of a compliant partner. Naturally, being mindful of my duties as Skipper and responsible for the safety of the boat and all aboard, I stayed where I was and did what was expected of me.

My R & R was disturbed by Dave who informed me that Turner had called and was waiting to take me back to his boat to meet one of his customer couples. I cleaned up and dressed in record time, minutes later stepping out to the stern with a smile on my face and a cheery, 'Good morning, Gary.'

'Morning, Harry. You ready?'

'Yep.' I stepped aboard his dinghy and was whizzed over to *Poseidon*, passing by the stern of *Gideon* on the way. Warren and Millie were sitting in the cockpit, and if I wasn't mistaken, I was the recipient of a murderous glare from Warren.

Turner noticed and gave a chuckle, 'He still doesn't like you very much!'

'Yeah, I'm starting to get that impression. But he'll be safe so long as he doesn't go prowling in the middle of the night.'

Turner chuckled again, 'That's his favourite time for making mischief. You'd better keep your eyes and ears open.'

There was a new boat anchored about a hundred metres away on the other side of Turner's, which I presumed belonged to the couple who'd been very careless with their girl.

'What's the go with these people, Gary? It's not like they can do a trade-in.'

'Correct. This is effectively a new transaction, which is why I thought you'd like to see the process.'

'Good-oh. Sounds interesting.'

The couple, a man and woman in their late forties, were introduced as Ben and Linda, no surname, and their fifty-foot cruiser was called *Joker*. They were quite jovial people and Ben had a firm handshake. Linda was attractive, pleasantly rounded, and seemed to be a generally happy person. However, by the looks she gave me, I figured she considered herself a real player and considered anyone was fair game.

We were made comfortable in Turner's saloon, and it was Corrine who served drinks, greeting me with a quiet, 'Hello Harry,' but wouldn't look me in the eye.

I had Linda beside me and she asked, 'Are you here to get a girl too, Harry?'

Turner turned from giving instructions to Corrine, and laughed 'Goodness me, no Linda. Harry has that enormous red catamaran not far away and it's totally stacked with lots of lovely young girls. If I didn't know better, I'd suspect he was trying to muscle in on my business.'

Linda patted me on the thigh, 'Oh, you wouldn't do that to Gary, would you Harry? He's been so good to us.'

I smiled, 'No Linda. I wouldn't do that. I haven't known Gary very long and was just cruising around with a couple of mates and our usual bunch of young lovelies. Got to do something productive, you know. Ha, ha. Sex, booze and more sex and booze.'

I felt her hand clamp down hard, 'Ooh, lovely! You sound like our sort of people. What do you think, Ben?'

By the bulge in the front of his shorts, Ben was thinking about all the things he'd like to do to Corrine, as he dragged his attention away from her naked body bits for a moment and tried to focus a slightly glazed expression on his wife. 'Oh, yeah… sure. Just like us… fit right in.'

I was saved from further questioning, but not her wandering hand, by the arrival in the saloon of the first of Turner's girls to be offered as a replacement. Naturally she was naked, apart from the ubiquitous black collar, which looked quite sexy, if you ignored its sinister and deadly purpose.

'This is Jay,' Turner said. 'She's eighteen, or thereabouts, perfectly healthy and works well around the boat. Turn around slowly, please dear. Let the nice people get a good look at you.'

She tried to smile, but it was a weak effort, as she slowly turned, keeping her eyes downcast.

'Oh, I like the look of her,' Linda exclaimed, 'Don't you, Ben?'

'Oh, yes. Very nice, dear.'

He turned his attention to Turner, 'What about that one over in the corner? Corrine. I like the look of her. She looks like she could be really feisty – I like them feisty.'

'Now, now, dearest. I don't think she's for sale today. Just wipe the corner of your mouth… that's it. No, there's more down your chin. Do try to control yourself. We'll have one again very soon.'

She looked at Turner. 'Right, Gary. Who's next?'

The second and third girls were remarkably similar in shape and age, and although the fourth one was a bit chubby, it sat well on her. Their names were Teri, Lena and Philippa, and Turner had them parade in the same way as Jay had.

'Naturally, all the girls are guaranteed clean and shave regularly, although they can let things grow out if that's your preference.'

'Thank you dear. Very thoughtful. What do you think, Ben? We must make a choice now.'

Ben grumped a bit, then said, 'Well. If we really can't have Corrine, then we'll take the chubby one. What's her name?'

'That would be Philippa, Ben,' Turner said quietly, 'and are you willing to confirm that Philippa is the one for you too, Linda?'

'Oh, I suppose so. Is she a hard worker? I don't like having to do housework, you know.'

Turner nodded sincerely, 'Oh, yes. Very good worker. Never makes trouble either. An excellent choice.'

'Very well, then.'

He turned to the girl, 'Alright Philippa. You've been chosen by these lovely people, so get dressed and pack. Be back here in ten minutes.'

She turned without a word and headed for the bow cabin she shared with the other girls.

'Now that's settled,' Turner said brightly, 'there's just the payment to make. Cash or transfer?'

Linda beamed at him, 'Oh, cash, of course. So anonymous, don't you think, Harry?'

I pasted a dumb smile on my face and said, 'Absolutely. I always use cash if I can. Much safer.'

That earned me another squeeze, and I was surprised she didn't already have my zip open.

Corrine stepped forward from her place in the corner and placed a piece of paper in front of Linda who was clearly the driving force of this partnership. She peered at the figures. 'Fifty thousand? That's the same as last time. Don't we get a discount for repeat business?'

Turner gave an oily smile. 'Normally you would if the loss was due to a fault with the collar, or the girl had a pre-existing medical problem, but this one was your fault I'm afraid.'

'Oh dear. Yes, I suppose it was. Very silly of us. Well, we won't be making that mistake again.'

She dug into the voluminous pocket of her spray jacket, produced a fat wad of green hundred-dollar notes, banded into $10,000 packs. She flipped five packs onto the table.

Turner nodded at Corrine, who stepped forward again and quickly counted each pack.

He waited until she'd finished and nodded approval, before he smiled and shook their hands.

'Congratulations. As you've done this before, I can dispense with reading the rules again, but Harry and I will come with you to bind her collar to your transmitter. Only takes a few moments.'

'Lovely, thank you, Gary dear. So kind.'

Philippa was waiting, holding a small soft bag which represented her only possessions.

Turner snapped his fingers, 'Come along, girl. Don't keep your new owners waiting.'

Corrine stepped forward and spoke quietly. 'Better turn off her collar, Gary.'

'Damn. That really would be an 'oops' moment. Ha, ha. Thank you, dear girl.'

He stepped back into the wheelhouse and presumably went

through the same procedure Corrine had used on Mary's collar. There was a click from it, and the join separated. Corrine carefully removed it, before handing it to Turner.

'Okay. Let's go.'

Philippa went with Ben and Linda in their dinghy, while I climbed into Turner's dinghy. He passed me the collar. 'Hang onto this for me, please Harry, while I drive this thing. It won't take long to reactivate and it will automatically bind with their existing transmitter.'

I scanned it carefully, while trying not to appear to be doing so.

'Do they ever go off accidently?'

'No. Never had a problem like that. Korey supplies them. They're made in Japan and he gets them direct from one of their criminal gangs. Ingenious little jiggers, aren't they?'

I turned the deadly piece of curved plastic in my hands.

'Quite amazing,' I said, sounding genuine, although my meaning was different to his as I filed another piece of the puzzle away. I wanted to keep taking advantage of his relaxed, talkative mood, but we were pulling up to the stern of *Joker*. It was a nice boat, well-built and equipped, providing additional proof that money wasn't an issue for Ben and Linda. They'd just dropped another fifty-grand on a replacement girl without blinking.

Turner took Philippa forward to the steering station, put the collar around her neck and had her hold the ends together. He shielded the panel from her sight, although I clearly saw that all he did was just a press and hold on the green button. There was the buzz from the collar, but it took longer for the LEDs to turn red, presumably due to the auto-bind process.

Moments later, after waving a small hand-held meter over the collar, he pronounced it fully functional.

He addressed Philippa. 'This is your new home, and Ben and Linda are your owners. You answer to them alone. They look after you, and in return, you do whatever they want you to do. No arguments. Do you understand?'

She nodded seriously, 'Yes, Mr Turner. I understand.'

'Good. Behave yourself, and you will have a very comfortable life.'

By the look on Ben's face and the dribble of saliva running down to his chin, I had severe doubts about the accuracy of that statement.

We shook hands with Ben and Linda and got out of there. On the way back to *Firebird* Turner said, 'That bloody Linda is a case. I saw how she was groping your leg. If they hang around, you'll probably get an invitation to drop over for drinks and a bit of sport, but be careful if you do. She's one crazy bitch when she's got some booze or drugs in her system.'

'Advice taken, thanks Gary.'

He continued. 'Although Ben doesn't seem too bad, he's different, and just as bad in his own way. You saw how he was drooling over the thought of getting his paws on Corrine? Girls take a while to recover from some of their extended sessions with him. I'm surprised they haven't asked for a second girl. Maybe I'll suggest it if they stay round here much longer.'

'Speaking of that,' I said, 'what's the plan? Stay or move on?'

He appeared to consider what to say while we idled up to *Firebird's* stern. 'My partner, Korey, is delivering a new batch of girls in the next few days, so I was thinking about moving to a quieter location. I don't want to go too far away though, and need good access from the mainland. Any suggestions?'

I was surprised by his request, which seemed to indicate that I was considered more reliable and trustworthy than either the two sets of his customers I'd met so far. Although Warren had seemed to be highly regarded by Turner at first, I saw his attitude changing as Warren seemed to be becoming increasingly unstable.

Despite putting on a brave face, Turner also had to be a bit rattled by Mary's apparent suicide.

With these fleeting thoughts buzzing around, I responded, 'Why not just move up to the west shore of Fraser/K'gari Island near Kingfisher Resort? There's a quiet anchorage with a sandy beach a couple of miles north of where the vehicle ferry from the mainland goes to Wanggoolba Creek. Transfers would be more private than here, and the scenery a lot better. Swimming will be a lot safer, too.'

'Not a bad idea, Harry. You've been in this area before, have you?'

'Yeah. Just passed through a couple of times, so I don't know it very well, but I learned to stay away from the mangroves if you want to avoid the bloody mozzies.'

He chuckled in agreement. 'Yeah, okay then. We might move tomorrow morning. I don't suppose you know how far it is?'

'Only thirty nautical miles or so, I think, so an easy few hour's run in the morning. Hopefully, the weather will have cleared by then.'

'Okay. I'll let the Collings know. I'm not sure about Ben and Linda. They may have other plans, but I'll invite them anyway.'

I hopped out and he headed straight for *Gideon*. I still wasn't sure how much I was trusted, or how deeply Warren was involved with his new scheme, but I thought it best to be patient.

Sandy, Kim and Sally were up and dressed warmly, as I updated them all and assured Dave that his lady appeared fit and well.

'We know,' he said, 'we had a long message from her while you and Turner were messing around on the other boat. She reported that the girls were very upset by Mary's death, but she hasn't let on to them what really happened. She doesn't trust their acting skills. Turner has warned them to expect another four girls in a few days' time, so they'll have to make room for them somehow. He suggested that some of them may not be staying too long, depending on how his plans work out. She also said that losing Mary was a big shock to him, and Warren's increasingly erratic behaviour is worrying him a lot.'

With the weather still foul, the pussies were very happy to snuggle up to whoever would sit still and pet them. Except when they'd just come back inside after a visit to their external toilet mat, when they were shooed away until they dried off. The cockpit doors stayed closed, the diesel heaters kept blowing lovely warm air, and we all gathered around the saloon table to enjoy the hot lunch whipped up by Bree and Hanh. Discussion revolved around the move north to the island, and the new bunch of girls coming in.

'How many girls can Turner's boat hold at a time?' I asked Mary, who was becoming happier by the day as she enjoyed the transition from captive slave to a welcome part of the crew.

'Normally four or five is the limit. He's still got three aboard, so another four will make conditions really overcrowded. It's odd that he's getting another four in one batch like this, unless he does have more customers lined up. He's never been able to sell girls that quickly before. The average has been about one per month up to now. Something else must be going on.'

What she said made sense, but we still couldn't connect any dots. As in – four extra girls coming in with three already in hand – needing access from the mainland – Slain Island – hand-guns and rifles – new scheme and big income. After a while, the crew started drifting off or settling down to read or look at videos. With the rain pelting down again, I was a bit keen for a romp in the sack, but Sandy wasn't for some reason, so I did some basic maintenance chores, including cleaning the solar panels.

At least with electric motors, I was spared the time-consuming task of frequent oil and filter changes on the diesels.

We had two small diesel generators for when we couldn't sail, or the weather was particularly bad, but even in the current low-light conditions when the solar panels weren't so effective, the wind generators were delivering a good supply of electrons to the battery banks.

The afternoon drifted quietly on, and I found myself sitting at the chart-table, jotting down notes about all the anomalous stuff we'd seen or heard, and trying to make some sense of it. Later on, as evening crept in, hardly noticed in the rainy gloom, some-one declared the bar open, and that got the evening off to an early start. Luckily, most of us were still bushed from last night's over-indulgences, so it wasn't such a pissy evening as I expected. Even so, Kim and Sally were keen on a repeat performance and came below when Sandy and I decided to head for bed. I was due to take over a watch at about 01:00, although I didn't get much sleep, since Sally wanted to swap places with Kim.

Once back in the saloon, I was joined by Mary who'd volunteered to stand a night watch. Normally, the pussies share themselves around the various beds, but tonight, Jasper was with us and acting unsettled. I tried talking to him, much to Mary's amusement, however he wouldn't sit still, so after telling Mary to keep out of sight, I rugged up and ventured on deck. The light breeze was cold, although the rain had eased off to a misty drizzle which still managed to wet everything thoroughly. There was very little light from the town, so vision was limited and I saw nothing unusual.

Purely on impulse, I went below and fired up the masthead camera, selecting its colour-coded infra-red mode for best night vision. I scanned all around, and spotted a couple of die-hard fishermen anchored some distance away, plus some others heading north toward the bar area.

Checking closer to home, there was a slight heat signature from *Gideon*, so I zoomed in. It firmed up and moved from the midships area toward the stern.

With Mary at my shoulder peering at the display, I zoomed in some more and was rewarded with the distinct outline of a human moving further aft toward the stern.

'Interesting,' I commented, 'maybe it's just Warren going to take a leak, but why get wet and cold for no reason?'

The resolution of the camera was excellent, even in infra-red mode, and once the person was in the open, clearly showed it was loading several small items into the dinghy.

'What are you up to, Warren?' I muttered rhetorically. 'And why do I have the feeling that you're about to be a very naughty boy?'

'What's he going to do, Harry?' Mary asked, getting a bit concerned, since I didn't seem to be doing anything as the figure rowed away from *Gideon* and headed for us.

I gave her a joyful grin, 'This idiot isn't about to give up and seems to hold a grudge for some reason. I think it's time Jasper had some exercise.'

'What's that mean?'

'It means that Warren is about to get his first and final warning not to mess with the *Firebird* crew.'

'He won't get hurt, will he?'

I laughed, 'No, Jasper won't, but Warren will. Big time.'

'Good! Having seen what Warren likes doing to girls, you won't hear me standing up for him – the vicious, depraved prick.'

'Glad to hear it, because this could get messy. I'll just have a word to Jasper, if you wouldn't mind staying here. Keep low and don't make a sound.'

I checked the camera again and saw the dinghy being rowed awkwardly against the wind, but it was only about twenty metres away.

Jasper was in the cockpit, his black fur blending into the night gloom.

'Bad man coming, boy. Wait until I tell you, then take him down. Quiet as you can.'

I never know how much of my words are understood, however he did have a good track record, and this time stopped his soft growl to huff at me.

I armed myself with a super-bright LED hand-held spotlight and crouched in the saloon doorway behind one partly opened door. There was a soft thump as he arrived and tied the dinghy up, then a faint metallic scraping, like a tin can being pushed along the deck. The faint lights of the town were off the stern, so his dark form showed in silhouette as he crept up the port steps carrying some items.

He stopped at the top of the steps and placed something on the cockpit floor. There came the metallic sound again, then the strong tang of petrol swirled around the cockpit.

I stood up with the torch above my head and flicked it on.

Warren was caught fair in the middle of the pure-white, super-bright beam, wide-eyed, like a kangaroo in a car's headlights. He had an opened can of outboard fuel at his feet with a rag stuffed in the hole, and an unlit cigarette lighter in his hand.

'Go boy' I called, and switched off the light just before a black shadow launched from the gloom at the cockpit side, hitting him high in the chest.

Dazzled, he didn't see what hit him, and gave a strangled grunt of shock and pain as he went over backwards, landing with a shuddering thump on the boarding platform. Then there was an all-too-familiar sickening, crunching sound. I knew what that meant, and called softly, 'That's enough, thanks boy. Hold him there.'

Which was maybe a bit superfluous, because I was fairly certain that Warren had abused his last girl. When he was turned loose like this, Jasper's trademark attack method was to crush or rip the victim's throat out in one big, tearing bite, which cuts down on noise and is guaranteed terminal.

Such was the case when I carefully shone a smaller torch beam down the port stairs. Jasper was sitting on Warren's chest, looking pleased with himself. There was a bloody mess where Warren's throat had been and by the rate of blood loss, he didn't have long to live.

Calling Jasper back, I stepped down to crouch beside Warren. He was understandably in deep shock, but still just conscious.

'You've been a very bad boy with the ladies, Warren, but coming over here to burn my boat and crew was going a bit too far, I'm afraid. I'm not sorry that you won't survive this little encounter, and with all your blood running straight overboard, I reckon there'll be several lads in grey suits lining up to finish off your worthless carcase. They never leave much for anybody to find, so you'll just disappear. Bye, bye.'

With those words and zero regret, I tipped him over the stern, right into the middle of his own spreading pool of blood. As expected, the ever-reliable bull sharks weren't far away, and within seconds, a series of splashes slowly drifting downstream were the last we saw of the very late and decidedly unlamented Warren Collings.

Mary was waiting at the top of the steps, very pale, but with a look of satisfaction on her face. Surprisingly, she gave me a hard hug, moulding her lovely body against me.

'Thank you, Harry. That was particularly gruesome, but I'm very glad for all the girls he's abused so terribly over the years.'

I nodded grimly, 'Yep. I'll second that thought. On a brighter note, when that sort of thing happens down here, the traces are easy to clean off. Which reminds me, I have to do that and clean Jasper's face.'

Demonstrating a pleasing sense of practicality and self-control, she said, 'How about I hose off the steps, and you clean up that wonderful overgrown pussycat.'

I kissed her on the cheek. 'Thanks Mary. Sounds like a very good plan.'

A look of pleased surprise flashed across her face, before I showed her where the wash-down hose and sponges were stowed, and she got busy. I left her to it and took Jasper over to the other side steps where the hand-held shower was located.

I had just finished washing pussy's face, when Alex appeared silently.

'Problems, Harry?'

'Not anymore.' I pointed to the can of petrol with the rag still poking out of the spout. 'Warren came calling with murderous intent, but Jasper was onto him early, and made sure he wasn't going to bother any girls ever again.'

He peered around, noting Jasper with a clean, wet face, and

Mary rolling up the hose. 'A grey-suit clean-up squad job, eh?'

'Yep. No disposal problems here.'

'How'd the lady handle it?'

'Excellent. Wasn't sorry to see him go. She's got some guts, that one. She's had a hard life with too many Warren's in it.'

He smiled, 'Well said, Boss. In that case, I think I'll go back to bed.'

'Yeah. We can cancel the night watches for now. Our biggest problem has been solved for the moment.'

'Goodnight Harry.'

'Cheers Alex, and thanks man.'

My final act in the disinformation game was to tow Warren's dinghy back to *Gideon* with our silent electric outboard, and quietly tie it up at the stern.

Back on *Firebird,* and as an unwinder, I made a pair of NQ teas for Mary and myself and we sat in the saloon, making a quiet fuss of Jasper who loved to be told when he's done a good job. I mean, he always knows he does a good job, but really loves to be told as well. Not much different to most humans, really.

'Are you sure you're alright after that?' I asked her, sipping quietly at my tea.

She gave a genuine smile, 'Yes, Harry. I really am. I actually feel a great weight has been lifted off my shoulders. Even hosing the mongrel's blood away seemed to banish a lot of demons. And thanks for being concerned. I'm not used to anyone being concerned about how I feel, so I'm really sorry for being so prickly. I've had to put up with a lot of bad things in the last few years, but seeing the end of a genuine monster was really good.'

We chatted about more light-hearted things for a while longer, then she went to bed, and I re-joined Sandy and the girls who'd slept through the whole episode.

TIN CAN BAY

Next morning, the sun shone from a sky washed clean by the rain, making the air so clear, the hills behind the coast looked close enough to touch. *Firebird* had received a good bath as well, with all the sticky salt washed off.

I was up on deck before dawn, leaving Sandy, Kim and Sally still asleep and snoring softly. A steaming mug of sweet tea in hand, I was joined by Jasper and gave him a lot of attention.

I was also joined by Reggie again, who asked, 'I thought I heard some odd noises last night. Everything all right?'

I made with a wry grin, 'Yes, you could say that. Warren came calling – but he's not going to bother anyone again.'

She looked around. 'He can't have gone far. His boat's still there with the dinghy tied up.'

I couldn't help a chuckle. 'Ah… yes. But Warren isn't.'

She screwed her face up in a puzzled look. 'Where is he, if not on his boat?'

I grinned, and pointed over the side. 'I'd say his various components are presently making their way through the digestive system of several bull sharks.'

'Fuckin' hell Harry! What happened?'

'He came to try to set fire to my boat and all of us, but he didn't allow for Jasper's acute senses. Actually, now I come to think of it, he didn't know about Jasper in the first place, but that was his problem. If he hadn't tried to be such a bad boy, he'd still be here. Anyway, Jasper ripped his throat out, and I tipped him overboard. There was a lot of blood which always brings the clean-up squad around, and that was that.'

'Oh, shit! So, Jasper killed him?'

'Hmmm… strictly speaking, no. It was the sharks who killed him, but he was nearly gone when I tipped him over. He wouldn't have felt a thing.'

She looked horrified, 'But the man is dead. Doesn't that bother you?'

I gave her my pissed-off Major glare. 'No, it doesn't! Not in the slightest. Go have a more careful look in the cockpit. That ten-litre container full of petrol you probably had to step around on your way up here isn't ours. When Warren put it there, it had a rag stuffed in the spout to act as a wick, and he had the lighter in his hand, about to flick it. Once lit, he only had to kick the can over and jump back in his dinghy. That much petrol flooding across the cockpit flooring would have the boat in flames within a minute. The resin holding all this fancy carbon-fibre together burns very nicely and very hot. Most of us or all of us would be dead – either suffocated by the toxic smoke, or burned alive and impersonating crispy critters. That's why I'm not bothered in the slightest. And nor is Mary who was with me at the time and saw the whole thing. She was delighted for all the girls he'd abused so severely.'

Her face fell as she stepped to the rail, looking decidedly green, 'Oh, dear Lord. What's going on? This operation isn't like I thought it would be.'

I stepped up beside her, gently turned her to face me and softened my tone.

'Look, Reggie. What's going on is that this is the real world full of bad guys and girls who don't hesitate to do serious harm to anybody who tries to stop them getting their warped, twisted way. Last night, one of those bad guys with a grudge against me, decided he wanted to take us all out in one of the nastiest ways possible. Thanks to Jasper, he failed and it barely disturbed your sleep. So now isn't the time to become full of remorse for the removal of a psychopathic piece of shit who has already caused immeasurable, long-term damage and pain to lots of girls, and who was about to kill all of us.'

She didn't reply, so I took a deep breath and continued in the same even tone. 'Understand this, Reggie. I've had a lot of accusations levelled at me over the years, when bad guys failed to turn up in handcuffs as expected, but I can honestly say that I've never deliberately taken out somebody who didn't truly deserve it.

I've never just acted on orders to kill people either, and nor has Corrine. From your lofty perch on the moral high ground, you can label us as mindless killing machines if that makes you feel righteous, but nothing could be further from the truth. As a police officer, how do you feel when you hear of a lazy judge who lets a murderer free on a 'technicality', only to have him or her kill a child 24-hours later? Or what's your opinion of those rabid do-gooders who scream that criminals have rights, when the victim has none? Is that fair or just? Maybe I do have a black and white view of the world, but when I see someone who can't stand up for themselves being abused by an arrogant shit of a bully, then the issue is crystal-clear. That's what works for me anyway. Take it or leave it, it's how I am, and I'm comfortable with myself. I always sleep well at night.'

By now tears were running down her cheeks, and she was sobbing quietly, something I've never been able to handle with females, so I resorted to the old standby, and gave her a hug. She held the embrace for a long time, but then lifted her head, looked past me and said in a still quavering voice, 'I think Millie has just discovered Warren's missing.'

I turned around to see Millie and their girl, Taylor, searching the upper deck, cockpit and the dinghy, calling Warren's name. Shortly after, Turner appeared on *Poseidon's* deck, jumped in his dinghy and motored over to *Gideon*. Minutes after that, he came calling on us.

'Good morning, Gary. You're up early. You must have peed the bed or something.'

'Cut the crap, Harry. Millie's cracking up because Warren's missing. Do you know where he is?'

I looked him straight in the eye and told the honest truth.

'No Gary, I truly don't know where he is. I could add that I don't particularly care, but you already know that.'

He returned my look, then nodded. 'Yeah, fair enough. Since his dinghy's still there, he can't have gone ashore, so he must have fallen overboard while taking a piss or something and hit his head. That's the only explanation I can think of if you don't know his whereabouts. I know there are a lot of sharks around here who'd finish him off if he was stunned and bleeding. I'd better go and sort Millie out. The silly bitch wants to call the cops.'

'What's she going to do? Is she a boating person?'

I wanted to know for Taylor's sake.

'Hmmm… good point. I don't really know. I guess I'd better find out. I only know she's a bloody hard woman, but without Warren holding her hand, things might be different. At the moment, she's cracking up big time.'

He returned to *Gideon* and disappeared inside, while I went into the saloon to brief the rest of the crew who'd gathered to hear what'd been happening. Everyone was grimly pleased Warren was out of the way – even Kim and Sally just shrugged. Warren had physically hurt both girls at Noosa, and they were well aware of how unstable he had been, so there were no regrets that he was no longer with us.

Bree and Mary got breakfast started, and we were eating when Turner returned, forcing Mary to quickly disappear below.

Strangely, this time he accepted my invitation to join us and also accepted a mug of coffee.

He looked badly shaken, as if the string of adverse incidents were finally sapping his confidence.

'This is all dead weird, excuse the pun,' he stated. 'Millie has accepted that Warren is gone. I said I'd found some skin and blood on the edge of the stern board where he could have slipped and hit his head. It was still raining last night and everything was wet. She knows nothing about boats, because Warren did all of that. I already knew she's very wealthy, and with him apparently gone, she just wants to walk away from the whole scene. She's not interested in the boat or the girl, and is packing up as we speak.'

He frowned as he pondered a moment, before looking at me.

'That leaves me with a big problem, Harry, because I really need that boat, but I've got no one to run it. I'm not going to ask Korey for one of his thugs to help. They're bloody animals and only good for bashing people up.'

He paused, and gave me a considering look. 'I don't suppose you'd like to take the boat over? You've got two spare guys here. It'd help me out and I can make it well worth your while.'

I pretended to think about his suggestion for a while. 'Yeah. Maybe we could come to some arrangement.'

Turner looked pathetically eager. 'Okay, what sort of deal will keep you happy?'

'I'm prepared to put Dave aboard to run the boat, and we'll keep it with us wherever you need to go, but, the deal is this. I take over the boat and the girl completely. I'll cover all running expenses and if you need it for any reasonable purpose, we'll do it. But the girl is mine to do with as I want.'

As expected, he ranted and raved a while, so I let him blow off steam before saying, 'Get a grip, Gary and stop being a big girl's blouse. That boat wasn't yours to start with, and as you've already been paid for the girl by the Collings, she's not yours either. Look at it this way. It's like Millie has put the boat and the girl on the open market with a one-dollar price tag and I paid up first. It's no use to you without a crew, since you can't run it alone, so I'm doing you a very big favour by taking over the running of it, and making it available for your use when you need it. At no cost to you. The girl is a bonus for me. You've already got your money for her, so don't be a greedy prick. I suggest you think it through carefully, because that's my deal or we're out of here.'

He did think it through, as after a bit more huffing and puffing, he agreed with a damp, limp handshake.

'Okay, deal. I'll take Millie ashore when she's ready, then your man can move in. I'd better show you how to de-activate the collar in case you need to take the girl off the boat at any time. Wouldn't want another accident.'

I gave him a hard look, 'No, we wouldn't want that. There have been too many accidents and weird things happening for our comfort, so everyone needs to be very careful from here on. People who work together doing stuff like this need to have some trust in each other.'

He nodded vigorously, 'Yes, yes. Trust. That's the word. You help me and I help you and we trust each other.'

I gave him a calculating look. 'Actually, it's called 'you scratch my back, and I'll scratch yours', but you've got the general idea. We'll play it straight and you will too.'

He insisted on shaking my hand again, then left to take Millie ashore.

The last we saw of her was a small figure sitting in Turner's dinghy as it sped away, giving us the traditional English archer's salute.

There was dead silence around the cockpit table as the sound of his outboard slowly faded in the distance.

Then Sandy spoke, a wondering tone to her voice, 'Correct me if I'm wrong, dear-heart, but did you just acquire a forty-foot boat and a slave girl for free?'

I grinned happily, 'Yep. How good is that? The boat, the girl, the collar system and an inside track to finding out what Turner and his mate are up to. That scheme of Yanos is possibly what he wants the boat for, but now we run it. It even comes with a built-in crew-person. Which reminds me. I'd better go over and tell Taylor there's been a change of management.'

I jumped in the dinghy and purred the short distance to *Gideon*, where Taylor met me at the stern. 'Oh, Hi Harry. Do you know what's going on? Warren's not here and Millie just packed some clothes and went off with Mr Turner.'

I chased her inside, and sat her down in the aft saloon. 'You need to know a few things. There have been a few changes since last night. Warren is dead and gone. He can't hurt you again.'

The look on her pretty face was almost indescribable, but was mainly happiness.

'Additionally, Millie has bailed out and gone. She doesn't want either the boat or you, so I've negotiated with Turner to take over the boat and to take over you as well. He doesn't have anybody to run this thing, so I've agreed to man the boat with one of my crew.'

Her face fell, 'Oh. I see.'

Her face revealed what she was thinking, and it was all bad.

'No Sweetie, I don't think you do. When we first met, you asked me to rescue you one day, and I said I would. Well, this is that day. When Turner comes back shortly after dropping Millie off, he's going to show me how to take your collar off safely, and I'm going to pretend that I didn't already know how to do it. My good friend Dave will drive the boat when we leave here later on, but you'll be without your collar. And you'll stay that way so long as Turner or Yanos aren't around. However, to keep up appearances, I need you to stay with us for a little while longer while we find out what these bastards are up to. After that, you'll be free to go and do whatever you want.'

It was a lot to take in at once, so I waited for the emotions displayed by the array of expressions flitting across her face to settle down.

'What happened to Warren?'

'You can't tell Gary this, but last night, he came across to burn our boat and everybody aboard, but my cat sussed him out and effectively killed him. Then I fed him to the sharks.'

She blinked a few times.

'Your cat must be pretty special to do all that. But is Warren really dead?'

'Yep. After he'd nearly bled out, I tipped him overboard and saw the sharks grab him. A girl we rescued off Turner's boat the other night, hosed his blood off the stern of my boat. He's gone. Kaput. Permanently erased. Not even a dead body. No coming back.'

A slow, beaming smile lit up her face, transforming her appearance and in a repeat of what Mary had displayed, it looked like a load had just been lifted from her shoulders as well.

'Wow! Radical! That's great. But what about Millie? Where's she gone?'

I shrugged, 'No idea – don't care. As best I know, she's just gone. Bailed out. Whatever. After Turner diplomatically told her that Warren was dead, she promptly stated that she wanted nothing further to do with the boat or you. Apparently, she's got plenty of money, so she just grabbed a few clothes and left.'

'Even better. She was almost as bad as he was. So, that part's all good, but what's the go with the boat and me. I mean, as bad as it's been, this is the only home I've got. I haven't got any money, very few clothes and haven't got anywhere to go. What happens to me?'

Happiness fled, and her expression grew bleak as she described her situation. With my white knight instincts kicking into high gear, I confined myself to just taking one of her hands as I said, 'We need to stick around with Turner for a while longer to see what he and his partner, this Korey Yanos fella are up to. They've got something nasty brewing that I'm sure we need to stop… whatever it is. Plus, I really want to put an end to this whole rotten slavery thing. Therefore, we need you to help us. In the short term, I had to promise to make this boat available for Turner when he needs it. I know there is a new batch of girls being delivered in the next few days, and since his boat is full, this might be where the new girls are housed. If that's the case, are you willing to stay here and help look after them? As I said, my good friend Dave will take over running the boat and there definitely won't be any slavery bullshit while we're in charge. My boat is also a bit full at the moment with two rescued girls plus my normal crew.'

'Am I really free to leave if I want to?'

'Yes, of course. We don't enslave girls. Everybody on my boat is there because they want to be there, and they're all having a great time. Not a collar in sight! And they want to take down Turner and end this slavery thing as much as I do.'

'Do I still have to wear the collar?'

'Only when Turner or Yanos are around. The rest of the time you can leave it off. I'll show you how to do it yourself. It's a very simple and quick operation. When we get organised, probably later this morning, we'll be moving further north up Fraser/K'gari Island to a nicer anchorage. Then we'll tie our two boats together and you can walk back and forth anytime you like and meet our crew. And my cats. No collar!'

She was happy with the first part, but looked a bit dubious about meeting the killer cats.

'You're not going to restrict me in any way, except for when Turner or Yanos are close, is that right?'

'That's right. You can do whatever you like, wear whatever you like and you don't have to take your pants off for anybody unless you want to. I'll have to wait for Turner to come back to do the collar-opening thing, but after that, we'll show you how your life is going to be without Warren and Millie. I just ask in return that you do as we ask for a little while longer so we can try to stop these rotten mongrels.'

She shrugged resignedly. 'Okay. I can't do much else, can I? How did you put it, 'you've taken me over'?'

As Taylor was virtually repeating Mary's self-pity rant, I didn't bother trying to make her realise how things had changed. Future actions would have to prove our good intentions. Nevertheless, I frowned in frustration at her cynicism, but I supposed being a slave to Warren and Millie would have made her lose all hope of ever being free again.

I heard the buzz of an outboard, went aft and spotted Turner speeding toward us. He saw my dinghy and came straight to the *Gideon*.

'Ah, good man. Meeting your new girl, eh?'

'Yeah. I thought we'd better get acquainted and check out my new boat as well. I'll need to go upriver to restock, refuel and fill the water tanks before we head over to the island. I had the thought that you might need the extra beds for this new batch of girls when they arrive. Your boat seems rather full at the moment.'

He looked at me sharply, radiating instant distrust, so I just smiled gently and made a patting motion with my hands.

'Cool it, sport. It's only a suggestion to try to help you out. There are spare beds here, and a collar transmitter to keep them under control. But that's entirely your call, since they're your girls. I'm quite happy to use the extra beds myself so my crew can spread out. In fact… forget my suggestion, that's what I'll do. All my crew will be more comfortable.'

I beamed happily at him, my minor problem solved.

He frowned. 'No… no… back up the bus. You agreed to help me as required, and I've decided that I like your suggestion after all. This will be the perfect place for the new girls, so I request your help to make it happen.'

While rejoicing internally, I frowned in return. 'Me and my big mouth. All right, but show me how this collar thing works. It looks like a neat piece of kit.'

Happy to have my reluctant agreement about housing the new girls, he became quite enthusiastic about the collar setup and quickly explained how it worked and its range of operation. Binding new collars to the same transmitter wasn't a problem, as I'd seen, but now he showed me how to de-activate and reactivate them, as well as the recharge process.

'That's simple enough,' I commented, 'clever design.'

'It is very clever. Some guy in Japan designed and makes them. Korey buys them direct and imports them as pet trackers. Nobody suspects pet supplies would be dangerous. The explosives aren't detectable by sniffer dogs as they're sealed in a plastic which has a strong smell anyway.'

'Neat.'

'Anyway, I'll go and let you sort things out. Call me when you're ready to head for the island.'

'Okay. But it might be a few hours before we're good to go.'

'No problem.'

Once he was gone, I poked around inspecting things, but for all his glaring faults, Warren must have been a good seaman. The engine room was very clean, fuel tanks at 50%, water about the same and the bilges clean and nearly dry. Food supplies were low, so without further delay, I showed Taylor how to take her collar off, fired up the engine, raised anchor and motored slowly over to raft up against *Firebird*. Dave and Alex were waiting with fenders and lines, and soon had *Gideon* secure.

I led Taylor across to meet the others, where she was delighted to recognise Mary, who explained that any stories of her demise were rather exaggerated. That helped speed up Taylor's transition back into civilisation, especially as everyone made her feel welcome.

'The boat looks to be in really good condition,' I said to Dave, 'but you'll need to fill the water and fuel tanks and stock up on food and other supplies.'

'Taylor and I will go across and make a list now,' Bree offered.

'Great, thanks Bree. Will you also allow for maybe another four girls to come aboard in two or three days? I've volunteered *Gideon* to be the overflow accommodation when Turner's partner brings this new batch in.'

'Clever boy,' Sandy said admiringly, 'we get four more girls under our control. How did you convince him to go with that?'

'I suggested it as a possibility, then when he became suspicious of my motives, I pretended to change my mind and said we'd use it instead. He couldn't over-rule me fast enough.'

Dave asked, 'So, what's going to be the plan?'

'While we can keep Turner at arm's length, Taylor can stay off the collar, but when he's close, and after the girls arrive, all their collars will have to go back on.'

Taylor nodded her understanding, for now just relishing the

freedom and slowly coming to grips with the realisation that she was permanently out from being under the control and violent intimate attentions of the Collings and Turner.

I looked at Dave. 'You can sleep on either boat until the new girls arrive, but then we'd like you to stay with them on *Gideon* so they don't do anything silly. You'll have to play the part of their jailer or guardian. Taylor will help you keep them settled and behaving nicely. We can't raft-up with the new girls aboard either, or they'll be wondering why our girls don't have collars.'

Alex asked, 'What about just telling the new girls what we're up to?'

I thought a moment. 'It'd make life easier, but I don't think we could do it. Not at first anyway, as tempting as that would be. It would mean we'd have to trust four strangers to keep a secret, and they'd want to have their collars off as well. Remember, they're still supposed to be Turner's, so at any time he might want to swap them around. Taylor will be the head girl and reinforce your control.'

Taylor was happy with that and knowing she was truly free, it made wearing the collar for a while longer no real problem.

TIN CAN BAY – FRASER ISLAND

I tagged along on the shopping and replenishment trip to the riverside of town and we gave Turner a cheery wave as we motored past, with Dave getting the feel of his new command. Taylor came ashore, collar-less in public for the first time since she was snatched.

The friendly folk at the Tin Can Bay Marina made us welcome and looked after the refuelling and watering, as well as loaning us a car to go shopping at the Dolphin shopping centre further up town. I asked the girls to take Taylor with them in case she wanted to get some clothes or other stuff of her own.

An hour later, suitably laden with a huge pile of bags, they were back, Taylor beaming happily with some clothes and personal items, as well as having enjoyed another taste of the freedom of just doing normal living activities. We returned to the anchorage, but didn't anchor, as Dave nosed up to the stern just long enough to let me jump off the bow over onto *Firebird*.

Before he left, I clipped Taylor's collar back on, disturbed to see the look of revulsion briefly cross her face as it snapped into place. I watched him ease up beside *Poseidon* to let Turner know we were setting off to McKenzie's jetty anchorage on the island, before he headed up the estuary at a sedate ten knots. Alex and I got *Firebird* organised for sailing, hung around with feathered sails until Turner got going, then tagged along.

POSEIDON

'Yeah Gary. What's the problem now?'

'Just wanted to let you know I lost my head girl, Mary, the other night.'

'Jesus, Gary! What the fuck's going on up there? You've lost two now and a customer has lost one! It's like a fuckin' epidemic! What's going to happen next?'

'Well, there's more I'm afraid, Korey. My unofficial assistant, Warren Collings, has disappeared without a trace. We think he must have fallen overboard, hitting his head on the way. There are a lot of sharks around here.'

'Shit! There's a lot of something going on around there, that's for sure. Is the wife going to carry on, and is that moron with the big cat still with you?'

'No. His wife bailed out straight away. Just walked off the boat, left the girl and went, but the bloke with the big cat's still here.'

'Oh. Well, that's alright then. You've scored a new boat and a replacement girl. We can use both.'

'Well, actually, Korey, it's not that simple. I know we need the boat but I haven't got anyone to run it as well as look after the girl, so Harry, the rich guy who owns the big cat, agreed to operate the boat for me, by putting one of his crew aboard to look after the girl. I'm going to put the extra girls on it because there's no room here.'

'Don't be a fuckin' idiot, Gary. You can't trust an outsider to run our spare boat and look after the new girls.'

'I don't have any choice. I just said there's no one else to run it. I needed someone who knew what he's doing immediately, and anyway, like I told you, this bloke's got so many girls on his cat, he even gave me one he wasn't happy with. His other girls don't need collars to make them stick around. They're all happy just being there.'

'Bullshit! He wouldn't just give you one like that.'

'Well, he has. He said she was acting really bitchy on his boat and upsetting the others, but she's turned out to be fantastic! He doesn't need any more girls, so he's not trying to poach ours, and he's quite willing to follow along and do what he's told. Apart from being very wealthy, he's a bit of a fuck-wit and thinks it's all great fun.'

'But he'll find out about the collars!'

'He already knows about them and thinks they're a great idea. As well as giving me a hand now, I reckon he could even be a customer.'

'Hmmm. We'll see. I'm not sure about this. I'll have a think about it and check him out when I bring the new girls.'

'Okay. When's that going to be?'

'Two or three days yet. I just picked up two Asian backpackers who don't speak English. Good-lookers, but it's taking time to settle them down. One is being a real pain in the arse.'

'Hmmm. I hope you aren't turning your thugs loose on them in your attempts to settle them down? The last time that happened, the girls were physically and mentally useless!'

'Don't you worry about what I do, Gary! Just try a lot harder to keep your own house under control.'

'Yeah, yeah. Anyway, we'll be laying up just north of the vehicle ferry terminal. Let me know if you're going to come over on it and I'll be there to meet you.'

'Yeah, yeah. Let me think about that too. In the meantime, you just try really hard to keep anybody else from blowing themselves up or disappearing. Okay? It sounds like there's a fuckin' X-Files body-snatching operation going on up there.'

FIREBIRD

It took the best part of an hour to catch up with *Gideon*, then with Turner leading, we held station close in beside Dave and followed. However, with the south-east breeze piping up nicely, I soon became bored with holding back to ten knots, so I called Dave on the marine VHF radio and told him we were going to squirt on ahead.

'I'll tell Turner on the way past, and anchor near the jetty ruins.

Your chart should show the place.'

'Yeah mate, it does. I don't blame you for wanting to have a fun sail. This thing goes alright, just slow. See you there.'

We unfurled the big code zero, sheeted in the other two sails, and accelerated past Dave, our speed building quickly toward thirty knots as we closed on *Poseidon*. I had Alex steer close in beside *Poseidon*, and toasted Turner with a beer as we swept past, just two metres away.

'The crew were bored,' I called cheerily, 'so we're going to have some jolly good fun. We'll see you at McKenzie's jetty.'

My words were backed up by a raucous, drunken-sounding cheer from the crew, several of the female ones sprawled on the forward trampoline netting, tanning their naked bodies.

The ruins of the old jetty lay on the western shore of the largest sand island in the world. Unusually for a sand island, there was abundant plant and tree growth thanks to a naturally-occurring fungus in the sand which supplied the nourishment to support plant life. The jetty was built in the early 1900s to ship timber to the mainland and its decaying remains ran from a shallow valley between the high, scrub-covered sand-hills lining the foreshore, out into the clean, clear waters of the Great Sandy Straits. Further south, the land became low-lying, swampy and bordered with mangroves, but around the old jetty and further north, the beach was sand, with deep, tide-scoured water less than fifty metres off the beach. Kingfisher Bay resort, a few kilometres to the north, even had a regular anchorage for decent-sized cruise ships.

As an anchorage for a few days, it was idyllic.

About an hour later, *Gideon*, followed by *Poseidon*, slid into the anchorage. I waved Dave to raft up, figuring we'd separate when the other girls arrived. This way, Taylor could join in and be part of the crew in the meantime. She was delighted with the arrangement and wore her new clothes in celebration.

Corrine apparently didn't have anything new to report, possibly because the man himself dropped by to bring me up-to-date, and as was his preference, stayed in his dinghy. Nevertheless, we kept the collar-less Taylor inside out of sight.

'I had a call from my partner, Korey. He was going to bring the new girls over in a 4WD wagon, but he reckons there's too many eyes around the ferry terminal, so the hand-over will be back on the mainland, at the River Heads public boat ramp at 22:00 in three nights time. You come with me and we'll run over in *Poseidon*.'

I shrugged, 'Yep. That's okay by me.'

'Good. Korey wants to meet you.'

I considered, 'Okay. That's alright. No problem. Always good to know who you're working with, eh?'

'Yeah. I'll let you know if there are any changes.'

With that, he drove away without a backward glance.

JAPANESE EMBASSY, CANBERRA

With the flaring yellow orb of the sun barely above the hills to the east, a polite knock sounded at the office door of the Japanese Ambassador to Australia, Sakura Ito. At his invitation, his aide, a tall, lean young man entered, bowed, and advanced to the Ambassador's desk, who noted the frown creasing his aide's brow.

'Yes, Mitsu. What is so worrisome to you this lovely morning, that it needs my attention?'

'Please forgive my intrusion, sir, but I have received a most curious telephone call.'

'Very well, Mitsu. You have my attention. Please explain this curious communication.'

'The caller named himself as Raijin Tanaka, the most senior of the senior bosses in the Yamaguchi-gumi Yakuza clan, and he made two requests. Firstly, he wished to know the contact number for Commander Stevens, although he only knew of him by reputation, not name. He asked for name of the owner of the red catamaran who was at Heard Island. Secondly, he advised that his 19-year-old granddaughter, Chiaki Yamada, is in Australia with a girlfriend, and has been touring the country as a backpacker. The girls insisted on travelling in this manner to properly experience the country and culture. However, she has not made contact for one week and her mobile phone is turned off. Apparently, this is most unusual and concerning behaviour for the young ladies. He asked if we could make discrete enquiries as to their whereabouts.'

It was the Ambassador's turn to frown. He knew, as did most Japanese, that the Yamaguchi-gumi clan was the largest and most powerful Yakuza group in Japan. The most senior boss was therefore an extremely powerful person, second only to the Kumicho or godfather. Although the clan was a declared criminal organisation, the vast spread of their increasingly legitimate business enterprises required that he be treated with considerable respect.

That he would make contact with a diplomatic outpost in a foreign country was unusual in the extreme, and to ask for help, virtually unheard of.

After a period of careful contemplation of the issues involved, Sakura Ito said, 'This is a most interesting situation, Mitsu. What is your counsel?'

Mitsu acknowledged the compliment.

'The very unusual nature of the two requests leads me to humbly suggest that we return his telephone call and supply the Commander's satellite number, and to say that we will initiate enquiries in regard to his granddaughter's location immediately. However, I would also suggest that we contact the Commander first, to ask if he wishes to receive Tanaka-san's telephone call.'

The Ambassador beamed. 'Excellent advice, Mitsu. That is precisely what I was thinking. Could I trouble you to place the call to the Commander for me?'

'Certainly, Excellency.'

FIREBIRD

Feeling in a pensive mood, I was sitting in my favourite early morning position, the port bow seat, looking back along the length of the freshly-washed red hulls, where the countless water droplets were winking in the early sunlight like thousands of tiny rubies. A steaming mug of sweet tea was in hand, and my lovely, lethal black cat, Jasper was sitting at my feet. The killer-cat was idly batting at a tiny spider who had parachuted aboard on a strand of silk, and claimed the hole in a safety-rail shackle for her new home.

The spider was winning the battle as Jasper's paw was way too large to have any hope of dislodging the tiny creature who displayed the stubbornness of her breed.

I scratched his soft, furry head, letting the peace and tranquillity of the morning seep into my inner being, while the accumulated stress and tension of the operation, temporarily at least, floated away with the tide.

As usual, that moment was all too short, as Hanh approached along the deck, the SatPhone in hand.

'Sorry to disturb you, Harry, but there's a gentleman on the phone saying that he has the Japanese Ambassador for you. He speaks good English, but I can translate if necessary.'

'Thanks Hanh. I didn't know you spoke Japanese. We must talk about that later.'

She smiled and handed me the phone, then sat down beside Jasper and hugged his warm body. His rumbling purr was seriously loud, but as always, I put up with it.

'This is Harry Stevens,' I announced.

'*Ahh. Good morning, Commander. My name is Mitsu, and my compliments to your young lady for the excellence of her Japanese. She is most fluent. However, if it pleases you, His Excellency, Ambassador Ito is waiting to speak with you.*'

'Good morning, Mitsu. I'd be delighted to speak with the Ambassador. Thank you.'

There was a soft click, then the clear, deep voice of Sakura Ito was in my ear.

'Good morning, Commander. Thank you for speaking with me at such an early hour.'

'It is always my great pleasure to hear from you, Your Excellency. I trust you are keeping well in our nation's capital?'

'Indeed I am, thank you Commander. May I ask where you are at this time?'

'Sitting on the bow of my boat with Jasper my cat, enjoying the peace of the sunrise over Fraser Island/K'gari in Queensland. This is a very beautiful anchorage. You should visit with us some time. It is guaranteed to temporarily remove all the stress of politics.'

He gave a genuine laugh. *'I have heard much about the therapeutic benefits of a visit to your boat and your cat, from your Prime Minister. Perhaps I will avail myself of your generous offer before long. My soul is badly in need of restoration.'*

'Excellent. In which case I shall try to convince Andy to take a break at the same time. But apart from inviting you to join us, how may I be of assistance at this time?'

'My personal assistant, Mitsu, has just taken an unusual telephone call from the most senior boss in the Yamaguchi-gumi Yakusa clan, Raijin Tanaka. He didn't know you by name, only by reputation, and requested your telephone number. Additionally, he has asked me to enquire after the whereabouts of his granddaughter, Chiaki, who is on a backpacking tour of Australia with a female companion. The girl has failed to report on schedule as required by her family, and they are very concerned for her safety.

Naturally, I will do what I can to locate the girls, but before I contact him again, I needed to ask if you were willing for me to pass your number to Tanaka-san?'

'That is most interesting, Excellency. My only contact with the Yakusa has been with a young man we called 'Sunnies', on our last operation. That was the occasion which caused you to present me with that wonderful medal on behalf of your Emperor and your cousin, the Prime Minister.'

He chuckled, '*Indeed. I remember it well. So, are you prepared to be contacted by Tanaka-san?*'

'Yes. Certainly, Excellency. No problem. Let's hear what he has to say.'

'*Very well, Commander, I shall do that immediately, and thank you again for your generous invitation to visit with you. Good day for now.*'

'Cheers, Excellency. Take care.'

I looked at Hanh. 'No translation necessary this time,' I said. 'Mr Ito speaks excellent English. His aide, Mitsu, complimented you on your very good Japanese. Where did you learn it?'

'The two people who rescued my parents and me after we were shipwrecked, had spent several years in Japan when they were still working, and were fluent in the language. They used it a lot on the boat to help them remain fluent, so I started to pick it up and soon that was all we spoke on board.'

'Good one. Apparently, two of the new girls are Asian, but I don't know if they're Japanese.'

She smiled, 'Well, of course I can also do Vietnamese in a pinch.'

Another budding smart arse. I thought I was enough for one boat, but was glad she was still in an upbeat mood.

I gave her a quick hug, then followed her aft, where breakfast smells were wafting around, attracting the crew from their bunks like bees to flowers, and told them of my early phone call.

'Will this mean trouble?' Alex asked.

'Quite possibly, but I guess we'll find out soon enough.'

Breakfast was just complete when the SatPhone rang again. I contemplated a smart-arse answer, but mindful of who might be on the other end of the call, restrained myself to a simple 'Hello?'

A voice with an obviously Asian accent, but fluent in English, said, '*Is that Commander Stevens?*'

'It is indeed. May I presume that this is Raijin Tanaka?'

'*Ahh, yes. You have been contacted by our Ambassador. This is good.*

I'm sure you are puzzled that I should be seeking to make contact with you.'

'Yes, Tanaka-san, I am puzzled. Although on reflection, perhaps it is in connection with the young gentleman from your organisation whom I met, under rather adverse circumstances, last year at Heard Island and again in Tasmania.'

'That is very perceptive, Commander. The young gentleman in question is Daku Tanaka, and he is my grandson.'

'Very interesting, Tanaka-san, but how does that affect me, as I understand he has been confined in prison for his crimes against Japan and Australia?'

'That information is regrettably out-of-date, Commander. Daku has been released due to a successful appeal against the length of his sentence. What might concern you is that he appears to bear very strong feelings of animosity against your crew in general and you personally, for what he believes you have done to him during your series of encounters. I hasten to add that I do not support nor share my grandson's beliefs. He acted very badly during that business and deserved to be punished. He has brought great shame on my family and on the organisation of which I am a proud member. This has caused him to be expelled from this organisation.'

'That is disturbing information, Tanaka-san. Do I understand correctly that this phone call is in the nature of a warning? And do you believe that your grandson intends to cause harm to myself and my crew?'

'Yes, Commander. It is a warning which I am anxious to pass on, as I have been informed that my grandson is presently on his way to Australia with the intention of locating you and exacting his idea of revenge. I must repeat that I do not share his views and that he is acting entirely on his own, without the approval or support of this organisation. It pains me to add that my Kumicho has ordered that he be seized on sight and returned to Japan to face discipline.'

I thought a few moments. 'I am very grateful to you and your Kumicho for your warning, Tanaka-san. It always helps to be prepared, and I am reminded of a quote by the Chinese general, Sun-Tzu, who said – 'Know thy self and know thy enemy.'

'*Ah, yes. Excellent advice. Perhaps the nature of my telephone call is best summed up by another Sun-Tzu quotation – 'Don't depend on the enemy not coming: depend rather on being ready for him'.'*

I laughed. 'That is even better advice, and I feel you have helped me do just that. I thank you for your warning and acknowledge that I am in your debt. Is there anything I can do to redress the balance?'

'*You show great respect, Commander, and have already proved that you embrace the warrior's code. This is unusual for a gaigin. Unhappily, I do have another problem which involves your country, but I fear you will not be able to assist.'*

'May I be permitted to hear of this problem, Tanaka-san? A problem shared is sometimes a problem halved.'

'*You continue to surprise me, Commander. Very well. To be brief, my granddaughter, Chiaki and her friend Fumiko, are presently in Australia, travelling as backpackers. My family was very strongly against the young women travelling in this way, but they were determined, and as with most young persons in these very liberal times, their will prevailed.*

However, one of the conditions of their visit was that they must communicate their location and status every two days. However, we have not received any communication for more than a week, and their mobile telephones remain switched off, so we cannot track them that way. I have asked our Ambassador to do what he can to trace their last known location, as we have become very concerned for their safety.'

'I'm sorry to hear that. However, perhaps I can assist, as I do have a lot of contacts with various Government agencies. Are you able to send photographs of the two ladies if I supply an email address?'

'*Yes, of course. I shall do so immediately, and I will be very grateful for any help you can provide.'*

I read out the boat's email address and completed the call by saying, 'This has been a most enlightening conversation, Tanaka-san. I can only hope that good things for both of us comes from it.'

'*I concur with that thought, Commander. I will call again if I have more news. Good day to you.*'

'Likewise, Tanaka-san. Ja ne.'

The crew were clustered around and had heard my side, so I filled in the rest.

Sandy looked troubled. 'Bloody hell, Harry. I thought we were done with Sunnies, or Daku and now the rotten little toad is heading our way.'

'Yes. I admit it's a complication we don't really need at the moment, although we don't know if he's acting alone or has a crew. I think for now, we just be prepared, but continue with what we're doing. I'll let my people know. They might have records of his legal entry into the country. Perhaps you could contact Bob Casey and get the word spread at least through Queensland Police circles, in case they have come to official attention.'

Alex nodded, 'Asking your people to trace Daku would be the best place to start, Harry. We need to know his movements if we're to be properly prepared.'

There was more discussion along similar lines, but nobody had anything useful to add, so I shooed them away so I could talk to my controller in private.

'*Good morning, Harry. About time you made a report. Bad boy. We've been wondering if you've managed to make any progress, or are you just swanning around in the sun, forcing yourself to act like degenerate yachties?*'

'Good morning M, it's a lot of both, actually. We are swanning around to maintain cover, but we're now doing so in company with Mr Gary Turner, one of two guys running this slavery gig. The other is a fella named Korey Yanos, who has a Greek father and a Serbian mother. He's supposed to be a very bad bloke all round. Perhaps you can pull up more info?'

I heard a keyboard being delicately taped for a minute.

'*Ahh… yes. Korey Yanos. Greek father and Serbian mother, close* links to the Australian, European and strangely enough, the Japanese *Yakuza* criminal gangs. No recorded convictions, but a great deal of anecdotal evidence linking him to many violent crimes, ranging from extortion, rape, violent assault and murder. Educated in the UK and rated highly intelligent. Not someone to underestimate.'

'That sounds like our man,' I commented, 'anyway, he's bringing four new girls here in a couple of days, and wants to meet me, so that'll be exciting.'

'Be careful, Harry. He seems to be a very dangerous man. His history indicates that he really does have a long history of extreme violence. On the upside, if he were to somehow meet with a terminal accident, there would be a number of very happy individuals around here.'

'Yes, ma'am. I shall extend my neck too far in the name of duty once again.'

'Very dramatic, dear boy. Just don't overdo it.'

'On another note, I received a couple of unusual phone calls this morning. One from the Japanese Ambassador in Canberra, and one from the 2IC of the largest Japanese Yakusa clan.'

'Dear boy. I'm highly impressed. You do move in exalted circles. Pray tell, what do these two gentlemen have in common, apart from being Japanese?'

'The Ambassador wanted my permission to release my phone number to the Yakusa bloke. Then the Yakusa bloke wanted to warn me that his grandson, who happens to be the character we knew as 'Sunnies' of Heard Island and Port Davey infamy, was out of prison and in Australia, gunning for me and my crew.'

'Excellent, Harry. You aren't nicknamed the 'trouble magnet' for nothing. I take it that the Yakusa in general aren't chasing you, just the grandson?'

'That's correct. Just Sunnies, although his real name is Daku Tanaka. Perhaps you would like to check airline arrivals for the last few weeks to see if his name shows. I don't know if he has a crew with him, but his grandfather says that because he's brought dishonour to the family, he's been kicked out of the Yakusa. If there is a crew with him, they'll on their own with no backup.'

There was the rattle of the keyboard again and a longer wait, but then M was back.

'Yes. Ten days ago, he flew in via Qantas out of Tokyo under his own name. Because he was supposed to be still in prison for a long time, there wasn't a red flag alert on the Immigration computers. There were three tickets booked at the same time, so it would be safe to say he has a crew of two for backup. Any weapons they think they'll need will have to be sourced locally. I mentioned earlier that this Korey Yanos had connections with Japanese criminals. I hope that your Tanaka-san junior wasn't one of his connections. That would really drop you in the poop, to coin a phrase.'

I chuckled at her rare wit. 'It's unlikely they would be in contact. If so, we have the chance to deal with them separately. Oh, one last thing. Tanaka senior informed me that his granddaughter, Chiaki Tanaka, and her friend Fumiko Yamada, have been in Australia on a backpacking tour. The girls were under strict reporting conditions, but haven't been heard of for over a week. I offered to assist where I could, so would you mind doing what you can to at least find their last known location?'

'Yep, sure thing. We can do that. But I'll have to get back to you later. It may take some time.'

'Excellent, M. I look forward to hearing from you. Ja ne.'

CHAPTER 22

For the rest of the day, Turner left us alone and I tended to keep to myself, my 'thousand-metre stare' firmly in place. Sandy warned the crew that this was a sign that I was thinking and the outcome frequently caused trouble for everyone concerned.

Next morning, I was up before dawn, once again on deck with my mug of sweet tea and with Jasper letting me know how happy he was that I'd joined him. With Warren no longer a problem, I had put the night watch routine on hold, but now we had another predator in the form of Sunnies, or Daku Tanaka and his mates chasing us. Accordingly, I thought we should start the watch again from tonight onwards.

I was surprised to be joined by Taylor, happily collar-less, a mug of coffee in her hand. She had decided to sleep aboard the *Gideon*, as she was familiar with the boat, and without the Collings to bother her, it was peaceful. But through the day, she hung with the *Firebird* crew, where she fitted in well and was well-liked by everyone.

After the usual pleasantries, she said, 'I want to thank you again for all you've done for me. I was in such a fit of depression, I was about to take that final step off the stern and end it all. Warren was a complete animal and I couldn't see any way out. I really feel for those girls on Turner's boat and the new ones coming in soon.'

I nodded, getting a sense of her dreadful suffering and feeling of hopelessness, and understood where she was coming from. 'It's a terrible thing to force another person to act against their will to that extent, and to confine them with no hope of escape. But here you are, and you'll only have to pretend to be in confinement for a short time. I hope to wrap this up very soon, since I feel we're getting close to the end game, but I've learned that at this stage of an operation, things often get a little bit worse before they get better.'

'I understand.'

I looked at her more closely than I had before, seeing a pretty girl, with a calm demeanour and intelligence in her level gaze.

'I didn't ask before, but how did you come to be caught up in this mess?'

She gave a bitter laugh. 'It's probably a familiar story to you by now. My parents died in a plane crash when I was young, and I lived with my grandmother for about five years. She was a really cool person to be with, and so delightfully wacky… we got on so well. She was very wealthy, but when she died, her dropkick of a son inherited everything and promptly kicked me out of the house with literally just the clothes on my back. It was a bit of a social adjustment to go from extreme comfort one day, to sleeping on friends' lounges for a day or two at a time, until I wore out my welcome.

Then one day, this guy came up to me on the street and offered me a trip on a boat for a day, if I'd act as hostess to serve drinks and food. He gave me one hundred and fifty dollars, and said I could eat and drink all I wanted, and there was a uniform provided. I just had to be nice to his customers for the day.

The boat was Turner's, of course, and the only time I left it after that day, was to be transferred to the Collings boat when I was sold. So, while I'm free of that slavery, thanks to you and the crew, I still don't have any money, few clothes, nor any place to live.'

She looked on the verge of tearing up, so to forestall that event, I hastily said, 'Don't worry about that for now. When we sort out these mongrels, I want to get the sales lists, then track down every girl who's been sold into slavery and recover them. We'll work out some sort of rehab program for everyone later. Money isn't a problem.'

Taylor looked wistfully around the dewy-red decks. 'Despite what I've been through, I actually love boats and being on the water, although I can imagine most of the other girls must hate it. This is a beautiful boat and I love the way it sails so fast.'

I considered her in a new light. 'That's an interesting comment. I thought you'd hate the water.'

'No way. The *Gideon* and being on the water were the only things which kept me sane. If I'd been a captive in a house ashore, I would have taken the walk long ago.'

She thought a moment, 'If you don't mind my asking, this boat and its running costs must be huge. Who pays?'

I laughed. 'No. I don't mind and it's a good question. When I left the Army, I soon decided I didn't like life ashore, so I had the original *Firebird* built to have a home I could also travel in, and I preferred sail to power. I was by myself, so thanks to my uncle's inheritance, I lived like a wealthy playboy for a while, but then, because of my Army background, I was approached by the Australian Commonwealth Police to keep on with what I was already doing, but to be available to take on undercover jobs involving maritime crime. I was given a couple of small jobs as trials, which worked out okay, and on one of those in strange circumstances, a Korean cook on a cargo ship gave me a big black kitten. He said if I looked after him, he'd look after me in turn. He said the kitten was 'very special'. That was how Jasper became my companion. There followed a series of much larger and more involved operations and I decided I needed a bigger boat as my crew and the equipment we were acquiring, kept on expanding. As for the financing, I get a salary and basic expenses from the ACP, but that would barely feed you lot for a day, let alone pay for and run this boat. But some time ago, while dealing with two seriously bad people, we hung onto the large amount of loot they'd accumulated. Then, in the course of dealing with a bunch of pirates up in the Indonesian islands who tried to take us out, we came across an accumulated heap of real pirate treasure. In both cases, we were outside Australian waters and because there was nobody left to lay claim to it, we kept the lot. My superiors quietly approved since they could cut out my expense account, and the proceeds from that windfall have kept us very well-funded ever since.'

Taylor's eyes were wide open. 'I saw what the Collings paid to keep their boat running. To pay for this boat and the running costs for this crew must be enormous.'

I smiled. 'Yeah. The costs are huge, but we've made a great deal of money and more is still coming in, so we actually have more than we could reasonably spend in our collective lifetimes. Plus, we've made a few good investments which keep additional income flowing nicely.'

'So, if it's safe to say you're seriously rich, why keep chasing bad guys? Why not just kick back and enjoy life? You're perfectly set up to do so.'

I chuckled and waved my hand around. 'But that's the whole point, dear girl. We already *are* kicked back and enjoying life. By taking on the odd bunch of bad guys occasionally, we just have a decent reason to be travelling around on a lovely boat, visiting lots of different places in the best way possible. Then there's the added mental challenge of out-thinking and catching those bad guys. Neither Corine, Dave, Sandy, Bree, Alex or myself could handle just sitting back sucking on booze every day, with the only mental stimulation being whether to have a snooze before lunch or afterwards. This life has all the ingredients to keep us mentally alive for a long time.'

'But Bree and Alex are paid crew. They don't need to stick their necks out and take risks. They could go where they want at any time.'

I shook my head. 'While you're right that they could go anywhere they want, they're not paid crew. They stay here by choice and as our business partners, are very wealthy in their own right. They choose to keep this lifestyle. Everybody who was crew on the operations where we acquired loot, received an equal share. That's always been the deal.'

I grinned at her amazed expression. 'Unfortunately for you, I don't see this operation producing much in the way of loot.'

'Oh… you mean that if it did, I'd get a share?'

'That's what I said. If you're crew and we have a bit of an earn, it's shared equally.'

She gazed around with a fresh perspective. 'I don't know much about boats, so I'm guessing this must have cost millions?'

I nodded gently, 'Yep.'

'Fuckin' hell!'

I chuckled, 'That's a polite way of putting it, and many before you thought the same thing.'

Apart from an occasional sighting in the cockpit or out on deck of *Poseidon*, we hadn't seen much of Corrine, and there hadn't been any new messages for a while. But later that morning, when we saw Turner messing with the outboard on his dinghy, a message came in from Bikini Radio.

'Hi guys. Sorry for the lack of contact, but I know Turner has been telling you a lot more now that you're almost partners. So I'll just try to fill in the gaps. There was a call from Korey this morning to say he wants to transfer the new girls tomorrow night. There will only be two of them coming here now: the two Asian girls who don't speak English. The other two will be taken directly to a house which Korey owns in a small village called Maaroom, back down the Strait. There are four men who are referred to as clients, flying in to Maryborough and being taken to the house tomorrow. The other two girls are going there to act as hostesses and to cook and clean. Two of Korey's men are going as well to act as minders, and the girls will have collars.

I can only suppose he's using Maaroom because it's close to Slain Island, which they both keep talking about, although I still don't know what they plan to do there. The chart shows it to be semi-tidal and mostly covered in mangroves. They're talking about doing something there the day after tomorrow.

Maaroom village has no facilities at all, except for a good boat ramp, and is about 20 kms from Maryborough. There's not even a pub or general store, so it's a very odd choice for a base. That's all I have for now. Miss you guys and please stay close.'

We had a round table to discuss the latest intel, although it seemed to add to the mystery, rather than clarifying anything. I let the talk bounce back and forth in case someone could join some dots, but when the dots failed to co-operate, I spoke up.

'I'm tired of us being on the back-foot with all this, so I think it's time to go pro-active.'

Sandy groaned theatrically. 'Oh dear. This'll be trouble.'

I poked my tongue out at her, 'Thank you dearest, for that vote of confidence. Anyway, this is what we're going to do.'

I laid my plan out quickly, since it wasn't very complicated. Dave took Taylor back to *Gideon*, while Bree and Sandy went below to dig out the cases holding *Dragonfly*, our high-tech Unmanned Aerial Vehicle or UAV surveillance platform.

I took the dinghy and headed over to where Turner was still stuffing around with his outboard.

'Gidday Gary. Got some problems?'

'Yeah. Got some water in the fuel, and now it's in the engine. I just need to pump it through, but it's a messy job. What's going on with you guys?'

I was amazed at the change in his attitude. I guess being promoted from rich, dumb guy, to rich, dumb, semi-trusted partner made all the difference.

'I just wanted to let you know that we're going down the strait a way to pump out our holding tanks. They fill up quickly with this crowd on board, and I don't like to dump it at the anchorage. Better to spread it out over some distance in the channels where the tide flow is strong. Dave's going to stay here at anchor while we're gone.'

'Oh, okay. Will you be long?'

'Nah. Maybe an hour. Just want to get away from the anchorage and that Wanggoolba Creek ferry terminal.'

'Okay. And just for your info, we'll be heading across to the River Heads boat ramp tomorrow night to pick up a couple of girls. About 22:00.'

'Only two? I thought you said there were four.'

'Yeah. Korey's changed plans. These will be the Asian girls, so there should be plenty of room on *Gideon*.'

'Fair enough. We'll be ready.'

The crew had *Firebird* untied from *Gideon*, and the anchor raised. We went under power as our course curved to the south and the south-east breeze was still blowing. I really just wanted to put some land between us and Turner's binoculars. Once masked by the mangrove-covered coast of Fraser/K'gari Island, the girls fired up the UAV, and with all checks complete, it lifted off on its mission.

I wanted to have a good look at Slain Island, to see what attraction might be there for Korey, Turner and their clients. I also wanted to look at Maaroom.

It was only about six nautical miles or eleven kilometres to Slain Island, which turned out to be as Corrine described – semi-tidal mangrove swamp. As a site for fun and games of any description, I couldn't imagine any place with less appeal. The lower the girls flew *Dragonfly*, the worse the island looked. They flew higher over Maaroom, which was a pleasant-looking village, but apart from the caravan park and the boat ramp, there was nothing to attract visitors except peace, tranquillity, fishing and a few gazillion giant mosquitos.

As soon as the girls had the UAV back on deck, we turned and headed north, our holding tanks unemptied, because I don't believe in polluting enclosed water-ways with sewage, even though it was partially treated on-board before discharge.

Once back at anchor, rafted up, and with the UAV stowed away, Dave hopped across, chuckling. 'Turner was like a nervous bride when you headed out. He had his binoculars on you until you rounded the point. Then he became even more nervous. He's only just gone back inside.'

I laughed with him. 'Yeah. We thought he'd do that.'

'See anything interesting?'

'Interesting yes, but informative? No. Slain Island is a semi-tidal, mangrove swamp, just as Corrine described it. It must have some deeply-hidden quality that makes it attractive to Korey and Turner, but I'm buggered if I know what it could be, so the trip didn't tell us anything useful. The same with Maaroom. It's a nice little village plonked in the middle of mangrove wetlands, without even a pub. Good boat-ramp though.'

'So where does that leave us?'

'Like a jigsaw puzzle with half the pieces and the original picture missing.'

The rest of the day went quietly, and as the sun slipped below the western horizon, a party developed on the trampoline nets. We did have a reputation to live down to, after all, so I made a bucket-full of Pina Colada. Although there was very little clothing worn, there was no fooling around amongst the girls, and certainly not with Mary, Taylor and Hanh, who were still a long way from getting over their experiences.

It occurred to me that it might be many months before they fully recovered and could enter into any sort of close relationship with a guy or girl, although that still didn't stop them from sucking up the lovely brew and getting giggly-silly like the others. All considered, it seemed like pretty good therapy.

Until it was fully dark, Mary and Taylor had to settle for standing on the forward cabin bunks, and poking their heads out of the deck hatch, although there was no sign of Turner prowling around. They still downed their fair share of the heady concoction.

The next day was hot and still, with that oppressive feeling to the air as if some bad weather might be brewing, although at that stage, the sky remained clear. The clear water over a sandy bottom encouraged the whole crew to get wet, although Alex, Dave and I took turns on shark watch, standing on the cockpit roof.

That evening, around 21:00, I had Alex run Dave and me across to *Poseidon* in our dinghy. Corrine was there to greet us, managing a quick hug for us both, before Turner strode aft, causing her to immediately revert to hostess mode.

'Ah. There you are. Good timing. I was just about to start engines.'

He was enough of a seaman to have red lighting switched on throughout the boat to preserve night vision, and the wheelhouse was well-equipped with radar, chart plotter and depth sounder. Five minutes after our arrival, we were heading for River Heads on the mainland. From our anchorage, it was a straight run slightly south of west to the boat ramp rendezvous, without any shallow or hard bits to dodge on the way.

The night air was still, close and hot, with a clear sky, although the weather charts had finally shown a small, but intense low rapidly developing to the north-east of Townsville. The water was glassy smooth, and with the scattered lights of civilisation reaching out toward us, it would have been a very pleasant run, if it weren't for the evil purpose of the trip.

Of the four girls aboard, only Corrine hung around. She offered drinks, which we declined, although there wasn't any opportunity to talk to her. The trip only took thirty minutes, so we were anchored just off the boat ramp well before the 22:00 deadline.

At that hour, there was no activity in the car-park, although a couple of tinnies were anchored a few hundred metres north of us, their occupants showing as dark, shapeless lumps with rods poking up like radio aerials.

At ten minutes past the hour, a large Toyota four-wheel drive wagon wheeled into the car-park and stopped near the ramp, killing its lights instantly. There was a double flash of a torch, which could be mistaken for anything, but prompted Turner to tell Dave to stay aboard, while he and I went ashore to meet Korey.

He turned out to be a huge man, barrel-chested, with massively thick arms and legs, and a bone-crushing grip which I had trouble resisting let alone beating. He had two other men with him, who I took to be part of the snatch and grab crew. They were also big and brutal-looking, but weren't introduced and didn't speak.

'So, you're the wealthy playboy Gary has told me so much about.

He says you like what we've done with our girls, although you seem to have plenty of your own.'

I shrugged in the dimness, as I reverted to my fatuous, rich guy routine.

'As I'm sure you know, plenty of money and a big boat attracts the young ladies. Show 'em a good time, give them whatever it is they want and they'll happily stick around, that's my motto. Ha, ha.'

He peered at me, as if trying to discern my true nature. 'Yes, perhaps. Tell me Harry, are you a sporting man? Do you like the thrill of hunting?'

Despite the tingle down my spine, I felt at the implications of the question, I forced a chuckle, 'Oh, I'm always hunting for more young ladies. Best sport of all. Love it.'

'Very funny,' he growled, his huge chest almost making the words reverberate. 'I mean, of course, hunting with a firearm. Like shooting large animals and such?'

'Maybe. It would depend on the prey, wouldn't it? To be really challenging, it should be something which can defend itself effectively or even shoot back. That would be the ultimate prey.'

He gave a long, rumbling laugh. 'Oh, very good, Harry. That is an interesting insight. I'd like to have more time to discuss this with you, but we are short of that for now. Later perhaps. Anyway, I have two new girls for my partner. I've had to restrain and gag them as they are still very unhappy with their situation. They also don't speak English. I don't know what country they're from, so that becomes your problem, Gary.'

Without further talk, he opened the rear tailgate door to reveal two slight girls, dressed in grubby shorts and T-shirts, with wrists and ankles firmly taped, and tape gags in place. There were two large backpacks and a cardboard box jammed in alongside them. With no effort, he plucked each from the load area and dumped them roughly on the ground, where they sat glaring furiously at him.

He handed me the two backpacks and the box.

'Put these in the dinghy, Harry. I need to have a few words with my partner for a moment.'

'Okay. See ya.' I awkwardly shouldered the backpacks, tucked the small box under one arm and headed for the dinghy. A few minutes later, Korey carried each girl down the ramp, one under each massive arm, and placed them in the dinghy on the centre seat.

'Don't untie them until they're safely aboard,' he warned, waggling his finger in my face – a particularly rude gesture which, in the past, had usually resulted in the offender receiving at least one broken finger.

I ignored him and held the bow while Gary scrambled into the blunt end, then pushed off.

As we motored the short distance to *Poseidon*, Gary said, 'I think he likes you, Harry.'

I shrugged, 'Can't imagine why. I don't go much on him, I'm afraid. But that doesn't matter. I don't have to live with him.'

'No, no. Of course not.'

To avoid any accidents, I carefully cut away the tape on the ankles of both girls, before trying to get them out of the dinghy, and with Dave helping, we soon had them safely seated in the aft saloon. Turner insisted on leaving their wrists and mouths taped until they were safely aboard *Gideon* and their collars were fitted.

During the return trip, Corrine sat with the girls and spoke softly to them, but that didn't seem to do much to reduce the intensity of their glares.

With all fenders out, Turner managed to ease alongside *Gideon* without exchanging too much paint. The girls, the backpacks and two new collars were transferred, and Turner insisted on setting the collars in place and doing the binding process himself. With red LEDs showing on both collars, he announced he was satisfied.

'I'll leave you to untie them,' he said with an oily smirk, 'but be careful. Korey said both were very feisty. They've been told about the collars using pictures, but you might like to remind them again, if you can. If they go over to your boat they should still be in range, but that will be the limit.'

That was good information about the potential range of the transmitter which I mentally filed away.

He then looked at Dave. 'Tomorrow morning, I'll be taking my boat down to an island just south of here for a few hours for some business with Korey. You stay here and look after the three girls. Okay?'

Dave shrugged, 'Sure Gary. Whatever you say. That's no problem for me.'

He nodded, 'Good,' then went back aboard *Poseidon*, and moved away a couple of hundred metres before dropping anchor.

CHAPTER 23

With Turner well clear, I left Dave to watch the girls, and went to fetch Hanh. She was in bed, but was just reading, and happily followed me over to *Gideon*, looking rather fetching in shorty PJs.

'I don't really know what their nationality is, but do what you can to communicate. I don't want to remove their gags or untie their wrists until they understand that we won't hurt them, but try to tell them that they have to stay here and be quiet for a few days until this mess is resolved.'

She nodded, 'Yes, understood, Harry. I'll do what I can.'

It took her just one look at the two new arrivals, then she launched into a gentle-sounding stream of what I took to be Japanese. Within moments, both girls nodded.

'Please remove their gags and wrist bindings, Harry. They are Japanese, will keep quiet, and understand we mean to help them.'

Dave and I quickly removed the offending tape as gently as we could, helping the girls up so they could restore circulation to their numbed hands and feet. A two-way dialogue ensued, with much bowing and smiles.

'I've taken the liberty of telling them what's going on,' Hanh said, 'otherwise they won't understand the need to keep up the pretence for the next few days.'

I nodded, 'Yep. That's good. Can you ask for their names, what they're doing in Australia, and how they came to be picked up by Korey and his crew?'

The next exchange was lengthier, then with a grin, Hanh

reported. 'Their names are Chiaki Tanaka and Fumiko Yamada and they're on a backpacking trip around Australia.'

I was shocked into a rare silence for a moment at the amazing coincidence that had dumped the two most sought-after girls in Australia in my lap, although upon reflection, there probably weren't too many kidnapping crews currently on the lookout for young girls. I also thought more happily of the pleasure of informing Tanaka-san and the Japanese Ambassador, Sakura Ito, that the girls were safe.

Hanh took my silence for understanding, and carried on.

'They say their parents are wealthy, so they haven't been looking for work, but were picked up as they left a pub in Brisbane, where they had just eaten, then were listening to live music. They like Australian pub food and the live music, but although the men who grabbed them were very rough, they weren't abused in any way sexually or otherwise. They weren't sure what the big man meant with his pictures of the collar, and don't know why they're wearing them now.'

'Oh, shit!' I looked at Dave, realising how close we had come to losing one or both if they'd tried to escape.

Hastily, I asked Hanh. 'Please explain what the collars do, but say that I'm deactivating them now, although when Turner comes around, they'll have to go back on.'

More dialogue and two shocked expressions followed, then I went to the wheelhouse, hit and held the right button and with a buzz and a click, their collars opened, so after carefully removing them, I left them near the transmitter.

With Hanh continuing to explain the situation to Chiaki and Fumiko in as much detail as possible, I went with Dave to confer with the crew. After I'd covered what was said on shore, and what Turner was doing tomorrow, Bree suggested, 'Sounds like we should put *Dragonfly* up as soon as Turner leaves. We should be able to at least see what's going on with that stupid island.'

'Good idea,' I replied. 'Make sure it's fully fuelled and park it in loiter mode over the top for the duration.'

'Another thing occurs to me,' Alex said, 'concerning these clients who Korey has in this little village, Maaroom. The only other boat we know they have the use of is parked next to us. Therefore, whatever they intend doing on this island, it involves Turner, using one or the other to get them all there and back.'

I nodded approvingly, 'That's exactly what he'll have to do, so if we track him the whole time, we can maybe find the house as well as get photo evidence of what's going on the island.'

The simple plan was kicked around a while longer, then we all headed for bed, except for the night watch. I made sure Chiaki and Fumiko had been settled in, and they assured me, via Hanh's translation, that they were much happier now they understood what was happening, and why they couldn't contact their parents straight away. I made sure there were no phones left lying around, just in case someone changed their mind.

Back on *Firebird*, I placed a call to my controller in Canberra, expecting to get a duty officer, but surprisingly, or perhaps not really, M answered after just a couple of rings.

'*Good evening Harry. All is well, I hope?*'

'Yep, all good thanks M. This is to let you know that we have acquired the two missing Japanese girls, although we are not informing parents or anybody else just yet. We have information that a climax of some sort in the sex-slave part of the operation may be approaching in the next day or two, so we need to keep quiet for now.'

'*Lovely work, dear boy. Both governments will be pleased, as will the Yakuza. You seem to be accumulating yet more brownie points with your powerful friends. I concur with your decision to keep quiet for now. I'll do the same, until you report again. Good work and goodnight.*'

There wasn't anything else to organise that night, so I left Alex and Bree on watch, and headed for bed.

Next morning, there was a buzz of excitement in the air, and most of the crew were up early, except for Sally and Reggie who'd had the early morning watch and were still asleep. Bree organised brekkie earlier than usual to get it out of the way, making an extra pile of pancakes for the sleeping watch girls, and stashing them away from sight of the hungry hordes. With everything cleared away, Bree and Sandy brought the *Dragonfly* cases up into the saloon, ready to unpack once Turner left.

It was around 09:00 when activity was spotted on *Poseidon* as the engines were started and the anchor came up.

As usual, there wasn't any acknowledgement from Turner as he motored past, so as soon as he was far enough away, the girls started assembling the UAV on deck. To fly it off *Firebird's* foredeck, the headsail sheets and the inner headsail boom had to be pulled aside, and the device programmed to only take-off on the clear side. Turner was well out of sight by the time the girls were satisfied with their preparations, and on command, *Dragonfly* lifted smoothly, pivoted 90°, then accelerated away in a climbing turn to the south. As distances weren't far, we would have live video coverage for the whole flight, and since Turner wasn't going very fast, Bree set a low, and very economical cruise speed at 2,000 feet to avoid detection.

It wasn't long before they reported *Poseidon* was in sight, where-upon Bree set the autopilot to perform slow orbits of the target at minimum safe flight speed. The camera stayed locked on the cock-pit using the AutoTrack function. As expected, Turner continued south past Slain Island, but deviated west of the main channel to approach Maaroom from the north-east. After he'd anchored not far off the boat ramp, Bree unlocked the AutoTrack and zoomed in on the ramp, where Korey, two of his men from last night and two other men we hadn't seen before, waited. Strangely, two golf bags were passed into the dinghy, which was over-crowded with six men aboard, especially one the size of Korey.

They all seemed to be in a happy mood with lots of smiles and high-fives being tossed around as Turner motored slowly back to the *Poseidon*, trying not to swamp the heavily-laden dinghy.

'How the hell are they going to play golf on that piece of shit little island?' Dave exclaimed in frustration. 'And why would anyone be so excited about even going there in the first place? This is nuts!'

Although the tingling on the back of my neck suggested that something was badly wrong and we'd missed some vital clues, I admitted that it still made no sense to me either, so we waited, impatiently watching through our secret eye-in-the-sky, for all to be revealed.

While Turner got his boat underway again, the guests gathered in the cockpit, where we saw Corrine serve tea and coffee. With lots of smiles and laughter on display, the mood still appeared very upbeat amongst the guests, although nothing in their behaviour gave a clue as to the purpose of this bizarre outing.

It was less than five nautical miles from Maaroom to the north side of Slain Island, so thirty minutes later, Turner dropped anchor in the muddy water close to shore. It didn't even look to be a good fishing area since there weren't any other boats nearby.

The mystery deepened, as one of Turner's girls appeared in the cockpit, without her collar, and was handed what appeared to be a long broom handle. She wore shorts, a long-sleeved yellow shirt, joggers on her feet and appeared to be receiving congratulations from the bunch of men in the cockpit. Even zoomed in from 2,000 feet, she looked happy, albeit a bit puzzled by all the attention. Turner waved her into the dinghy, then ferried her ashore where she was seen to head south along the length of the island, which was covered in low trees and bushes, with many swampy-looking patches along the way.

Turner then returned to the boat where he picked up the two strangers, complete with golf bags, and ferried them ashore.

There was some pantomiming, with Turner tapping his wrist several times and pointing to the other two with both hands raised, fingers splayed. He then motored the dinghy down to the other end of the island where there was a small patch of sand which could, at a stretch, be called a beach. Then he pulled the dinghy up and seemed to settle in to wait for something to happen.

Initially, we were still totally perplexed by this round of extraordinary behaviour, but as the high-resolution video from *Dragonfly's* slow orbit continued to display the unfolding events, I spotted the girl in her yellow shirt, running along the edge of a rare patch of open ground. She'd barely reached the south end of it, when one of the men appeared at the northern end of the same patch. What caught my attention was that he wasn't carrying a golf club bag any longer, but a rifle.

I slumped back in my seat, cursing, feeling a wave of dread and revulsion sweep through to my soul. 'Oh, those rotten, filthy, sick bastards!'

Sandy looked at me, her face stricken, 'Is this what I think it is?' she asked in a whisper.

I nodded, barely able to speak, but then said louder for the others. 'Those fuckers are hunting that girl. She's unarmed, they're going to shoot to kill, and there's nothing we can do about it. Absolutely fucking nothing!'

There was a chorus of disbelieving, 'what' and 'no way' from some of the other girls, although Sandy, Alex, Dave and Bree worked it out at the same time as I did, so I gave a brief explanation.

'The girl has had her collar removed and has been told her task is to get to the other end of the island where Turner will be waiting to take her to the nearest town and set her free. What they don't tell her is that two sick fuckers, who will have paid a lot of money for the privilege, are put ashore behind her with rifles, and are trying to kill her before she reaches Turner.

I'd also bet anything that even if she does get to him, he'll shoot her anyway. There's no way they can afford to let her get away to tell this story. If we weren't watching this with *Dragonfly*, nobody else would have a clue what these miserable, sick fucks were up to. If it's the last thing I ever do, this mob are all going down. Hard!'

As much as I would've liked to shut the video feed down and stop the recording, we just had to watch, a seething rage building inside me. We saw the man in the clearing, suddenly lift his rifle and saw the silent puff of smoke from the barrel. 'Judging by the recoil, they're using at least 5.56mm or maybe .243 calibre,' I commented. 'Turner better keep his head down if they get much closer or he'll wear a bullet as well.'

It occurred to me, that unless the guys were military-trained, they were going to have to get quite close to hit the girl, since there were a lot of scrubby trees and large bushes which would easily deflect high-velocity, small-calibre bullets. Plus, trying to run in boggy ground was tough going for a man with a rifle. As the viewing angle changed again, I noticed that the top part of the island, where the girl had started from, was cut right across by a diagonal channel, perhaps five or six metres wide at one end, but narrowing to just one or two metres at the other end. There was no way to tell how deep it was until someone tried to cross it, but it was yet another obstacle in this deadly hunt.

Watching with the dreadful frustration of not being able to intervene, we kept catching little flashes of yellow between the trees as the girl initially made good progress, but since the hunters were wearing dark or camo clothing, they were more difficult to spot. We'd already seen one guy track in the girl's footsteps along the edge of the open ground, and this put him well ahead of his partner who had to fight through the scrub on the northern side. The girl suddenly appeared on the edge of the little channel, and without hesitation, jumped in. It was deeper than I expected, as the water went almost up to her shoulders, but just a few slow strides and she was scrambling for a handhold and footing up the other steep bank.

That delay allowed the first man we'd seen to catch up as he nearly fell into the channel in his haste to close the distance. As she hauled herself out of the water, he fired a snap-shot which missed, despite the point-blank range. But then he paused and fired a more controlled shot, hitting her in the side.

We all thought that one more shot would be the end for her, but the guy was too eager to claim his trophy, and jumped into the water. Apparently, he thought it would be shallow, or maybe he was just vertically-challenged, but he went completely under, rifle and all. He surfaced without it, but then ducked under and came back up with it. Then he made a bit of a mistake. He had retrieved the rifle by its stock, and in his excited haste, lunged for the bank, losing his footing for a moment.

He struggled to keep himself upright by using the rifle as crutch, but just ahead of him, the girl made it to her feet, a spreading patch of red on her left side. This galvanised her attacker to awkwardly lift the rifle to a shooting position and take aim.

'Uh-oh.' I said with grim satisfaction, 'this could get very ugly.' The others thought I meant that the girl was about to be shot from about two metres distance, but that wasn't the case. There was a large explosion as the breech of the rifle disintegrated in his hands, removing one hand and turning his face into raw mince-meat. He slumped back into the water and sank in the middle of a spreading patch of red.

'What happened there?' someone gasped. 'Did the girl have a gun?'

'No gun needed just then,' I said with grim satisfaction. 'That's what happens when you try to fire a cheap rifle with the barrel plugged hard with mud. All the energy has to go somewhere.'

We mentally cheered the girl on, as she ripped the yellow shirt off, tied it tightly around her middle across the wound, then moved away at a slower pace.

She elected to angle toward the west side of the island where the vegetation was less dense, but that was where the second hunter had been headed. I thought he might have been drawn to the east by the shots fired, but maybe he was smarter than his mate as we caught glimpses of him still moving down the island at a good pace. He crossed the channel at its narrowest, where it was almost jumping distance, but he still got wet.

If he was looking for the yellow shirt, there wasn't much to see since the girl was still bleeding heavily and the yellow had largely turned red. She looked to have a decent tan, and that helped her blend into the foliage a bit better, but she kept moving, and that was what gave her away.

Her pursuer must have caught sight of her, as he stopped, aimed carefully and fired.

It was a miss, but it looked like the girl was hit by wood splinters on one arm and her back. More blood flowed, although she kept moving.

Unfortunately, her executioner was faster and closed the distance, apparently eager for the kill – which happened a few minutes later in a smaller, more open area on the south-west edge of the island. She had crossed the area quite quickly, and was almost to the trees on the south side, when the man caught a good look at her, stopped and fired. He was a much better shot than his partner, and the girl immediately dropped in the loose, tangled sprawl which only the dead can properly achieve. He seemed to have hit her squarely between her bare shoulder blades, and I was thankful she had fallen face-down. Nobody needed to see the exit wound.

The hunter closed on her body, prodded it a few times with the muzzle of his rifle, then pulled a small hand-held radio from his pocket, presumably to report the successful end to his day's sporting activity. We saw Turner push the dinghy off the southern shore, and motor up the west side to where the brave hunter had waded out from the mangroves. The two of them returned to the girl's body and dragged it to the shore, where it was draped across the bow like a trophy. There was much hand-shaking and back-slapping as the brave, victorious hunter climbed in, but also a lot of use of the radio, presumably trying to contact the missing man.

Turner headed the dinghy back around the south end of Slain Island, and some way out into more open water, where they unceremoniously dumped the girl's body, fairly safe in the knowledge that bull sharks would provide their usual efficient and speedy disposal service.

Back at the boat, it looked like a search was organised for the missing hunter, and it wasn't long before his body was found, snagged in mangrove roots near the mouth of the small channel he'd come to grief in. Their care and compassion were further demonstrated when they left his body to the attention of the crabs and other marine scavengers, before returning to the *Poseidon* in obvious high spirits.

Turner up-anchored shortly after and headed south down the inner channels to Maaroom.

We kept *Dragonfly* overhead and saw Korey, his two men and the victorious hunter get dropped ashore, amid another round of handshakes and backslapping. Turner returned to *Poseidon,* raised anchor and headed north.

The girls tracked Korey and crew back to a house not far from the boat-ramp, took a few screen-shots of it, then chased after Turner, but it was obvious he was simply returning to base, so I asked them to retrieve *Dragonfly* and pack it away before he came too close. Naturally, they were way ahead of me and already had the wonderous UAV inbound.

To say that all of us were absolutely gutted was an understatement.

CHAPTER 24

FRASER ISLAND, MAAROOM, PAYBACK

While Turner was making his return trip, I sat thinking quietly in the cockpit, slowly and silently joined in ones and twos by the others, everyone dumb with shock at the depth of depravity we'd just seen on display. We watched numbly, as Turner brought *Poseidon* into the anchorage, whereupon the FM radio crackled into life.

'Harry, Harry. I hope you can hear me, as I'll only have a few moments. I'm sure I saw Dragonfly overhead a few times, so I'm presuming you know even more about what these sick fuckers did than I do. That girl was just seventeen, and I intend to avenge her. That is, unless my action would totally screw up your plans. If so, set off a red smoke flare in the cockpit. Make it seem like an accident if you do. If I see nothing in the next five minutes, I'll take that as approval for some payback. Gotta go, love ya' all and hope to see you soon.

Everyone looked at me, silently waiting for me to leap into action, but I just sat calmly, a gentle smile on my face. Over the way, *Poseidon* dropped anchor, reversed back to set it, then the engines cut. There was only one other boat in our vicinity, and it was five or six hundred metres up the beach. All was quiet for a while, until a male screamed, then a minute later, Turner was marched out onto the rear deck. He was bleeding profusely from a cut across his forehead, masses of blood sheeting down his face blinding him, and with his wrists bound behind his back. Corrine was encouraging him along with a large kitchen knife stabbing into his back.

She manoeuvred him down onto the stern-board, turned him to face her, then with her right hand, made what looked like a blurringly-fast criss-cross motion in front of him, before stepping smartly back a pace.

There was absolutely no religious significance to her motions!

Two red lines opened up, one right across his belly, the other vertically down from his breastbone to his crotch, allowing thick, ropey strands of creamy-pink intestine to spill down past his knees, while his mouth opened in a silent scream of shock and pain. Then she reached forward and gently pushed him overboard. Just before he hit the water, I glimpsed a black band around his neck.

As the deep channel was just out from our sterns, and the tidal current was strongly to the south, it carried Turner, wildly kicking and struggling, toward us. However, when he reached about the halfway point between the two boats, there was a sharp crack, and his head slowly lifted into the air, surrounded by a large cloud of fine pink mist, then plopped back to sink beside his now lifeless body. Corrine gazed at the spot, went inside briefly, then untied the dinghy and came over to us.

She had removed her collar and left it aboard *Poseidon*, and had a joyful reunion with all the crew she knew and met the newcomers.

'Bloody marvellous job, Mouse. Well done!' I enthused, hugging her tightly when I got the chance. She got a bit emotional for a few moments, a rare occurrence for Corrine, but she quickly recovered.

'That was a tough gig, Harry,' she said quietly, 'maybe I'm getting too old to stick my neck and body out like that anymore. The only good part was slicing that rotten mongrel's guts open and blowing his head off.'

I carefully looked her in the eyes. 'I hope you're not completely done yet. You and I and Jasper are going out tonight to sort out the rest of 'em. You up for it?'

'Fuck, yeah!' was her positive reply, a grin mostly replacing the distressed look she been wearing.

'Good. We've got some housekeeping to do first, but kick back and take it easy for now. How are the remaining two girls on

Poseidon coping?'

She looked serious, 'Not good. We soon realised what was going on, and before Turner got around to choosing who was to be the sacrificial goat, we were all shitting our pants, wondering if we were going to be the one. So, the other two are mentally shattered for now. They'll need a lot of TLC.'

'Understood. We might move *Poseidon* over here to raft up to *Gideon* and get the girls over here. We'll be taking *Firebird* on the op tonight.'

'Thanks Harry.'

I left Dave to stay close to his lady and took Alex with me over to *Poseidon*. We found the stern-board still covered in blood, but that was quickly cleaned off. As Lena had been the girl shot, the two remaining girls, Jay and Teri, were huddled together in the saloon clad only in brief panties, shaking with fright and wondering what the hell was going on.

I took in their state at a glance, and sat on the steps leading down from the cockpit, about as far from them as I could be and still talk easily.

'Hi girls. I'm Harry, and my friend up on deck is Alex. We're from the red catamaran. You might remember me from the other day when Philippa was sold.'

'Yeah. We remember,' the blonde girl said cautiously, 'but where's Corrine?'

I smiled, 'She's on my boat. That is, on the catamaran. She's actually a very close friend of ours.'

'What's happened to Gary Turner? Corrine seemed to attack him.'

'She did exactly that. I hope you'll be pleased to hear that Gary Turner is no more. He met with a most painful death at Corrine's hands, and won't be able to hurt you, or anybody else again.'

'Do you mean that he's gone? As in, like, finished?'

'Death does that, I'm afraid. Although in his case, I'm very glad.'

The girls looked at each other, daring to hope my words meant what they thought. 'So, we're free? Is that what you're saying?'

I nodded, 'Yep. As soon as I take your collars off, you are. Although I'd really like you to stick around for a little while longer.'

'You can take these things off? Really?'

'Sure can. Just a minute.' I went forward, careful to avoid frightening them, and did the trick with the button, being rewarded with two buzzes and two clicks as the collars opened.

Returning to the aft saloon, I saw the girls were too afraid to touch the collars, even though they hung partly opened around their necks.

'I'm just going to remove them,' I said gently, stepping close and carefully removing the lethal plastic bands and laying them on the table.

'There. That's fixed that little problem. Now, I have a few things to tell you, so please listen carefully.'

They nodded seriously, still not daring to hope too much and afraid to move.

'As I said, Turner has been taken care of, but there's still Korey Yanos, four of his men and three of Korey's clients. One was killed today on the hunt, and I'm very sorry to say that Lena was also killed.'

They nodded dumbly, having already worked that out from the discussion when the fearless, noble hunter returned to the boat.

'Tonight, Corrine and I will be going into Maaroom village to take care of them. As the remaining partner and his clients are all together, we will be permanently terminating them and therefore this foul, depraved scheme. Tonight, we'll have to leave you with the other girls we've rescued, and the two motor boats will be tied up together. But while we're away taking care of business, I need you to stay with the others and not to try to go ashore, even though I've said that you are free. It's just that if you told anybody what's been going on, you could put all our lives at risk, including your own. Are you willing to help us?'

They looked at each other again, then blondie said, 'Of course we will Harry. Anything! This has been a lot to take in, all at once. Earlier on, we were fearing for our lives, then Lena was taken ashore and killed. And now Corrine has killed Turner and you've taken those horrible collars off and told us we're free. Of course, we'll help you. You just saved our lives! But we won't be trying to go anywhere, because we don't have anywhere to go, and no money anyway.'

'I understand. Do you have any family you could go to when this is over?'

'No. We're both orphans and were mostly living on the streets when Korey and his animals picked us up.'

'Okay. This is becoming a very familiar story, but we'll sort it out eventually. Don't worry too much, as I can promise that you won't be just dumped back on the streets. Money won't be a problem and we'll do something about finding a decent home and jobs for you all. The important thing is that there are a few nasty things still happening, so I really need you to do as I ask without argument. We have a lot to think about and do, so not having to worry about you for a few days will be a great help. Is that okay? You'll help?'

They both nodded vigorously.

'Sure. We can do that, especially if you really are going to look after us and stop this slavery thing.'

'That's exactly what we're going to do, but for the moment, Alex and I are going to move this boat over to tie up beside the other motor boat. You will be free to move about between all three boats and meet all the others. I think you'll meet an old friend who'll be very happy to see you. When we come back from Maaroom, you can come back here to sleep, but we'll feed you all on my boat.'

'Can we get dressed?' Blondie asked.

I laughed, 'Of course you can! Nobody will ever tell you what to wear again. You can suit yourselves. You could even go sleep on the other motor boat if you prefer to avoid bad memories. I'll leave that up to you. Anyway, I'll let the others tell you what else has been going on. We've got a lot to do and time is running out.'

'Thanks, Harry. I'm Jay, and this is my sister Teri. I promise we won't cause any trouble.'

'That's really good to hear, Jay, I appreciate that.'

I left them to it and hastened forward to find that Alex was ready to start engines.

'This is a really nice boat, Harry,' he enthused, 'not very fast as we've already seen, but very well set up. Anyway, all good with the girls?'

'Yeah, they'll be fine, I think. But let's move. I've got some calls to make and some mayhem to organise.'

Five minutes later, we were tied up beside *Gideon*, where Jay and Teri were ecstatic to be re-united with Mary, alive and well. I figured she would be a great help in settling them down and explaining what was still going on.

My first task was to call M.

'Harry, dear boy. I must apologise for not getting back to you earlier about Daku's movements.'

'No problem M, we've been rather busy as well, but before I report, I urgently need some information.'

'Go ahead.'

'Will you find out from the real estate agents who look after properties in Maaroom, Queensland, the address of the house purchased by Korey Yanos? The agents will be located in Maryborough. We've looked at the place briefly from the air, but I just need to be absolutely sure of the address. I'd hate to blow up the wrong house.'

'Ahhh… don't say stuff like that you naughty boy! But give me a moment, and I'll get that address search started'

She was only a few minutes, then I brought her up to speed on what the whole nasty operation was all about.

'My goodness, Harry. You really did step in deep doggie doo-doo this time! It was a great shame to lose that young girl, but at least you have the chance to stop it dead. May I presume there won't be anybody left

to tell tales or for us to prosecute after tonight?'

'That's another story M. After tonight, if all goes to plan… then no. The last few heads will be removed from the Hydra, if I may quote Greek mythology for a moment and using a nasty pun. However, as far as loose ends go, there are another thirty-nine boats out there with a slave girl or perhaps two aboard who need to be freed. The aftermath of this operation might last a while, but I have half a plan to fix that. More when I think of the other half.'

She gave her throaty chuckle, *'I look forward to hearing that one. Now. Your friend, Daku and his men are not only in the country, but are in your area right now. It appears they know your precise whereabouts, courtesy of your other dear friend, Korey Yanos.'*

'How the hell did that unholy alliance happen to come about, M?'

'Three guesses who is the supplier of those very nasty bang collars you've been playing with?'

'Oh, no. The Yakusa. And even though Daku was in prison, he would have known about the supply contact with Yanos. Hence the intel leak. Bugger it!'

She chuckled again, *'Precisely. I think you would call this a right royal clusterfuck. Such a delightfully descriptive phrase. The question is, what are you going to do about it?'*

'First things first. We have the Yanos problem to resolve now, then I'll tackle Daku. Don't forget that I have Chiaki Tanaka who is Raijin Tanaka's granddaughter and Daku's sister, under my control. They'll have to be my ace cards.'

'Ah… yes. The young ladies. They are well, I trust?'

'Extremely well now. Having a great time. They hadn't planned on a boat cruise, but it seems to agree with them already. It's handy that Hanh speaks Japanese so well. They're very comfortable and already starting to inject Japanese food styles into the on-board menu. More to the point, the crew really like it. Culinary events aboard may never be the same again.'

M gave way to a rare fit of girlish giggles, before regaining a measure of decorum. *'Delightful, dear boy. My staff haven't come back with your address yet, but I suspect it won't be long. May I email or text you?'*

'Either will be fine, thanks M. We'll talk later. Bye for now.'

I returned to the cockpit to find that as huge as it was, it was getting seriously overcrowded with fourteen or fifteen people milling around, most sucking on booze. I pulled Sandy, Dave, Alex, Bree and Corrine back into the saloon to confer.

'How are the plans going, Boss?' Corrine asked, already sounding more like her normal, confident self – thank goodness.

I frowned, 'A bit slow at the moment, I'm afraid. By my reckoning, the house has Korey, four of his thugs, three hunting clients and two girls in residence. I'd like to give Korey a taste of what he gave the girls, and take the rest out in one hit, but we have to get the two girls out safely first.'

Corrine just gave me a look. 'Is that all you're worried about? Too easy, Boss. Don't forget that I've brought my full kit with me. I've even got my dart kit with some of that lovely blue-ringed octopus venom left. And there's always the sleepy spray.'

'Good call, Mouse. I'd almost forgotten about the octopus-juice. Gee, that was really something, wasn't it? It would be really nice to hit Korey with that, but probably what he deserves is to have a collar strapped around his greasy neck and cop a round of the same treatment you gave Turner.'

She shrugged, 'No problem with that option either, although we might need Alex to help move the big lump. How about we get the girls and Korey out, then set fire to the whole rotten place?'

I thought a few moments. 'That's a thought. Although maybe we can achieve that goal without having to do too much heavy lifting. How about this for an idea.'

I quickly ran through the rough plan, then the others kicked it around until we had what we figured might be workable. To check one thing, I asked Mary to join us.

'The collar base-station transmitter has battery back-up, is that right?'

'Yes, Harry. It plugs into either boat power or normal mains power, but if that fails, the internal battery is good for 24 hours or so.'

'Okay. Thanks Mary.'

I looked around. 'That's it then. It's a plan.'

I decided that the shore party would be myself, Corrine, Alex and Jasper, while Bree and Reggie would remain to look after the two motor boats and the collection of girls. Dave and Sandy would come along, but would stay on *Firebird* to secure our exit strategy, and the trip time there would take about ninety minutes.

The plan called for us to hit the house when the occupants were well asleep, which meant around 02:00 to be safe. I wanted to take *Firebird*, because with the dagger boards raised, it had the shallowest draft of the three boats for navigating the shallow, twisting channels to Maaroom which we weren't familiar with. The electric drives also made it super quiet, although we could sail some of the way to save on power.

Departing our two rafted-up powerboats at midnight, we sailed as far as possible while we had good water, but when the forward-looking sonar showed the bottom becoming uncomfortably close to our delicate bottoms, I raised the dagger-boards and reluctantly furled all sail. The motors purred into life and we slowly followed the shallow channels, our 1.5 metre draft not causing any problems.

It was an uneventful run and we were anchored just off the rough shore near the boat ramp at Maaroom by 01:30. *Firebird's* red hulls blended in nicely with the darkness, although we saw no activity on or off the water. The gusty south-east breeze rattling through the various trees in the shore-side park covered any small noises we made. I'd fired up the masthead camera, and selected infra-red, night vision mode. This let us check the surroundings carefully.

The address of Korey's house, which M had emailed through

earlier, was the one we thought we saw Korey and crew driving to. It proved to be a large, single-level house of rough wood construction, sitting high on raised pilings in the Queensland fashion for both ventilation and flood-proofing. It had a wide, covered veranda around it on all sides, with sets of steps at the front and rear leading up to the veranda.

We were able to see two sides of the house using the camera, since the mast-head was 35.5 metres above sea-level, and the thermal imager showed there wasn't anyone on guard in the grounds or on the veranda.

I didn't really expect Korey to bother with guards, as he didn't know he had anything to guard against. What a shame!

CHAPTER 25

As we didn't really know what to expect, tension was high as Sandy ferried Alex, Corrine, Jasper and myself ashore so they'd have the dinghy in case of trouble, and I had a UHF CB radio for comms when we needed a pickup. We looked a motley collection as we picked our way in silence across the rough ground toward the first street. Three of us wore backpacks, and the hulking form of Alex dwarfed Corrine's diminutive form, while the lean black shadow who was Jasper padded silently at my side. At night, he was easy to pass off as a long-tailed dog, which was what people expected to see walking the streets.

Like most of the houses in the street, there wasn't a fence or hedge fronting the property, but the neighbour on the southern side had a few trees along his boundary which gave us some cover while we checked the house and grounds at close quarters. I spotted a half-cabin fishing boat on a trailer, with a big outboard motor bolted to its stern parked under the house, and a large four-wheel drive wagon beside it.

We paused for a while under the trees as a final check for insomniacs or someone doing a bladder dump, but all was quiet. The breeze was just gusty enough to gently rattle tree limbs and make enough natural noise around the eaves to mask our movements. Nevertheless, Corrine waved us to stay put while she made a recon. She was far better at this covet stuff than Alex or me, so we crouched down and patiently waited as she silently flitted across the open ground to the house.

She took a lot longer than I expected, but re-appeared silently in front of us, scaring the crap out of me as usual when she does that trick.

'Fuckin' hell, Mouse. I do wish you wouldn't do that. I'm getting grey hairs.'

'Man-up, Harry,' she retorted, 'it's not me giving you grey hairs! It's this degenerate lifestyle you insist on leading. Not good for you older chaps. You can't take the pressure.'

'Get stuffed, Mouse.'

'I plan to. Frequently and often by my lovely man, just as soon as we can wrap up this mob.'

'So, what's the go?' I asked.

'Okay. What we have is that they're all seriously pissed and fast asleep, with the doors unlocked, and all windows open. They've apparently been celebrating the successful hunt – the kitchen table is covered with beer bottles and a few empty rum and vodka bottles for good measure. There are five bedrooms with two beds in each. The two girls are sharing one room.

'I've already given all the men a puff of my favourite sleepy-spray, so they'll definitely stay asleep for twenty to thirty minutes. That should be plenty of time.'

'Great work, Mouse. Let's go do it!'

With nobody around, and having full confidence in the effective-ness of Corrine's sleepy spray, we walked straight up the steps and in through the front door. The place stank of spilled booze and curry. As reported, the kitchen, with a large table in the centre, was a mess. Our first job was to get the girls out of bed quietly, so while Corrine looked after that, Alex and I searched the room for any papers which might help our search for the other 39 girls. All we found was a locked cupboard in the lounge room, which yielded easily to Alex's Ka-Bar knife blade. There was a large kit-bag which looked to be more than half-full of banded bundles of cash, and a small stack of manila file folders. I stuffed the folders in with the cash and placed it outside on the veranda by the stairs.

While we'd been doing that, Jasper had been searching the rooms, and returned, growling softly. I squatted down beside him, 'Very bad men boy. No men are to leave the house. Bite to kill if any try. Two girls are good people, so be nice to them.'

In the gloom, I could swear that he pulled his lips back in a grin, but he did 'huff' gently at me.

Moments later, Corrine appeared, leading two girls, naked except for their black collars. They looked even more terrified to see the hulking dark shapes of Alex and me. Luckily, they didn't see Jasper, since he'd gone outside to prowl the veranda, desperately hoping someone tried to escape.

'Have you told the girls anything?' I murmured to her. Murmurs carry far less than the higher pitch of whispers in a quiet environment.

'Just that they're being rescued and mustn't make a sound.'

'Don't they have any clothes?'

'Effectively, no. They've been ripped off them so often, they're in tatters. They'll be alright. They don't care about flashing some skin after what they've been through.'

'I meant that maybe they'd be cold.'

'Really Harry, you pick the strangest times to worry about a girl being naked. Stop it – they'll be fine.'

I turned to the girls. 'Good evening girls. I'm Harry, this is Corrine and the large gentleman is Alex. As Corrine has already said, we're here to rescue you, and to do some harm to these animals who've been abusing you, but you must be super quiet. What are your names?'

A short girl with dark hair spoke softly. 'I'm Renee and this is Stella. Are you really rescuing us?'

'Yes. But before we do anything else, I'm going to remove your collars.'

'Oh, yes please. That'll be great.'

'But first, even though you're now free and can do as you wish, you must promise not to run away just yet. For now, I need you to come with us to our boat. We have a lot of other girls we've rescued, and we need to keep you all in one place under protection, until we shut this entire obscene business down.'

They both nodded, and Stella gave a bitter, mirthless laugh and echoed the words we'd been hearing much too often lately. 'No problem Harry. We've got no clothes, no money and nowhere to go anyway, so we'll do whatever you say. Just get us out of here, please.'

'Good-oh. Just wait here until I find the bloody transmitter.'

Renee spoke, 'It's just over there on the far kitchen counter. Right in the corner beside the coffee machine. You can just see the red light blinking.'

I looked around, 'Oh, yeah. Great. Silly me.'

I had the girls go around and close all the blinds and pull the curtains where they could, then turned on a couple of dim lights.

I had to give some credit where it was due – Korey had an excellent eye for attractive young ladies! Therefore, despite my earlier concerns, the girls looked very attractive wearing just their black collars, but I dragged my mind back on track and stayed with the program of carrying out the disable routine. There was a sigh of relief from the girls, as both collars clicked open, so I gently removed them and handed one to Corrine.

'I think one on Korey, then tape his wrists behind him, and a hobble on his ankles. I'll get you to wake him up when we're ready to pay homage to Guy Fawkes.'

'No probs. What about his gorillas and the intrepid hunters?'

'We'd better not give the local law too many odd problems at once, so just a second dose of sleepy spray, please. I'll round up some booze for them.'

Alex had made a search of the bedrooms, and came out from Korey's room with a large, heavy pilot's briefcase, which he placed outside next to the other bag. I got Renee and Stella to help me collect some full bottles of vodka and rum. We visited each bedroom, where we tipped half a bottle over each sleeping form, making sure the bedding was soaked and then left the part-filled bottle on its side beside the bed as though it'd been knocked over. That let a fair amount of the contents escape, while the girls gave a few stifled giggles.

'Won't this wake them up,' Renee asked quietly out in the hallway after doing the last room.

'Nah. Corrine hit them with some knock-out spray before she got you two up.'

'Really? We didn't hear a thing until she woke us.'

'Yeah. She's very good at doing stuff like that.'

'What's going to happen to all the men?'

'It's better if you didn't worry about them for now. I gather they weren't very nice toward you?'

Both gave a shudder and Renee said, 'No. I won't go into details, but they're really bad. Especially, Korey and his men.'

I patted each gently on the shoulder. 'Excellent. In that case, you won't be upset by what we do to them.'

By the time each sleeper had been suitably anointed, Corrine had delivered a second spray to everyone except Korey, who was showing signs of stirring. With Alex's help, she had very effectively bound and hobbled him. I'd figured it would be easier if he walked to the dinghy by himself, rather than us having to carry the big lump.

As he had a fat neck, Corrine had to force Korey's collar ends in place while I activated the transmitter, the two halves sealing with a satisfying buzz and a click although it looked as if he would have trouble talking, it was so tight. I carefully checked that the transmitter had a battery fitted, before unplugging it from the mains power and tucking it into my pants pocket.

It gave a soft beep as the mains power was disconnected, but the indicator lights remained on and steady.

One last check around, and I announced, 'Okay boys and girls. It's time to get the flock outta here.' With Alex's help, Corrine managed to get Korey to his feet, but it took several very hard slaps across his face to keep him vertical. Alex wasn't very gentle and seemed to enjoy it.

After the third slap, Korey managed to mumble, 'What the fuck's going on? Who are you guys? Why am I tied up? Do you know who I am?'

I stepped up to him. 'It's a shame that your degenerate lifestyle has made you forget your own name, but hopefully it'll come back to you. But for now you can save the questions.'

I pulled the transmitter from my pocket and showed him the slowly blinking red light.

With difficulty, he focused on it.

'Careful with that. It looks after the girl's collars. You've got it unplugged. It's running on the battery now.'

I gave him my best evil grin. 'If you care to look around, you'll see that while the girls are no longer wearing collars, or anything else for that matter, you are.'

It took a few moments for that piece of information to penetrate his alcohol and drug-clouded brain, but then he realised the tight constriction around his neck was a collar.

'Oh, fuck! I've got a collar on. Hang on a minute, I know you. You're the smart-arse with a bunch of girls on the red cat. I told Turner you looked dodgy. What do you think you're doing?'

I stepped close to him and said my favourite words. 'You've been a very naughty boy, Korey, and I'm afraid you're going to have to come with us. Try to keep in mind that I've got the magic box in my pocket and the collar is to make sure you do what we say, stay very quiet and very close to me.'

Despite the odds stacked up against him, he still tried some bluster. 'You won't get away with this. Gary will arrange to have you lot sorted out.'

I smiled this time. 'Gee, Korey. I'd forgotten to tell you about Gary. He received some tragic news and seems to have totally lost his head and his guts over it.'

As the significance of that statement slowly sank in, he seemed at a loss for words and the slight slump of his shoulders suggested that he was resigned to his fate. But as he still radiated a powerful aura of menace, we didn't dare relax our guard for a second.

Although very groggy he got the message, so it didn't take much to get him shuffling outside and downstairs, where Alex slapped a piece of tape over his mouth, then looped a length of clothes line around his neck and held the free end. Corrine carelessly knocked over a few more open bottles of rum and vodka in the kitchen before joining us downstairs, a golf bag looped over one shoulder. I made sure Jasper was lurking well in the background, away from Korey and the girls, since they hadn't had seen him yet.

Corrine and I went under the house to where the boat sat on its trailer, and I was pleased to see that my expectations were correct. There were a pair of large fuel tanks strapped to the floor of the boat, and more fuel stored in eight 20 litre jerry cans, neatly lined up on the dirt floor, along with some assorted junk like broken chairs, and an old table with one leg-less corner propped up by a fruit box.

It was the work of minutes to screw in the boat's drain bungs and empty three cans of petrol into the boat, with the remaining five stood upright on the floorboards. Almost immediately, the smell of alcoholic spirits dripping through the wood floor boards of the kitchen directly above us, was overwhelmed by the eye-watering stench of petrol.

Corrine dug in her backpack and unrolled a length of pyrotechnic safety fuse. It's all too easy to underestimate the explosive power of vaporised petrol, as those who have tossed some onto a BBQ fire have regretted while on their way to hospital. In this case, the length of fuse would give us about five minutes to get clear of the immediate vicinity.

She waited until we'd got Korey moving, slowed by his awkward, shuffling gait, then lit the fuse and trotted after us.

If we'd looked a motley crew coming ashore, we must have looked even weirder heading back. The huge form of Alex was still holding the leash of the slightly smaller Korey, hands behind his back, and taking small steps like a Japanese lady in a kimono. Beside me walked three girls, only one of whom wore any clothes and she had a golf bag slung over her shoulder. Bringing up the rear was a large, lean, black cat padding silently, still hopeful the 'bad man' would do something suitably bite-worthy. I carried the bags holding the cash and other papers.

We were about half-way across the tree-filled park between the street and the shore, when there was a soft bass 'whump' behind us and a flash of yellow light briefly washed through the trees. That first flash had barely dulled, before it quickly bloomed into something much brighter, and the sound grew quickly into a dull roar as the fuel tanks heated and vented blow-torch-quality flames at the flammable resin of the boat hull.

Less than a minute later, we saw the flames were already inside the house, courtesy of the rum and vodka leaking through the floorboards, and reaching up the walls in the kitchen and lounge room. Moments later, there were a series of yellow flares of light from the bedroom windows on this side of the house as the alcohol trails, carelessly spilled along the hallway to each of the bedrooms, caught and flared.

Then what sounded like five hundred dogs all started barking at once, and lights started to appear in the bedrooms of surrounding houses. Even if the Fire Brigade lads were standing ready in the next street, there was no way they were going to put that lot out. It was just as well the houses were well separated, because the heat was getting intense, with fountains of burning embers pouring out of each shattered window driven by greedy yellow tongues driving up toward the silent, uncaring sky.

It quickly became apparent that nobody was prepared to be a hero, as the neighbours were too busy with hoses wetting down their own walls and roofs, and putting out spot fires in their gardens.

Mr Fawkes would have been very proud.

As a dedicated pyromaniac, I looked over at Corrine and grinned, 'Absolutely top job, Mouse.'

She gave me a return grin and a thumbs up, even though her first preference was to make big explosions. In this case, the fire was going to do a much better job of eliminating all evidence of foul play, and the forensics mob should be able to write it off to careless storage of fuel and too much alcohol, both spilled and taken internally.

With the fire visible from twenty kilometres away, there was no need to radio Sandy for a pick-up and she was waiting with the dinghy nosed up against the rocky shoreline. Beyond her, *Firebird* was far enough out to just be a distant shadow, but we weren't in any mood to hang around. Somehow, we all squeezed aboard, with Korey balanced precariously right up in the bow, hoping Sandy didn't rock the boat too much.

He and the two girls received a dreadful shock when Jasper leapt lightly into the middle of the huddled mass of humans. I made brief introductions to the girls as Sandy motored silently and slowly out to *Firebird*, Korey receiving a threatening deep growl with the full bared-fangs routine.

Sandy's first words, predictably, were, 'Really, Harry. One day you're going to find some girls with clothes on for a change. At least these ones are dry and aren't leaking claret. Hello girls, I'm Sandy, and we'll get you dressed as soon as we're aboard.'

Renee and Stella giggled, and said, 'Hi Sandy. But we're not worried. We're just glad to be out of the hands of those animals, although Harry's brought the worst one with us, for some reason.'

Sandy gave a grim smile in the reflected firelight which hadn't diminished yet. 'Don't worry, dear girl, I suspect we won't have to put up with his company for very long.'

When she nosed up to the stern of *Firebird*, Dave was there to drag

Korey out, and at my direction, sat him on the edge of the boarding platform. Dave looked admiringly at the two naked girls, until Corrine punched him on the arm to get his attention.

His head spun around. 'Oh, hello, dear. Good to see you back in one piece.'

'I'll give you one piece, my lustful friend. Take these bags and be very careful.'

'Yes, boss.'

'Fuck-off, smart-arse.'

He grabbed the bags and trotted up the steps, 'Yes, ma'am. Fucking-off as instructed.'

Renee and Stella giggled again and followed him to the cockpit, Corrine behind carrying the golf bag. Alex went straight to the controls and commenced raising the anchor. With that done, we motored silently away from the quite spectacular blaze which, despite the best efforts of the locals, seemed to have spread to the neighbouring fences, trees and gardens.

The return trip was mostly uneventful, and as the batteries were holding up well, we stayed under power all the way instead of shagging around with sails, dagger-boards and dodging sandbanks. In fact, the only event of note, was that once in the main channel, with the tide still running south quite strongly, Corrine and I went aft to visit Korey still perched on the side of the stern platform.

'Who's your contact in Japan for the supply of the collars?' I asked, after Corrine took great delight in ripping the very sticky gaffer tape off his mouth, taking half one lip with it.

'Nothing to say to you, smart-arse. But they're already on your trail and not far away.'

I smiled. 'I don't suppose it would be Daku and his two mates, would it? He's not long out of prison, I believe.'

Korey looked shocked at my use of that name.

'Yeah, well. I spoke to him this morning with an update on what was happening. Anyway, there's more behind him.'

'Oh. Did you really think his grandfather, Raijin Tanaka, of the Yamaguchi-gumi, Yakusa clan was sending another hit squad? I've already been speaking with him. Lovely chap. We got along like a house on fire – pardon the pun, but I'm afraid he doesn't approve of what his grandson has been doing, so there's actually no support coming from there at all.'

'How the fuck did that happen? No. Don't tell me. I'm not saying another word.'

'Good-oh. No problem for me. You've just confirmed what we thought anyway, plus I've got all the other information I need. We took the liberty of collecting all your papers before we torched the place. Should make interesting reading.'

'Get fucked, little man,' he growled.

I gave a mirthless smile, 'Gee. Such aggro in the face of adversity. However, thanks to you and Daku, we have a really neat way to deal with that, big guy. Bye, bye.'

I nodded to Corrine, who braced herself, planted a foot in Korey's broad back and pushed hard. He gave a terrified shriek as he slid on the wet surface and went straight overboard and under, surfacing moments later, obviously kicking frantically, his mouth open in a soundless scream. Fortunately, the darkness astern swallowed him before we heard a sharp 'crack'.

With a sense of relief, I removed the transmitter from my pocket, turned it off and walked Corrine back to the group in the saloon, where Korey's departure had gone totally un-noticed and un-lamented.

CHAPTER 26

BURRUM HEADS, BUNDABERG

Our arrival back at McKenzie's Jetty anchorage was only noted by Reggie and Bree, who were on watch on the power boats. But the noise of anchoring and rafting up soon had all the girls up and milling around to make the new pair welcome. Renee and Stella were happy to be re-united with Chiaki and Fumiko, especially when Hanh could do some basic translating for them.

Even though it was now 04:45, discussions were put on hold until everyone had some sleep. I'd found out the hard way that planning when over-tired was flawed at best. Therefore, beds were found for Renee and Stella and I chased everyone else back to theirs.

Jasper was left to watch over us, and did his usual, quietly competent job. Or maybe it was because nobody came calling. Regardless, I didn't stir until mid-morning, with a full bladder and an empty stomach driving me out of bed. Just Sandy, Alex, Bree, Corrine and Dave were up and about, and Bree quickly fetched a lovely hot breakfast she'd set aside for me. As I ate, Sandy explained that they'd been discussing our next move.

I finished a mouthful. 'Despite the amazing collection of young ladies, and two spare boats we've acquired, the most serious concern at the moment is that Daku has had good feedback on our location via Korey. Their last contact was just yesterday morning, so he knows exactly where we are.'

'Ahh, fuck it!' Dave exclaimed disgustedly. 'That makes life a lot harder.'

I nodded agreement, 'Yes, it does. Our ability to deal with Daku is restricted by our need to protect all the young ladies. Therefore, I think our first priority is to change locations ASAP and hopefully disappear as best we can, now that Turner and Korey can't report our movements any more. That'll buy us time to re-group and plan. We've successfully done this before, so we can do it again. I want this next encounter to be on our terms, not his.'

Sandy patted my knee. 'Yes, my dear man, but not with a bunch of homeless, penniless innocents depending on us to keep them safe. Perhaps we could park them somewhere?'

It was Corrine who voiced my thoughts. 'There's a problem with that, unfortunately. I think the rescued girls will be happy to continue to be looked after for a while, and won't cause a problem, but there's Sally and Kim who have a normal life to get back to. The issue with letting any of them go is that if they mention what's been happening, even innocently, the word will spread and the media will pick it up. Then the thirty-nine boats with a girl or two aboard, will drop from sight.'

I backed up her words. 'That's right. Amongst those papers on *Poseidon*, there should be a list of Turner's customers. Mary will know for sure – she said she used to keep his books. So that becomes the next job straight after we cope with Daku. I'm hoping we can resolve that one peacefully, but we need to be firmly in control to make that happen. Things can go horribly wrong when a psychotic character as fucked-up as Daku is pulling the strings. That's why we need to drop out of sight for a while to re-group.'

'But we can't try to hide three boats and eighteen crew,' Bree calmly pointed out.

I differed. 'I think maybe we can. If we head north shortly, we can spend a night or two at Burrum Heads. It's a small village just thirty nautical miles up the coast. Three hours, so long as *Poseidon and Gideon* have enough fuel.'

'*Gideon* is nearly full and *Poseidon* is about 75%.' Dave commented.

Some additional thoughts suddenly popped into mind, so the others waited silently, having become used to my mental processes.

'Okay. Hold the bus a moment. How many bunks on *Poseidon?*'

'Around eight, I think, including the master stateroom,' Dave said.

'Good. We have ten or twelve here on *Firebird*, so that means we can accommodate everyone on just two boats if some girls don't mind bunking together in the few double berths. So how about we call a yacht broker in Hervey Bay and drop *Gideon* off with him to sell on consignment. We were going to have to sell it sooner or later, so doing it sooner will make us more mobile and just a little less conspicuous.'

Our business brain, Bree, spoke up. 'We don't have official title to it, Harry. We can't sell it without officially owning it.'

I looked at Corrine, who nodded. 'No real problem with that. I'll take care of it. Do we have any personal information on Warren and Millie?'

Dave piped up, 'There were a bunch of papers in a drawer when I was searching the whole boat the other day. Looks like Millie didn't bother with any of them either when she bailed, I didn't stop to look closely, but they might have what info you need.'

She waved him away. 'Go get 'em, big boy. I've got work to do.'

I looked around the small group. 'Are we all happy to proceed like this for now? We can start some detailed planning about the Daku problem when we get all the girls more settled, and are somewhere other than where Daku thinks we are.'

While Dave went on his paper hunt, I said to Sandy and Bree. 'We need to strip *Gideon* of all food and drink, Taylor and her gear, and any stuff left from Warren and Millie. Just the basic boat stuff can stay there. Would you mind starting on that?'

'Sure, but where will we put Taylor?'

'How about in the forward port cabin with Mary for now? They seem friendly enough and Taylor deserves her own bunk. I'll have a briefing with everyone shortly, then we'll have to get going. I'll call a broker in Hervey Bay to line this up first.'

While they went to move Taylor and clean out the boat, I went on-line and looked up a likely-sounding broker.

'*Hervey Bay Yacht Sales, Jarrod speaking. How can I help you?*'

'Gidday Jarrod, my name's Dave Robson and I've recently bought a forty-foot cruiser from a deceased estate. The fella was a mate of mine so it was sort of a favour for his widow, but the wife and I have decided we don't want to keep it after all, so we want to put it on the market. Can you help us out?'

'*Yeah, be happy to, Dave. Where's the boat and when can I take a look at it?*'

I gave an embarrassed-sounding chuckle. 'This is all happening a bit sudden, I'm afraid. We've been invited to go cruising with a friend, but he's suddenly decided he wants to go today, so if I could bring the boat to you in the next hour or two, that'd really solve a problem for us. Is that alright with you?'

'*Ahh… sure, Dave. No problem at all. I'll just need the Bill of Sale, do an inventory then get you to sign some papers.*'

'That's terrific, thanks Jarrod. Once it's in your hands there's no real urgency about when you sell it.'

'*No problem, Dave. It's a popular size, so if it's in good nick and you set an attractive price, it should move quickly. Anyway, give me a call on VHF channel 73 when you get to the harbour entrance, and I'll direct you to a temporary berth.*'

'Fantastic, thanks Jarrod. See you soon.'

Alex raised his eyebrows at me. 'No point leaving your name for Daku to follow, eh?'

I grinned, 'That's the idea. Dave can handle this deal.'

Taylor soon appeared, looking a bit sleepy, but with a bag in hand.

'Sorry to kick you out of home,' I said, 'but we've decided to cut-down the fleet by selling *Gideon*.'

She shrugged, 'That's not a big problem for me, Harry. Even though it's been my home and is a great boat, there really are too many bad memories, even with the Collings gone. Sandy said I could bunk in with Mary. Is that right?'

'Yeah. It's the forward cabin in the left side hull, just forward of the laundry and workshop. You have your own bathroom as well.

I think I saw Mary a few minutes ago… ahh, here she is.'

Mary came in from the cockpit, laughing delightedly at the wriggling antics of a little furry, black bundle of arms and legs she was trying to hold.

She dumped Krazy on the settee and scratched her belly, starting the purr rolling immediately. 'The little devil was on *Poseidon*. We might have to put a bell on her.'

'Thanks Mary. I'm afraid you've scored a cabin-mate for a while. I've had to boot Taylor out of her home, because we're getting rid of *Gideon*. We'll all have to fit on two boats now.'

She smiled. 'Oh, okay. No problem, Harry. There's heaps of room, and you're very welcome, Taylor. Follow me and I'll show you where we are.'

'Thanks, Mary.'

I wandered next door to *Gideon* to find a growing pile of groceries and other foodstuffs stacked in the cockpit awaiting transfer. Dave had already dug out some personal papers belonging to the Collings and passed them to Corrine who had started drafting up an official-looking Bill of Sale in Millie's name.

'Have a look at this, Harry,' Dave said, holding out a heavy fabric shopping bag.

I peered in to see stacks of money nearly filling the bag. 'That's looks nice. Where was it?'

'Up the back of a locker right up in the bow. It must have been their fun money, and Millie forgot about it in her rush to bail out. There's something like $250 thousand. Maybe a lot more.'

I grinned. 'I think I made the rash comment to Taylor the other day that there wouldn't be any loot from this gig to share around, but with the bag of cash from last night, plus this and whatever Turner might have had stashed away in bank accounts, there could be a nice little earn after all.'

He grinned happily. 'I'm sure we'll find something good to do with it.'

I left them to it and went further across to *Poseidon* where sleepy girls in various stages of undress were wandering around and chatting about last night. Most were in the aft saloon, and brightened up when I walked in to a chorus of, 'Good morning Harry,' followed by a round of laughter. The girls were happy!

'Good morning, ladies. We have some plans to briefly discuss with you, so could you come over to *Firebird* as soon as you can? And wake up anybody still in bed, please. Oh, and on the way, would you mind helping move all that stuff in the cockpit of *Gideon* over to *Firebird?*'

There was a chorus of, 'Okay Harry', so I beat a hasty retreat from the disturbing collection of nubile bare flesh, stopping just to tell Sandy and Bree about the briefing. As the girls assembled, they hadn't bothered dressing too much, and some not dressed at all, although each had collected some gear from the *Gideon* stack on the way.

When they were all gathered in the cockpit, I stood in the saloon doorway. 'Although yesterday's event and last night's operation removed two of our major problems, we have another issue to deal with in the next few days, in the form of an upset and psychotic Japanese gentleman who has come to Australia to try to inflict some hurt on my me and my crew. I know this doesn't involve any of you directly, but as you are here and under our protection, until this character is defused one way or the other, he remains a common problem.

On top of that, there is the much larger problem of thirty-nine other boats out there somewhere, with girls just like you on them. We plan to recover them all as quickly as possible, and I think you can all appreciate the urgency of that.'

There were a lot of nods and grim looks on their young faces.

'Therefore, until we get things sorted out, we're going to change location immediately, and are getting rid of the smaller boat, *Gideon*. There was only Taylor camped aboard, and she's on this boat now, so are the rest of you comfortable where you are?'

There was another chorus of agreement, as those on *Poseidon* had already spread out to suit themselves and with Gary gone, there was the spare master cabin as well. 'Lovely, thank you. With the main bad guys now out of the picture, there's no need to wear collars for show any more, or ever again, for that matter.'

That last comment stirred a loud cheer from the girls, which somehow made my eyes go itchy for a few moments.

'Therefore, please leave any collars you still have, or find, on the chart table on this boat. As they still contain an explosive charge, they are potentially lethal. As I've already mentioned, you're all free to do as you want, but with the threat of this Japanese fella hanging over us, we'd appreciate you staying with us for a few more days, or until we get this latest mess sorted out. Then we'll work out a plan to retrieve the others and look after everyone. I have promised that ultimately we would see everyone settled safely where you want to be, and I meant it!'

I looked around for any objections, since what I diplomatically didn't say was that we really couldn't allow any of them to go roaming free to tell their story to the media. Yet! Fortunately, there weren't any wanting to do an immediate runner, so we didn't have to come the heavies with any rebels.

'When we move on, *Poseidon's* new skipper will be Dave, but he'll sleep aboard *Firebird* each night, as we'll always travel together and raft-up at night. Any boat-related problems, please see him. Any other problems you have, personal or otherwise, let Sandy or me know. We'll be leaving here shortly, stopping at Hervey Bay Marina to drop off *Gideon*, then pushing on to park at Burrum Heads for a day or two. We'll do some shopping and more planning from there. When we're travelling, it doesn't matter which boat you're on, but bear in mind that we'd prefer not to have to stop to make any transfers under way. That's it for now, thanks for your co-operation and we'll talk more tonight and tomorrow.'

The group broke up, with eight girls either drifting back toward *Poseidon,* or ratting around in *Firebird's* galley for breakfast. I had a quick word to Bree about perhaps doing mass catering for the main meals. She agreed.

My next job was to take Sally and Kim aside.

'Sorry I've been a bit busy over the last couple of days to talk much business, but I need to know what you guys want to do. We could have a real problem with this Japanese gentleman and two of his men who are chasing us because of a dispute from our last op. He's a genuine psychopath and an ex-member of a Yakuza gang. I'm confident we can sort him out, but we need to deal with him on our terms, not his. We can't release all these girls to roam the country – they haven't got anywhere to go, don't have any money, and precious few clothes, but we can sort that out later. However, as I said earlier, we can't risk them talking to the media and spreading their story until we rescue the others, or we'll lose them for good!'

'Are there really another thirty-nine girls out there? In slavery?' Kim asked, still looking very upset at the thought.

'Yes. That is, there are thirty-nine boats, and most should only have one girl aboard. We'll know more when we have the time to go through Turner's paperwork.'

The sisters looked at each other with that silent communion thing that so many close twins have.

'Perhaps we can help in some way. I know we told you after you rescued us from Warren's attentions, that we worked in a law firm. We do, but in fact we're both lawyers. Very new and junior I'm afraid, but unless you prefer to use your own, we'd be happy to help with whatever legal issues might be involved. Plus, we can extend our holidays a bit longer if work is going to be involved. I've already spoken to the boss. He's our father.'

I laughed, 'That must be fun. Working in the pressure cooker of a law office with Dad as the boss.'

Kim smiled, 'It's not as bad as you might think. The practice is fairly small, so it's very laid back, and we're getting a good grounding in law at an easy pace. So, that's our position. We're happy to stay if you want, or go if you don't, but we would like to help if we can.

Plus, the side benefits here are very attractive.'

I laughed with them, 'Deal. Maybe you could go over Turner's papers to see what you can find about who he sold girls to, and make a list. Mary can show you where the papers are.'

They eagerly went to find her, the light of the challenge in their eyes. I felt reassured to know they were lawyers and could possibly be a real help in sorting out our rescuee's problems.

With *Gideon* double-checked for any more loot and cleared out of everything except basic boat gear, Alex and Dave had already readied both power boats for departure, so I let them lead the way, and played with sail settings to take advantage of the brisk southerly breeze to stay with them.

With a distance of only 15 miles to run to the Hervey Bay Marina, it was just over an hour until we were holding position off the breakwater, and I heard Dave calling Jarred on the VHF. He was told to bring *Gideon* into the enclosed harbour, where he'd be met by a bloke in a workboat who'd show him the way to the berth. He had Corrine aboard to help with lines, and she had the freshly prepared, back-dated paperwork ready, as well as an inventory list of all the small, boat-related items, like fenders, lines, anchors, fire-extinguishers, etc.

I'd dropped sails and just used the motors to hold position close to the side of the breakwater arm, with Alex keeping *Poseidon* hovering nearby.

Dave was nearly an hour before he called on the VHF radio for a pickup. Sandy ran in to get them, and they reported that all was well, with Jarred accepting the documentation and the cover story without question. With Dave's approval, he was going to list the boat at $150,000 and was confident that at that price, he could move it quite quickly, since he considered *Gideon* to be in excellent condition and even had a couple of prospective customers on his books waiting for such a boat. As soon as Dave and Alex had swapped boats, we motored away from the marina for a couple of miles, before hoisting sail and cracking on for the little fishing village of Burrum Heads. It was a short run of twenty miles, so by 16:30 we were dropping anchor off a sandy beach on the deserted north side of the main anchorage, a good mile from a boat ramp giving access to the small shopping centre. I saw Bree running around checking supplies on both boats as well as checking with each girl, with the list in her notebook getting longer by the minute.

There were quite a few other boats moored in this peaceful and pretty estuary, but over on the north shore, we were by ourselves and as anonymous as an 83-foot red-hulled catamaran could be with a 65-foot motor cruiser rafted up beside it.

'Are we staying here tomorrow?' Bree asked, once the arrival activity had settled.

'Yes, I think so. Plenty of time for shopping in the morning,' I added.

She grinned back, 'I think your idea of centralised cooking and eating will be the best. I'll use the fridges and freezers on *Poseidon* for the extra food, but it'll be much easier to cook in just one place.'

'Good oh,' I replied, 'just make sure you've got plenty of helpers.'

'No problem there. They all want to help with something. No one is slacking off and they all appreciated your talk this morning. It seems to have eased a lot of concerns.'

'That's good to hear. So, no one has said they would like to bail out anytime soon?'

'Nope. Not one. They realise they've got nowhere to go and no money to get there, so are more than happy staying here being fed, looked after and not molested. I hope you're working on a plan to do something to help them all when this is over.'

'Yeah. I'm definitely working on it.' Which was technically correct, although I didn't explain that I hadn't got very far with it. Bree knew me too well by now as she gave me a tight grin, a brief hug for encouragement and continued list-making.

I was in the cockpit, mulling things over and idly scratching Jasper's head, when Sally and Kim climbed over the rail from *Poseidon*, lugging a bulging briefcase and a large boxy bag like pilots and lawyers love to drag around.

'Find some interesting stuff?' I asked.

'Yeah. It looks like all the information we need will be in the stuff in the briefcase, so were going to go through it on the inside dining table. But jammed up the back of a locker in Turner's cabin was his stash.'

Kim opened the boxy case, unfolded the top leaves and showed me that it was nearly full of cash. Some fifties, but mostly hundreds going by a quick look, but still a lot of money.

'That's nice,' I commented, digging down amongst the layers. 'Turner obviously didn't believe in leaving too many paper trails with bank accounts. This will be the skimmed takings from his girl sales, I reckon. I'm working on an idea to put all this loot to very good use. Thanks ladies, we'll count it later.'

After taking the bag down to our cabin and stowing it safely with the other cash from the Collings and Yanos, I took Jasper and Krazy cat over to the beach for a good romp for them and a long, quiet think for me.

It was a very tired and subdued crowd around the dining tables that night, due to the late-night raid and the trip north, so yawns were frequent, and girls started drifting off shortly after the clean-up was finished. Bree loved having so many willing hands to help with all the domestic chores. Krazy cat also loved having the choice of so many new humans who were anxious for the soothing comfort of a soft, purring cat. Not that Jasper wasn't immune to all the extra cuddles available, once all the new girls got over his size and the length of his fangs, they discovered that he was just a big pussy cat of similar temperament to Krazy. With people he liked that is, and he did seem to like all the girls.

CHAPTER 27

Next morning, I was up early, fully refreshed and thinking clearly for a change. Tiredness slows the thought process and makes everything seem worse than it really is. It also masks the ideas which lead to good solutions for bad problems.

Everyone must have slept well, as two of Bree's sous chefs started an early breakfast, and the smells of bacon and sausages called to the rest of the crew like an open packet of hot chips to a flock of seagulls.

With eighteen bellies full and clean-up done, Bree organised Alex and Dave with both dinghies, to head across the broad estuary to the boat ramp close to the supermarket. It was a long run in the dinghies, but I wanted to keep as low a profile as possible. Two of the rescued girls, Jay and Teri off *Poseidon* wanted to go with them to help, as well as go ashore for once. I said yes, since I thought that two guys and three girls weren't too many to be obvious, and with the length of Bree's shopping list, their help would be needed.

Chiaki and Fumiko were quite happy to stay on board, but as we were anchored close to the beach, most of the other girls jumped into the shallow water and went ashore. I kept an eye on them, with some splashing about in the water, while others lay on the sand, or went for a run along the beach.

At the west end of the beach there was a small settlement, some six hundred metres away, with just thirty-odd houses, some of which looked permanently lived in, and a public boat-ramp, but there were very few people in sight and no one showed any interest in our activities.

The shopping expedition took well over an hour, and they returned heavily laden, motoring slowly to keep from splashing the goodies.

'Luckily the check-out chick was used to boaties stocking up big,' Bree laughed, as an endless stream of bags and boxes came aboard, the bottoms of cartons being carefully inspected for cockroach eggs before being allowed into Bree's pristine galley and pantry. The beer and wine stocks had taken a big hit since the girls were rescued, since nothing alcoholic was on Turner's shopping list for his captives.

I browsed the internet and placed a call to the Bundaberg Port Marina, where they obligingly rented us two adjacent berths for a week. *Firebird's* length and beam limited us to an outside berth, but I was used to that and very happy that they were able to accommodate two big boats at such short notice.

As the run up to Port Bundaberg was only three hours, we stayed where we were until after lunch, serving plates of sandwiches and drinks on the stern platforms for the girls messing about on the beach, who waded out when they felt hungry. Naturally, after their previous life of incarceration and abuse, this was the ultimate in luxury holidays for them and it was uplifting to hear their happy calls and laughter. I soon got the feeling that when the time came for all the girls to be re-located, we might have serious trouble convincing some of them to leave.

If it weren't for the spectre of Daku and his mates hovering in the background, I'd probably relax a lot more as well. Even Chiaki and Fumiko joined in the laughter and were enjoying themselves.

However, by 14:00, the beach set were tired, sunburnt, and more than happy to come aboard and to carefully hose off before ascending to the cockpit. I shared Bree's aversion to sand aboard, where it ultimately finds its way into every crook and nanny. I also didn't mind the parade of naked, and near-naked bodies hosing off and towelling dry in the cockpit. It seemed odd to me that despite their experiences, most of the girls were quite comfortable being naked most of the day, possibly because now it was their choice.

My normal bodily reaction to their display was the cause of much hilarity, and while I was willing to stand my ground with two or even three girls, eight or nine was too much, so as soon as all were aboard, I took my shattered dignity to the helm station to set about raising the anchor. Sandy didn't help by joining in the laughter at my condition, and all girls chose to stay on *Firebird* for the sailing run up the coast, so Corrine went with Dave as crew on *Poseidon*.

'We might have to help de-tune that condition Harry seems to have got himself in,' Kim cheekily said to Sandy, who agreed it might be an excellent idea, but it would be best if they waited until I'd navigated to Burnett Heads.

All three smirked at me, then went to change.

With *Poseidon* in front, I stayed with electric power until we'd cleared the shallow, twisting channels at the mouth of the inlet and had turned north. Then the electrics were switched off and sail power took over, the regenerative, automatic prop system rapidly pouring charge back into the battery banks.

The approach to Bundaberg Port Marina was very safe and easy as the river entrance was wide and deep, kept in shape by a training wall on the north side of the river, extending nearly one kilometre out to sea. A call to the marina on VHF channel 81 produced a helpful set of instructions of where we were to go, and several friendly staff were there to take lines and position *Firebird* so we didn't get in the way of anyone else.

Our length and large beam meant we were on the outside of a jetty arm where a cross-piece made a T-shape. Being of more normal proportions, *Poseidon* was allocated the adjacent slot berth just inshore of our stern, and as the pontoon jetties were floating, there was no need to adjust lines for the tide.

On shore, a bar, restaurant and take-away looked after the food and drink needs, while the large, multi-machine laundry was the first item the girls wanted to use. A shuttle bus was available to take everybody to the city, some fifteen kilometres upstream by road. Sandy told me the girls were looking forward to visiting a proper city for the first time in many years for some of them.

'There's a couple of somethings I wanted to discuss with you,' I said to Sandy, as we showered and changed for the walk to the restaurant and the evening meal. Although she enjoyed cooking, Bree was delighted to have some time out of the galley, as the demands of feeding eighteen mouths was a bit different to the usual four when we were in home port.

With an inquiring expression, Sandy sat on the bed, looking very fetching wearing nothing at all, so I dragged my attention and gaze two stations north and said, 'Sally and Kim have been going through Turner's papers, so they might as well do the same with all the stuff we scored from Korey's room. The other thing was that the cash we recovered from Korey and Turner could be split up between all the rescue girls. They've got nothing of their own, so some cash will let them buy clothes and other girly stuff. Maybe there will be enough to set each up with a starter nest-egg.'

She considered my words. 'Good thinking, my darling man, and we should do just that. But two questions. What about the thirty-nine plus girls still to be tracked down? And just what are we going to do with all these girls when we recover them? There are seven here now, not counting Chiaki and Fumiko who will go home soon, but then maybe thirty-nine more if we track down everyone. Maybe we can dump some of them back into society if they think they could trust their families which is unlikely from what we've heard so far, but most haven't got a clue how to get a legal job and set themselves up. Many have been in this slavery bullshit since their early to mid-teens.'

I nodded seriously, 'That's one of the main problems I've been turning over in my mind. But let's see how much money we've seized.'

I dragged the various bags and cases out of the secure locker built into the bedhead, keeping Korey's papers to one side for Sally and Kim to go through later. We then separated Turner's money from Korey's.

'How about this for an idea.' I said, 'We could say that Turner's stash was made up of income from the sale of all the girls.'

Sandy nodded.

'Therefore, it could be said that it belongs to all the rescued girls.'

She nodded again.

'So, we could set that aside to be split up at a later date when we see how many we eventually recover.'

'Okay. That's fair.'

'Now. Korey's money came mostly from the four hunters, with some perhaps from Turner for services rendered or other sources. That money has little to do with the thirty-nine girls we've yet to find, so could be split with the seven we have here.'

She nodded again, 'Sounds reasonable, but let's see what we've actually got. We might have to tip some in ourselves.'

'Yeah. I was thinking that too. No problem doing that with the gem auctions still bringing in so much.'

She giggled. 'It's tough not having to worry about slinging a big lump of cash at some homeless girls.'

I set Turner's heavy bag aside, and dragged Korey's heavy bag onto the bed. It was packed to the top with bundled banknotes and took some digging to get them out. We ended up with a pile of cash, but someone, maybe Korey, had been methodical by banding the $100 notes into packs of $10K each. As I'd found out in the past, $10K was a surprisingly slim bundle when laid flat, but was still worth $10K!

Without counting every note, we soon ended up with one hundred and thirty-five packs, for a total of $1.35 mil Aussie dollars.

That was slightly unexpected and Sandy's comment was, 'Well, fuck me.'

I glanced distractedly at her nakedness, 'Later dearest, later.'

'Okay. What's in Turner's bag?' she demanded, so we played Scrooge McDuck and roughly shovelled the first stack of pretty green plastic aside and dragged the other very heavy bag on the bed.

That proved to have more of the same, to the tune of one hundred and fifteen packs for a total of $1.15 mil Aussie dollars. However, Turner's bag had some ballast in the bottom, consisting of four, 1 kilo gold bars issued by the Perth Mint, which guaranteed 999.9 purity and could be sold for around $71,000 each. That raised the total of Turner's stash to $1.4364 million.

'That's a hell of a lot more than what Mary was writing up in his ledger when she did his bookwork. I heard her say that he was barely breaking even on girl sales and should increase his prices.'

Sandy was hastily scribbling in a memo pad. 'Korey's stash, divided amongst the seven girls here comes to nearly $193K each girl. That's a goodly piece of shopping change.'

She scribbled some more. 'And the thirty-nine, if we get them, would get $36.83K each. Which is a lot less, but still better than a poke in the eye with the proverbial.'

'Hell, yes. Anyway, let's pack this stuff away. I don't think we should announce this just yet. We can if asked, but I don't think any of those girls are ready to properly handle nearly $200K in cash. We'll need to set something up legally, like trust funds perhaps, using Sally and Kim and their dad's firm. Getting some business tossed their way might be a way to include them in the profit sharing.'

Sandy smiled and suggested, 'Or maybe we just pool the lot and use it to assist the rehabilitation of all of them.'

'Even better thinking dear lady. But for now, let's just go have a good feed and relax.'

It was good we'd booked the restaurant, since eighteen people in one unexpected hit would have been a challenge for the chef, but the staff good-naturedly shoved several tables together and with the promise of some good income for a few nights at least, proceeded to wine and dine us very well. The food was excellent and the service just as good. It was therefore a bunch of very pissed possums who steered an unsteady course back down the Marina jetty late that night.

The promised relief mission by Sally and Kim didn't happen that night, as they had trouble finding their beds, let alone anything smaller. But it did happen next morning, severely delaying our appearance at breakfast.

I was enjoying a post-breakfast mug of tea, seated up on the port bow, when I heard the deep-throated rumble of several large, twin-cylinder motorcycles. A deep chill ran down my spine, as I had an immediate flashback to a previous operation at Tin Can Bay when we were being chased by several gangs of bikies. We had survived that chase at great cost to all involved, especially the chasers, although the menacing sound on this quiet morning brought back a host of very unpleasant memories. Especially when the bikes in question slowed to turn in at the marina gates. There were four of them, the riders all wearing colours on their greasy vests, although I was too far away to make out the branding.

They stopped briefly at the end of the entry road where it narrowed down to a walkway leading onto the first jetty, and looked carefully around. I might have been imagining it, but they seemed to pause their scan to look carefully at the red decks of *Firebird* at the far end of the jetty. With the marina manager and the receptionist standing outside the office looking concerned, they then burbled slowly out of the quiet driveway, turned into the main road and roared away.

I turned to see Corrine, Sandy, Alex and Dave standing close-by.

'Recon?' Corrine asked.

I nodded, 'Yeah. Reckon so. With Daku's links to organised crime in Australia, it's natural he'd use bikies to do the running around looking for us. It wouldn't take long for a few bikie gangs to cover every marina and anchorage on this whole coast, especially when he already knew the general area where we'd be.'

'It's a shame we've got to bugger off so soon. This is a really nice place,' Dave commented.

'Hang on. We're not going just yet,' I countered. 'I think we're pretty secure here in a crowded marina. He won't risk an attack outright with so many people around, so there's a good chance he'll talk first. It's me he wants most of all.'

'You sure about this, Harry?' Corrine queried.

'Reasonably so. We stay, but let's keep a good lookout. Maybe even a night watch, just in case he tries a sneaky night attack.'

We split up, everyone going to do their own stuff, while the girls started planning domestic chores like more clothes washing. Dave, Alex and I had already washed both boats down with fresh water from the marina, and topped the tanks, so it was later that morning when Sandy and Bree loaded up the marina trolley cart with loads of sheets and headed for the laundry. We had a washing machine aboard *Firebird*, but it was too much to ask it to cope with the demands of this large crew.

Yet another benefit of staying at a marina for a few days or so.

CHAPTER 28

PORT BUNDABERG

Sometime later, I was kicked back in the cockpit, yarning with Alex, when one of the marina staff walked down, holding a folded piece of paper.

'Mr Stevens?' he politely asked. 'A chap left this at reception for you.'

I took it from him, thanking him for his kindness, and opened it out.

An icy feeling of dread gripped me as I read the hastily scrawled words.

'I HAVE WASHING WOMEN. SOUTH HEAD PARKLANDS IN ONE HOUR. NO POLICE OR WOMEN DIE. YOU SILLY MAN.'

The wording left no doubt as to who wrote the words, so I showed it to Alex who jumped to his feet, fists balled in rage, staring up the marina toward the laundry, as if Bree and Sandy would miraculously appear, laughing at a shared joke as usual.

As often had happened in the past, the lead-up to combat was the worst, but once the enemy had shown his hand, my brain functioned calmly and much more smoothly.

'Cool it, big brother,' I said, placing one hand on his massive arm, before calling out for Dave and Corrine to join us. They were in their midships cabin, putting new sheets on their bed. Dave swore when he read the note, but Corrine just nodded, and I knew from experience that she functioned the same as I did in the face of an attack.

Save all your emotions and strength for planning how to turn a disadvantage into an opportunity.

'Shit, Harry. That prick must have been really close to get here so quickly.'

'Yeah. Probably based himself at Bundaberg as a central spot, and we conveniently parked right on his doorstep. He must be laughing fit to bust at my stupidity!'

Corrine went straight to the chart table and called up Google Earth, quickly locating South Head Parklands, which looked to be a broad, 'L-shaped' expanse of grass, with a small, fan-shaped parking area in the angle. The parking lot was bordered on the south side by a grove of trees, then there were more open grass areas, with the ocean to the east. The entrance came off a sharp bend in the road, on the south-west side, with houses opposite.

There were the usual toilets and shelters with BBQs for the obligatory Sunday family picnics in the park, but being midweek, it would hopefully be deserted.

I led off with my hastily-contrived plan, Corrine refined it, and Alex and Dave tossed in their thoughts. I found Reggie, Hanh, Jasper, Chiaki and Fumiko, showed them the note, and told them what was happening. Via Hanh's translations, Chiaki was terribly upset at her brother's actions and said that he had always been impulsive and violent, and that she totally condemned his actions. She added that her grandfather would be very angry to hear of the kidnapping.

I said to Reggie, 'You're in charge here while we're gone. Let the others know what we're doing, but they must all stay here. No argument! Don't let anyone leave the boat for any reason. We need to know that you're all safe in one place, just in case this is a two-pronged attack with the bikies involved. Get your fully-loaded service pistol and keep it on you, but out of sight. Perhaps bring all the girls onto *Firebird* until we get back.'

She rose to the occasion and nodded soberly, 'Okay Harry. I'll look after things. Just be careful.'

As per our plan, we made some preparations, before I went to the reception office.

'Good morning, Mr Stevens,' the pleasant and helpful young lady said. 'I hope you're all enjoying your stay with us?'

With some difficulty, I pasted a smile on my face, as I checked her name badge, perched nicely on the upper slope of her perky left breast.

'Yes, indeed Petra. Everyone has been very helpful, and we love the restaurant.'

She laughed, 'I know the chef loves having you guys too. It's been a bit quiet lately. Not all our guests eat there regularly.'

'I understand, so we'll keep doing our best to boost the local economy. But there is something you might be able to help me with.'

She raised her eyebrows. 'Of course. Anything is possible.'

'We need to hire or borrow a large car or a van for about an hour. Not a taxi. We won't be going far, but something has come up and we need it in the next twenty minutes or so. I'll be happy to pay whatever is necessary.'

'Let me talk to Laurie, our Manager, and we'll see what we can do.'

If necessary, I'd buy a bloody car if one was for sale, but that would draw too much attention.

Minutes later, she was back, still smiling, a key ring dangling off her finger. 'Laurie is quite happy to let you borrow his own car. It's an older Holden Caprice, but is very roomy. He won't need it until he goes home later this afternoon, if that would fit your plans?'

'That'd be wonderful. We'll look after it.'

'I'm sure you will. Here's the key, and it's the dark blue one just outside. Enjoy.'

'Thanks Petra, and thank Laurie again. I'm greatly obliged.'

'No problem, Mr Stevens. Happy to help.'

I hustled back to the boat with the marina luggage trolley in tow, to find that the girls, in a very subdued mood, had already retrieved all our washing from the laundry, and our party was assembled.

I addressed Hanh. 'Chiaki and Fumiko know what they have to do? They mustn't move until I tell them, no matter what happens.'

'Yes, Harry. They understand and will do exactly what I have told them. Chiaki has never been close to Daku, although family bonds are still strong.'

'Okay. That's good. I'd like to have you there to be sure, but we have too many bodies already.'

'I understand. They're keen to do their job.'

Nobody took any notice as our small group pulled the trolley with an old blanket draped over a lumpy shape up to the car-park. Fortunately, the Caprice was parked out of direct sight of the reception and the office windows, so slipping Jasper into the back seat was the work of moments. While the others climbed aboard, I ran the trolley back to its storage bay at the head of the jetty, then took the driver's seat. Corrine had written down the directions and after only a couple of wrong turns, I stopped briefly in a cross street to the west of the park, then drove on, stopping again near the east end of another cross street, this one on the south side of the park. Three more passengers got out, organised themselves, then strolled slowly away toward the open expanse of grass on the south side of the trees which bordered the parking area.

I turned around to retrace my last couple of turns, so that I was approaching the carpark from the west. I stopped at the entrance, and as I hoped, it was empty, apart from a white Mercedes-Benz Vito panel van parked facing the entrance, its left side adjacent the grove of trees. It was just as well there were no other visitors, as the van was effectively blocking the exit lane.

Standing at the front of the van, leaning back against the bonnet, was the sneering lout we had dubbed 'Sunnies' for his arrogant habit of wearing mirrored sunglasses day and night. Beside him was a larger Asian man. The van doors were closed, so Sandy, Bree and presumably the other thug, must be inside.

I eased the Caprice, with its heavily-tinted windows, forward until the two vehicles were facing each other, ten metres or so apart, before checking the left side rear-view mirror, where I glimpsed, in the distance, a single person walking briskly across the grass over by the north-west side of the park, roughly heading our way. He was swishing at the taller strands of grass with a long walking stick, an aid becoming popular with serious walkers. I turned off the engine and climbed out, leaving the door open and standing behind it.

Daku and his mate glanced around, obviously dismissing the lone man in the distance to the north-west as being too far away to be a threat, then they checked toward town, to the south, where a young couple were slowly strolling across the grass toward the ocean beach, and tossing a Frisbee for their black dog who was having a lovely time running and jumping to catch it. They too, weren't regarded as a threat, but could possibly become witnesses if things became violent, so they returned their full attention to me.

'Who clever now, silly man?' Daku sneered. 'We have someone you want and we want you. We trade, yes? Two for one, good deal.'

I regarded him silently for a while, then stepped around my door, standing out to the side, but still didn't speak.

After a minute of silence, his face contorted and his permanent sneer gave way to naked anger.

'What wrong with you? No can speak? Stupid man lost washerwomen. Maybe we come take more girls. My men and I have plenty good time. You learn not play silly games with Daku. I beat you. You finished now.'

He had become increasingly agitated, leaning forward to emphasise his words, spittle flying with the force of his anger, but still I didn't speak.

'What wrong with you?' He suddenly screamed. 'You think I not hurt women? You cannot defy me, stupid little man.'

'I want to see the ladies,' I said quietly.

His mood changed instantly, making me wonder if he was bi-polar. 'Ah… this better. You speak. Good request. See ladies. Okay. We do.' He raised one hand and snapped his fingers. The sliding door in the side of the van opened and the other goon stepped out, then reached back in to drag Bree and Sandy out.

Their wrists were taped together, with a piece of tape across their mouths as a gag.

Daku made a theatrical gesture. 'There. You see? They unhurt for now. So, you come here, maybe I let them go.'

I took one slow pace forward, concentrating their attention on my movement. 'What if I don't want to go with you?' I asked. 'I don't like you at all, and I don't like your men either. They look dirty and probably smell.'

'What this you say?' he said, puzzled by my remarks. 'You not come – I hurt washer-women badly. Then my men hurt them too. Many times. We show your women what real men be like.'

He made an obscene gesture with his fisted arm, which was apparently intended to reduce me to quivering acquiescence, but he lacked the poise to carry it off.

I laughed, 'You wouldn't know a real man if he bit you on the arse. Which is all that ape beside you is good for. And the same goes for that other piece of shit holding the ladies. The three of you are an insult to real men everywhere.'

He spluttered, 'You… you stupid man! You dare insult me and my men, while we have your women? You are fool!'

I smiled and inclined my head, 'For once we agree on something, as indeed I am at times. But in this particular instance, I'm not the one with a gun pointed at the head of his man holding my women.'

Daku looked puzzled again as he translated my words. 'What you say? This bullshit stuff. You no have gun on my man!'

'Quite right, my dear little dickhead, I don't. But the young lady standing behind your man does. And she's a lot better with it than I am.'

Daku paused again to sort that little lot out, then spun around to his left, to see Corrine standing right behind the goon at the side door, a PMR-30 pistol, with a long suppressor attached, almost touching the back of his head. Dave and Jasper were just out to the side, Jasper's lips drawn back in a ferocious snarl exposing his intimidating fangs, while a deep rumbling growl reinforced the shift of power.

Both goons must have had trouble understanding me, as they were slow to react, but when they did, the one by the side door let the girls go and tried to lash out at Corrine, who just stepped back smartly, dropped her arm and shot him in the foot. It was a good shot, naturally, so to prove it wasn't a fluke, she shot him in the other one as well.

He had considerable trouble standing after that, and sagged to the ground with a howl of pain, but then the other goon had a belated attack of the braves, and started to charge around the front of the van to get to her, but Jasper was ready for that and with one bound followed by a flying leap, hit him in the chest, his jaws clamped firmly around his thick neck.

'Hold only, boy,' I called as the terrified man fell hard on his back making gurgling sounds, Jasper attached like a limpet, all four sets of claws dug in hard, doing his infamous impression of the octopus-like creature in the first Alien movie.

Daku froze momentarily, then spun back to his right to run away, only to slam rather comically into the fleshy brick wall of Alex's chest. A pair of arms, thicker than most people's legs, clamped around the smaller man's body, trapping his arms. Then Alex started squeezing slowly.

I distinctly heard three ribs pop, before I said quietly, 'That should do for the moment, thanks Alex. Best leave enough breath in him so we can have a brief chat with the stupid little turdburger.'

Alex relaxed the pressure enough to turn him to face me, then squeezed again. Daku looked to be on the verge of panic, when I said, 'I was actually prepared to talk sensibly with you, Daku, before you went and made some very nasty threats directed at my ladies. I find that to be quite unacceptable. For that, you will pay. Big time.'

He gasped for air, until at my nod, Alex relaxed the pressure some more.

'But you must trade! You must pay for insults. You make me look stupid.'

I smiled, 'No. Once again, you have made yourself look stupid by being so arrogant and having idiots as crew. Everything has been your fault. Down at Heard Island, at Port Davey, and now here. Your grandfather is extremely unhappy with what you've done so far. After this latest fuck-up, you'll be in serious trouble.'

'What you know of my grandfather? You know nothing! You still silly man.'

'Oh, Raijin and I have had a very interesting talk. He sounded like a good man.'

'This more bullshit! He not speak with Gaigin. He man of honour.'

'Yes, he is. I agree entirely. Which is why he thinks you have no honour and has kicked you out of the family.'

He spluttered again, 'How you know this? More bullshit.'

'Oh, no, you silly little dickhead. He told me himself. You are history. You couldn't even get a kidnapping right. Raijin will be terribly disappointed in you. But I will at least bring a ray of sunshine into his life when I return his grand-daughter, your sister that is, and her friend to his family.'

'What you talk of now? What this talk about my sister?'

'Oh, dear. You didn't even know your sister and her friend had been kidnapped by that piece of garbage partner of yours, Korey Yanos, to be sold into sex-slavery? You remember Korey Yanos, don't you? He's the one you sold all those explosive collars to. I'll bet you didn't know that those collars you liked so much, had been fastened around the pretty little necks of your sister and her friend. All ready to go bang if they moved out of range of the transmitter. When I tell him, Raijin will be even more upset with you, if that's humanly possible.'

Daku looked stricken. 'How you know all this? Why you say this? It not true.'

I forced a laugh. 'Oh, but it is. Perhaps you should hear it from the little lady herself? Unfortunately, I don't think she likes you very much, but don't worry, Perhaps Alex will protect you.'

I stepped back and opened the rear door, letting Chiaki and Fumiko step out, Chiaki glaring at her hapless brother and unleashing a screaming torrent of Japanese. I had no hope of understanding a single word, but by the look of dismay, then horror on his face, I guessed she was saying a heap of stuff he didn't want to hear.

When her tirade finally wound down, I bowed them back into the car and closed the door. By then, Dave and Corrine had bound and gagged the bloke with the perforated feet, and wrapped gaffer tape roughly around his wounds, boots and all. They did the same with the one who Jasper was still trying to choke, before I called him off. Between us, we hauled them into the back of the van, then bound and gagged Daku and tossed him roughly on top.

The only evidence of violence was a small amount of blood that had pooled on the blacktop from the bloke with the perforated feet, but a bottle of water soon dispersed that well enough.

As there were no outraged neighbours jumping up and down, or hanging out of windows, I counted it as a successful operation. The ladies were suitably grateful and assured us they hadn't been hurt.

'Okay. Time we returned Laurie's car and I make a phone call or two.'

Fifteen minutes later, Laurie's Caprice had been returned, with thanks, its fuel tank filled. Jasper had been uneventfully transported back aboard, and Sandy and Bree had been tearfully welcomed back by the crew.

We parked the van across the road from the marina in the boat storage area, with the three inept kidnappers totally immobilised in the back, a tarpaulin shielding them from casual sight.

A well-earned beer in hand, I parked at the chart table, looked up a number, then placed the call. After giving my name to several intermediaries in turn, I finally reached the main man.

'Good afternoon, Mr Stevens. It is a pleasure to hear from you. Do you have news for me?'

'I do, Tanaka-san. Both good and bad, I'm afraid.'

'Ahhh… then in this case, shall we have the good news first? I find that usually softens the impact of the bad, would you agree?'

'But of course, Tanaka-san. A wise choice. The good news is that I have recovered your grand-daughter and her friend. They are well, are here with me now, and most anxious to speak with you.'

'Ahhh… Mr Stevens. You make an old man's heart much lighter. This is truly wonderful news!'

'One moment, sir.'

I passed the phone to Chiaki, who cried when she spoke, but then her tone hardened and her facial expression grew stern as she continued with what I presumed was her side of the bad news part of my report. Soon after, she ran out of words and passed the phone back to me, her cheeks still wet with happy tears.

'Please understand that my family and I will always be indebted to you, Mr Stevens, for this great service to us and to Fumiko's family as well. They are also a very influential family in Japan, on close personal terms with our Prime Minister.'

'That is very good to hear, Tanaka-san. As it happens, I too am acquainted with His Excellency, Ito-san. Forgive me if I do not use the correct form of address, but I think Shinzo will excuse me that.'

'I understand, Mr Stevens. I have heard about your medal presentation for services to Japan, and hasten to add that the organisation of which I am a part, was not a supporter of the failed coup. We appreciate stability for our various business interests, and your efforts greatly assisted with that. But to return to matters at hand, may I assume that you have detained my grandson and his two colleagues?'

'That is so, Tanaka-san. Regretfully, despite my official standing, I am not in a position to do so for any great length of time. What are your wishes in this matter?'

'If you are able to detain them for another three or four hours, I shall have some associates call by to relieve you of the burden.'

'That will not be a problem, sir, and I can tell you that they are already in the transport they used to abduct my two ladies, so that should make their collection easier. How shall I know your associates when they arrive?'

He chuckled, 'Oh, there will not be any problem with identification, Mr Stevens. Will you be on your boat at 7 pm your time?'

'We will be in the marina restaurant by then. I have a large crew to feed. But I also must ask. Is it your intention that Chiaki and Fumiko remain with us, or are they to go with your associates? Naturally, they are very welcome to stay, as they have proved to be most charming and delightful company.'

'My apologies. My associates will also take charge of the two young ladies and look after them while I make arrangements for their speedy return home.'

'Ah, I see. In that case, I shall have them prepared for travel.'

'I understand. Your care and kind treatment of the young ladies brings great honour upon you. We shall speak again soon. Ja ne, Mr Stevens.'

'Ja ne, Tanaka-san.'

By 18:30, we three guys and our fifteen-strong female football team were wandering up the jetty toward the restaurant, drawing the usual array of curious, lustful and some frankly envious glances from fellow boaties. Given their looks, it must have seemed more like a model's convention in an unusual setting.

Our now usual long table was ready and we were greeted by several other boaties we'd become friendly with.

At 19:00 on the dot, the sound of two, large and noisy twin-cylinder motorcycles could be heard approaching the marina at speed. The dining room fell silent as they turned into the access road, stopped right outside and killed their engines in perfect unison. One minute later, heavy boots sounded on the floorboards outside the door, and two large bikies in their full uniform of jeans, T-shirt and leather vest with colours, strode inside, then separated to take up position either side of the door, arms folded and glowering expressions on their hard faces.

The manager and the waitresses looked stricken with panic, and were on the verge of calling the police, when a tall, slim Asian gentleman, immaculately-dressed in what looked like a dark-grey Armani suit, with white shirt and subdued blue tie, stepped quietly between the bikies, looked around, bowed to the manager, then approached our table.

He delivered a deep bow to Chiaki and Fumiko, then asked, 'Commander Stevens, please?'

I stood, then walked around to meet him, holding my hand out.

He bowed first, then shook my hand enthusiastically. 'Ah, Commander. I am Hiroto Sakamoto, and it is my pleasure to have been asked by Tanaka-san to escort Chiaki-chan and Fumiko-chan back to their families. I do hope the appearance of my associates has not caused too much distress, but they are tasked with escorting Daku-san and his associates.'

'I'm very happy to see the young ladies are in such good hands, Sakamoto-san, although Tanaka-san did say that I would readily recognise their escort. Allow me to show you where Daku is located.'

The two girls were already saying their tearful goodbyes to our crew, with hugs and kisses around the table, and after collecting their backpacks from behind the bar, followed us outside. As I passed the bikies, one held out his hand and said, 'Good evening Commander. I'm Jack Perry, Outcasts MC. I hope we didn't interrupt your dinner too much.'

I laughed, 'No, not at all, Jack. I'm just glad to be able to hand these clowns over to you.'

He smiled, 'Our pleasure. Lots of brownie points in this little job for us.'

'Yes. I imagine there will be.'

He spoke again, but quietly. 'I've also been asked by the same very well-connected person, to say that should you require any assistance with your work in the future, our Club and several others in the larger area with whom we associate, are available. That is, of course, so long as your request doesn't interfere with our normal activities.'

He passed over a professional-standard business card with contact numbers on it, and I found it ironic that these could very well have been the guys searching for us in the first place. Or even a couple of years ago when I pinched all their drugs.

But such is the modern world, where irony was the new normal, and strange allegiances were readily made depending solely on what was considered most expedient.

I went to move, then stopped and said, 'Actually, Jack. There may be some help you could provide, but I need to plan it some more. It would involve a lot of riding. May I call you in a day or two?'

He grinned, 'Riding is what we do, Commander. And as I said, helping you scores us even more big brownie points with the big man, so call when you're ready.'

'Thanks, Jack.'

In the carpark was a stretch limousine, sleek, black and comfortable. A driver stood holding the rear door open for the girls, who stopped to deliver me a very formal bow, followed by a very modern hug which made my ribs creak. I didn't know what they said, but the intent was clear. I kissed both on the forehead, hoping I wasn't committing some grave social gaffe, but Hiroto smiled benignly.

When the girls were settled, he said, 'I'll just check on Daku and friends, if I may, Commander, before Mr Perry escorts them away.'

A third bikie was standing by and must have been the designated driver, as there were only two bikes, both single-seat Harleys. I led the way across the road to the boat storage hardstand, where the white van was parked and gave Hiroto the key.

The three men in the back were alive and very unhappy, especially the two under Daku, as it smelled like he'd had to relieve some bladder pressure, and the results had soaked all three.

Jack and the other two hauled them out and stood them up, except that the one with a bullet hole in each foot, immediately collapsed with a muffled howl of pain. Daku's other helper had dried blood down both sides of his neck where Jasper had held him.

Hiroto smiled, 'Damaged goods, Commander. I presume they objected to being detained?'

'Afraid so, Hiroto. But only these two. Daku may have some cracked ribs, but no claret leaks.'

He laughed with delight. 'Claret leaks. Excellent. I love the Australian humour and learn something new every day.'

He ceremoniously passed the key to Jack, who passed it in turn to the designated driver. Between them, they arranged the three bound men a little more comfortably on the bare metal floor and closed the sliding door.

'May I know what are the transport arrangements for the young ladies?' I asked.

'Of course, Commander. Tanaka-san has dispatched his Gulfstream IV jet to the closest customs airport, which is the Sunshine Coast airport. The aircraft is on its way as we speak, and ETA is 03:00. We will deliver the girls, and after they have been cleaned-up, Daku and his men as well, to the aircraft for direct return to Tokyo. Daku will be severely chastised by Tanaka-san for the trouble he has caused, and the dishonour he has brought to his family and his grandfather's name.'

As the last was said without any hint of humour, I could only imagine what Tanaka-san's form of 'chastisement' would take.

'In that case, it has been a pleasure to meet you, and I wish you a safe journey.' I shook his hand, and Jack's as well.

'I hope to be in touch, Jack. Ride well, my friend.'

I received a surprisingly warm smile in return. 'You too, Commander. You lead an interesting life.'

I returned to the restaurant, just in time for the main course to be delivered, a succulent rib-eye steak which deserved and received my full attention, after which I gave the troops a brief outline of the goings on. While it might have seemed like the end of the operation to some, I knew better, and the kernel of an idea I had concerning Jack and his merry men kept churning around my brain.

Recovery next morning was slow, but I had some more ideas in mind. Talking business to Sally and Kim was top of the list, but chasing them out of our bed first was another matter and took some time.

Therefore, I decided to hold a crew meeting after breakfast, mainly addressing the rescued girls.

'Although yet another major problem has been resolved and duly disposed of,' I said, 'there still remains thirty-nine or so other girls out there in similar circumstances to what you've experienced. Finding and rescuing them, if they want to be that is, is now our highest priority.'

There weren't any arguments about that idea, so I continued, 'It still means we have to keep a low profile, to make sure news of the demise of Turner and Yanos doesn't spread until those girls are safe. Therefore, I have to ask that you stay with us for a while longer, and not to make contact with any friends or family.'

Mary, as the senior and longest-serving girl, had been elected to speak for the girls, and said, 'No problem, Harry. I think we are all so very grateful to you, Corrine and all the crew for your efforts to help us already. None of us have anywhere to rush off to anyway, except back on the streets or to crash pads. Having luxury accommodation and great food is a giant step up, as is not being molested or expected to perform on command. I can assure you, the relief is huge! If we can help the other girls, that will be a bonus for all of us.'

There was a murmur of agreement, so she went on, 'You mentioned you were working on a plan to help us find good accommodation and work. Has that progressed any?'

I had to shake my head. 'Not much further at the moment, although I do have an idea which will need more work and consultation. But whatever happens, you will all be looked after, physically and financially. I say again that you have my word on that, and I can promise you won't be turned out on the streets with nothing.'

I must have said the right things, as there were a few teary eyes in the group, so I hastily wrapped it up, and went to find Sally and Kim.

I found them on the foredeck with Sandy.

'Good morning, Tiger,' Kim said with a lecherous grin.

'Good morning, yourself pussycat,' I replied, grinning back, 'it's obviously your fault for saying you weren't tired.'

She tried to look sheepish, but failed.

'Anyway, to business for a change. You've been looking through Turner's papers, and I need to know if you've found a list of his customers?'

'Sure have,' Sally said. 'Mary helped. There are names in the ledger she used to write up, but we found another two lists which gave more complete details, like the customer's name, contact numbers, the girl, the boat, where the deal was done, as well as how much was paid. As Mary showed us in the ledger, he didn't seem to charge very much. She told him he was barely breaking even.'

'Yes. I heard that too.' I didn't mention that we'd found his cash stash and that the fees he'd actually charged were a lot more than he'd let Mary know. The ledger was probably for Korey's benefit, in case he checked.

'Would you mind summarising that info on a single sheet with just names, boat and contact details, please? The task of tracking these people is huge and we're going to need all the help we can get.'

'No problem. We'll do that now.'

I found the boat's mobile, and called Canberra.

'*Good morning, Harry. All well?*'

'Yeah, very good now thanks M. I'm happy to report that Gary Turner and Korey Yanos won't be culling the ranks of homeless young females again.'

'*Excellent. No loose ends, I trust?*'

'Not associated with their removal, but the nine rescued girls we had with us, are now down to seven, plus another thirty-nine or so still out there on boats.'

'*Ah. Would that be the reason for the arrival of a large business jet at the Sunshine Coast International Airport early this morning, direct from Tokyo. It departed immediately after refuelling with an additional five passengers.*'

'Yes. That was the one. As well as the girls, it carried Daku Tanaka and his two heavies. Grandpa wants to have a little chat with him. I suspect it won't end well for Daku.'

She gave her throaty chuckle, '*I can imagine how it will go. The Yakusa doesn't take kindly to rogue operations, or operators for that matter. But what are your plans for finding the other girls?*'

'If I email you a list of customer names and boat names, can you trawl your resources and find out where those boats are at the moment? The various Harbourmaster's reports should be the best place to start. The majority should be in Queensland waters, but that's not one hundred percent certain.'

'*We can do that,*' she replied, '*it may take a while, but I'll get the details ASAP. How are you going to chase everyone down? It'll be a big task with just your two boats.*'

'Oddly, I've been offered the resources of several local Outlaw Motorcycle Clubs. At the prompting of Raijin Tanaka, I might add.

I'm sure it wasn't my sparkling personality that made them offer to help in any way they could, short of interrupting normal business.'

'*Well done, dear boy. Friends in the right places this time. I presume they would like a degree of immunity as well if they help with the search?*'

'I haven't gone into details with them yet M, but to a limited extent, that'd be a nice sweetener to toss on the table.'

'*I'll see what I can do, but if this goes ahead, tell them to behave as best they can while on official business.*'

'Good-oh, I'll do that.'

'*Okay Harry. I'll get back to you when I have the boat locations.*'

'Thanks, M. Talk later.'

I placed a second call to the Japanese Embassy in Canberra, quickly being connected to the Ambassador, Sakura Ito.

'*Good morning, Commander Stevens. It is good to hear from you. I hope all is well with you?*'

'Good morning, Mr Ambassador. All is very well here, thank you. I won't keep you long, but wanted to report that after I last spoke with you, and was in turn contacted by Raijin Tanaka, I have been fortunate enough to recover his grand-daughter Chiaki-chan and her friend Fumiko-chan, safe and well. Both girls had been abducted by a group who were selling girls into a sex-slavery ring. However, they fortunately came under my control before they had been abused or hurt in any way. Chiaki-chan's brother, Daku Tanaka, was associated with the slavers, has been detained and returned to Japan with the girls at the request of Tanaka-san.'

'*I am more than impressed, Commander. Your speedy, discrete and successful handling of this situation does you great honour. I imagine that Tanaka-san was very pleased.*'

'Indeed he was, Mr Ambassador, and I was very pleased to be able to inform him of a successful outcome to his problem. However, I have to say that I was very fortunate to be in the right place at the right time to recover the young ladies.'

'*Your modesty does you further credit, Commander. You won't mind if I make mention of this business to my cousin? He has taken a keen interest in your activities since the affair in the Southern Ocean and Tasmania.*

I was amused at the thought of the Japanese Prime Minister taking an interest in my doings.

'That is very kind of you to say so, sir. Please extend my fondest regards to your cousin.'

'*Indeed, I shall. However, I shan't keep you any longer, Commander, but I thank you most sincerely for an excellent job, very well done.*'

'My pleasure, sir. Good day now.'

PORT BUNDABERG

'What's the plan when you get the info from M?' Dave asked, after I'd brought our executive group up to date.

'I initially thought we might take advantage of the offer Jack Perry made, and ask him to send pairs of the nearest Club members out to the various locations to confirm the presence of the boat in question and see what's happening on-board. That would save us a lot of running around. We could control the whole search from here.'

There was a round of approving nods at that.

'If a girl is on a particular boat, we can go have a chat with the owners and make an official arrest on a string of charges, starting with kidnapping. We'll have the evidence in writing from Turner's paperwork, and the girl will be wearing an explosive collar.'

'That'll still be a lot of running around,' Sandy put in.

'Yes, it will. But this is where it becomes messy and brings my plan undone. If we try to turn the arrest over to the local police, which is the current protocol, they'll take time to get up to speed on the back-story. Then there's the issue of the collar disarming, plus the girls themselves could be held in limbo for months with no one looking out for them. I regard that as a totally unacceptable outcome for the welfare of the girls involved. I mean – can you see the local coppers doing even a fraction of what we're doing to help rehabilitate the girls? Then there will be thirty-nine different stories being spread around about who snatched them in the first place and the guy who sold them to the boaties. Standard enquiries would soon involve us and totally blow our undercover usefulness.'

'I see what you mean. If the boat owners are being arrested, the girls truly can't be kept out of the system!' Sandy said despondently. 'That won't work. I know you want to help every girl, but apart from disarming the collars, you really would have to let the system process each girl's kidnapping and slavery confinement at its own, glacial pace. We could maybe try to help them later when the system eventually releases them, but that's going to be a big task keeping track of each girl and the associated court proceedings.'

I was glad she was seeing the problem we faced and had one final argument against my initial plan. 'But from the moment the first arrest is made by the local coppers, there will be such a flood of publicity, that will cause the end of any more arrests. The people who have the girls are going to get rid of them ASAP. Therefore, at best, we might save three or four girls. The rest will disappear. There'll be headless bodies clogging the waterways from the Gold Coast to Yeppoon!'

Sandy had to acknowledge the truth of that statement. 'Yeah, bugger it! You're right.'

There was silence around the table for a few moments before Sandy spoke again, choosing her words carefully.

'What if we try one arrest ourselves, just to see if the situation with these other girls is the same as what we've seen so far. Then we might see a better way to proceed.'

I shrugged, still not convinced that this was a viable way to rescue all the girls, but no one had any other ideas. 'Okay. I guess we can try that. But we need to find one who is reasonably close.'

We agreed to do nothing until M got back to us.

Things were more relaxing, now that no one was actively looking for us, so everyone was in a fairly upbeat mood. It wasn't until next morning that M called to tell me that she had emailed a list of the whereabouts of all the boats on my list. Some of the information was old, meaning that the boat could have stayed in the same place for a long time, or moved on without telling the Harbourmaster.

Regardless, there were a lot of boats with their current position information to choose from.

'Look. There's one of them right here in Bundaberg.' Sandy was peering over my shoulder, her breath tickling my ear in a mildly erotic manner. 'Mid-Town Marina. That's just up river from here. We could borrow that bloke's car you used the other day and go take a look.'

I knew I'd get no peace until I agreed, so I did, then said. 'We might be doing a bit more running around if we do have to chase more of these boats, so we may as well hire a car. Then the crew can go to upriver to Bundy whenever they want.'

'Okay. Good idea.'

I recognised the boat name, *Joker*, as belonging to the weirdly-odd couple, Linda and Ben, who had come to replace their misplaced girl with Philippa. It was the transaction I'd been invited to witness by Turner.

I looked up some hire places and after several phone calls, managed to track down a mini-bus, and an obliging lady named Pat Hamilton who said she would gladly deliver it to the marina within the hour, provided we ran her back to town. That suited our trip to the Mid-Town Marina, so I booked it for a week.

'Bring your credentials, 'cuffs and a gun, please dear,' I requested. 'Just in case we need to come heavy with these turkeys.'

I kept a lookout, and just over an hour later, spotted a white van driving down the entry road. I called the previous number, and suggested to Pat that she park it and bring the paperwork down to the boat for us to sign.

She was happy to do that, and turned out to be a happy, attractive and slightly chubby lady around forty, who loved the boat and Krazy cat, who always pounced on any fresh human, looking for extra affection. Obviously she thought she didn't get enough. With paperwork signed and a decent cash deposit paid, Sandy, Pat and I headed back up the jetty.

'I'd love to stay longer and see more of your boat, Harry,' she gushed, 'but I'm on my own today, so I need to be back at the office soon as.'

'No problem, Pat. To speed things up, how about you drive, and we'll take it from there.'

The van turned out to be a near-new Toyota Hi-Ace Commuter with 12-seats. In appearance, it resembled a refrigerator laid on its side, with a wheel stuck on each corner. But to be fair, it was quiet, roomy, and seemed to drive well, although the seats definitely weren't designed for long journeys. Still, for shuttling our tribe to the shops and back, it was ideal. If we had to go further afield, we'd get a decent sedan.

The marina where our first target was supposed to be, surprisingly lacked a jetty where boats could actually tie up, which was a bit of a puzzle, until some bloke in an office explained that the name was a bit of a misnomer, as it was actually just a ship's chandlery, and that any real boats were at the jetties directly opposite across the river at the separate and independent brokerage. Slightly mystified by the peculiar arrangement, we took our trusty van over the bridge and along to where a side street afforded a view of a couple of short jetties with boats attached, and a bunch more sitting high and dry on a dirt hardstand.

Enquiries at a nondescript office revealed that it was in fact a brokerage, and the boat we were looking for, *Joker*, was tied up at one of the jetties.

The yacht broker himself was a broad, red-faced man who had the appearance of someone who had sampled the town's most famous product way too often. However, he was most amiable and said, 'If you want to see the boat, it's only just been listed, but you'll have to wait until the owners finish clearing their gear off.'

I stared at him, 'Listed? Do you mean listed for sale?'

It was his turn to stare back. 'Yeah, of course. That's what I do. Sell boats. What did you think I did?'

I smiled to settle him down. 'Sorry. My mistake. We wanted

to speak with Ben and Linda. We thought they were staying here.'

He settled, his eyes drifting distractedly sideways to assess Sandy's generous chest. 'Well. They were camped here for a while, but then they suddenly said they wanted to sell the boat and move ashore. I must say it was rather unexpected. I hope there wasn't any problem with their girl. She was a pretty thing, but she went off with another bloke one day. That was just before they listed the boat. Most odd it all was.'

He tore his eyes away from Sandy and added, 'If you leave me your mobile number, I'll give you a call when they've finished clearing out. This should be their last load this afternoon. Probably tomorrow you can make an inspection.'

I could see that he wasn't going to let us down to the jetty to talk to Ben and Linda in case we made a private deal and he lost his commission. So to avoid raising any suspicions, I handed him my number and we gracefully retired to the carpark and the van. While I was thinking things through, Sandy cunningly relieved me of the keys and took the driver's seat, having suffered my horrible driving habits way too many times.

'Where to now, big dog?' she cheerfully asked, happy to have the steering wheel firmly in her grasp and out of mine.

'Drive out, straight across the street, do a U-turn and park facing the river, please.'

'Okay, but what's the go with that?'

'If they're clearing out their boat, Ben and Linda must have somewhere in town where they're storing their stuff. Might be a storage locker, or even just a motel. We're going to follow them and have a chat. I want to know where their girl, Philippa, has gone and why.'

We only waited thirty minutes, before a small, white rental truck with a high, boxy back, nosed out of the boatyard opposite and turned left toward the bridge, a man and a woman in the cab. Sandy eased out behind them, and at a comfortable distance, we followed them back over the river and out to the east side of town, where they finally turned into the driveway of a self-storage park full of variously-sized lock-up units. They triggered the sliding gate with their key-card, and drove through.

The large, sliding gate was ponderously slow in each direction, making it easy to wait well back, then drive through, after they'd turned down the second row of units on the left. Sandy drove slowly straight ahead, then turned at the far end of the first row, and parked.

We hopped out and walked to the end of the row, where we peered around the corner. Anyone watching would have called the police, given our furtive behaviour, but the place was deserted, except for the small truck backed up to a unit just three up from where we stood. The unit door was up, and from the noise, unloading of gear was in progress.

I wanted to make an open approach, so we just strolled up, chatting inanely about nothing, just for the sake of making some noise.

It was Ben who stuck his head around the side of the truck body to see who was coming, so I called, out, 'It is you. Hi Ben, it's Harry. We met on Gary Turner's boat, remember?'

I turned to Sandy and said loudly, 'See, dear. I told you it was Ben and Linda. I never forget a face.'

I turned back to Ben to see that Linda had stepped out of the storage shed, her face sweaty and chest heaving with exertion.

'There's Linda. Hello, darling lady. It's Harry, from Gary Turner's boat and this is my Sandy. When you picked up Philippa…'

That made them quickly spin around to see who else might be listening to this loud-mouthed idiot, but we were still alone.

Ben wiped his own forehead and said, 'Ah… yeah. Gidday Harry. Hello Sandy, nice to meet you. What are you guys doing here?'

'Oh, we decided to hang around the area for a while, so we hired a storage unit here. There's always too much stuff aboard, and we're going to sell some off. But what are you putting in storage? That looks like a lot of stuff. Your boat was plenty big enough for the three of you, surely?'

They exchanged a quick look, before Ben said, 'Actually Harry, I can tell you that we've decided to sell the boat and move ashore for a while. Therefore, all our gear has to come off.'

'Oh, dear. That is a shame. I hate to see people giving up the boating life, but I guess you have to do what seems best. Anyway, how's that girl working out? She looked really good to me. It was Philippa, wasn't it?'

'Yeah, that's her. She was really good, but we don't have her any longer.'

'Oh, no. Not another accident, I hope?'

I saw Linda give an involuntary shudder. 'No, no. Nothing like that. Very good for us, actually. We were contacted by some bloke who got our number from Gary, and said he wanted to buy our girl.'

'Buy her? But you'd only just bought her!'

He nodded, 'Yeah. I know. Crazy, isn't it. But he offered too much money to say no to. Much more than we paid for her.'

I looked puzzled, and it wasn't an act. 'Why didn't he just buy one from Gary? It would have been much cheaper.'

'Well, what he said to us was that he wanted a lot of girls, all at once, and Gary couldn't supply them that quickly. Money wasn't any problem, so long as he got the girls quickly.'

'Bloody hell. How many did he want? We've got a few spare ones we could part with for the right money.'

Ben shrugged, 'He said he needed thirty or forty. Gary must have given him the list of past sales, but talk to Gary. This dude might still need some more.'

'Good one, Ben. We'll do that. But did this bloke say what he wanted the girls for? Our spare ones are quite young.'

Ben got a strange, distracted look in his eyes for a moment, and he licked his lips slowly. 'Yeah, he did. He said he was setting up a private club-type resort on an island up the coast, where anything goes, if his member clients have the money. With what he paid for our girl, I wished we had more to sell. You're lucky if you've got some you can spare.'

'Yeah, sure. That's not the problem. I just need to know if he wants really young ones, like under sixteen, or if all the girls must be aged twenty or more.'

Ben replied. 'As you probably know, Gary only sells girls eighteen or older, but I'm sure this new bloke wouldn't mind some younger stuff. We like younger stuff too, don't we Linda?'

'Yes dear, we do, even though it's becoming harder to get. But do try to control yourself, you're dribbling again. Just wipe… yes, that's got it. Good boy.'

Unloading obviously forgotten, Ben had allowed himself to become deeply involved in giving Sandy's T-shirt and tight jeans a very close scrutiny, so Linda spoke for him.

'I've got this bloke's name and number if you want, Harry. It'll save going through Gary who'll probably want a commission. I think he took one on our sale, the cheeky bugger.'

She looked up her phone then scribbled a name, number and the island name on a scrap of cardboard torn off one of the heaps of boxes in the truck.

'There you go. I hope it helps you sell a few girls. Maybe you and Sandy would like to come back to our motel with us? They have a lovely bar overlooking the water.'

'Thanks, Linda. Kind offer, but we were just dropping off some more junk, and have to get back. You've both been very helpful. We'd love to take you up on your offer some other time, though. Are you staying in town long?'

'Just until the boat sells, so it might be a couple of weeks. Then we'll see where we want to live.'

'Okay. We'll catch up soon. Bye.'

We strolled away, but as soon as we were around the corner, sprinted for the van. Sandy got it turned around and we drove back out the way we'd come in, the gate set to automatic opening for outgoing vehicles.

Once on the road back to Port Bundaberg, we both burst out laughing.

'I hope you enjoyed that virtual undressing and fondling session you copped from Ben,' I said. 'I'm fairly sure that wet patch on the front of his jeans wasn't sweat.'

She giggled, 'You should talk. Linda nearly got off on you, too. I hate to think what would have happened if we'd gone back to the motel with them.'

'It would have been very interesting. Maybe we should go and get Sally and Kim and come back. That'd make a really interesting mix.'

That started Sandy giggling again and made her steering a bit wobbly for a few moments.

'And maybe we just keep it in the family, so to speak. Linda could be alright, but that Ben is a real nutcase. That fuckin' drooling bit! He's psycho!'

'Yeah, but how about this bloke buying Philippa at a premium price. We might have to rethink this whole search, or at least do some serious checking. There may not be any girls to rescue.'

'Too easy, my darling man. I have a simple plan to take care of that. Wait 'til we get back.'

We finished the trip in silence, with only the occasional giggle from Sandy.

'So, are you saying there's a possibility that all the girls have been bought by this rich dude with the island?' Dave asked, as a few of us sat around sucking on wine and beer, the sun settling low toward the western horizon.

'Basically, yes,' I replied. 'I mean, if he wanted thirty or forty of them, why would he pay so much extra just for one girl. She was a nice girl, but not that special. If he's staffing up a private resort for no-holds-barred sex action, that might explain his haste and need for so many at once. And if money really is no object, the girls are ready-made for what he wants. Mind you, I'm only guessing here. Reality might be totally different, but it makes a sort of twisted sense to me.'

Alex and Bree nodded, and Alex rumbled, 'Yes. That makes sense to us, too. But we still need to make sure.'

Sandy added her piece. 'That's why I thought Dave should call a couple of Turner's customers and pretend to be Turner. You know – 'Hi guys, just checking to make sure everything is going alright with your girl and do you want another one?' That sort of stuff. Mary can check your speech pattern, although I doubt they've had too many phone calls from Turner, so it shouldn't matter too much how he sounds. Just have all their information in front of you at the time.'

Dave nodded slowly, considering, 'Yeah. That could work. Have we got all their details?'

'Yep. Well, the basic ones, anyway, but that's all you'll need. The phone number, their names and the girl's name are really all you need. Sally and Kim made a list.'

He shrugged, 'Good-oh. Let's have it and I'll call the first one now. Pick a name.'

While Kim went to get the list, I went over to *Poseidon* to get Turner's old mobile, so at least the calling number display would show the right name.

Sandy picked George and Michelle Gibson, whose boat, the *Wanderer* was shown as having recently arrived in Gladstone, and staying at the Port Curtis Marina.

… 'Is that George?'

… 'It's Gary Turner, George.'

… 'Yeah, good thanks mate. Good to hear you too.'

… 'No. No problem. I'm just checking that everything is going alright with you guys and Stephanie. No dramas?'

… 'What! Really? I can't believe it. I mean, a few weeks back, I had some bloke asking how many girls I had available, but had to say that I didn't have any presently in stock. He must be really desperate to pay that much. I assume it's the same guy. Like, what're the chances of two guys wanting a whole bunch of girls all at once.'

… 'Yeah, yeah. Kazemi. That's him. Oh well. I guess I'll give him a call to see if he still wants more in a few weeks. I've got more girls coming in then.'

… 'Yeah. Understand. Sounds like I'd better put my prices up.'

… 'No, I don't have any at all right now. That's the problem. Anyway, you've made a good profit. But if Kazemi doesn't need any more, call me in a few weeks if you want another one and I'll give you a discount for being a good customer.'

… 'Good on you, George. All the best to Michelle. Cheers, mate.'

He hung up and I asked, 'Same story? Paid heaps extra for a girl straight away?'

'Yep. $75K – no questions asked. Sent a couple of goons to pick her up and collect the transmitter.'

'Bugger! Okay. Try two more, please, and if it's the same story, we'll have to presume most if not all of them have been purchased and taken to this island.'

He placed the calls, and the outcome was the same. An unexpected phone call – the offer of an immediate 50% profit – the girl collected within twelve hours.

The last contact added extra information. He said that Kazemi had made them an additional offer to join his very exclusive Resort Club, which was where their girl and the others, were going. The Resort was located on an island imaginatively called No-Name Island around 70 nautical miles south-east of Mackay. It was in the Duke Island group, and between Bamborough and Hunter Islands.

'Did he ask what was so special about this very exclusive island club?'

'He did, but all Kazemi said was that it was a luxurious resort, 5-star accommodation, with great food, and staffed by lots of girls who'd do anything that was asked of them. There were some young guys for the customers who preferred male company. He didn't say anymore, just invited them to join the club. $30K annual fee, and $4K per day when they were on-site, all inclusive, and they were the discount rates.'

'Bloody hell! It must be really good for that sort of money,' Sandy commented, eyebrows raised, 'but I know what you're thinking Harry, and you need to consider that there must be a lot of security to look after so many male and female staff.'

I grinned at her disturbingly uncanny way of divining my thoughts.

'Yes, my dear. But maybe not too many goons if Kazemi is using collars on all the girls and boys to keep them in line. If there's no need to guard them, he only needs a few heavies to make sure the guests don't get too rough with the staff, and that uninvited visitors don't gate-crash the party.'

'My point exactly. There's no way to get on that island without being bailed-up.'

'We don't know that yet. Let's check Google Earth for a look at the place.'

I knew Corrine and Alex were thinking the same as I was, so we crowded around the computer screen. It was a small, rocky island, shaped like a badly-made horseshoe, with one arm longer than the other. The longer arm poked up to the north-west, and the shorter one angled more to the north. The two arms enclosed a beautiful little bay with a dazzling-white sandy beach, while the shoreline from the south-west, right around through south to the north-east, was rocky, with no easy landing places.

As the images were several years old, the resort didn't show, but the interior of the island had what looked like a large, depressed sand patch just back from the beach, and this would probably be where the resort would now be. With the whole island just 800 metres by 650 metres, no one was going to get lost, even if they tried hard.

Right on the western tip, was another very small, sandy beach. The surrounding water was shown on the charts as mostly shallow over sand, although a deeper channel allowed safe access by large boats to the main bay from the northeast.

Maximum height above sea-level was around 26 metres, and three smaller islands lay in a casually-scattered arc to the south, the closest to No-Name was about eight hundred metres away. The chart also showed the water as shallow all the way south to the largest island in the group, Marble Island, which was also privately-owned and inhabited.

NO-NAME ISLAND

I placed a call to my controller to bring her up-to-date.

'Copied all that, Harry. What's your next move?'

'We'll stock up, top fuel tanks and head that way tomorrow. We need to recon the place to see what's feasible in the way of a raid, and make plans from there.'

'Let me know what you're doing please, as soon as you work it out.'

'Yes, Boss.'

Sandy had made contact with her boss, Superintendent Bob Casey, and he was delighted with our progress so far.

While we'd been bringing our superiors up-to-date, Bree had been busy looking up property records.

'Look at this, Harry,' she called out. 'The cheeky bugger!'

She showed us a web page where the island was shown as having been purchased for $900K by a company named 'Black Collar Holdings Pty Ltd'.

That jogged another thought loose, so I grabbed the phone and the business card from the other night in the marina restaurant.

'Outcasts,' answered a cheerful voice, sounding totally at odds with their name.

'Is that Jack?' I asked.

'Yep. And you are?'

'Harry Stevens, Jack. We met at the Port Bundaberg Marina.'

'Of course, Commander. I'll not forget your name. How can we help you?'

'Actually, Jack, I just called to say that it appears we may not need the help I thought you could provide, as the situation as just changed, possibly in our favour. But I did want to thank you again for the offer of assistance.'

'*No problem, Commander. The offer still stands, if you ever need a hand in the future.*'

'Thanks Jack. Ride well and stay upright.'

'*Cheers, Commander.*'

Then it was round-table time, with most of the girls drifting in from the cockpit as well, drinks in hand, given that it was happy hour.

'What's the plan?' Dave asked, kicking back with a cold beer.

'Top off fuel, water and food stocks, then head north to the Duke group of islands in the morning. What sort of range has *Poseidon* got?'

He thought a moment, 'At a cruise of twelve knots, I reckon about 700 nautical. How far to the island?'

'There's a place called Tynemouth Island three miles south of the target, which should be a good place to lay up while we do a survey run or three with *Dragonfly*. It's about 215nm or 18 hours at twelve knots. But to avoid doing a night cruise, our old stamping ground, Hummocky Island, is exactly halfway, so if we can fuel, water and provision early in the morning, we can make Hummocky in daylight.'

Dave nodded, then Bree commented, 'Food stocks are still good, but going into an unknown situation with the possibly of acquiring a much larger crew, I think we should stock up with extra while we can. The local IGA opens at 07:00.'

'Great, thanks Bree. When we go up to have a feed, I'll arrange for *Poseidon* to be refuelled early.' There wasn't much more to discuss at this stage, so everyone got back to enjoying happy hour, then we went up to the restaurant.

We had a great night, but an air of excitement and nervousness was evident, particularly amongst the new girls who didn't know what to expect. Not too much booze was drunk either, and once back aboard, everyone tended to drift off to their own beds sooner than later.

Next morning by 09:00, we were heading out through the wide, safe harbour mouth of Burnett Heads, before swinging north. As usual, Dave set the pace and *Firebird* idled along comfortably off to one side, with the light south-easterly breeze just keeping the sails filled. We needed the big lightweight code zero at first, until the wind speed rose, then we rolled it up and stayed with just the main and the small, self-tacking stay-sail.

Three of the girls who normally lived on *Poseidon* had come over the *Firebird* for the day since we had a lot more room, and they quickly discovered the delights of laying on the trampoline nets soaking up the sun, or watching the waves slipping by just below. There was usually a pod or two of dolphins playing around under the bows, and they seemed to enjoy splashing their human observers.

It was a very pleasant, relaxing sail and around 18:00, the twin green humps which gave Hummocky Island its name, poked above the northern horizon. The pretty little island formed an L-shape with the southern side steep, rocky and covered in grass and low, scrubby bushes. On the western end, a finger of low, steep-sided rock poked northward, partly enclosing a delightful little bay made up of half rocky foreshore and the other half a short, sandy beach. Protection from most winds, except a northerly, was excellent. We gave a wide berth to the two nasty-looking outcrops of bare rock which guarded the southern approaches to Hummocky.

With plenty of daylight remaining, we anchored close-in to the beach, which encouraged most of the crew to leap into the water and swim ashore. I launched the dinghy and took Jasper and Krazy ashore for a run on the sand. I doubt they remembered their last visit to the island, so presumably for a cat confined to a boat most of its life, any beach is a good beach for a run and play. As it had been a warm day and the night remained so as well, Bree decided to have a simple beach BBQ over an open fire. Steak, chops and sausages, with foil-wrapped potatoes and a fresh salad with Italian dressing, washed down with wine or beer was perfect for a hungry crew.

The pussies loved the unexpected treat of being allowed to stay ashore for so long with all their new human friends to play with. As usual, Jasper kept a close eye on the younger, troublesome one, and brought her back near the fire several times after she'd chased some insect or lizard into the scrub.

Promptly at dawn next morning, both boats raised anchors and quietly motored north. Most of our crew remained in bed as long as they could, but drifted out looking bleary-eyed when Bree started cooking bacon and eggs. Nearly all the new girls followed the habits of our female crew and spent the day either naked or with miniscule pants on. Since being rescued, most hadn't had much of a chance to improve their tans, but were certainly making up for it now. Neither Alex nor I minded in the slightest.

I must admit that after what they'd been through, I still expected the girls to be excessively modest, but Sandy suggested that now they accepted they were truly free of slavery, and with a brighter, if unspecified future, they relaxed and finally felt they could do what they wanted.

She did deliver me a stern warning. 'Just remember, dearest, you've made these girls some promises about their future that we're going to have to honour above all else. I'm sure you've considered it already, but I just wanted to remind you. Also, keep in mind that you may not be able to save everybody we come across, although knowing you as well as I do, I'm sure you're going to give it a bloody good try.'

I couldn't think of a suitable reply, so I resorted to old faithful and just kissed her. Works every time. Well, mostly.

While yesterday's run up to Agnes Water and Seventeen-Seventy, then past Gladstone had been fairly boring scenery-wise, today's sail was more interesting as we kept close in to the Keppel Islands, of Great and Northern fame. We stayed close to the coast, dodging smaller islands until we entered the southern end of an area quite crowded with beautiful islands, large and small, which stretched north to and beyond the stunning Whitsunday Island group.

Several of these islands were privately-owned with just large houses on them, some with resorts, while others were National Parks. Our target island was in the Duke Islands group, three of which were privately owned.

Sandy called my attention to an internet page where Bamborough Island, immediately north of our target island, was for sale, complete with several houses, livestock and all facilities.

'There you go, Harry. Any offer over $2 mil will be considered. Not a bad bit of real estate. That would be a good place for a resort if we didn't want to keep living on a boat.'

I had a look, and checked it on Google Earth. 'Yeah. It looks good. Plenty of great beaches. But I'd go nuts listening to guests whinge and whine about being sunburnt, or how there was a bug in the swimming pool, when there's the beautiful ocean fifty metres away.'

She laughed at me, but a seed of an idea had been planted in my mind. To test out the theory, I called Mary over to have a look.

After she'd read the listing and looked at the photo, I asked, 'What do you think of that?'

She grinned, 'Sounds absolutely idyllic. It'd make a terrific laid-back resort. Getting and keeping dedicated staff would be the biggest issue, but that would be a great place.'

She wandered off, as Sandy looked at me. 'You have that cunning plan look in your eye. What are you up to?'

'Nothing, dearest. Just speculating.'

'Bullshit!'

By early afternoon, we had passed the tip of Townshend and Leicester Islands, part of the extensive Australian military training area of Shoalwater Bay, and were approaching the Duke Island group, with our first anchorage being at Tynemouth Island.

Tynemouth had a stunning stretch of white sandy beach on

the north-western side, nearly eight hundred metres long and this was where we dropped anchor in the lee of a high hill. There was another hill at the southern end of the island, and a wide, low valley in between, covered in grass and a few trees.

Someone had dug a few dams in various places, making sure there was good water for stock although there didn't seem to be any in residence at the moment.

The hill directly above our anchorage was about seventy metres high, which would provide good exercise for a lookout, and allow a good view of our target, No-Name Island, just three miles to the north. Naturally, the best view would be gained by putting up our super-capable UAV, *Dragonfly,* and this was what I asked Bree and Sandy to get organised as soon as we had anchored safely and the boats were rafted-up.

As *Poseidon* had more open deck space, the girls set the aircraft up there, and after all the checks were done, they launched to the cheers of an interested audience.

'Two thousand feet orbit, and a wide view to start?' Bree asked, as the UAV tilted its engine pods forward and accelerated into wing-borne forward flight, banking into a climbing turn to the north.

'Yes, please Bree. That should keep us invisible from any of the bad guys.'

She left the camera lens on wide-angle for the short flight to No-Name Island, giving us a spectacular view of the beautiful pale-green shallow water, with the various islands of the group mostly to the east of the flight path. It was obvious that the Duke group of islands lay on a broad, shallow, sandy bank, with deep water to both west and east.

I looked at Dave and he shrugged. 'Looks fairly shallow, but not too bad.'

I nodded, 'Yeah, but let's check. Bree, would you mind turning back and dropping down to about fifty feet, and just skirt the west shore of that island to our north-east that looks like a fish hook?

I'd like a better look at the water depth.'

'That's called Hunter Island,' Sandy added, looking at the chart, 'and it's supposed to have two to three metres of water at low tide along the shore.'

The UAV was by now doing a low and slow pass along the shoreline, showing that indeed the water had reasonable depth, despite the extensive sand shoals shown on the chart.

'Okay, thanks Bree. Back to the flight plan.'

The view on the screen widened out as the aircraft entered another climbing turn and headed north again. Minutes later, it was at cruise height and coming up on our target island. The view was the same as we had already seen from the satellite photo, but what that hadn't showed was the new development of the resort buildings mostly set, as expected, in the sandy depression in the centre of the island.

There was a long, low building fronting the beach, plus several rows of small huts with what looked like thatched roofs and connected by a network of pathways, on the south side of the main block. I counted forty of those. There were also two long wings angled back from each end of the main building which semi-enclosed the thatched huts and could be staff quarters, store rooms and places for all the supplies and stuff necessary to run a resort. Offset well clear on the eastern side were several small buildings, one with a large silver tank-like object beside it.

'Generator shed,' Dave muttered.

To the west side, on the beach just up from the water, were a few more sheds. One had a set of rails running down into the water.

A large RIB, about six-metres long and with two huge outboards bolted to the stern, was pulled up on the sand, while near-by, a cargo barge, with a load-space big enough for a small vehicle, was being unloaded by a tracked bobcat. The cargo consisted of boxes of various sizes on pallets, and they were being transferred to a long trailer attached to a 4x4 ATV ag truck. Three large power boats were anchored in the bay, along with a vessel with an unusual shape docked into a U-shaped pontoon attached to a short wooden jetty built out from the beach. It was sort-of like an aircraft, but with very broad, stubby, triangular wings, and looked to be about 18 metres long.

'What the hell's that thing?' Dave asked, peering at the screen.

After a closer inspection, I chuckled in amazement. 'It's a WIG. A wing-in-ground-effect craft. I wondered how they'd cope with getting their VIP clients out here in rough weather. Although it actually flies, it's classed as a boat, because it can't fly higher than three to four metres above ground or water. This one is called the Airfish-8, and is built in Singapore. It's much faster than a boat, and by being able to fly over the waves, it's not affected in the slightest by wave motion.'

'It looks a bit weird, but I like the idea of travelling above the waves on a rough day.'

'Yeah, that's a big plus. It carries eight to ten passengers, uses a big V-8 car engine to drive those twin air propellors at the rear, and goes about 100 knots. It can make the trip from Mackay in less than an hour, without making passengers sea or air-sick, and land on water on arrival.'

'That's really neat.'

The girls moved the visual scan around, concentrating on the outer perimeter, zooming in to look for patrols, but we saw nothing.

'Why aren't there security guards everywhere?' Reggie asked.

'It must be like I suggested. If they're using the collars on all the girls and boys, then there's no need to worry about them running away. And where would they go anyway?'

'But this place is much bigger than a boat. They'd have to cover the whole island to make it safe. How can they do that?'

It was a good thought, so I suggested, 'There's no reason why not. All it should need is a more powerful transmitter and a higher antenna. Look for a mast a few meters high on top of a building. That'd be enough to cover the whole place.'

We soon spotted a slender mast mounted on the roof above the last room on the east wing, which angled off the main building. It had a cross-bar on top holding several other antennas of different lengths.

'That'll be it!' Dave exclaimed, stabbing at the screen with his finger. 'They'd need to be able to talk to the boats and the Airfish-8 as well as look after the collars.'

As the scan moved across the lines of huts clustered behind the main block, we spotted two figures leave one hut, and walk slowly toward the main building.

'Zoom in on them, please Bree,' I quickly asked.

She did, and as the focus sharpened, we saw a girl and a guy walking toward the main building. The girl was wearing brief panties, while the guy wore a G-string pouch and both had the distinctive black collars around their necks.

'Excellent,' I muttered.

'Why excellent?' Reggie asked. 'The poor buggers are wearing those rotten collars!'

'Because it shows the presence of both girls and guys, and the fact that they're wearing collars suggests that hopefully most of the staff are therefore under restraint. That should reduce the number of guards and security staff we have to worry about.'

Sandy looked at me. 'I'm guessing, or should it be hoping, that you have one of your cunning plans running around inside that warped mind of yours? But how can you remove thirty-something girls plus a few young guys, from a private island under the noses of the security staff?'

'I'm working on that.'

That earned me a disbelieving look which I choose to ignore. Some people have no faith!

I had the UAV crew video the whole resort in close-up detail, including the three boats anchored in the bay. There was no sign of crew on the boats, so presumably everyone was ashore. With all video recorded for later analysis, the ladies brought the UAV back to *Poseidon's* foredeck and shut it down. While they checked it over and prepared for another flight after dark, we broke up the impromptu conference to indulge in our own happy hour.

As I drank and relaxed, I let a few ideas fizz quietly through my brain. I also exchanged some thoughts with Corrine who became quite excited.

The late afternoon had become rather hot and humid, so most of the crew decided to jump overboard, parking their drinks on the stern platforms. That resulted in a regular procession of wet, naked females wandering past fetching fresh ones and giggling at my reaction. I became sure they were doing it deliberately when the same delightfully-shaped girl went past twice in quick succession.

When she could get my attention, Corrine said, 'With no posted guards or regular patrols during the day, it'll be interesting to see if things change at night. I'm thinking we should do a night recon before planning too much further.'

'Yeah, I agree, Mouse. But a covert one, please. We'll do an aerial survey tonight with *Dragonfly* using infra-red, and see what's happening.'

Thanks to the steady supply of drinks, the swimming party was getting rather raucous, so at Bree's suggestion, I fired up the big stern-mounted BBQ, while she and Sandy made salads. As the sun sank below the western horizon in a fantastic display of orange cloud swirls fading through to purple as darkness closed in, we enjoyed a simple feast, everyone perched where they could, although with the size of *Firebird's* cockpit, there wasn't any serious overcrowding.

CHAPTER 32

With full darkness, Bree and Sandy started up *Dragonfly* and activated the automatic flight plan. The UAV revved up, lifted off smoothly, and purred off into the gloom. With the infrared camera selected, a reasonably sharp picture in grey tones was displayed on the main monitor, with the island coming into view within minutes. To mask the muted engine noise, Bree kept it at two thousand feet and used the stabilised zoom to great effect. She scanned the island perimeter for signs of guards without any indication of activity. Closer in toward the buildings, the light output swamped the night vision camera, so she switched to the daylight camera, but there wasn't anything additional to see that we hadn't picked up during the daylight run, so it was back to infrared.

After a few more orbits, I asked the girls to bring it home, and while they were doing that, Corrine pulled Dave and me aside for a quiet word. 'I'd like to make a recon now,' she said. 'There aren't any guard posts or regular patrols, although there could be random ones.'

I shrugged, 'True. Their security seems to be very lax, or maybe Kazemi believes the collars are all the security he needs. Either way, if you're happy, then let's do it.' Corrine beamed, and went to change and collect the usual few items she liked to take on this sort of recon.

Ten minutes later, she was back wearing a new night camo suit I hadn't seen before. On previous night recon missions, she had always favoured tight, dark clothing to minimise rustles and snags, but this suit was very thin, very slick and absolutely skin-tight. She may as well have been naked, as it did a superb job of moulding itself intimately to her body to the extent where a toothpick would have shown up.

There was a hood with built-in mask, and the whole thing was finished in a dark grey and black mottled pattern. A small black bum-bag buckled around her waist completed the outfit.

'Bloody hell, Mouse,' I exclaimed, 'if any guard does see you, he's more likely to try to rip that off first, instead of calling for help.'

She grinned, 'Thanks, Harry.'

We went in *Firebird's* RIB with the electric outboard motor, where the loudest sound was that of our foaming wake at twenty knots. Close to the island, we slowed to reduce the noise and the visual impact of the white wash of disturbed water. I approached the island in a curve from the west, aiming for the tiny beach on the north-west arm, which was nearly six hundred meters from the resort. The vegetation had looked sparse from the aerial survey, and there even seemed to be a bit of a worn track leading to the end of the small rocky spit.

We were each wearing a radio headset for short-range comms, and I nominated an alternate pick-up spot at the boatshed on the main beach if she got into trouble. The rest of the shoreline was too rocky for safety.

As soon as the hard keel of the RIB crunched onto the shore, Corrine was feet-dry over the bow, and disappeared from sight. Five minutes later, we heard her murmur in our headsets, *'All clear. Approaching the west arm of the main block now.'*

I clicked my mic twice in response.

To be ready for a quick getaway, Dave hopped overboard and held the dingy steady against the small waves, which rolled around from the south-east. It had been the prevailing direction of wind and waves for the last few days.

Fifteen agonisingly long minutes later, Corrine spoke again. *'Still no guards. I'm checking the east-arm rooms. All the activity seems to be in the main block so far. That's where all the lights are and where all the noise is coming from. There's just some very dim path lighting around the huts.'*

There was another wait until she reported the east wing searched, and that she was heading for the small cluster of buildings away to the east, one of which we thought housed the generator. Then there was a much longer wait of thirty minutes or more, until she suddenly appeared, scaring the hell out of me and Dave.

She giggled at our reactions, as she slipped aboard, hardly breathing hard.

'Any chance you two can get your arses into gear and get us out of here? I'm starting to get a bit cold. This suit's pretty thin.'

Muttering under his breath, Dave shoved off, I twisted the throttle and we moved slowly and silently away until it was safe to open up and scoot for home.

Back aboard and dressed more warmly, Corrine sat in the saloon, sipping a mug of steaming hot chocolate. Most of the girls had gone to bed, but Sandy, Bree, Mary, Alex and Reggie joined us.

'There aren't any lookouts at all that I could find,' she started her report, 'and all the activity was in the main building which has a large dining and lounge area, a bar, plus a big room done out as a casino along the front. Of the staff I saw, the girls are mostly naked, the boys wear G-string pouches, and they all wear black domino-type masks. The casino dealers and pit bosses were dressed normally. There were twenty or thirty guests, mostly older men and women, but all dressed casually.

I caught a glimpse of a tall, darker-skinned man dressed in a white tuxedo, who is probably Kazemi. He's got a thick mane of white hair, brushed straight back off his forehead which gives him a very dramatic look! The large kitchen and store rooms are directly behind the dining room and are accessible from the courtyard. There are two offices at the back beside the kitchen, one of which looks much better furnished than the other, so it's probably Kazemi's private office. The other is probably the real working office. There's a very luxurious bedroom beside Kazemi's office, which I guess would be his too.'

She paused to sip more hot chocolate. 'The huts are made of large slabs of rough wood – like old railway sleepers, with an imitation thatch on the roof, but there's a solid corrugated roof under the thatch. Apart from the thatch, I guess they would stand up to a cyclone very well, which would be a necessity in this area. Inside, they're very luxurious with a huge bed and all sorts of weird gear and sex toys laying around. The west wing is all staff rooms, each quite small and basic with two beds per room and shared bathrooms and toilets down the end of the corridor. The east wing has several general store rooms, some extra staff bedrooms which don't look to be occupied, and on the end, furthest from the main block, is the radio room.

Nothing is locked, and it looked like the collar transmitter is there. It's a bigger unit than the one on *Poseidon* although the face is similar in layout, and there are several other radios as well.

The few sheds to the east, up a small gully between the sand dunes, are the generator with its fuel tank, and several garages holding four of those small 4X4 utility vehicles we saw earlier today. There appeared to be the top a large, underground tank, presumably for water storage, although I couldn't see where they get supplies from. There's no accommodation up there, nor any signs of patrols. The sheds on the beach are only for the large RIB and a couple of jet-skis. There are three dinghies tied to the jetty, presumably belonging to the power-boats out in the bay. There's also the 'U'-shaped dock for that neat flying boat thingy.'

She looked at me, 'So that's it, boss. Sex-slavery catering for all sorts of weird and depraved tastes and an illegal casino all in one neat package.'

'Great work, Mouse. That might be enough excitement for one night, so you get some sleep, I'll do some thinking and we'll have a planning session tomorrow.'

I actually didn't get a lot of thinking or sleep that night, since Sally and Kim were feeling frisky after the afternoon playing in the water and getting pissy, but they were a lot of fun so no complaints from Sandy or me.

Next morning after breakfast, I held a planning session with the executive crew.

With her devil's advocate hat firmly on, Sandy asked a good question. 'I presume we're going to launch a raid on this island, rather than notify the Mackay coppers and let them do it?'

'Yes. Apart from the difficulty of getting them to respond quickly, along with the publicity problems we've already discussed, my thoughts are that there are bound to be guns in the hands of the senior staff. If we turn the bust over to police who can't tell the bad guys from the innocents, the raid will turn into a giant clusterfuck with a good chance of innocent guys and girls getting killed and the serious bad guys, like Kazemi and his depraved customers, likely to get away.'

'C'mon Harry. The local Mackay guys wouldn't be that incompetent.'

'No. And actually I'm not suggesting that they are, but remember they would have no prior knowledge of what's been going on, and coming in cold turkey like that, wouldn't know the good guys from the bad ones. It would be too easy for Kazemi to create mass confusion by just turning off the collar transmitter and blowing the heads off thirty-nine young persons.

That in turn, would give Kazemi and all his cronies a chance to bail. Plus, if there are well-known VIPs amongst that lot, and past experience says that most of them will be, they also might escape.

We, on the other hand, have got intimate knowledge of the collars and how they work. We've already done two aerial and one ground reconnaissance and know the resort layout very well. We know who's the good, the bad and the ugly ones – plus, we're better trained and equipped.'

That raised a general laugh, and Sandy grinned, 'Yeah, alright. I'll grant you most of that. But you'll have to get the Mackay coppers involved sooner or later.'

'Yeah, I know. And I intend to, but I'm still working on how to tip them off without having to answer embarrassing questions later.'

She subsided briefly, muttering softly, but then rallied with a question, 'Putting the jurisdictional issues aside for the moment, have you worked out the priorities? That's going to affect our planning.'

'Absolutely, and it's a no-brainer. Prime task is to get the collared staff clear and de-activate the collars before we deal with Kazemi and his crew. Hopefully, that'll minimise accidents.'

I then asked Mary a question which had occurred to me a few nights ago. 'What's the possibility that any of the collared crew won't want to be rescued?'

She went to speak, then paused and thought a moment. 'That's an interesting point. I know for sure that none of our lot would have wanted to stay where they were. But I suppose it's possible someone might have a case of the Stockholm Syndrome, or are desperate enough have come to actually enjoy what they're doing. Unlikely, but possible.'

'Okay, thanks, Mary. We'll plan for 100% willing to be rescued, but be prepared for a dissenter or three.'

'What's the plan for dealing with Kazemi and his core group?' Sandy asked pointedly.

I shrugged, 'To my mind, none of them are any better than Turner or Yanos, so they all deserve the same treatment.'

'What about the clients on the island?'

'I'm inclined to class them as just a bunch of depraved arse-holes, so if they want to step aside without trying to cause us trouble, we let the coppers deal with them later if they can round them up.'

Sandy nodded approval. 'Good call. But then there's the other non-collared staff, like the dealers, cooks and boat drivers?'

I gave an evil grin, 'Easy one. Anyone who fights back gets taken down. No second chance. But those who really are innocent won't provide any resistance, so we can let them, or even tell them to get out of the way and be collected by the coppers when they arrive.'

That assessment drew sober approval from the team.

'And how do you intend to stop anyone leaving?' Sandy asked with that one raised eyebrow trick. 'There are three big boats, several smaller ones, and that WIG thing for them to choose from.'

I shared a quick glance with my dear demolition expert in the slender, innocent-looking form of Corrine. 'Short of swimming, I don't plan on there being any way for those left on the island to escape before the police arrive.'

Sandy levelled her eyes at me. 'Okay dearest. I know you didn't have much time for thinking last night, but I suspect you have an action plan?'

I tried to look humble and wise, but failed miserably. 'Well, yes. As you know, I do try to rise to the occasion…'

A hail of abuse and several cushions were launched my direction, so I went back to looking serious.

'However, this is what I think might work, but speak up if you see any flaws.'

About an hour later, we'd hammered into shape what everyone thought was a risky, but possibly workable plan, then split up to round up the various pieces of equipment and supplies we thought we'd need.

With that done, I went over the sections of the plan affecting each of the participants to make sure they knew what they had to do and when. As I always believe in planning for the best, but expecting the worst, we developed several contingency plans as well. Dave was pissed at not being part of the raiding party, but I needed him as a backstop.

With all that in place, we deliberately kicked back and rested as much as possible, double and triple-checking gear and plans every few hours.

The operation kicked off at twilight, with the launching of *Dragonfly*, with a full tank of fuel. It was to remain overhead for the duration. Bree and Sandy operated it as usual, although Sandy had a second part to play later on. The evening weather forecast was for light to moderate south-easterlies, a partial cloud cover with high tide at 22:00.

Aerial video from our faithful UAV showed no change to the position or number of boats or anything else around the resort, so we waited until dusk had settled in before very carefully moving *Firebird,* in complete black-out mode and with *Poseidon's* crew aboard as well, across the shallow water to the western shore of a small islet, just one kilometre south of No-Name Island.

Here we anchored, and while we waited, I placed a SatPhone call to the Mackay police station to say that I was on a trawler, the *Mary Jane* and could see a big fire engulfing some buildings on the little island immediately south of Bamborough Island in the Duke group. I hung up quickly to forestall any questions or further explanations.

CHAPTER 33

At 21:45, after another aerial check that there were no roving patrols in the area, we raised the anchor and silently motored the short distance to the tiny beach on the western tip of No-Name. I kept the forward-looking sonar running as we carefully avoided threatening rocks and extra shallow sand patches, until we were less than fifty metres off the tiny beach. The surrounding water was infested with more rocky outcrops breaking the surface. With the main anchor on short scope, and the south-east breeze holding us bow-in to shore, we were safe from drifting sideways onto any of the nasty hard stuff.

The shore party of myself, Jasper, Sandy, Alex, Corrine, Mary and Reggie, assembled at the stern and loaded our gear into the dinghy. Alex, Sandy, Corrine and I had comms headsets, and could talk to each other as well as back to the boat. Sandy ran us ashore, where we secured the dinghy, then headed off without delay.

The rearmost, or southern part of the cluster of guest huts was our first objective, and we made it without any human encounters, although I was still suspicious of the apparent lack of security, and didn't want to take any chances. We were all in dark clothing, while Corrine was in her super-sexy, camo jump-suit with a small backpack and a waist belt with a holster holding a PMR-30 pistol with a suppressor fitted. She quickly checked the six guest huts in the rear row, confirming they were empty.

Alex had his job to do and melted into the shadows beyond the wing of the main building to the east. Mary and Reggie stripped off all their clothes, immediately grumbling about the cool breeze on bare skin, and each put on one of the domino-type masks which Corrine had reported all the girls wearing. They were already wearing a collar, but these were only taped closed and weren't activated. Otherwise, they looked the same as any of the other thirty-odd girls on the island.

While the girls were stripping, Corrine went to the staff wing on the west side. There was a door on the end, which presumably opened into an access corridor. Sandy had blankets to keep Mary and Reggie warm while we waited, a good thing, as Reggie's goose-bumps had been getting almost bigger than her nipples. Corrine was quite a while, but returned with a surprise haul of five girls trailing along, luckily all fully and warmly dressed.

Corrine eased up beside me with a tall, dark-haired girl in tow. 'This is June. She's one of the senior girls and is delighted to be rescued. She's got some info you'd better hear first-hand.'

June surprised me by giving me a hard hug, then standing close, her lips beside my ear. 'Thanks for the rescue, Harry. Corrine says that you want to get all the collared crew out?'

'Yeah. That's the idea. It might get a bit messy soon, and I want you guys and girls out of the way.'

'Fuckin' brilliant. But Corrine said you were going to send two of your girls inside to talk to the others. I can do that a lot better, since they all know me. You had a good idea, but your girls would stand out too much as we all know each other very well by now.'

'Great. So long as you're happy to go for a wander around. Do you think everyone will want to come with us?'

'All the girls, guaranteed. Between our time on the boats, then coming here, it's been a very nasty experience so far. However, there are three of the guys we don't trust, because we think they're either moles, or are enjoying themselves too much. I wouldn't invite them. What do you want me to do?'

'This is terrific, June. Are you able to get small groups of girls away from the clients without raising too much attention?'

She nodded, the cool breeze blowing her hair around and tickling my face.

'Sure. Girls are always coming and going, although I can't get them all out like that. It'd be too obvious.'

'Understand. Tell everyone you trust, and get as many as is reasonable, to leave one or two at a time. There won't be time for everyone to get dressed, but for those who can, tell them to grab something on the way out. Getting as many as possible out of there and back here without raising an alarm is by far the most important thing. Tell the ones who need to stay, to act normally until the main lights go out. That'll be their signal that the action is about to start. There will be some dim, battery-powered emergency lights which will come on immediately, but that's when all those girls who are left inside, should make their way straight back here, as fast as possible. That's very important, since there will be a lot of noise, fuss and confusion.'

'Okay, Harry. Anything else?'

'Yeah. What other staff would you class as innocent workers?'

She didn't hesitate. 'The kitchen staff are just contractors. They've been good to us when and however they can.'

'Good. If you can, also tell them that when the lights go out, they should leave the building immediately, and head for the east arm of the island where the generator shed is. They'll be rescued later by the police. We can only take your group. Can you do all that?'

'No worries. It'll be a pleasure. So, it's most of our group back here before the lights go out, the rest as quickly as possible after they do. Then the cooks to the east arm. What about our collars? We've been told they set off alarms and do something nasty if we leave the area around the resort.'

'Yeah, they certainly do. But you can tell the others that I'll disable the collars straight after the lights go out. They'll all be unlocked at the same time, so everyone can just take them off, but each girl must bring her collar with her. Don't throw them away. That's very important!'

'I can do that. When do I go?'

'Right now, please, and get the first few out here as quickly as you can. After they arrive, I'll have the lights killed.'

I was impressed that she didn't waste time asking more questions, just peeled off all her clothes, grabbed Reggie's mask, and headed up one of the dimly-lit paths to the back of the main building.

'Okay, Mouse,' I said to Corrine, 'time to go get some records from Kazemi's office.'

She immediately turned and trotted up the path behind the quite spectacular form of the naked June, who was just going into the main building.

'Can we please get dressed now?' Reggie asked plaintively, her voice trembling with cold.

I grinned at her, 'Oh. Sorry about that. Yes, you can. Since Plan B is now in operation, June will do that job.'

As soon as she and Mary were decent again and warming up, I said to Reggie, 'Now that you're staying here, I have another job for you. I showed you the collar disarm procedure on the boat, so I want you to go to the radio room on the very end of the east wing, and as soon as the lights go out, press that green button three times, which will disarm all the collars. When the mains power failed, the transmitter will have automatically switched over to run on batteries, but that won't change the procedure. Just take your time and do it properly.'

She nodded seriously and went over the procedure to confirm it with me. 'I remember that, and I'll be very careful, Harry.'

'Good. You can go there now to find the transmitter before the lights go out.' Sandy passed her a small LED torch, after checking again it was working, then she trotted off.

Sandy then said to me, 'Back to the boat?'

'Yes, please dear, but a slight change of plan. Take Mary with you, plus these four girls, then come straight back.' I replied. 'Mary is to keep them by the dinghy until Reggie disables the collars. I don't want to risk anyone getting out of range until Reggie does her thing.

They mustn't try to go out to *Firebird* before the collars click open! And make sure they bring all their collars with them. I don't want any left on the island.'

We'd discussed the possible range of the transmitter, and decided that for safety, and the continued health of his expensive investments, Kazemi would have made sure the transmitter could cover the whole island, but I didn't want to risk them going any further. I also reminded our crew that as the island girls apparently hadn't been told about the lethal nature of the collars, they were to stick close to all the newcomers until we finished the job and unlocked the collars, in case someone tried to do something stupid like go for a swim!

Sandy waited until I'd briefed Mary, then they jogged away with the small, grateful flock trotting behind. Then I called on the hand-held radio.

'Sandy, Mary, plus four inbound, Dave. Mary is staying on the beach with the new girls until collars are unlocked,' I announced on the radio.

Alex would have heard that and would know that his action time was getting close. I kept waiting to hear some sounds of alarm from the main building, but there was only the hissing grumble of waves breaking on the rocky shore behind us, and the muted murmur of voices from the casino, with the occasional excited female laugh rising above it.

To our left, the rear door to the staff wing suddenly opened, and five naked girls spilled out into the cool night breeze, milling around in confusion, until I coughed to get their attention. They moved hesitantly toward us, uneasy about seeing a dark figure lurking in the lee of the nearest hut, although they settled down when I held out a couple of blankets.

'Good evening, ladies,' I spoke quietly. 'I'm Harry. I believe June told you we're here to rescue you?'

One short, delightfully rounded blonde girl, spoke up. 'Hello, Harry. I'm Ella, and this is Steph, Ann, Isabel and Mia. Yes, June did tell us what's going on and that we were to come straight out here without taking time to get clothes.'

'That's right, Ella. Things are in motion as we speak, and I couldn't take the risk of any of you getting caught again. We'll get you wearing something before long, but at least you'll be free.'

'Thanks, Harry. But we've still got these collars on. June said you could do something about that?'

'Yeah, we will be. But not immediately. Shortly after the resort lights go out, they will unlock and you can take them off safely, but please hang onto all of them. Do not throw them away. That's very important.'

She nodded vigorously, setting blonde curls and other very attractive bits bouncing. 'Understood, Harry. Do we just stay here with you?'

'Yep. No matter what happens, don't move. Very soon, my lady is coming to take you back to our boat.'

The five huddled together under the shared blankets for warmth, since the breeze was picking up quite a lot. Everyone jumped, when Corrine appeared in our midst like a ghost, laden with two heavy cases.

'Jeeze, Mouse,' I hissed, 'I wish you'd knock. You scared the shit outa me! Again!'

'Get stuffed, Harry,' she panted, 'these things are fucking heavy. Come and give me a hand, 'cause there's three more, plus I grabbed the computer hard drives.'

I didn't argue, but ran after her to the dark opening in the rear wall of the main building where Kazemi's office was. Two more medium-sized suitcases, very heavy, sat just inside the door along with a plastic box and a bulging soft leather bag. We hauled them back to the rear of the huts, to find that Sandy had just arrived.

'Well done, dear man,' she said slightly breathlessly, 'five more naked girls, and a pile of luggage.'

'Yes, dear,' I replied, 'just living down to my justly-earned reputation. But you need to get the girls and these bags back to the boat immediately. After the lights go out and the collars unlock, Mary can take them aboard, but you come straight back here again please, to collect the next batch.'

She was immediately back to being all professional, just nodding, then said to the girls, 'If you all want to get out of here, leave the blankets for the next lot, then grab a bag each. We've got about six hundred metres to walk, so swap the loads between you when you get tired. C'mon. Let's go as quick as you can.'

Her official Inspector's voice had the desired effect, as five girls dropped the blankets, grabbed a bag and staggered off into the darkness behind her.

'Good work, Boss. There was a shit-load of good stuff in that office, plus the safe was totally stuffed with cash from the casino, so I couldn't leave that behind. I guess the membership fees didn't cover gambling debts, or maybe members just paid everything in cash.'

'Well done. So, there's nothing of value left in there?'

'Nah. I grabbed every bit of paper I could find, plus the cash. He had this in a desk drawer, too.'

She reached behind her, pulled a Glock 17 from her belt, and handed it over. I checked the load and found it was part full. I jacked one round into the chamber and shoved it in my waistband in the small of my back.

'Okay. I'm about to tell Alex to pull the plug. Are you going to wait for Kazemi in his office?'

'Yeah. When the lights go, he's bound to want to check that his loot is safe. I'll grab him then.'

'Good. I'll give you thirty seconds, then call Alex.'

She disappeared without a word. I waited the time, then called Alex. 'Lights out, please Alex, then hustle.'

He replied with two clicks, then abruptly, all lights went out. There was an immediate chorus of feminine screams and male shouts from the front rooms of the main building, and the occasional crash of breaking glass. A few, very dim patches of light showed from the scattered battery-powered emergency lights, plus several torches were soon seen, their beams swinging wildly as the holders were jostled by hitting obstacles or being run down by panicked patrons. There was about five minutes of relative chaos, then a stream of naked girls poured from the main rear entrance, and headed down, what was to them, all too familiar pathways through the huts toward us.

I shielded a torch and flashed it at my feet as a guide, and we were soon surrounded by a chattering flock of naked girls, plus two guys wearing G-string pouches bringing up the rear. Thankfully, June was with them, and quickly found her clothes and dressed, while I passed the few blankets around the new flock.

'Terrific job, June. Thanks very much. It's made our job a lot easier.'

She gave me a tearful hug, 'Thank you, Harry, for doing this. This really is amazing if we can get away.'

'Oh, we'll get away alright,' I promised, 'we just need to redress the balance first. If you can help keep everyone together and under control, that'll be a big help. Things will be a bit crowded aboard at first, but we'll sort that out. So long as we have everyone safe and aboard, they're the most important things.'

She nodded, too overcome with emotion to speak further.

At that point, a breathless Sandy arrived and bent over to catch her breath.

I turned to the group and had to raise my voice to be heard.

'Quiet, please. Quiet.'

They shut up like I'd thrown a switch. 'That's better. I'm Harry and this is Sandy. If you want to get off this island and out of this slavery gig, please be quiet and do exactly as I say. If anybody wants to stay, please stick your hand up. Right now.'

Nobody even twitched, the guys included.

'Good. Very glad to see that. At any moment now, your collars will be de-activated and will unlock. When that happens… ah, there they go. Perfect timing. As I was saying, please remove them and hang onto them. Do not throw them away under any circumstances. Take them with you. As soon as we are joined by Reggie, the lady who just opened your collars, she and Sandy will escort you to our boat.

It might help you to know that both Sandy and Reggie are serving Queensland police officers. However, to continue. Do not leave the group or the track, and do exactly what my crew tell you to do without question. We'll be leaving the island within the hour, probably much less, and we won't have time to mess around finding any strays. If you wander off, for whatever reason, you get left behind. Is all that understood?'

There was silence, then a muted chorus of, 'yes sir's,' travelled around the large group. I had to admit, that even in the dim torchlight, I'd never seen such a large group of young, naked females before, and probably never would again.

Reggie re-joined us at that point, goggling at the assembled crowd.

'Fuckin' hell, Harry. This is amazing! If I didn't know better, I'd say you were being a bit greedy!'

I gave a short laugh – glad she was collected enough to make feeble jokes. 'Yeah, Reggie, very funny. But you're right, it's a night of firsts, that's for sure. Great job with the transmitter, by the way. I'm much happier now that's off.'

'No problem. It worked just like you said and I bashed it with a hammer until it's lights went out, just to make sure it stays off.'

'Good thinking. We won't be needing it again.'

I looked out over the flock again, 'Okay, girls and boys. Time to move out. Sandy and Reggie will escort you back to the boat. Just remember what I said about straggling, and do exactly what you are told. I know you are cold, but you'll be in warm shelter very soon.'

Heads nodded here and there, and more than a few started crying. Hopefully with relief or happiness. The two young guys pushed to the front, shook my hand and gave me a tight hug, which due to their state of undress was rather more intimate than I would have preferred, but I was happy to return their hug as it was worth it to see both with tears of relief streaming down their cheeks.

Sandy clapped her hands for attention, then led the way boat-wards, and the group slowly followed in a long straggling line, with Reggie bringing up the rear trying to keep them moving and on track. I counted as they went past, and came up with twenty-four fresh bodies, so I called Dave on the radio.

'Reggie and Sandy incoming with twenty-four new ones. Two are guys. They don't have any clothes, so best put everyone in the saloon with the heaters on. We'll worry about getting them dressed later. If anyone needs the toilet, ask them to hang over the stern. The on-board system will freak trying to cope with thirty-three extra sets of bladders and bowels.'

'Copied that,' came the laconic reply from Dave.

'And don't forget to hang onto all collars.'

'Copied.'

A few minutes later, Alex arrived, the big man barely panting, even though he had a pole balanced across his shoulders, with four twenty-litre jerry cans tied to it. Nevertheless, he grunted as he lowered his burden to the ground.

'Well done Alex, great timing. Any problems?'

'All good, Harry,' he growled in his deep voice with the lilting South African accent I liked so much. 'I didn't disable the generator, just flipped off all the circuit breakers and turned the fuel off. They might have some trouble restoring all that in the dark because I took the emergency torch as well.'

'Excellent. When you're ready, we'll just splash a liberal amount of this diesel fuel over all the rear hut walls in this row, and the two main building wings as well. But don't forget to leave this nearest hut untouched. I want the police to find a room with all the toys intact. The moment Corrine joins us, we'll light 'em up!'

It was the work of less than five minutes to soak the other four hut walls with diesel, then do the same with the end rooms of both wings. We hadn't long finished, when Corrine appeared from the back of the main building, pushing a tall man in front of her with the muzzle of her pistol. He had trouble walking, as his hands were taped behind his back, with a short length of electrical cord lashed between his ankles. His beautiful white tuxedo was in tatters, and blood smeared his face.

He also sported a black collar around his neck.

Corrine jerked him to a halt in front of Alex and me, and handed over a slim notebook and a portable collar transmitter, its battery light flashing.

I turned the torch on and considerately directed it in his face.

'Good evening, Mr Kazemi. It's regrettable that we have to meet under such circumstances, but I'm afraid you've been a very naughty boy.'

He glared at me through squinted eyes. 'Who the hell are you?' he demanded. 'You'll never get away with this. You can't just rob me and my guests like this. There are some very important people inside there. They can and will cause you a great deal of trouble.'

I smiled gently. 'Oh, we're not concerned about how wonderful your guests think they are, and we didn't come just to rob you, Mr Kazemi – we came for all the girls and boys you have enslaved and abused. For that crime alone, you are going to pay a very steep price. And as for all those very influential, sick arseholes you have here in this den of depravity, very shortly they won't be in a position to worry about me and my associates.'

He lost some of his bluster. 'What steep price are you talking about? Look, I have some money here, and can probably get more. Tell me your price and I'll pay it. If you leave immediately, I'll convince all my guests this was a horrible mistake and that all the fuss is over. Let me go back inside, turn the power back on, and everything will be back to normal.'

I smiled grimly. 'Oh no, Mr Kazemi. Things will never be

normal for you or your guests ever again. I did say you have to pay a very steep price for the untold amount of suffering you put all those girls and young men through. And I'm afraid to say that you really don't have enough money to settle that debt. And as for those depraved lunatics you attracted to this island with the promise of unlimited sexual pleasures with the girls and boys, they can explain to the police just what they are doing here. I imagine they'll have some very creative stories, but the evidence we've gathered won't support their lies for one second.'

He regained some bluster. 'You're a fool. Nobody will be here when the police arrive. Four boats, two jet-skis and a WIG aircraft will take care of staff and guests, and I know the girls won't talk.'

I shook my head, although he couldn't see it. 'I'm delighted to tell you, you foul, greedy shit-head, that they are already talking, but enough of this crap. Remain here for a moment until we complete our task, then we'll be taking a little walk.'

I passed him into Alex's not-so-tender care, took the last can of diesel and went to the back wall of the main building, splashing fuel generously against the walls and inside the open doors of the central hallway and Kazemi's office. I dropped the empty can and was walking away, when there was a scream of outrage behind me, and I heard the sound of a shot.

There was a strong tug and a sting at my left side, which made me stumble and trip over one of the pathway light pedestals, which probably saved my life, as several more shots rang out and I dimly heard the buzz of bullets passing by my ear, one of them close enough to graze my scalp. That meant I was a bit disoriented for a few moments, with a pain in my side and another over my left ear.

From my disoriented, horizontal position, what I didn't see, was a dark shape which launched from the shadows at the rear of the building, and briefly melded with the white-clad figure standing in the hall doorway, still wildly waving a gun around looking for someone else to shoot at. The wet, crunching sound which most certainly followed, would have been lost in the general background sound of screams and yells from the guests, as was the thump as the lifeless body of Kazemi's personal body-guard hit the ground. Soon after, I felt a dripping wet muzzle nosing around my face, then felt strong hands lifting me upright, and Alex's voice in my ear.

'I've got you Harry. Take it easy, man. Sandy's really going to be pissed! You've been shot. Again!'

As the mental fog cleared slightly, my mind suddenly decided to start working, and as I registered his words, I also noted a strong, pulsing wave of pain from my side and another from my head. Alex painfully stripped my jersey off and tied it tightly around my middle, putting some pressure on the main wound. Apart from the two sources of rather intense pain, I was mostly functional, and said so. Jasper appeared again and leant against my leg in support.

'You've got blood all over your face, Harry. Did you get shot somewhere else up there, as well as the side of your head?'

'Nah. That was Jasper giving me some CPR. He must have bitten someone and it's theirs. I really can walk, thanks Alex, but we need to dig out the old kitchen matches, sport. It's bonfire time and I can hear the ghost of Mr Fawkes calling us.'

He gave me a look that clearly said I must be in shock and was babbling, but he followed me to the rear of the huts where we lost no time starting the hut and wing walls burning. Being diesel, the flames were very slow to start, but with the wind blowing, I had confidence they would do the job, so we lost no time heading for the boat. I stumbled a few times, but Alex always seemed to be there to catch me, although by the time we reached the beach, I was feeling decidedly ordinary, and needed his full-time support.

Corrine kept her prisoner moving and his hobbled pace was about the same as mine.

Back at the dinghy, Sandy started straight in by giving me an earful for getting shot yet again, but for once Alex and Corrine over-rode her concern-motivated tirade, and got us all aboard and out to *Firebird* without further incident or delay. Once there, Corrine turned Kazemi over to Alex and headed for the foredeck. Sandy tried to look at my side and head under the red night-lights which made the blood on my face, sheeting down the side of my neck and down my side look black, freaking out some of the young ladies.

'For fuck's sake, Harry, you look terrible! You need to lie down and let Bree slap some of our magic green goop on those wounds.'

'Not yet, dearest one. We've got some things to make happen first. I'll lie down afterwards. I promise.'

She subsided, muttering dark things under her breath, but reluctantly let me make my way forward. There was no chance of getting into the saloon anyway. It was literally wall-to-wall, chock-a-block with mostly naked females, although more blankets and towels were being passed around to cover up all that delightful flesh. I was curiously pleased that I could still notice.

Alex followed me for'rard, half-carrying Kazemi by his neck, where we stood back while Corrine happily set up the Russian RPG-7, rocket-propelled grenade launcher. Dave had two packs of rounds stacked ready, and was in the process of loading the first round into the launch tube.

I waved grandly at Corrine, who was holding the loaded RPG-7 across her body, and looked like something dreamt up by the Star-Wars SFX team. My grand wave included the resort in general, the boats moored in the bay, and woozily, I nearly fell overboard in the process.

'See, Mr Kazemi,' I slurred. 'This is why I was sure your guests would be still waiting for the police to arrive. I'm afraid there won't be any WIGs, moustaches, boats or jet-thingy whatsits to remove them from the scene of their depravity. All those young people in the saloon behind you were enslaved by you for lust, greed and money. They're looking for justice and so am I. There won't be a team of smart-arse, over-priced lawyers to save you from the consequences of these crimes, my dear fat cockroach. But before we do anything about that, I want you to witness the end of your warped dream.'

In the middle of the island, flames were starting to rise above the roof-tops as the thatching on the huts eagerly caught fire, which greatly helped spread the fire as it relentlessly marched toward the main block. The ends of both wings were also burning well, the whole blaze driven by the gusty south-easterly, and the shrieks of alarm from the guests had turned to real fear as thick, choking smoke increased the dimness throughout the buildings. In an undignified pack, they jammed the exits as they started spilling out the front of the building onto the beach.

As the first groups stumbled toward the jetty and the boatshed, Corrine called, 'Fire in the hole.' A tongue of flame shot from both ends of the launch tube, the one at the front propelling the bulbous missile streaking toward the jetty. There was a deeply satisfying explosion as three dinghies, the WIG and half the jetty erupted skywards, leaving behind a spreading pool of fiercely-burning petrol.

Dave smoothly reloaded the tube, patted Corrine's shoulder, and with another warning, she sent a missile into the boatshed, converting it and its contents to splinters and another eruption of petrol-fuelled flame.

That was enough to send the lead elements of the panicking crowd scampering back toward the resort for the dubious shelter it offered. In case some brave soul wanted to take his or her chances with the local shark population, Corrine lobbed three more rounds at the boats lying at anchor. Two were direct hits and the targets simply blew up, while the third suffered a near-miss which still created enough of a hole in the side to allow it to quickly sink.

As well as sharing my love of destructive fires, Corrine really gets off on blowing things up, as the broad grin on her lovely face clearly showed.

'Well done, Mouse,' I enthused, 'great shouting... ahhh, shooting... I think!'

'Yeah. Wasn't bad, was it?'

Kazemi's face told another story as the bright orange light from the now raging fire, slowly consumed his version of the ultimate pleasure palace and cash cow.

I nodded at Dave, who quickly made his way aft. Moments later, the anchor winch started grinding as the chain was retrieved. There wasn't much out, so within a minute, we were easing backwards away from the rocky little beach.

That move prompted Kazemi to have another shot at me. 'I don't care what you say or think. My lawyers will have me out of the hands of the police with hours, and I'll use all my resources to come for you.'

I waved at the two lovely girls, Sally and Kim, standing beside me, watching me with mixed expressions or horror and concern, as I continued to leak puddles of claret onto my very expensive already-red decks.

'Gee. That's interesting. My lawyers here tell me quite the opposite. If I were to be stupid enough to turn you over to the police, they reckon you'd be in jail for the rest of your life, based on the evidence we've left in your otherwise empty fire-proof safe. But I can assure you that despite appearances, I'm not really that stupid. A bit silly sometimes, like now, but…. here, enough talk, let me show you what I mean.'

I could see that he was still trying to follow my convoluted line of discussion, so I took hold of one arm, and led him forward to the port bow. Pointing down, I said, 'Look – down there. That's what I'm talking about.'

Naturally he looked, then all I had to do was give him a gentle push so that he rotated across the safety railing and landed flat on his face in the water. He frantically tried to swim, before discovering he could just stand, although the slippery rocks made that difficult.

He also started screaming, and would have clawed at his neck if his hands were free, as the terrifying reality of his position set in.

Dave backed us up a good fifty metres, before turning to retrace our course back to where *Poseidon* was parked, and soon after, a sharp 'crack' echoed across the water. Thankfully, it was too dark to see details, but I stood staring at the small area of disturbed water lit by the orange flames ashore for a minute, before I realised Sandy had my arm and was trying to lead me below, while Jasper was mewling softly and nudging me to go with her.

CHAPTER 34

HOUSEKEEPING

There were still a few things I needed to organise before I submitted to being treated, so I asked Sandy, 'Have the Mackay coppers been alerted?'

'Yes, dear. Remember? You made the call well before we went ashore. They should be here shortly if they had a boat available.'

'Oh, good. Now, how about all the girls and the two guys? We need to get them dressed and bedded down for the rest of the night.'

'Organised, dear. When we pick up *Poseidon*, all our crew are going to donate basic pants and tops. It might be a stretch to get them all covered, but we'll manage until we get to civilisation. Where did you want to go?'

I sorted through some more fuzzy thoughts, feeling an intense, dragging weariness which even made coherent thinking increasingly difficult. 'We need to clear this area immediately and Yeppoon is the closest town with what we want. That beaut Keppel Bay Marina would be good value if they have space for us at short notice. From memory, it should be about seven hours away, once we get crews and boats sorted.'

Sandy and Dave were happy with that, and eased me through the crowd and down to our cabin where I was relieved to be told that one bullet had only grazed my left side, although it had painfully removed some flesh and scored a rib along the way. The one which grazed the left side of my head had made a decent crease, taking some more flesh and hair, along with a fair load of claret. It hurt like all buggery, especially when Bree insisted on washing out both raw grooves with Betadine antiseptic solution applied with what felt like a steel-bristle brush.

'Lucky, Harry,' she commented, ignoring my bleating as she expertly spread a thin coating of the magical green goop on all the hurty bits, and wrapped both my side and head with non-stick dressings and bandages. 'No stitches necessary and with the help of the green goop, they should heal nicely giving you two more handsome scars to brag about.'

She dosed me up with Panadine Forte, and pronounced me fit to live another day or two. Jasper wanted to try to speed up the healing process with his trick saliva, but we managed to convince him I wasn't about to fall off the perch just yet.

By then, Alex was easing us in beside *Poseidon*, so as the pain was already easing, I pulled on my oldest, softest favourite football jersey, and went up on deck to find we had already rafted up alongside the smaller boat. Corrine had washed Jasper's head and muzzle, then had to settle the mass panic which erupted amongst the new arrivals when he first wandered happily into the press of bodies, looking for heaps of affection from all his new friends. Little Krazy avoided all the feet by assuming her usual perch on his shoulders.

Sandy took charge of the looming clothing crisis, by first sending the *Poseidon* crew over to dig out all the clothes they could spare, while our lot did the same. We ended up with all the girls sort-of dressed, mostly just in a shirt, which still left me lots of bare bits to look at, which must help to speed my recovery. I think.

Settees, lounges, spare fenders and loose cushions became makeshift beds, and once both boats were underway heading south, everyone except the watch crew had their heads down. The huge stern daybed hanging over the stern was popular and held seven girls packed in like sardines.

Despite the pain-killing effects of the green gel, I was too wired to sleep, although the thought crossed my mind that it was probably best that the aphrodisiac side-effects of the magic gel hadn't kicked in, as Sandy let three girls take over our bed, with two more on the floor, and joined me on watch. With the wind on our nose, we had to motor for the first hour, but then as our course bent more south, I found that we could just make headway into the south-easterly with jib and mainsail set close-hauled. The further south we went, the more our course allowed me to bear away a little more, increasing speed. For once, Dave had to slow down to let us keep up.

This situation was one of the few drawbacks to having an all-electric sail boat, although if time was critical, I could have motored by running the two small generators flat-out, but since we weren't in that much of a hurry, I didn't bother.

With an ETA of 09:30, I called the Marina at 07:00, and was lucky enough to score two adjacent berths, so I booked in for at least two days, which I figured would give us time to work out the next step.

The same smiling, helpful crew directed us to our berths, and helped us tie up. I noticed a lot of amused looks and lifted eyebrows at the sight of nineteen crew on *Poseidon* and another thirty one on *Firebird*, most of them very attractive young ladies. The minimal standard of dress of most of our girls drew a steady parade of male marina workers who seemed to have a need to fix, paint or grease something on the jetty walkways nearby.

Curiously, many of the girls responded happily to the attention, perching prettily on the sterns and daybed to chat with their newest best friends. My head bandage drew a lot of sympathetic attention from the girls, which I milked as best I could when Sandy wasn't close-by.

I asked Sandy and Bree to organise a shopping list for the troops, with clothes, medical supplies, air mattresses and bedding as priorities, and Bree called a maxi-taxi when they were ready.

With that happening, I held a conference with Sally, Kim and Corrine. We had to retreat to *Poseidon* as the more extensive lounging areas on *Firebird* were occupied by small groups of rescuees, slowly relaxing and getting used to being freed from slavery, each group including at least one of the girls who'd been rescued earlier to answer questions and hold hands where necessary.

I looked at Sally and Kim. 'Two jobs, please ladies. First – go through the paperwork Corrine grabbed from Kazemi's office, and see what's interesting from a legal perspective. Secondly – you may wish to call your father, because I want to put your firm on retainer to help sort out what to do with forty-odd homeless young adults who've been severely traumatised. I intend to entrust their welfare to the government system, so I've been working on a few ideas which I need to think about further, but there could be a fair amount of legal work and added income for your small business.'

Both girls beamed. 'That'll be great, Harry. We don't get a lot of work, and Dad will love to be involved in this. Everyone's over the age of eighteen, so there aren't any custody battles. They're free to make up their own minds about what they want to do.'

'Yep. That's the way I see it too. With what loot we've recovered, money won't be a problem, but we aren't just going to hand each girl and guy a bundle of cash. I don't believe that helps anybody, and often totally stuffs people up if they're not well used to handling money. What I want is to create something more permanent for them to look forward to. Something worthwhile for them to do with their lives after they recover from this very nasty experience.'

They both nodded in agreement. 'Dad will agree with you completely. Let us know your ideas when you firm them up. But in the meantime, where's Kazemi's papers? We'll get started on that.'

Corrine went to her cabin where she'd stashed all the stuff from the island, and dragged up a suitcase stuffed full of papers. Sally and Kim took it to their cabin and started sifting through it.

As soon as they left, Corrine pulled up her shirt and slipped a slim notebook out from her waistband. 'This was on Kazemi's desk. I only took a quick look, but it seems to be a list of all the members of his 'Resort Club'. Both your lot and the Mackay coppers might be interested in checking them out.'

'Brilliant stuff, Mouse. I'll call M in a moment.'

Corrine giggled, 'Do you really call her M?

'Yeah. She started making cheeky references to my lifestyle being like James Bond, so I started calling her 'M'. The dear lady seems to like it, so it stuck. But what I need to talk to you about is we need to count the cash. You said there was a fair bit in the safe?'

'Yep. There sure was. Mostly flat packs of $100 notes, but other denominations as well. I needed two bags to stuff them all in. I presume it was all casino takings. But what was the other thing you wanted to talk about?'

I had a rare moment when I wasn't sure what to say, and just looked helplessly at her.

'Mouse, I don't know what to do next with all these young people. This is the first time in my life I've run out of ideas.'

She reached across the table, grabbed my hand and squeezed hard.

'It's okay to sometimes not know everything, Harry. Remember that just twelve hours ago you were shot, including one to the head. That scrambles your thinking for a while and takes some time to get over, even for you. You're trying to accomplish a very complex task way too quickly. Back off, Big Dog and chill.

Secondly, if you look around, you'll see a bunch of young people laughing, sharing stories and indulging in their own version of therapy. It's a much better system than a roomful of over-paid shrinks. However, inside each one is a psyche which has been ripped apart by these mongrels. These are still just kids. They haven't seen war like you and I have, or had prior experience of the scum of all nations, who prowl the streets preying on innocents like themselves.

Most may have come from abusive family situations, but they weren't equipped for that either. Whether you like it or not, you've given them hope for the first time in their short lives, and they trust you to turn their lives around.'

I nodded at the truth of her words. 'But what's the next move?'

'You've already started the healing process by rescuing them from slavery. Letting them see that hell-hole of a resort going up in flames was more great therapy. It showed that the old and dark part of their lives was gone. Burnt to ashes, along with the mongrels who enslaved them. The kids are still pretty messed-up inside, but as I just said, most seem to be starting to put the bad stuff behind them and are ready to start looking forward to something a lot better. We're here to help you achieve that, and when we do, it'll be the best thing we've ever done.'

I squeezed her hand in silent thanks, and she understood that no further words were needed.

'How about we get Dave and Alex counting the latest batch of cash, while you and I have a brief word to each girl and guy to get basic stuff like name, what their home status is, and what they want to do. That will give us a starting point for planning.'

I nodded, once again terribly grateful for Mouse's mental strength and clarity of thought. My head currently seemed to be stuffed with cotton-wool, while I seemed to be hearing weird buzzing sounds.

'Good thinking. Although I might speak to them all together first.'

While Corrine organised Dave and Alex to do a cash count, I went back to *Firebird* and mustered all the girls and the two guys together.

'First up, thanks for being cool with everything which went down last night. I know it wasn't easy, or pleasant, but we did what we thought badly needed doing.'

There were a lot of encouraging calls of 'Yay', from the group.

I smiled, 'I'm glad you approve. However, we want to keep moving forward, so I need to have a brief chat with each of you in turn, just to get some basic details, and find out what you want or would like to do. Have a think about that while you're waiting your turn. If you could all wait here, please, Corrine will come and get you one by one in a few minutes.'

I turned to go, when there was a brief outbreak of clapping, to which I just raised a hand in acknowledgement and kept moving, although it sent a shiver of pleasure down my spine and brought an unfamiliar tickle to my eyes.

Corrine and I set up in *Poseidon's* saloon, and as we finished with one rescuee, we asked her to send another one over.

By the time Bree and Sandy were back from shopping, we had worked through the whole bunch. Interestingly, their replies showed that while many still had a home they could potentially go back to, none wanted to take that option under any circumstances. Without having to ask why, enough girls volunteered the information, saying that they had either a sexually or physically abusive parent, parents, siblings or other relatives.

The two young guys were gay and had suffered the usual torment from parents who refused to accept that sometimes an individual's sexual preference doesn't conform to what used to be considered to be the social norm.

The other answer common to all and without exception, was that none knew what they wanted to do, except that, if given a choice, they didn't want to go back to their previous life on the streets either.

That dumped it back in my lap, but by this time, I had a glimmering of a serious idea.

I called base, brought M up-to-date, told her my idea, and asked her to make a few discrete enquiries. I talked my idea over with Sandy, Corrine, Dave, Bree and Alex.

'I've been totally out of ideas as to which was the best way to go forward from here. But thanks to Corrine's input, I think I have the start of a plan which might look after both the short and the longer-term problems, but as usual, it will require a lot of different things coming together to be successful.'

I went over my idea in general terms, and they were enthusiastic.

'Great. In that case, we'll proceed as though it's all a goer until told otherwise.'

Sandy and Bree had bought some airbeds, extra sheets, a few blankets and enough basic clothes so that those who'd donated clothing to the girls could have their own back. A more comprehensive shopping trip for all the rescuees would have to wait.

Bree told me we were good for supplies, *Poseidon* was good for fuel, so I decided we'd leave in the morning.

At another group meeting, I passed on the first part of my plan.

'We're working on a plan to look after everybody, and the first part of that is to leave here first thing in the morning. Our first brief stop will be Noosa to drop off Sally and Kim to collect their car, but there won't be any shore leave I'm afraid.' Nobody voiced concern about that, so I pushed on.

'We'll then be heading for our home base, the Gold Coast. I know some of you had homes there, but we won't be dumping any of you ashore. You'll all stay on these boats until our alternate arrangements are ready. Dave and Corrine have their own boat there, so you'll be able to spread out a bit more. It'll still be a bit cramped, to the extent that you'll have to share a cabin, but at least everyone will have their own bunk so you won't be inconvenienced too much, and hopefully, it won't be for too long.'

Mary called out from the back of the group. 'Don't worry about that, Harry. Compared to what we've all had to put up with, this is heaven.'

There was a round of cheering agreement, and it was encouraging to see them still in such an upbeat mood.

'That's great, thanks Mary. Now, Sandy and Bree have some air beds for those who have been bedding down on cushions and more sheets and blankets. We'll try to spread everyone out between both boats where there's some vacant floor space, because our first leg south will be an overnight sail. That means the boats will be rocking and rolling a bit, but I guess you're all used to boat motion by now. We also need space for the night watch to move around, so please don't block passage-ways. After we drop Sally and Kim off, it's just a day sail to the Gold Coast where those sleeping on the floor can have a proper bunk again.'

I made sure I had their full attention. 'By the time we get there, I hope to be able to tell you what happens next, but all I can say for now is, that if things work out as I've planned, I think you'll all be safe, properly looked after and hopefully happy.'

I was gratified to see a bunch of smiles and more than a few tears.

Afterwards, I took Sally and Kim aside. 'I can't tell you what I've got planned yet, but if I can call in a few favours and it works out, I'll need you guys to do a bunch of legal work shortly and in the future.'

They both nodded happily, 'No problem, Harry. We'll be ready when you are.'

'Thanks. If it's going to work, I'll be calling on you quite soon.'

Bree settled all accounts with the marina, and we enjoyed a lovely meal at the restaurant that night, our extended group nearly filling the place. Sandy and I reclaimed our bed, but as we had the biggest cabin, we had room for one girl on an air mattress. The girl was Philippa, who I'd seen sold to Ben and Linda, the weird couple who'd lost their first girl overboard in Bundaberg. She was very pretty, pleasantly rounded and had a bright, happy personality.

'Thanks for letting me stay here,' she said, as she worked the foot-pump to slowly pump up her bed, 'I'll stay out of your way as much as I can. Just pretend I'm not here.'

Sandy grinned in reply, 'You'll have to put up with Harry's habits, I'm afraid. He's always jumping up through the night to check on things around the boat. And he doesn't always remember to put his pants on first.'

She giggled. 'That's not a problem for me. If you need some private time, just say so and I'll disappear for a while.'

Sandy snorted. 'That won't worry Harry either, I'm afraid.' Philippa just giggled.

No night watch was set while we were in the marina, so everyone got a good night's sleep, although I must admit that I waited until Philippa seemed asleep, before becoming re-connected with Sandy. Twice even. Having to be subtle and quiet was a new experience, but interesting.

There were a few times when I thought Philippa might be awake, but she always seemed to be breathing evenly and deeply.

HEADING SOUTH

For our departure next morning, the weather gods took pity on us and turned the ever-present south-easterly into a light northerly. This made for very pleasant sailing and encouraged nearly all the crew to get out in the sun, mainly on the forward trampoline netting or the aft daybed. Bree had several helpers in the galley and a steady stream of drinks and snacks headed forward and aft. Jasper and Krazy loved having the undivided attention of so many new friends, and spent most of the day with them.

Bree got with Sandy and me during the day when the saloon was mostly empty, to catch us up with the money situation.

'Dave and Alex counted all the cash from Kazemi's safe,' Bree opened with, 'and the total was $4.8 million. I guess he hadn't been to the bank for a while, although even a fraction of that amount would have raised red flags. Anyway, added to the $2.786 mill from Turner and Yanos, that's a bit over $7.5 mill in cash. I've kept the $250K from the Collings as expense cash, so that's not counted in the total.'

I whistled and Sandy blinked a few times. 'I think I said to Taylor that I couldn't see this trip producing any loot, but I'm very glad to be wrong.'

She smiled, and continued the briefing. 'Naturally, we can't dispose of that amount of cash in Australia, so I suggest we plan another run to Vanuatu as soon as we can. But in addition to that, Corrine was able to access Kazemi's operating bank account, since he'd conveniently left his bank details and passwords in that notebook she rescued.'

I grinned and interrupted. 'I knew she was hiding something, our clever little Mouse.'

She grinned back, 'Yeah, well. It seems she can't help being good – it just comes naturally to her. Anyway, there was another $6.7 mill in there, which she's already transferred into that holding account we set up at the Bank of Vanuatu after the Indonesian operation. So, the total from this op is a bit over $14 mill. That should be plenty enough to kick off your cunning plan for the girls, if everyone else co-operates. Naturally, we'll draw on our accounts if we need more funds in the short term, then replace those funds with the cash when we get around to banking it. Although I doubt that we'll need to go that far, and will hopefully have enough left over to make a decent profit for ourselves, even after looking after the girls and guys.'

I looked admiringly at Bree. 'Well done. That will work very nicely. I love it when the bad guys get to pay hard currency for the damage they've caused. It's almost a shame they aren't here to get their knickers in a twist over losing all that lovely money, but then… just as well not.'

It was just before lunch when Mary brought the SatPhone over to where I was on duty at the wheel, while I gave Alex a break.

'Call for you, Harry,' she said with a grin, 'it's some lady I think, calling herself Charlie and she sounds very excited about something.'

'Thanks Mary. If it's the Charlie we know so very well and love, she gets excited about everything!'

'Hi, Charlie. Great to hear from you.'

That throaty, husky voice said, *'Harry. You lovely man. How are you?'*

'In general, moderately well thanks, although I do have a sore left side and head.'

She chuckled, *'Did Sandy punch you for being a naughty boy, again?'*

'Nah. Nothing as exciting as that. I sort of got shot a couple of nights back.'

Her voice sharpened, as she slipped effortlessly into her main persona of the Personal Private Secretary to the Prime Minister of Australia.

'Oh? Where did this happen? I haven't heard of an operation going on.'

'It's been a very low-profile undercover operation and is a bit of a long story, Charlie. I'll have to catch you up on it when we meet next. But apart from that, what can I do for you.'

'I heard about an enquiry originating from an office in the ACP, asking delicately about the current status of a certain property south-west of Beaudesert which was the former training base for that EarthCare mob. The enquiry had been hand-balled around several departments, trying unsuccessfully to find the right ones, since no one seemed to know anything about it.

All I can say on this phone is that a whole bunch of red flags were raised, your name was front and centre, so therefore I need to know where you are at the moment.'

'Well. I can confirm that I did originate that enquiry which seems to have stirred up a bit of a hornet's nest. But as for our position, we're currently sailing south in company with another boat and are almost abeam Gladstone. We plan to put into Noosa tomorrow to drop off two ladies, then continue on to the Gold Coast.'

'When will you be in Noosa?'

'Roughly about 08:00 tomorrow morning.'

'Hmmm. What about your position later on this afternoon?'

'Hang on a minute… We should be abeam Bundaberg, or at least Port Bundaberg at the mouth of the Burnett River, by around 18:00.'

'Standby Harry.'

I was on hold for a couple of minutes, then she was back. 'Okay. We've just received some more intel, so the Boss says this is urgent enough to justify a Falcon flight. I see there's a Port Bundaberg Marina at the mouth of the river. Can you pull in there at 18:00 to pick up a package?'

By now I was thoroughly mystified, but replied, 'Sure Charlie, we can do that.'

'*Great. Gotta go. Be in touch soon. See ya.*'

Mary had hung around and heard my side of things.

'She sounds an interesting lady.'

I smiled, 'You don't know the half of it. She's the Personal Private Secretary to the PM, and does more to run the country than Andy does. He'd be lost without her.'

Mary's eyebrows headed for her hairline. 'You mix with people in very high places, Harry,' she said carefully. 'Could it be that you're a lot more than you pretend to be?'

I gave my best enigmatic smile, 'Hell, no. Not me… I don't pretend to be anyone, but I do suspect we're going to have a visitor this evening. We've been asked to call in to Port Bundaberg Marina this evening to pick up a package.'

'Oh. Is this going to be trouble?'

'Nah, not for us. That's the beauty of being the good guys. We can get all the high-powered help we need. I don't like to call on that help very often, as it tends to bugger-up our hedonistic lifestyle cover, but sometimes we need assistance. Although I must admit that I don't know what the problem is this time. I haven't asked for help yet, or at least I didn't think I did.'

Sandy, Bree and Alex wandered out and I gave them an update.

'Should I try to find another bed, just in case?' Sandy asked.

'Yes please. If it's Charlie, she'd better share our cabin. Ask Philippa if she wouldn't mind camping on the floor in another cabin.'

'She can move into our cabin for the night, if that'll help,' Bree offered. 'There'll be a spare cabin up for'rard from tomorrow morning on, when Sally and Kim leave.'

'Terrific. Thanks Bree. So Philippa to Bree and Alex's cabin, and Charlie, if she's the mysterious package we get, in with us. I hope Andy doesn't decide to come as well. That might stretch things. She didn't shut up long enough for me to tell her we were overbooked.'

Sandy laughed, 'That sounds like Charlie. She'd talk underwater with a mouth full of marbles!'

Mary had a slightly horrified look on her face, 'This Andy you talk about. That wouldn't happen to be the Prime Minister, Andy Friar, would it? Like... he might come here?'

I grinned at her look, 'Yeah. That's the Andy. He's been here before, sailing with us, but I don't think he'll make it this time. They sounded pretty busy.'

Mary subsided with a puzzled frown and a quietly awed, 'Oh, I see... I think.'

I went inside to the chart table and called Dave on the VHF radio,

'Sorry to wake you up, old mate, but we have a slight schedule change.'

'Get nicked Harry. Cheeky prick! Anyway, where are we going now?'

'Just had Charlie on the blower. Can't say anything here, but we've been asked to call in briefly at the Port Bundaberg Marina to pick up a package. I worked out an ETA of about 18:00. Is that what you make it?'

'Yeah, close enough. What sort of a package?'

'You know Charlie. Didn't really say, but I suspect the usual. We'll go in and just stick our nose in where we can fit, so you can hold off outside. More later. Cheers.'

'Cheers, mate.'

The afternoon rolled quietly on, as we gently rolled and pitched steadily south, so that around 15:00, a party developed on the foredeck with most of the rescued crew. That in turn stirred Bree into making up a bucket of Pina Coladas, a *Firebird* staple. I called the marina and asked for a place to make a quick pick-up, and was told the outer 'T' of the central arm was free for now and they'd be happy to accommodate my request.

'Someone may turn up looking for us,' I explained, 'if you wouldn't mind pointing them in the right direction.'

'No problem, Harry. See you soon.'

The next little piece of excitement happened about 17:15, when from out of nowhere there was an ear-splitting roar directly overhead, accompanied by screams of fright from the bunch of freshly-pissed possums on the foredeck, as a very sleek, swept-wing jet with three engines mounted at the rear and RAAF roundels under the wings, screamed very low overhead, before pulling up into a very steeply-banked circling turn. It made one low 360° orbit of our boats, then levelled out on course for Bundaberg, rocking its wings as it went.

Mary came aft from the party, a strange look on her face. 'Was that your Charlie?' she asked.

I grinned, 'I strongly suspect it is. And you can relax – Andy won't be there. They wouldn't do that with the Boss aboard.'

'Fuckin' hell. It scared the living shit outta everyone!'

BUNDABERG AIRPORT

That afternoon, plane-spotters and other interested persons at the airport, were intrigued to see the very rare sight of a sleek Dassault Falcon 7X tri-jet in RAAF markings, make a circling approach and land on the main, two thousand-metre runway. It taxied to a position close in front of the main commercial terminal, but kept the engines idling as the forward air-stairs unfolded and a short, stocky woman, casually dressed in jeans and a bright orange shirt, made her way down to the tarmac where she was met by a uniformed attendant from the terminal. They headed for the terminal and disappeared inside.

Those inside would have seen the ground-staff member peel off as the sole female passenger headed across the terminal to the outside, and got straight into a taxi.

She drew a lot less attention than the Falcon, which had retracted its air-stairs the moment their passenger stepped clear of them. The engines spooled up as soon as the passenger and her escort were safely clear, before it taxied to the runway end, paused briefly, then with a thundering roar, accelerated quickly and departed the circuit area in a steep climbing turn to the south-west.

FIREBIRD

Approaching the Port Bundaberg Marina just after six o'clock with all sails furled, almost felt like coming home. Two figures stood waiting on the designated portion of the jetty, one tall and lean, one short and slightly rounded. I picked my way for'rard through the party still in progress, my nifty remote manoeuvring controller in one hand. Looking like a PlayStation controller, it gave me full control over both engines and the rudder, including the anchor, so I was able to show off by easing one of *Firebird's* slim bows gently against a fat fender the marina dude had considerately placed in position.

Our passenger was indeed Charlie, barely able to stand still with excitement. She carried a briefcase, and wore a small backpack. She tossed the briefcase to me, then with commendable agility, hopped over the safety rail and fairly launched herself at me with a huge hug, to the vast amusement of the fifteen or so bodies sprawled around the foredeck.

'Harry! Darling man,' Charlie cried with delight, although her eyes were busy assessing and cataloguing, 'but what's with the party? Where the hell have they all come from?'

I carefully disengaged myself, trying not to scrape our bow against the dock, as our shore-side helper grinned lustfully at the collection of naked flesh draped all about, and regretfully pushed us clear.

'Hang on a second, Charlie while I just back us away from this jetty. I had to promise the nice man that I wouldn't run into it.'

'You're still a smart-arse, Harry, and just as well… oh, thank you, young man. A Pina Colada. Just what I wanted and I must say that's a lovely, large thong you're almost wearing.'

'He's gay, Charlie.'

'That's alright, Harry. It's the same tackle and I can still look, can't I?'

'Of course, you can, dear lady. Anyway, come aft and we'll get going again. Everyone loved your fly-over. Most impressive.'

She giggled. 'I couldn't resist and I must say the Squadron Leader didn't take much convincing to have a play. It's a lovely little toy. But by the size of this crowd and that head bandage, you've got quite a story to tell.'

'Yes, I have. And apparently you do too. But wait until we get sailing again, then we'll talk. You're going to have to bunk down in our cabin, by the way. We're a bit tight on accommodation.'

Charlie looked around the saloon with neatly made-up airbeds with folded clothes on them. 'I can see that. I didn't think to ask if you had room for me. Please tell me you didn't just go cruising with two women's hockey teams for extra company?'

I laughed, delighted to see her and her irrepressible attitude again. 'Nothing as simple as that, I'm afraid, and there's another team camped on the other boat waiting outside the heads for us.'

She had a lovely time catching up with Alex, Bree and Sandy, while I took the wheel. I tagged onto Dave's stern quarter after we cleared the river mouth, then resumed our southerly trek into the lowering gloom, the north breeze holding steady.

I handed the watch over to Alex, and as the foredeck party was breaking up due to the drop in temperature and heading aft looking for clothing, we left Bree and her helpers heading to the galley, while Sandy, Charlie and I went down to our cabin for privacy. I pointed to the airbed on the floor.

'We moved a girl out so you could have this one, Charlie. Not the usual standard we like to offer VVIP guests on *Firebird* but it's the best we have at the moment.'

'Oh, that's fine for me, Harry. You know that.'

'Good-oh. We'll have a bunk for you tomorrow night, if you're still with us. But what's so important that you had to fly up here at such vast expense?'

'Okay. I'll tell you my story first, but then I need to hear what you've been up to. Twenty-five or so extra crew, and most of them nubile young females, is a bit over the top even for you, dear Harry.'

'We've got more of them on the other boat, but you've got a deal. Now let's hear your stuff.'

'First up, apart from telling Alex and Bree, this intel mustn't leave the cabin. I know you're all cleared Top Secret, but the Boss had to over-ride the objections from a lot of heavy-hitters to let me tell you this.'

We nodded agreement, so she went on.

'That enquiry you had your controller, the quaintly-named M, make about the ex-EarthCare property near Beaudesert, raised a heap of red flags. The reason is that soon after you and your team dismembered that ratbag mob, several government departments became interested in the place because it was there, set up appropriately, and naturally isolated. I won't bore you with the details, but the military training-base side of the complex has been expanded a lot, and now houses a rotating contingent of Army troops who find the dry bush environment sufficiently different to the jungle training facility at Canungra, to be good value. But the training base does double-duty as cover and protection for a ultra-high-security section within the base, which is under the control of both ASIS and ASIO. They keep all their terrorist detainees there. That is, the ones they deem too radical to be confined in general prisons. It was quickly realised that the average impressionable, stumble-bum criminal would be too susceptible to conversion to radical fundamentalism if these turkeys were allowed to mix freely in general prison population.'

I grinned, 'Sort of like our version of Guantanamo Bay?'

She nodded seriously, 'Yep. That's exactly what it is, although no one will ever admit it. So, you'll understand that not the slightest hint of this place can be allowed to leak. Especially to the media. We'd have all the bleeding-heart liberals screaming persecution, and every radical organisation in the country trying to bust the inmates free.'

'Yeah. That makes sense. I can understand now why my enquiry caused a bit of a furball.'

'Yep. But the big question I've been ordered to ask is – what's your interest in the place? Unless you're looking to give up the sailing life and go bush?'

'No way, Charlie. The very short story behind my enquiry, is that we have a total of thirty-eight young ladies and two gay guys on our hands, most of whom we managed to rescue from a sex-slavery resort. Before that, they were all in a sex-slavery situation on private boats up and down the Queensland coast. Despite their happy appearance at the party this afternoon, they've all been severely mentally and physically traumatised and most still are. Some have physical scars which are slowly fading. Nearly all have come from abusive family backgrounds which they had run away from and were living on the streets, which is where they were kidnapped by a dedicated crew. After being stored on the ring-leader's boat for a time to be suitably brain-washed, they were then individually sold into sex-slavery, but most ended up at a private resort up near the Whitsunday's which offered luxurious accommodation, 5-star food, a casino and a do-what-you-want-with sex-slave for each Club member. Then we came on the scene, although the details of how they got to that point and their rescue will make up a much longer story which I'll be happy to explain at another time.

There is another much darker aspect to this operation which we managed to shut-down, but not before one young girl was shot and killed.'

Charlie looked shocked. 'What do you mean, 'shot and killed'? You mean accidently, don't you?'

I grimly shook my head. 'Afraid not, my dear. The plan hatched by the leader of the kidnap crew was to sell the rights to extreme hunters to chase and shoot at a girl. They found a deserted, swampy island in the Great Sandy Straits where two brave arse-holes armed with rifles, got to chase down an unarmed girl. It was a shoot-to-kill deal, and one poor girl found out the hard way!'

Charlie was quiet as her extraordinary mind recorded every word and nuance of my tale. 'Dear God, Harry. That's almost unbelievable! But you said that you'd stopped that operation. What happened to the people involved?'

I gave a grim smile. 'Totally off the record, there is no trace of any of those persons to be found. In other words, no loose ends!'

Charlie looked thoughtful a moment, then said, 'Right. That'll do at this stage, but I will need a full verbal report at a later time, if you don't mind.'

I smiled gently at her. 'Of course not. I know it's going to the right place.'

She patted my leg, 'Thanks, Harry.'

With that awkward moment covered for now, I carried on. 'I've stuck my neck out and made the promise to all the young people that we'd look after them somehow, and I intend to honour that promise. They're good young people – none are hooked on drugs, thank goodness – who've had to endure some truly horrible things, like wearing range-limited explosive collars, as well as be subjected to the grossest sexual excesses their owners could think of to inflict on them.'

The look on Charlie's face was again of shock. 'Explosive collars! What's this about explosive collars? What the fuck's been going on?'

I held up one hand. 'Chill, Charlie. As I said, we've been there, done that, Sandy's already designed the T-shirt. It's been stopped. The guys who started it are no more. All the surviving victims who wanted to escape are right here with us on these two boats, and the sex resort and illegal casino has been reduced to ashes. The Mackay water police should still be sifting through the ashes and conducting interviews with a small, but high-profile group of VVIPs who happened to be stranded on the island.'

Charlie showed a range of emotions at this brief summary, finally letting out a large breath, before holding up her own hand.

'No more summaries, dear man. Tell me the whole story from the start.'

At that point, Bree, with commendable foresight, brought several plates of hot and tasty finger foods down to us, along with wine for the girls and beer for me. While we got stuck into the food and drinks, I fossicked around in the pile of loose boxes beside Charlie's bed and produced a collar and a transmitter box.

Charlie was alternately amazed, disgusted and finally dismayed as I explained the workings of the device and sat for long minutes, turning it over in her hands, muttering vile expletives. We spent the next couple of hours going through the whole operation in fine detail, right from the time we first heard about Hanh from Mike Adams. Although Charlie had an amazing memory, before long, she pulled a legal pad from her briefcase and made copious notes as the tale unfolded.

She also interrupted my narration several times to clarify a point.

'So, there's a boat being sold in Hervey Bay which used to belong to one of the owners of a girl?'

'Yep. In fact, it should be sold by now. We only asked $150K and it was in very good nick. The other boat trailing off our sterns with girls on it that Dave's driving will also be sold, but not until we have a home for all out strays. It should bring in a fair bit more than the one at Hervey Bay. Like maybe $500K or so.'

'Okay, so two boats to be sold. What happens to the proceeds?'

'They go into the general pot. We decided to set aside all the proceeds of this operation to take care of the rehabilitation of all the girls and boys.'

She nodded. 'That's generous, Harry. But I hate to point out that even six hundred and fifty grand isn't going to go far with re-hab on the scale you're talking about.'

Bree poked me in the ribs. Luckily, not the shot side. She was getting as bad as Sandy at that. I jumped, coughed gently in surprise, then said, 'Actually, Charlie, there's a bit more than that already in the pot!'

She sat back and cracked a grin, 'Why am I not surprised to hear that, knowing your propensity for covering operating expenses with what you delightfully call 'spoils of war'. How much have you tripped across this time?'

I looked at Bree who was the business manager of our team, and she smoothly replied, 'Aside from some cash we've kept for immediate expenses and purchases for the troops, and with the Hervey Bay boat sale plus various bits and pieces, it's close to $14.5 mill. Additionally, the motor boat we're following can also be sold soon. That should be another $500K at least, so we're looking at somewhere around $15 mil.'

Charlie looked slightly stunned. 'Fuckin' hell! You guys don't mess around do you? So, do you reckon all the loose ends of the sex-slave operation have been wrapped up? Apart from the forty-odd girls and couple of boys?'

I nodded. 'Pretty well. I know the rescuees won't take too much convincing to keep quiet. It's not exactly a life experience they'll want to share with anyone else or put in a resume. There was a little bit of carnage along the way, unfortunately. The shootings at Slain Island left no trace. A house, a car and trailer boat at Maaroom village, just up from Tin Can Bay were burnt down, as was the casino-resort, three member's boats, sundry small boats and a Wing-In-Ground effect aircraft on No-Name Island, located south-east of Mackay. It was Turner and Yanos who conceived the scheme, and they're both gone, never to return. That character Kazemi, was the resort owner and he's gone too. The couples on the boats who Kazemi bought the girls and boys from have been well-paid for their investment and they definitely won't be doing any official complaining or loose talking, for that matter. Interestingly, since they've come to like the experience, some are actively looking to acquire more girls, so they certainly won't be talking to police or media!'

Charlie added more notes to her list. 'Good. Now, what was your plan behind the enquiry about the EarthCare place? Even your controller didn't know why you wanted the info.'

I shrugged. 'We decided we needed somewhere safe and isolated to place all these young people. There was no way we were going to dump them either into the official public system, or back on the streets. That's how they ended up here in the first place. It'd be a total, unmitigated clusterfuck if either option were forced on them! I had the notion that perhaps we could buy or lease the health-retreat side of the place, and engage some professional people to look after them. I didn't give any consideration to the military barracks side of the place, since I didn't know that it had been activated, or there was even much still there. We've interviewed all the rescuees and they have nowhere they can, or even want to go. As things stand, they literally have nothing – no home, no clothes and no money, apart from the few basic clothes we've already bought for them. As I've mentioned, I made them a promise that one way or another, they'd be looked after and they seem to be relying on us to do just that. It's something we can do in the short term, but is impossible for us to carry on alone in the longer term. We've got $15 million to toss into setting up something to look after them and we're happy to tip in more if that's not enough. But we need assistance to carry this on in the long term.'

Charlie looked thoughtful as she continued scribbling, so I continued.

'We thought they'll need a psychiatrist, at least a couple of counsellors, a doctor and medical support staff, cooks, trainers and a resort maintenance crew. Looking further ahead, I had the thought that as the girls recovered, those who were so inclined could progressively take over the running of the place with the longer-term aim of opening it up to outsiders as a health-retreat business. All the infrastructure is there. The kids would need the right training, of course, but we could engage proper administration people so they could provide the training. It would be good therapy for the young people to learn something useful and interesting. Those who took on jobs there would get paid a proper wage, and it could be a business that each could perhaps acquire a financial share in. The fine details of this plan are a bit sketchy at the moment, but before any of that could be developed, we just needed somewhere safe for them to recover. I thought it would also be helpful for them to be away from mainstream civilisation while they recovered. After chatting with them these past few days, it just seemed to me they badly need a purpose to their damaged lives and this could provide that purpose. So, as I said, if the fifteen-odd mill isn't enough, we have a healthy bank account and plenty of income, so we can top it up for a while.'

Charlie had suspiciously damp eyes after that lengthy explanation of my plan, and said, 'I don't quite know what to say except that it's a fuckin' brilliant plan, Harry and you guys are incredible! If things work out as I expect, I'm almost certain that we won't need all of your $15 mil, but I'll revise my notes and let the Boss know in the morning. The way I see it at the moment, it could work to the advantage of everyone. The military compound and detention centre would have the additional cover of a genuine, functioning rehabilitation health retreat, and the girls and boys would have a place to recover in peace. But that call is way above my pay grade. Maybe we should go mingle with the troops now while I digest all this. I'd like to get a sense of what they're like first-hand.'

CHAPTER 36

BACK HOME

It ended up being a funny night. When she changed hats from being the PM's PPS to a normal person, Charlie was a charming, bubbly, and a very charismatic, down-to-earth lady. The girls still had a buzz going from the afternoon indulgence of Pina Coladas, and responded to Charlie's light-hearted chatter in a very positive way. We didn't say exactly who she was, just suggested that she was a wealthy friend with connections in very high places. I don't think any of them had noticed that the jet was in military markings, except Mary who knew our guest was a seriously VVIP.

It was late when we went to bed, as I'd sent Alex off early to get his head down, while I took the first watch.

The main challenge that evening was to give the northern tip of Fraser Island a wide berth as the broad area of shifting sand bars made it a good spot to avoid. Then we had a clear run south to the mouth of the Noosa River.

I handed the watch over to Alex at 01:00 and went below to get my head down. Charlie and Sandy were asleep in separate beds, and stayed that way, so I actually had a decent sleep until 07:00, when we started our approach to the shallow, twisting entrance to the Noosa River, including the usual bit of fun with breaking waves on the outer bar. There was a public access jetty just downstream from the bridge in the middle of town, and with Sally and Kim packed and ready to go, I did my party trick with the remote controller by nosing one bow in against the jetty, allowing them to step off in a reasonably elegantly manner.

We attracted a fair amount of attention, even at 07:30, as the sight of an 83-foot red cat dropping two attractive young ladies off in the middle of town was apparently unusual enough to draw a small crowd.

'I hope your car is safe,' I called out whilst allowing the out-going tide to drift us slowly away from the jetty.

'We'll be fine, and thanks for everything, Harry. It's been a real hoot. Talk soon.' called Sally.

A parting wave, then we pivoted in a tight turn and headed back to the bar channels and the open ocean. Dave was loitering just outside the shallows, so I slid in behind him, the north-easterly allowing us to sail comfortably without using power.

After an early breakfast, Charlie grabbed the SatPhone, commandeered the port bow seat and called the Boss to give him the summary of what she'd learned last night.

Luckily for our phone bill, she kept it to the short version, after which she gave me a thumbs up and a grin. 'Good one, Harry. The Boss likes the concept, particularly since firing up the health retreat won't cost the taxpayer anything. Even though a lot of work had been done on the military camp side, the resort place has been in very basic caretaker mode since the demise of EarthCare. There's just a small administration staff and basic maintenance staff.

He's going to run it past the other agencies involved to make sure they don't have any particular concerns, but he really liked the idea of having a functioning health retreat as extra cover for the military side of things.'

We discussed a few other aspects of the idea as the low, watery hillocks slid peacefully and unobtrusively past our slim hulls, and the crew and passengers lay drowsily around in the sun.

'They do seem a happy lot, when one just sees them like this,' Charlie observed, 'but after talking with them even for such a short time, I can see they really have a lot of emotional baggage weighing them down.'

'Yeah. That's the big problem. It wasn't until I promised that we wouldn't just turn them loose on the streets, that they'd even smile again.'

The time was getting on for 17:00 before we were approaching the Gold Coast Seaway, and another fifty minutes before we were docking beside *Poseidon* at the Yacht Club marina where I'd arranged temporary berths for both boats. I still had a permanent mooring out from the marina where I normally preferred to park, but with such a large crew aboard, it would be much easier for everyone to be able to come and go straight onto dry land instead of via endless dinghy shuttles. The berths were also conveniently close to Dave and Corrine's sleek and fast Italian power cruiser, *Seeker*.

Sandy had moved Charlie into the cabin vacated by Sally and Kim, and after much discussion with Corrine, they worked out how to spread all the girls and the two guys between all three boats. By dinner time, everyone had their own bunk, although some were more palatial than others. We also decided to eat locally in the club restaurant for at least that first night back, our party nearly filling the place and generating a huge amount of talk amongst the local bar-flies.

During dinner, Charlie took a phone call from the Boss and after a few minutes, leant over to ask quietly in my ear.

'Is there anywhere close by where we can get picked up by a helicopter?' she asked.

'No problem. Just up toward Seaworld, past Marina Mirage and the trawler wharves, there's a large grass area on the south side of SeaWorld's carpark which itinerant helicopters often use.'

She passed that on, then terminated the call.

Back aboard, she made another lengthy call.

'Seven-thirty tomorrow morning, south end of the Seaworld carpark,' she said cryptically, 'you, me, Sandy, Corrine and Bree.'

I scored another good sleep that night as Charlie stayed in her cabin, and both Sandy and I were tired. Life can be tough sometimes.

I was up early next morning, using shore water to hose the salt off the decks, sails and fittings, hoping to get back into my relaxing home-port routine as soon as possible. Generally, after an operation, there was a period of looking over one's shoulder for more bad guys, but in this case, we still had forty homeless young people to look after, which constituted a sizeable mental distraction. I looked over at the next berth and saw Dave coming out of *Poseidon*'s cockpit, hose in hand, ready to do the same, so wandered back to chat.

He and Corrine had moved back into their palatial cabin on *Seeker* as soon as they docked, but he still wanted to look after *Poseidon* while it acted as home to a bunch of girls.

'Gidday, mate. All your troops well?'

He grinned, 'Yeah, all well. Everyone's got their own bed, so they're happy. Rather cheerful lot, really, considering the circumstances.'

'Yeah. I agree. While I think of it, will you go and poke Mouse in the ribs and tell her to be ready to roll at 07:15. Charlie's laid a trip on for the five of us, with a 07:30 pickup over at Seaworld. We'll take the dinghy.'

'Yeah, sure mate. But how about you do it? I've got some hosing to do.'

'Bugger that for a joke! I know what she's like first thing in the morning. You do it. You live with her.'

'But I'm really busy.'

'Man-up, Dave. Show her who's boss and all that cave-man stuff. Besides, I'm not sick of living yet. Don't forget, we leave at 07:15.'

'Pussy!'

'Big-girl's blouse!'

Despite Dave's trepidation at stirring Corrine too early, she and Dave were waiting when we swung past *Seeker*'s berth with Alex driving the dinghy. It was a brief run across glassy water to the sand beach where a large area of grass bordered the vast sealed carpark of what was the best theme park in the country.

Alex dropped us off, and headed back to talk someone into making him breakfast, since we'd pinched his favourite cook.

All was quiet at that hour, with the small fleet of trawlers at their wharf just inside the next little bay to the south, and a few houseboats nosed up to the shore, their owners out on deck with morning tea or breakfast. We exchanged cheery waves with some, before we heard the distinctive throbbing beat of a large, multi-bladed helicopter approaching at speed. The two local helicopter operators, Seaworld and Helitours, were still closed, so hopefully it was our ride.

The noise swelled as the helicopter approached, until with a thunderous roar and a massive blast of down-wash which made the trees by the water's edge trash wildly, an Army Blackhawk made a straight-in approach from the west. The touch-down was gentle by Army standards, which meant the oleo struts on the landing gear only compressed most of the way. The crew-chief immediately jumped out holding five headsets with dangling mike cords, routinely checked the tail clearance, signalled the pilot, then trotted across to our group.

Tossing me a quick salute, he said, 'Commander Stevens, Ms Langley plus three? If you'd all put these on, then follow me please.'

We gladly did so, since the noise level of a Blackhawk, even at ground idle, was in the painful range when standing close.

I was interested to see that we only rated the utility version interior, with webbing seats, but at least we could plug into the communication circuit, which I did straight away.

I immediately heard, 'Commander Stevens? I'm Captain Tanya Walsh, your pilot for today's mission. Although we've been placed under your command for the day, my instructions, should you approve, are to fly to a military-controlled, prohibited area in the scrub south-west of Beaudesert, land wherever you indicate and we can fit, then wait for you and your party to complete your business. My crew and I are then to return you to this location. Does that meet your requirements at this stage?'

Luckily I had a fair idea of what Charlie's little surprise entailed, and replied, 'Good morning Captain. That plan will be just fine as stated, thank you. You may or may not know that there is a civilian facility immediately adjacent to the Army controlled installation. We only need to visit the civilian facility, so please land where there should be a large, clear grass area suitable for this aircraft just out front of the main building.'

'Very good sir, and thank you. We'll depart immediately if there's nothing further?'

'All good, Captain. In your capable hands.'

The turbines spooled back up to flight idle, then when stabilised, pitch was pulled and the aircraft lifted smoothly, rotated neatly on its axis, then accelerated in an alarmingly steep nose-down attitude out across the sparkling expanse of the Broadwater, before climbing hard for altitude prior to reaching the built-up area of Southport as we headed south-west. The power and acceleration of the nearly empty helicopter was very impressive.

With only twenty-seven nautical miles to travel in a straight line, the Blackhawk ate up the distance in just twelve minutes. We flew over scrubby bush once past Beaudesert, until a cleared area became visible through the forward windshields, where a wide, paved road led off from a smaller country road we'd been more or less following. There were two distinct groups of buildings, the closer ones difficult to see as the various buildings were painted in camo patterns to blend into the scrub, and there had been minimal bush clearing around them.

The other was in total contrast, and looked like a hotel, with a large, white central building in a boomerang design, with the inner curve embracing two rows of two-story buildings. There were several other small buildings isolated from the main ones, and the whole thing was surrounded by lush, green lawns, and a tall wire fence. On the eastern or military side, the encircling cyclone fence was ominously topped with loosely-coiled razor-wire. Entry to both compounds was via a gatehouse established beside an arch supporting a substantial sliding gate. From our height, I caught a fleeting glimpse of a wide, metallic slot across the road, suggesting that a steel barrier was ready to be instantly hoisted into place to stop any unwanted vehicles who showed signs of not wanting to stop.

The road forked once past the gatehouse, with one road leading to the camouflaged military area, and the other sweeping grandly in a circle around a huge expanse of manicured lawn and flower beds, past the two-story main entrance portico, itself supported by tall, white pillars.

Captain Walsh made one brief circuit, before landing gently on the lawn, the massive downwash doing fearsome damage to the rose gardens. Once the motors were idling and the pretty, multi-coloured petal-storm had subsided, the engines were cut, dying with a fading whine. As the rotor was braked to a stop, the crew-chief opened the left sliding door and shepherded us out.

Behind us, Captain Walsh and her co-pilot were heads-down in the cockpit, busy writing pilot stuff in log-books.

A tall, well-groomed woman clad in a pale-blue suit, complete with Hermes neck scarf, and who looked to be in her late forties, stepped briskly down from the portico onto the driveway. There was a frown on her face as she contemplated the slightly ragged group dressed in super-casual clothes facing her. At least Sandy had talked me into jeans and a polo shirt. Her frown deepened, and her mouth developed a full-blown cat's bum scowl, as she took in the imposing sight of the Army Blackhawk helicopter parked behind us on the lawn, its camo-paint work temporarily, but heavily decorated in freshly-shredded, multi-hued rose petals.

In a prim, school head-mistress type voice, she announced to our group in general, 'Commander Stevens, I presume? I'm Camilla Ellis, caretaker of this government complex.'

I shook her firm hand and introduced Charlie, Sandy, Corrine and Bree.

Although I took an instant dislike to her imperious attitude, to try to be a good boy by way of further explanation, I stated. 'Ms Johns and Ms Welsh were here when it was an active EarthCare base. Ms Johns shuttled between both camps, while Ms Welsh was only on the military side. Let's just say they had other duties at the time.'

Camila's eyebrows raised in surprise, 'Hmmm. I see,' she said, before turning to address Charlie and Sandy. 'May I presume that one of you is the Administrative Services person I was told about? I received a call from someone in the Prime Minister's office saying that a person would be coming here to make an inspection of the facility. I really don't know why that is necessary as I send in detailed reports every few months, and it is such terribly short notice… really most inconvenient! And on top of all that, that dreadful helicopter has de-headed half the roses. I'll have to speak to that arrogant fool of a pilot. Absolutely no consideration, some people. The damn military think they can do what they want – when they want.'

I could feel the tension radiating from Charlie as she was winding up to explosive levels beside me, so as I gently touched her arm, I hurriedly asked, in my mildest tone, 'Have you held this administrative position very long, Ms Ellis?'

She blinked at the odd question. 'Well, yes. About eighteen months, in fact. May I ask why you need to know that?'

I ignored her question. 'And may I presume that you have enjoyed being the administrator of this excellent establishment?'

She blinked again. 'Well. Yes, of course. Although it's very hard work keeping things in shape and watching over the staff. Terribly lazy lot they are. I have to watch over them all the time.'

'Yes, I'm sure they are. But before we proceed with the inspection, I'd like to correct a couple of misconceptions you seem to have. Firstly, the person who informed you that an inspection was to be made today, was actually the Personal Private Secretary to the Prime Minister, and was acting on his direct instructions.'

'Oh, really. But how do you……?'

'Furthermore, the person who is making that inspection today, along with myself and my other two colleagues, happens to be the self-same Personal Private Secretary to the Prime Minister.'

'Oh… oh dear. I say… I…'

'No, please don't! Under the circumstances, I think you've said more than enough. Furthermore, the pilot of that helicopter was acting under my direct orders. I think the roses will grow back just fine, don't you? I'm told they need some pruning occasionally for best growth. And now, we'd all be obliged if you would return to your office as we have Ms Johns to show us around. She knows the place extremely well, having been second-in-command of both facilities in her time here. On our inspection tour, we'll decide for ourselves just how well you've been caretaking this valuable government facility, and consider whether it should even be left in your hands any longer. In the highly unlikely event we need anything else from you, we know where to find you. Thank you, Ms Ellis. Bye for now.'

Given no opportunity for a rejoinder, and with an ashen complexion, she stumbled as she turned away, then regained some composure before stalking back inside, her back stiff in outrage as though she had a broomstick up her bum. Behind me, I heard several poorly stifled giggles, then Charlie broke down and said, 'Oh, Harry. That was absolutely superb. Anytime you want a career change, just let me know. You'd be a shoo-in!'

I turned with a grin on my face. 'That really was fun, wasn't it? What a stupid woman. She'll be the first to go. Anyway, let's get on with the tour. Ms Johns, if you'd be so kind as to lead on?'

Corrine poked me in the ribs as she passed. What is it with female fingers and my ribs?

The marble-tiled, spacious entry foyer, with an empty reception desk offset to one side, had several lounge suites and armchairs scattered around for casual chat groups, all under a soaring atrium with glass panels letting in copious amounts of natural light. An operating fountain held centre stage and several small trees and native shrubs in decorative pots were dotted about, with several of the ubiquitous sparrows flitting about, their cheery chirps helping to dispel the empty feel of the place, by bringing the outdoors, indoors.

The standard of the former EarthCare VIP base was very high, and the forty rooms for senior staff and guests were spacious and luxurious. Even the twenty smaller rooms for service and maintenance staff were 4-star comfortable. The main block housed a kitchen with every modern convenience, adjacent to one large dining room with a smaller one which could be partitioned off from it for small, private briefings or VIP dining. As per Corrine's reports, there was a full medical suite including X-ray facility, pharmacy and even a small operating theatre. A spa and various specialised treatment rooms, conference rooms, two pools, the indoor one was heated, the outdoor one wasn't. That completed the list of facilities.

The buildings were surrounded by immaculate lawns, and were in turn ringed with seriously high cyclone fencing in good condition. The view to the north wasn't terribly inspiring, being just a vast expanse of low trees and scrub stretching to the horizon. I took note that apart from the razor-wire on top of the eastern fence, no indication of the presence of the military compound was visible from anywhere on the resort grounds or from the buildings. A small cluster of low hills dominated the view to the south.

The cleanliness and near-perfect condition of the facility and grounds were such that we soon realised it was Ms Ellis who was 'dreadfully lazy' and not the staff. The few we came across were all happy and helpful, but developed a sour look whenever Ellis's name was mentioned.

Once back out front, Charlie asked, 'What do you think? Will this be suitable for your collection of waifs?'

'Oh, hell yes. Absolutely perfect, in fact. And with the right people in charge, there's no reason why selected outsiders in genuine need of a health retreat-style treatments shouldn't be accepted much sooner rather than later. I can't see any problem with them mixing with the girls and boys. The income will help offset costs, and the psychiatrist, counselling staff and medicos can be kept busy treating the paying guests just as well as the girls and boys. When we get the young people installed, we can see how many are willing to help run the place, under the supervision of the experienced personnel. They would get paid for working, of course. I can also see how it would be excellent cover for the military base activities.'

Charlie smiled. 'The Boss and I agree with all that, and for that reason alone, I think he will be delighted to fast-track the project. We'll look after the staffing arrangements, as they'll need to be approved by the Department of Defence. So, if you're prepared to make some funds available, I'll set up a trading account with a local bank.'

Bree duly noted that and said she could arrange funds transfers as soon as the account was established.

At that, we told the greatly subdued Ms Ellis that we were leaving, but would return soon. She didn't seem overcome with happiness about that, becoming more so when I baldly stated that perhaps she should start sending her resume to prospective employers in the commercial sector.

Following more damage to the rose-heads, the competent hands of Captain Walsh and her co-pilot delivered us safe and sound back to the Seaworld carpark, where Alex was waiting for us.

Back aboard, I arranged for a group conference aboard *Firebird* later that afternoon, where I explained what was being arranged for them. I had just finished and called for questions.

One girl put her hand up. 'I'm not wishing to sound ungrateful for all you've done for us, I'm just looking at options. What if any of us don't like being stuck out in the middle of the scrub?'

'No problem,' was my short reply, 'if you just want to go to town for the day to look around, and go buy personal stuff, a minibus will take you and bring you back again.

However, if you want to go try the big, bad world all over again, or hook up with friends, then just leave! Despite the substantial fence around it, the resort itself is not now and never will be a prison. The gates aren't locked, so there's absolutely nothing holding you there. If you do take that option, you'll be handed $5,000 in cash by the receptionist as you leave, in order to get you started on whatever you want to do, but after that, you're totally on your own. Which simply means that if you do decide to leave, there's no coming back if you change your mind later when you decide the big, bad world is still very big and can be very bad. It has to be a one-way trip.'

'Of course, for those who do stay, you'll continue to get fed, housed and generally looked after by the medical and counselling staff. If you want to learn a useful trade, take up a job on the staff for which you get paid. If you learn enough about your chosen job and build up your bank account, you may want to leave anyway and get a job elsewhere. But by then, you will be in a healthy frame of mind to cope with living in the world again, and will be much better equipped to do so successfully with a talent, training and some money behind you.

'You say the gates aren't locked?'

'Not for departing persons. There are military guards at the gate, but they're only concerned with who comes in or out of the bush training base which is close-by. As I said, you can walk or be driven out from the retreat anytime you want, no questions asked. But if you want to stay away longer than a day, then there's no returning.'

The girl subsided, looking a bit conflicted, so at the risk of being repetitious, I added, 'Allow me to say again that this isn't a jail, people. This place was there, not being used, so it's the best idea we could come up with to give you all a chance to get over the dreadful experiences you've been through. This isolated recovery will also allow you to avoid you being exposed to the world which has given you such a rough start to life. It's a very comfortable, safe and totally non-threatening environment. There will be professional support people there to watch over you, help you and for you to talk to as you want or need. As I said earlier, my longer-term plan is that some of you might like to learn how to help run the place as a genuine health retreat for others who need help getting their own lives back together. You're already well-qualified in adversity.'

That at least raised a few chuckles.

'To be honest, since I'm no rehabilitation expert, I don't know how well this will work out, as that depends entirely on you. But at least it gives you time to decide what you'd like to do with yourselves. Having that time means there's absolutely no pressure for any of you to make hasty decisions about your future, especially if the place can start to support itself by earning some income from outsiders. Our pockets are deep, but not that much!'

There was a general laugh at that feeble joke, and a lot more questions about the training needed to get a job, showing that many seemed to be at least thinking about getting involved in the running of the place. The idea that paying customers would be slowly allowed to come to the retreat for treatment, seemed to go over well, especially when I suggested that it would probably help with their own integration back into a normal lifestyle to be mixing with both professionals and some slightly messed-up paying guests.

In general, they all seemed eager to see their new home, and settle into a fresh, safe and stable life.

EPILOGUE

... Charlie's version of fast-track was quite impressive for a government operation, since just three weeks later, she called one morning to say that when my flock was ready, I could charter a coach to take them to their new home. As shopping trips had already happened, they all had a suitcase each with new clothes and personal items. Strangely, and thankfully, there were very few medical problems amongst the group, but regardless, all were checked over thoroughly by our own medical team at the Pain Relief Centre, headed by Roger and Jill.

With everything done we could think of, there was no reason to delay the trip to their new home. Bree organised the coach, and next morning, the flock said a tearful goodbye to Alex, Bree, Corrine and Dave. Sandy and I went with them to see the arrangements for ourselves.

While the trip seemed to hold everyone's interest, their attention was sharply focused when the coach pulled up at the gatehouse guarded by several armed soldiers, and a uniformed sergeant saluted, checked my ID, then waved us through. As our coach moved off, I noted the soldiers still watched carefully to make sure our driver took the resort side of the driveway.

We took the right bit of road, which first wound through a stand of trees, then there were sounds of appreciation when they took their first look at the retreat's main frontage, shining clean and white in the morning sun. Sandy's and my concerns were eased further when we were met by a cheerful woman who radiated an air of relaxed competence, and we were pleased there was no sign of the obnoxious and self-serving Ms Ellis.

While several equally cheerful staff appeared, and efficiently organised getting the chattering crowd of girls and boys checked in, baggage sorted and shown to their rooms, Sandy and I met the medical team, and in turn, the rest of the support staff. We were very impressed with the competence and attitude of all the key staff, and after a quick private lunch with them, left with the feeling that our young people were in excellent hands, would be looked after properly, and that we'd achieved our objectives. The rest was up to the healing properties of time, and the young people themselves.

#... Naturally, in the days following our return to civilisation, Sandy and I had been in regular contact with our superiors, but after returning from the resort, I placed a long-overdue phone call to Tom Webb, the Bundaberg detective who was involved in the investigation of the death of the first girl whose collar had regrettably performed as advertised. He had a hard time accepting that the case was closed, not leaving any bad guys for him to run through the court process. I had to come on a bit heavy with my ACP credentials, before he grudgingly accepted there really was nothing left to investigate, as all the perpetrators and witnesses had disappeared in various ways. I honoured my promise to Mickey Cook, the Bundaberg Coroner, by calling her with a brief explanation of the bang collars, and their nasty purpose. She was used to keeping secrets, so I was comfortable she wouldn't ask questions of the wrong people.

#... We also heard via Sandy's work grapevine, that the Mackay police who had been called to No-Name Island, faced a very puzzling scene. The boat captain who had made the initial call to them was unknown to all the local fishing skippers, as was his boat. When they had roared into the bay in their 45-foot police boat, they found the information from the mysterious skipper was correct, as a bunch of buildings were still fiercely ablaze, and there were several large patches of burning fuel or oil in the small bay. Ashore, there were two widely-separated groups of survivors. The main group, which was also the most vocal in denying their innocence, long before they were accused of anything, contained three very prominent politicians, four senior clergy, including two archbishops, three TV celebrities, two judges, assorted magistrates and several near-naked young men. That group were huddled together on the beach, in front of the blazing ruins of some sort of complex which wasn't on any local or state DA records, and officially weren't supposed to be there at all. A separate group, consisting of a number of white-coated persons who looked like catering staff, cooks and chefs, were clustered around some buildings further to the east, and refused to have anything to do with the group on the beach. They did, however, prove to be most helpful and provided nearly all the information about the depraved activities associated with the mysterious buildings, the persons involved in operating the place, and the extreme range of perversions practiced there.

The slowly cooling debris yielded the partially-destroyed remains of gambling equipment, sex toys, S & M equipment along with several unidentifiable bodies.

Intensive questioning slowly revealed the extent of a very nasty sex-slavery operation and an illegal casino. The catering and cleaning staff continued to happily add a great deal of information to the picture, as did the membership list of a very select Club, which was discovered in a closed, but un-locked fire-proof safe which had performed as advertised. Along with a large selection of very incriminating photographs and videos on flash-drives, two very curious items were also in the safe, one being a black, plastic collar and the other a small control box of some sort. Upon examination, it was found to contain a micro-electronics package and a strip of high-explosive.

A scrawled note taped to the collar warned against messing around with the control box within a hundred metres of the collar.

It took some time for the description of the rescue to filter down to the Bundaberg station, but once it did, it prompted Tom Webb to make a call north to his colleagues. Tom passed on to the Mackay guys the old 'National Security' line of bullshit I'd had to lay on him to ensure that he and Harriet kept quiet.

I might be a bit silly sometimes, but I had become quite good at avoiding digging unnecessary holes for myself.

Coppers hate loose ends and unanswered questions, so I could understand their frustration. However, I hoped that my continuing silence would encourage them to confine their investigations to the bunch of survivors on No-Name beach, and the clues found in the resort remains. Apparently that worked well enough, since in time, sufficient truth came out, which led to many well-known persons, who should have known better, being incarcerated, so the dark mutterings from up north slowly diminished.

Despite the note left in the safe, and to prevent a nasty accident, I did feel obliged to call Tom Webb at Bundaberg, and ask him, in turn, to clue the Mackay coppers in about the operation of the collar and transmitter. That sparked a fresh round of heated mutterings from up north, but they too, faded when their enquiries led nowhere.

#... We had several meetings with Sally, Kim and their father, Peter. They were delighted to handle all the legal processes associated with putting forty-odd homeless young adults into a rehabilitation retreat and worked closely with Mike Adams who looked after the financial bits.

Mike had to shuffle funds around from our personal accounts to cover the amount required to get the retreat staffed and functioning, but that amount was easily covered by the seized cash, and would leave a very healthy profit after all. Our bank accounts would be replenished when we got around to visiting Vanuatu, where they didn't ask awkward questions about the origin of large amounts of cash.

#... Our boats seemed empty after the crowd departed, but we kept busy by cleaning up the *Poseidon* and getting it ready for sale.

Two brokers were happy to list it and we were pleased when it sold quickly for $650,000. Nobody questioned the rather basic ownership documentation.

#… After a few weeks, I was intrigued to receive a phone call direct from Raijin Tanaka, the chief under-boss of the Yamaguchi-gumi Yakusa clan, who again expressed his gratitude for my assistance in restoring his granddaughter and her close friend, Fumiko to their families. He again declared that he considered himself deeply in my debt, and I could call on him at any time for assistance of any description. I understood that to be a very large concession for a person of his stature and position to make.

#… No one was in a rush to make our banking run to Vanuatu just yet, because we wanted to see how things shook down at the retreat, but we did plan to make the trip once the cyclone season was past.

#… The one and only, surprise bail-out from the retreat was Mary, Turner's original head girl, who contacted me asking if she could come to live on *Firebird* with us for a while. She stated that she wasn't necessarily abandoning the retreat, but just wanted to sample boat living again under more normal circumstances. I hadn't thought that such a request might pop up, and spent much time in talks with Sandy, Bree and Alex, before reluctantly agreeing to a trial period sometime in the near future to see how it would work out.

#… One final question arose, via a phone call from the rehabilitation resort, concerning the status of Hanh Tran, who was an illegal immigrant. I promptly handballed that one upstairs to Charlie, who assured me she'd take care of it. Charlie's efforts resulted in an immigration Visa being granted.

Sandy and I officially offered to sponsor her, and arranged an offer of permanent work at the Resort, which meant that at the next Australia Day ceremony, Hanh Tran was granted Australian Citizenship.

#… In consideration of the trauma the two boys must have suffered with the discovery of the severed head which kicked off the investigation, Harry and Sandy hired a car and made the trip to Bundaberg to visit Jake and Will. He spoke to their parents first to clear the way for Jasper's visit, but all worries were groundless as the two boys were utterly delighted to meet Jasper and play with him. When it was time to leave, Jasper and the boys were reluctant to part, while their parents agreed that the visit would go a long way to easing the boy's nightmares.

The End… until the next adventure begins…

ALSO BY THE AUTHOR
BOOK THREE IN THE FIREBIRD SERIES

An Eco-terrorist organisation formed with lofty ideals…a ratbag wealthy industrialist egomaniac…a plot to overturn the entire Australian political process…a major natural gas processing plant at risk…a giant crocodile…RAN patrol boats…an assassination contract targeting the PM. All the ingredients for a Firebird cocktail…definitely shaken, not stirred!

Book 3 in the Firebird series sees the Special Marine Strike Force (SMSF) head for the Pilbara to deliver their own special brand of mayhem and retribution on the bad guys.

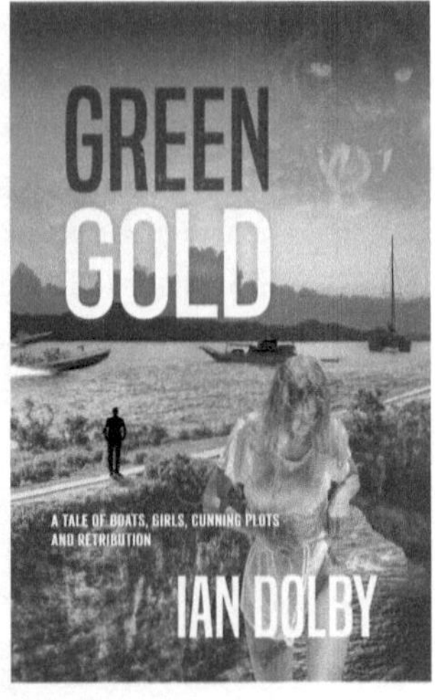

Driven by intense personal interest, including a shoulder with a bullet hole in it, Harry takes the Special Marine Strike Force across the Timor Sea to Indonesia in pursuit of the escaping Earth Care principals. Retribution and reward follow in the best Harry Stevens tradition, before the Strike Force take some well-deserved R&R and head for West Indonesia to keep their promise to their friends, Roger and Jill, in the search for the highly elusive and remarkable Green Gold.

Greedy islanders and pirates plying their age-old trade, do their best to complicate the process, but more treasure, along with the body count, keep piling up for the crews of the two boats, before some seized papers reveals details of an assassination plot against the Aussie PM and names the shadowy figures who were financing the EarthCare debacle!

Harry's not the only one with cunning plans - the special envoy who arrives to collect the papers comes up with a hare-brained scheme to safeguard the PM, but more strange alliances are formed as an old adversary unexpectedly re-surfaces.

A final round of havoc brews up that attracts Harry's particular brand of retribution, but who wins...who loses, and is the job really finished?

ALSO BY THE AUTHOR
BOOK FIVE IN THE FIREBIRD SERIES

With former Australian SAS Major, Harry Stevens and the Firebird crew heading home from their harrowing, but lucrative Indonesian operation, a call from the Australian PM sees the crew despatched to beautiful Lord Howe Island to investigate some disturbing events.

How can a beautiful and tranquil sub-tropical paradise have such a rotten core? Harry's disconcerting habit of attracting trouble strikes again as he encounters:

+ A wife-beating police officer...
+ A homicidal maniac terrorising young female tourists...
+ A major international smuggling operation, involving stolen uncut gemstones...
+ A very profitable smuggling operation dealing in protected Australian reptiles...
+ Are any of these linked?
+ Is putting two of Harry's favourite ladies in serious harm's way justified?
+ Can Harry's passion for coming up with complex 'cunning plans', save the ladies?
+ And what does one do with a homicidal Police officer in the absence of witnesses and 'smoking gun' evidence?
+ Who guards the guardian?

Doubts and misgivings plague Harry's waking thoughts as the darkest side of humanity increasingly shows its ugliest face.

At least with the diminutive, but deadly Corrine helping Harry and Jasper, there is possibly a way.

www.ingramcontent.com/pod-product-compliance
Lightning Source LLC
Chambersburg PA
CBHW020250120726
47904CB00001B/151